Peter

THE GRIMOIRE

Matador
9 De Montfort Mews
Leicester LE1 7FW, UK
Tel: (+44) 116 255 9311 / 9312
Email: books@troubador.co.uk
Web: www.troubador.co.uk/matador

ISBN 1 905237 46 4

Typeset in 11pt Stempel Garamond by Troubador Publishing Ltd, Leicester, UK

Matador is an imprint of Troubador Publishing Ltd

DAY ONE

OCTOBER THE THIRTIETH

DIVERSE PATHS

CHAPTER ONE

Sophie Gillett looked up from the newspaper draped across the bench as the old Morris Marina roared into view from behind the White Lion public house on the corner. The edges of her lips curled slightly upwards at seeing the banger, and she plucked another cheese and onion crisp from the packet and popped it into her mouth. Plump-bodied pigeons around her high-heels jerked their heads and took unhurried and methodical steps between the grass towards some pieces of stale bread. Gillett crunched the crisp and as glanced up at the tall, Victorian clock tower on her right, reading the time to be ten to twelve.

With her violet-coloured eyes, the twenty-five year old was just over six foot tall with a lean shapely physique and a tanned complexion that had been under the sunlamp a fraction too long. She had a long face with angular features framed by a rough auburn crop that was currently hidden under a wig. Gillett wore brown boots and a navy blue, pleated skirt and a long-sleeved blouse concealed by a red three-quarter length coat. Diverting her attention between the Marina, which was presently slowing as it crossed her field of vision, she zipped open her leather handbag and shoved the crisp packet deep inside before rummaging through the rest of her personal effects. Ahead of her, the old vehicle pulled up alongside the curb directly outside the combined village shop and post office.

Slanting rays of watery autumn sunshine descended from an almost clear blue sky, brightening the late October morning, drenching the houses with hazy warmth. Road signs glittered sharply. Red oaks were scattered about the main thoroughfare, their branches of bright crimson foliage ruffled in the gentle breeze. An elderly man took a moment to halt and unbutton his jacket in obvious pleasure as he felt the mild heat upon his face before letting his panting, Yorkshire terrier drag him hurriedly past Gillett who had finally fished out a dark, compact walkie-talkie. She pressed the talk button and raised it to her lips while focusing her attention back onto the Marina. The bearded driver had got out of the car and was now slamming the door shut behind him.

"Hawk! Scout here!" She uttered in a heavy east American accent, assessing the situation before her. "Jenkins has arrived at second pick-up point as source indicated, dead on time." She watched the sixty-one year old man walk around the back of the car and step inside the post pffice, empty handed. "Presently he's vulnerable, en route to collect the merchandise off Rutten. Do you copy over?" She explained. Brushing aside a length of her wig's blonde hair, she pressed the device to her ear as she glanced down to close up the tabloid she had been reading.

"Roger that scout." The male voice replied loud and clear from the receiver. "We're on the way and should intercept in about thirty seconds. I advise you sugar to get your pretty tail out of there as fast as you can because there's no telling what's going to happen when we arrive. Over!"

"Acknowledged Hawk," she answered, smiling at the speakers open concern for her. Slipping her thick handbag strap over her left shoulder and rising to her feet. The pigeons scattered. "I'll meet up with you at rendezvous A, in a couple of hours from now. Over!" Carrying the newspaper, she walked slowly away.

"Received and understood sweetheart!" The voice certified. "Out!"

* * *

The tranquil atmosphere in the picturesque, Lancashire village of Cuilfield was suddenly ripped apart by the screeching of brakes and the high-pitched whine of locking tyres. The sounds echoed sharply off the grey stone walls of the rows of cottages lining the high street. When the silver people-carrier finally skidded to a stop in the middle of the road a couple of yards behind the parked Morris Marina, the seats inside vibrated and the engine continued to rumble as the front and rear passenger doors of the Volkswagen Caravelle were flung wide open and villagers, alerted to the noise, dropped whatever they were doing to hurry to the windows of their homes in fear of seeing someone they knew that had been tragically knocked down.

Instead of a grisly accident, their eyes widened in shock from their various vantage points as they witnessed a pair of armed robbers tumble out of the Caravelle. The men were of different height and builds, wearing heavy walking boots and dressed in the same dark, baggy boiler suits with broad bandoleer belts worn over one shoulder and across the chest, with pockets for carrying ammunition; while woollen ski masks covered their heads. Both men were brandishing a firearm.

"Dear lord!" A pensioner muttered to herself as she peered through her net curtains at the unfolding scene across the street. "Dayne," she shouted to her daughter. "Call the police. There's a robbery taking place over the road."

Inside the Post Office-shop, Ralph Jerkins whipped his head around at the noise and addressed the post master behind the counter. "Blimey Abe sounds like an accident..." Out of curiosity he turned and made his way to the front of the store to find out.

"I don't know Ralph." Abraham Rutten declared anxiously, flipping aside the hinged section of the counter top and slipping through the gap in hot pursuit. "But I hope to god it's not mother. She said she was going shopping this morning and she isn't as lively on her feet as she once was."

Outside, shots rang out from a .357 Magnum Colt Python. Each time the bullet was released, the barrel of the gun kicked back in recoil. Dogs barked and pigeons were startled by the bangs. They flapped their collected wings and took to the sky. Several passers-by saw the sunlight glinting off the barrels of the firearms, and shouted frantic warnings and began to dive to the ground or scurry for the nearest cover. One fleeting look at the robbers was enough for shopping bags to be dropped, causing belongings to scatter. A woman fainted, collapsing in the midst of the screams while nearby a man on the same side of the street tripped as he hurried to get away from the scene, grazing his knee on the pavement as the owner of the Magnum pointing the smoking mouth to the fore, dashed onto the pavement, heading for the door of the Post Office. Grenades hanging loosely in-between the extra ammunition magazines on their bandoleers, swung back and forth with the loping strides.

A motorist who'd drawn up behind the Caravelle, saw the guns being flourished and quickly put her Peugeot in reverse and accelerated back down the road, passing a detached bungalow and a cottage as fast as she could. With her attention distracted however, she didn't see another car approaching from her rear until it was far to late for either car to brake. Gaining velocity, hydraulics screeched but the two vehicles still collided with force, buckling and folding the front of the Metro like a concertina. A geyser of steam erupted from the radiators. Upon impact, windscreens cracked into spider webs; the man inside the Metro sustained cuts from splinters of glass; the airbag instantly inflated to protect him but the seatbelt bruised his shoulder when he lunged forward. The engine pushed back snapping the bones in his feet and ankles and he grimaced in pain before losing consciousness. The woman in the Peugeot suffered severe whiplash injuring her vertebral and the muscles in her jolted neck.

Meanwhile the robbers advanced. The scuff of footfalls was heard as Jerkins scraped the floor of the store with his feet. Jenkins emerged in the open doorway holding a bunch of keys in one wrinkled hand while in the other he grasped a heavy brown, canvas bag that resembled a mail sack. The pouch was large and was sealed at the top with a basis lock. He shuffled forward a pace then blinked when he focused on the gunmen moving towards him. The sexagenarian went wide-eyed in surprise and froze, blocking the doorway much to the annoyance of Rutten, shadowing him.

"What is it Ralph?" Rutten enquired in irritation. "What happened out there?" He added, approaching the older man. "Is it something bad? Tell me man."

Before Jenkins could answer, he shivered with foreboding for his life when the shorter robber aimed the barrel of his weapon at him. An instant later, the powerful handgun discharged twice and the bullets slammed into his chest, his heart exploded as the slugs exited his back, retaining force enough to shatter the shop's display glass. Blood sprayed the air and Jenkins' rangy body was hurled backwards through the bow window. Rutten gasped at the ear ringing booms and uttering a shrieking cry of incoherent fright, he turned to run as the stocky figure of Kyle Klugman passed through the cloud of cordite smoke and crossed over the threshold of the Post Office. He grinned when he saw the postmaster retreating further into the interior and lifted his Colt Python. He fired again and Rutten crumpled in his tracks. Bits of brain matter and blood erupted from his disintegrating head in a messy pulp.

"Check inside." Klugman ordered gruffly. "And do what you have to. I'll get the stuff off the courier."

"I know the procedure Paul," came back the reply, using the pseudonym Klugman had picked for himself just for this heist.

Without wasting time, Adrian Cummings glided forward in a half crouch between the aisles of display shelves, treading onto the body of the Post Master. Bones crunched under his size twelves and blood oozed up to fill the treaded soles as he made his way into the store to see if there were any more canvas bags lying on the counter. The CCTV security cameras high above the shelves of newspapers and cigarettes captured Cummings snatching another pouch only after he'd rotated his Colt 45 horizontally as he gave his surroundings a quick extensive survey in case someone was lying in ambush to waylay him.

Behind him, Klugman was bent over Jerkins' body, and had already slipped the man's keyring into his side pocket. He was now in the act of forcibly wrenching the first bag from the cold hand. It came free abruptly and he straightened. "All clear Roy?" He shouted a question, stepping across glass shards, out of the bow window onto the pavement.

"Everything's fine." Cummings said curtly. "Let's go."

Backtracking together to the boot of the Marina, the raiders panned the barrels of their guns in a wide arc and shot off a few rounds apiece high into the air in front of them to discourage any would be heroes. At their rear, Jerome Thaw sat behind the steering wheel of the people-carrier and shook his head, working the bolt of his weapon before contributing to the general effect of the chaos by sticking the UZI out of his open window and pulling the trigger.

Thaw was in his early thirties but looked a few years older. He was about five foot seven in height with a lithe, athlete build that was devoid of excess flesh. He had a number of tattoos of various designs decorating his torso and on his upper arms. Over his head, his ski mask concealed a hard-featured face. Half of it was covered with dark stubble and wreathed with dark closely-cropped hair. He had steely cobalt-coloured eyes set between thin lips and a receding hairline and a widow's peak. Underneath his boiler suit Thaw wore a pair of sun-bleached jeans and a white tee-shirt. White flames erupted around the mouth of the semi-automatic as nine millimetre shells were sent clattering skyward. The spent brass, bullet casings spitting out of the top of the weapon cascaded down to clink and ping when they landed on the road.

Across the road, a middle-aged woman crouching behind a dry-masonry, garden wall jumped and uttered a petrified scream when more shots rang out. Kneeling not far away, beside a hedgerow, Sophie Gillett hoisted up the mirror of her cosmetic case above the gatepost and, using it like a periscope, she tilted the case's mirror at an angle and peered upward at the reflection in the hope of following what was happening directly opposite. Leaves from the trees hampered her view.

Klugman took a quick glance inside the Marina and saw nothing of value lying on the seats. Having a vague inkling there would be more money stacked in the boot, he called out to Cummings as he pulled up to the Caravelle and tossed the pouch inside. "Roy! Grab this. I've got to do something." He then stared at Thaw, observing him raise two fingers up above the dashboard. Klugman nodded at the gesture and knew they could linger only for another two minutes before their timetable urged them to get out of the village.

With a sigh, Cummings holstered his Colt 45, caught the pouch and shoved it forcibly beside the other onto the rear seats, carefully not to disturb the green rucksack anchored by seat belt straps to the furthest chair. He clambered inside and shut his passenger door with a loud slam.

Standing beside the Marina's boot, Klugman produced the key ring and under time pressure, fumbled and almost lost his grasp on them. Feeling his heart race and adrenaline careering through his blood, he selected a key and shoved it into the lock. But when he tried to turn it, the key wouldn't budge. "Fuck!" He shouted. "It's stuck." He forced it to turn only to hear a snap as the metal broke in his hand. Snarling he pointed his Colt Python at the lock and squeezed the trigger. A hollow click resounded telling him the gun was empty.

Behind, Thaw glanced at the clock set in the dashboard, not liking what he saw.

"Come on man," he said to himself. As the seconds slipped by, a niggling doubt began to steadily grow within him, knowing if Klugman didn't get a move on then they might not get away at all. Going beyond the deadline meant throwing off the schedule and allowed the police helicopters time to catch up and track their movements from the air. He swallowed involuntary at the prospect and was aware the damn things would direct Stinger units or allow police to throw road blocks across every possible escape route; and most certainly send armed response teams on ahead at certain sites, to set up a field of fire with their Heckler and Koch machine carbines.

Cummings banged the top of his head on the ceiling as he stared up through the sunroof to see if he could glimpse an earlier sighting of any specks in the sky. "Is he still at it Jerome?" He uttered nervously. Wincing when he felt his sorely bruised head. Sweat breaking across his forehead.

"Yeah," he confirmed with cold fury in his voice. "The greedy bastard. He can't be content with the money we've got. Oh no he wants more. Huh," he expressed his contempt with a grimace. "Even split five ways my share will be enough for my purposes. My ex-employer will have to find another lackey to sweep the floor of his barber shop tomorrow. I'm taking early retirement." He shook his head and came out of his reverie. "See anything out the back?"

Adrian Cummings was forty-four years of age and under his ski mask had a broad face with crumpled, bloodhound features. He was clean-shaven with a bulbous nose and a craggy forehead framed by a shock of brown hair peppered at the sides with gray. Cummings was built like an old brick outhouse. Easily six foot four in height, he was strongly constructed with broad-shoulders, a barrel chest and bulging muscles along his upper arms that were almost as big as coconuts. Beneath his boiler suit straining at the seams, he wore a brown collared-polo shirt and a pair of Chinos. A fifteen inch long knife with a single broad edge was housed in a sheath in his left boot.

"No! But it won't be long I wager." Cummings declared anxiously, pulling his sidearm free. "One of the villagers must have phoned the police by now." He awkwardly spun around his powerful, hulking frame between the seats to peer over the front headrest, passenger seat at Klugman. "The way we're going, we won't get a chance to spent any of the money because we'll be either ending up in jail tonight or just resting on a slab in the local morgue."

Speaking with a Geordie accent, Adrian Cummings was a career law-breaker having spent the last couple of decades of his life behind bars for one unsuccessful crime or another. He'd attempted to go straight in the past but couldn't get a job however hard he tried, given his track record and threatening appearance, he found that no one wanted to hire him. And the money he got to live on from his unemployment giro he actually believed was a joke. So when this venture appeared out of the blue from Thaw, an old cell mate of his who needed the assistance of a particular talent only he was enable to do, well the lure of quick, easy money was just to much for him to past up.

"I hear you, Adrian," came back the reply. "Don't get excited. It won't happen. I'll make certain of it." Thaw scanned his surroundings, noticing a villager here and there raise their heads above a hedge or a wall before ducking back under cover again the second they saw the raiders were still there. "I ain't leaving anyone behind who can finger us." Again he decided to stuck the UZI out of his window. He fired a short burst on this occasion to attract Klugman's attention.

Klugman finished loading his Colt Python as he heard the collection of shots clatter out. He turned and lowered himself into a crouch, expecting trouble sneaking up at them from behind, only to see Thaw withdrawing his UZI. "Get a move on, man!" He shouted desperately. "Thirty seconds to go." He removed the empty ammunition magazine from his weapon. "Whatever isn't in here by then is left behind to be worm food. He shoved a second nine millimetre clip home. "Understood?"

Klugman straightened and nodded briefly at the threat. Returning his gaze to the boot of the Marina, Klugman scowled and as he felt blood pounding in his ears, he cocked the hammer and shot the lock off. He heard the engine rev up as he pushed the lid up, reached inside and to his overwhelming relief, pulled out a third money pouch. Klugman hoisted up the canvas bag to his chest and sprinted towards the Caravelle. Seeing this, Thaw changed his mind, placing his UZI carefully in the long compartment-pocket alongside his door as Klugman made it to the opening and quickly passed the pouch over the top of his contoured seat to the rear of the vehicle. The alarm on Kugman's watch picked that moment to began beeping a high-pitched electronic signal, warning that his time was up.

Cummings reached up, taking the package with both hands and had to haul the pouch through the gap between the headrests with a strong yank when it became fastened for an instant against the ceiling of the Caravelle. Klugman got in, collapsed into his chair and had barely shut his passenger door when Thaw released the hand brake and pushed his foot down hard on the accelerator. The vehicle zoomed along main street, past the outskirts of the village, flinging the occupants back into their seats momentarily like they were being subjected to G-forces as the Caravelle sped on into the countryside. A speed camera flashed when the vehicle exceeded the road limit, capturing a clear image of its license plate.

With his eyes burning with rage, Thaw gave Klugman a quick piercing look as he grabbed hold of the top of his ski mask and yanked it off his head, to reveal a narrow hawk-like face of a man in his mid to late twenties with piercing blue eyes and a small pointed goatee beard. A wide grin split his almost handsome countenance. Beneath his coiled neck, he had a strong thickset frame and was just above average height. The boiler suit he wore covered a pair of dark trousers and a casual baggy shirt.

"Phew!" He said, brushing a strand of his long, greasy flaxen-coloured hair away his eyes. "That was tight going."

"Yeah!" Thaw replied, turning his gaze back to the road, freeing one of his own hands as he did from the steering wheel to pull off his knitted headgear. "You bloody idiot, Kyle!" His eyes glancing at the rearview mirror to see if they were being pursed.

They weren't, yet.

"Another couple of seconds delay," Thaw said, "and that would have been fatal to you mister. Do you know that? Was your reckless greed for an extra money pouch worth you nearly losing your life over?"

Sitting behind them, Cummings followed suit and tugged off his mask to leave his short hair disarranged and untidy like the others in front. The grin faded from Klugman's pinched face as he took in the question and the menacing warning behind it in the driver's voice. He whirled his head to the open passenger window on his side and spat arrogantly out through the gap where presently fields stretched away from ditches and wooden fences flanking both sides of the road. Klugman sniffed haughtily and when he returned his eyes, he levelled an unwavering stare at Thaw.

"Jerome," he said, his face taking on a forbidden expression that was reflected in the seriousness in the deep pitch of his voice. "You're too wired up. I would change to drinking de-caf if I were you and don't be so sodding well naive and jump to rash conclusions in future because I had it all under control." He smirked nastily, pulling up the sleeve of his boiler suit to reveal an expensive looking watch. "You heard the alarm on this. I knew exactly how long we had. I would've dropped everything in a heart beat if it had been necessary."

"Huh!" Thaw expressed in derision, stealing a glance in his direction. "The hell you say!" He growled, his eyes cynical as he met Klugman's cold gaze squarely without flinching. "Who said we were following Nathan's advice. We agreed killing Jenkins was absolutely at the last resort and when was the post master in the equation?" His words radiating boldness and courage while his stare returned to the country lane ahead.

"It made sense." Klugman said, seeing a crossroads about a hundred yards head. "Both could have stopped us. I decided I'd be spontaneous. There was no time to think it through like you and Adrian like you do."

"That maybe so Kyle." Cummings replied. Again squinting at the sky, peered up into the glare slanting through the sunroof. "But we didn't sign on to aid and abet a double murder. We looking at life imprisonment if we're caught."

The vehicle reduced its speed as Thaw turned sharply to the right, sending their people-carrier careering with a loud screech around the hedged-corner. Not having his seatbelt on, Klugman was slammed against the door, making his shoulder throb, wiping off the last fraction of his smirk from his face.

"Guns aren't toys Adrian." Klugman grunted, hurled back into his seat when Thaw floored the accelerator. The Caravelle cut along the other road. "Nor are explosives." His eyes narrowed to glitter with hatred at the driver. "I'm used to a lot of leeway and if you've pissed with me now, you're going love me after the distractions go off."

At those words, a stunned look appeared on Cummings face. His heart began to beat faster and he grimaced in displeasure. His massive scarred and callused left hand closed around the Ivory-hilted knife tucked away in his boot. A farm driveway flashed by.

"You, what?" Thaw shouted incredibly. "More death." His blood boiled and enraged, he released his right hand from the steering wheel and glancing into the compartment pocket where he dropped the UZI, he reached down to pick it up, with a mind to rid himself once and for all of this oppressive burden. Klugman heard something rasp like metal scraping against leather at the rear of him. Before Thaw could do anything, from the corner of his left eye, he saw Klugman interpret their reactions by pulling a hand grenade from his bandoleer, and slipped his middle finger casually through the ring atop of the bomb.

"So what Jerome! Cooks have to break eggs to make omelets. My field of expertise is the same," he said smugly. "Don't forget I can do stuff that's not exactly in the yellow papers you know."

The fences on either side of the road transformed now from wood to low stones walls.

Klugman smirked arrogantly. "There's no harm done really? We're on schedule, and we'll still lead the police a merry dance." He said, glancing at Thaw who feeling a knot of fear in the pit of his stomach, swallowed hard and his hand twitched unseen behind his leg as he saw a shrew and calculating look staring back at him before he turned his attention back to the road, his face a livid mask of rage.

"And if we do get any bother from them then we'll just throw a couple of these when they get close." Klugman held the grenade up higher to let Cummings see the bomb for himself over the top of the seat just in case he hadn't seen it before. "One way or another that should knock the fuckers off our tracks for a bit."

Catching sight of the grenade had a tremendous effect on Thaw. His face drained of all of its colour and his hand withdrew from the door's pocket as he abandoned killing him, focusing all of his attention again on their overall priorities. Behind him the grenade was enough of an incentive to cause Cummings to slam the blade back home in its sheath, his knuckles shone white as he tightened his grasp around the hilt. Concealing his panic extremely well, Thaw wiped beads of sweat from his forehead. He was scared of no man and was loathed to think he had to back down when he normally would rise to any dangerous challenge but this was no modest gamble instead this was for high stakes that had no chance of a winner yet plenty of opportunity for losers. If he shot Klugman now there was a possibly he wouldn't kill him out right, that he could still have enough life in him to pull that pin as a final defiant gesture before he died. Rather than cancel out his plans for Klugman, Thaw simply sighed heavily and decided to put it off and rectify matters later when he wouldn't be holding that hand grenade in such close proximity to him.

"Yeah, it should." Thaw agreed anxiously, giving him a fleeting steely glare. "Just be careful and put it away until we need it, okay?" He took a deep breath. "We traveling along old roads and we don't want an accident if we hit a pothole or something now do we?"

Klugman nodded. "Of course!" He uttered, his voice dripping with false sincerity. His finger withdrawing from the ring before attaching the small bomb back to the bandoleer. "I'll keep my hand near it merely as a precaution you understand. You never really know when trouble will come along."

Still ashen-faced, Thaw changed gear then the vehicle zoomed passed more open fields giving away to thin clumps of pine and larch trees, and denser clusters of oaks and beeches, among patches of heather. "No," he said bitterly, with a dark scowl and a slight edge in his voice. "We don't."

Unbeknown to them, hidden behind a length of dry stone wall, a man wearing a balaclava and holding a palette knife, dripping with oil paint, rose from his canvas when the vehicle roared passed at reckless speed. The artist's first thought was the people-carrier might have been stolen by joyriders. So memorising the license number and the direction it was going, he jotted it and the time down on a piece of scrap paper then focusing once more, he sat down to make use of the remaining light and when back to mixing his colours and applying his paint.

* * *

Behind the speeding people-carrier, the minutes dragged by and dazed and shaken up by the whole experience, the villagers slowly came out of hiding. A few of the citizens rushed over to the bodies and knelt in the crimson pools, reaching for the carotid artery to check if they could detect any vital signs. While others visited the injured in the crash site to offer first aid until medical help arrived on the scene. Still more residents in this close community, embraced family members or old friends tenderly, happy and thankful to be alive after surviving this most terrible of ordeals.

Elsewhere down a side street, a grin thinned out on the features of Sophie Gillett who had slipped away unnoticed from the gathering and quietly made her way in a slow and leisurely gait to where her motor scooter was parked outside the 14th century church. Once there, she dropped the newspaper into the rubbish bin, plunked the helmet from where it dangled on the handlebars and slipped it on. Adjusting the helmet straps beneath her chin, Gillett casually let her eyes wander to survey her surroundings. Except for a breeze blowing some pieces of waste-paper along the road; and a young, corpulent, ginger tomcat grooming itself in the sitting room window of a cottage across the way, the street was deserted. The rest of the populace had rushed to the high street to see what the tumult was all about.

Satisfied she wasn't being watched and having a pang of regret she didn't have time to finish off her crisps, Gillett pulled the key out of her coat pocket, seated herself and started up the engine. She racked the throttle then released the clutch. With a final glance over her right shoulder, she saw no oncoming traffic and accelerated away, turning right after fifty yards, down another road in the opposite direction to where the Caravelle had headed. She was long gone by the time the villages heard the rotor blades of the police surveillance helicopters flying fast overhead, and the wailing sirens proclaiming the approach of the ambulances and the patrol cars.

CHAPTER TWO

It just after twelve-thirty when Thaw finally slowed and turned off the country lane through a gate; the tyres trampling down the fields long, meadow grasses as he quickly left the track and made a beeline for the thick growth of trees and underbrush covering an extensive tract of the land before them. Once they were between the deciduous hardwoods, he parked the Caravelle in a pre-picked site beneath the spreading canopies of oak and maple; and alongside a row of towering hedges which concealed them from the road. Then as one the associates disembarked in orderly fashion and went about their assigned tasks with drilled military precision, Cummings and Klugman flitting around the vehicle, opening doors to remove the cargo, a rucksack and for other purposes while Thaw closed the gate behind them before backtracking to a location where he began to keep a lookout at the sky and the surrounding landscape.

"Jerome!" Cummings announced, withdrawing from the Caravelle's crowded boot, a folded bundle of patterned material. "The camouflage netting's ready to be deployed." He straightened and saw Thaw using his binoculars to scan the activity of the livestock in the next field over, grazing on rows of winter fodder.

"Understood Adrian," came back the reply. Relaxing his vigilance by lowering the binoculars and whirling around to stand in front of the unloaded money pouches.

"What did you see?" Cummings asked, opening the folds of the stretch netting for immediate use. "Any potential trouble?"

"Negative! Just cattle! Nothing in the air!" Thaw answered before addressing Klugman who was kneeling beside the drivers seat, delicately unwinding a continuous length of cord from a spool he held. "You nearly done with your surprise Kyle?" He watched him connect the end of the fuse to a electric device no bigger than a matchbox under the interior handle of the driver's door.

"Almost but I can't rush it. It's bloody awkward work getting this right especially wearing gloves." Klugman said, about to explain. "I soldered the container and impregnated the proximity fuse with chemicals last night. I've inserted the detonator, the frequency is already tuned in to the remote control and another minute and I'll activate the mechanical trigger then it's all set to go off one way or the other."

"Good!" Thaw nodded, glancing at his watch. It read 12:41. "When you finish, we'll drape the net over the Caravelle and then the hell out of here."

"I'll cover the door on this side myself Jerome." Klugman volunteered before disclosing why. "I've adjusted the key to act like a hair trigger. The slightest pressure on it will ignite the lead azide and detonate the charges."

"The jobs yours," Thaw declared as an afterthought occurred to him. "Kyle! Is there any chance this masterpiece of your could be defused by the bomb squad?"

"Naw," Klugman replied, not taking his eyes off what he was doing. Fitting a ceramic coil into the casting of the device. "The semtex is odourless and hidden by the tinted windows. it's rigged to detonate when the twenty-four hour timer has elapsed or sooner by remote if necessary." He flipped a tiny piece of plastic across the opening to hide the circuitry then inserted a screw and began twisting it home. "Failing that and the Caravelle is found then some unsuspecting fool will still set off the explosives when they simply open the door." He slipped the screwdriver into the pocket of his boiler suit and slowly got to his feet. "Finished!" He added, closing the driver's door, the key still in the lock, the length of fuse going slack beside the compartment. They all heard a beeping from another of Klugman pockets. "That's my indicator! Now our little surprise is active."

* * *

Picking up a canvas bag apiece, the robbers abandoned the disguised vehicle and proceeded on foot through the forest along a little known animal trail that winded through the bushes and trees. Cummings took the point and as natural as breathing, lead the way like his father had for him, many years previously when he was a lad, accompanying his parent on countless poaching trips in this wooded region as they trespassed upon private property to hunt game and fish. Thaw came next and Klugman still stroking his hand grenade brought up the rear, his rucksack strapped over his shoulders. A couple of miles passed without incident. Watery early afternoon sunlight shone through the semi-naked branches of the deciduous trees and filtered down between the evergreen foliage, a carpet of leaves crunched loudly beneath their boots surrounding islands where green and browning grass jutted up, the long blades beaded with a few moist drops of surviving night dew.

Klugman removed the earphones of his radio iPod. "Guys! The latest news reports say the police have identified our getaway vehicle to be a Volkswagen Caravelle but still haven't found it as yet. Traffic on all major arteries has slowed to a crawling 1.5mph on all many routes due to the filth having set up road blocks as well as currently searching all luggage at rail and bus stations they've staked-out in the region."

"Huh!" Thaw uttered, sandwiched between the two, in single line. Stepping over a tree root. "No surprises there then. That's caused a bit of chaos and a few migraines all round especially with the spate of road works and the sporting events already tying up a lot of the police resources."

"You ain't kidding Jerome." Cummings replied with a smile, tramping on. "The plan is working perfectly. The more distance we cover, the further our lead widens and the colder our trail becomes."

"What's the score so far on the match anyway Kyle?" Thaw asked, changing the position of his pouch and hoisting it atop of his shoulder. "Is united still ahead."

"Yeah by one!" Klugman answered, replacing the earphones. "it's nearly half time. I'll keep filling you both in as we go along."

Thaw and Klugman adhered to Cummings steps like they were walking through a minefield. Their passage in the silent wood was noisy and distinct, and in a bid to leave as few footprints as possible in their wake, they tried with almost caution to avoid breaking twigs on the trail and circumvent soggy areas where the recent wet weather and the repeated passage of animals had trampled the bare ground underneath into mud. The companions trotted along at an even pace, another thousand yard fell away behind them. Every so often, Cummings would turned right or left, away from their previous line of direction as well as ducking behind bushes or come to a dead stop in the trail, gesturing to his associates to do the same, clenching his jaw and throwing furtive glances at the surrounding terrain for a tense moment. Most times it was the sounds of rustling leaves being carried by the wind but one occasion the shrubbery shook after the wind had died down. Pushing the barrel of his colt 45 in front of him, Cummings strained his ears only to exhale a gusty sigh and relax when he heard the familiar scurrying of a roe deer behind the foliage.

* * *

"it's almost time Nathan," Gillett said, bringing the gear stick down to second as a sharp corner approached in the narrow country road ahead. "Get the remote out. This is where things start to get really interesting."

"I'm on it," Bisset remarked, taking his eyes off the wild overgrown hedges lining the lane. He opened up the glove compartment and reached inside as the car rounded the bend and sped on along the straight section of road. He produced a box like device Klugman had given them. It was about the size of a paperback book with a collection of tiny bulbs jutting up adjacent to a single row of switches. A big red button was located at the bottom of the box. Bisset pulled up the aerial at the top right hand corner, the antenna extended, sliding out of the overlapping sections like a telescope. "All done Sophie!" He added, stealing a glance at her. "Just give me the word and I'll execute it from here."

"Initiate one through four together, now!" She commanded, checking her wing-mirror out of habit, and seeing no one behind their Escort.

Bisset flicked a switch. The bulb alongside it turned green. He then repeated the procedure three more times lower down. "Active!" He declared, pressing the red button once. "Accomplished! That should keep the police happy for a while."

She nodded and slammed her foot down on the accelerator.

* * *

Many miles away from Gillett and Bisset, and driving along the northbound lane of the M6, the shadow of another overpass drifted steadily towards the cabin of the petrol tanker as Stuart Darley squinted his eyes in the watery sunshine and quickly lowered his visor to shade them. Fresh air flowed through the open tanker window while the tonal effects of a trumpet and a saxophone blared out jazz rhythms from the compact disc player inside. The forty year old was just shifting his attention from the road to check his tachometer when he suddenly heard something sharp and loud like a clap of thunder from above. The windscreen immediately shattered as his gaze shot up, peppering Darley with glass fragments, causing a long deep cut in his forehead while his right eye exploded in absolutely agony. Warm blood poured down his cheek, staining the shoulder of his knitted jumper bright crimson. Tears flooded his other eye, sliding the contact lens he wore from the cornea.

The roadway shook, the concussion force of the blast violently shuddered the moving tanker but the lighter weight of the Ford Mondeo alongside Darley and many more cars in the additional lanes were swept up and flung end over end high into the air, people screamed as a red Alfa Romeo fell and smacked into the flow of traffic moving along the motorway. The roof of an F-reg Astra Estate crumbled with a loud smashing noise, killing the driver and her passenger instantly when it landed upside down in the midst of the crash barrier, metal tearing and twisting in the central reservation. Petrol began to spill from the ruptured fuel tank towards a lit cigar thrown from the driver's hand.

More cars behind the pile up, locked their tyres but kept moving forward, rubber smoking. A Nissan Primera and Vauxhall Vectra fishtailed out of control, colliding powerfully into the rear of a five door saloon and a courier van at forty miles per hour as flowing flames not far away roared to swallow up the damaged Astra and then spurted high into the air, clothes and flesh burned fiercely inside the wreck, smoke churned around the asphalt. Darley's blurry vision didn't see the aftermath of the detonated plastic explosive as a massive fireball descended from beneath the ruined flyover only a yard ahead of him. Terrified, deaf from the concussion and in pain from his injures, he felt something like a cold hand clench his heart as he shivered in the advancing hotness, instinctively plunging down on the brake peddle.

The intense heat burned Darley's face. His eyebrows singed, exposed skin blistered and smoke began to smolder from his hair. The fire reflected off the tanker's bonnet and semi-trailer in the process of it ploughing on through the curtain of flame. At the same time steel reinforcing rods and lumps of concrete from the shattered flyover span, the sides of which were charred and darkened to carbon black fell from the sky, obscuring the slanting sunlight, raining down death to anyone in their path. A passenger was impaled in her chair by a pointed steel rod which lanced through the windscreen and pierced her neck. Blood splashed over her startled husband who only had time to blink in horror at the appalling sight, before he could make even attempt to staunch the flow, a nugget of cement struck and broke a hole in the hull of the tanker, the sparks then ignited the petrol within.

The semi-trailer and Darley's cabin obliterated, vanishing as fire blossomed about the disintegrating vehicle with a crackling roar. Flames leapt into the afternoon sky like flicking tongues and black smoke billowed up after it. Fed by the air and the tanker fuel, the blaze spread, rippling outward across the lanes of the motorway to engulf and devour the gridlock of vehicles. An elderly man lying unconscious where he had been thrown from his E-reg Yamaha motorbike never regained consciousness. The bright, reddish-orange wall rolled right over the biker, cooking his brain and the fluids in his body erupted into steam. The temperature reached a melting point and the asphalt below the surging inferno boiled and softened. Powerlines became severed, cutting of electricity for miles around. Trees and bushes lining the road flared up, grass blackened and withered in the heat, traffic cones melted and people injured and trapped inside their cars, screamed until their voices gave out, their lungs burned and shrivelled in the heated air and their larynxes became consumed as they too underwent combustion.

Further back, an overspreading pall of panic descended over the families in the cars stuck in line. Doors were flung open and people stampeded away from the approaching fire barrier in overpowering fright as fast as their legs could carry them. At their rear, additional cars exploded, more oily smoke arose, and soon after that, the blast spent its fury: the wind weakened and died away and the tongues of flame just as suddenly shrunk back, receding and evaporating leaving the wrecks of gutted cars and wisps of smoke rising from the blackened remains of charred corpses, cracking loudly in pools of fire.

* * *

A reasonably-sized clearing at the base of the hill, blanketed by evergreen shrubs and ringed with clumps of small laurel trees was the site Cummings choose to take a breather but as they rested briefly, the men found that they weren't really able to free their minds from the unwavering concentration they were experiencing.

"Hey Adrian," Thaw exclaimed to attract his allies attention when they had set off again. "When you were reconnoitering the route last month, did you happened to notice a phone mast erected around here?"

"Naw!" Cummings replied with a shake of his head as he lead the way up the steep incline. "Why?" He frowned. "Who are you gonna call Jerome?"

"Nathan!" He replied wheezingly. "I wanted to check the accuracy of the facts the journalists were reporting in comparison to what the version the police were communicating to each other on their private frequencies."

"You think it's not accurate." Cummings asked. Without looking back, he continued onward, mushrooms grew about them, varied by their shape and colour.

"Not sure!" Thaw admitted. "I reckon some of it is."

"Hmmm," Klugman uttered, giving thoughtfully consideration to what had just been said. "I can't see any of the mobiles working out here," he announced, slipping off the earphones, "not with all these trees around us distorting reception."

"True!" Cummings said, seeing the top of the hill in sight, trees thinning out slightly as he crushed the umbrella-like cap of a mushroom beneath his boots. "But we'll be at the summit soon enough, Kyle. There's hardly any trees up there from what I remember and it's nice and high. We could try and call Nathan then."

"Yeah!" Thaw said with a nod. "Worth a go!"

* * *

The dappled sunlight filtered through the colourful dome-like crown and the wide-spreading branches of the Maple trees as Thaw slowly took a step followed by another two across the grassy top of the hill, the white noise emitting from his mobile phone was extraordinary loud, drowning out the ruffling tree leaves caught in the wind above him.

Behind them, Cummings had set his pouch down and sat heavily upon a sewn-off tree stump. "Keep going Jerome," he encouraged. Seeing his ally turn down the volume on the mobile to curb the sharp interference from blasting into his earhole before dialing the number again with his thumb. "You're sure to get a connection in a minute."

Thaw nodded, with the handset pressed tight to his ear as he stepped forward and to his relief was rewarded not with static but rather with a burring tone. "I've got them. it's ringing." He stopped dead in his tracks.

"Must be in a straight line with a mast," Klugman determined. Unwrapping a toffee and popping it into his mouth, standing beside the other two pouches lying on the ground.

"We're through!" Thaw spoke directly to his companions before addressing his further comments down the phone. "Nathan! it's Jerome, how are things your end?"

A thin voice speaking very softly cracked on the other end of the line. "Fine! Though our fingers are suffering a bit from RSI from all of the dialing we've done to the police switchboard."

"I can well imagine," Thaw replied with a narrow smile. "We got a very bad connection here so keep to the bare facts."

"All right!" Bisset agreed. "Shout to me to repeat anything if you don't get all of this, Sophie is with me and she got rid of the scooter. it's at the bottom of the lake. Operation deadlock commenced under way ten minutes ago with four objectives being detonated. As an aftermath of the first and second disturbances, power has already cut-off hundreds of houses in the area. From all accounts half of Lancaster is in confusion and uproar."

"I know!" Thaw said matter-of-factly. "Kyle has been keeping us well acquainted with the low-down. Delays caused a riot with the football fans at the train station not to mention the police are actually saying a gas main is responsible for the explosion at the intersection. Just wait until the other distractions go off in fifteen minutes. Did you managed to miss the congestion by the way?"

"So far," Bisset declared. The chain of slight, distinct popping sounds was like dry wood burning. "We're about ten minutes from refuge. How are you faring and any idea what's your estimated time of arrival?"

"We're okay!" Thaw said. "The lads hung on for their lives though when I was driving at speed. They thought we'll actually be going back in time."

Laughter came from the other end of the line. Klugman shook his head and muttered wanker under his breath.

"They'll get over it. it's nothing a good stiff drink won't cure." he went on, putting his hand over the mouth piece and staring at Cummings. "Adrian! What's our current ETA?"

Cummings looked up and squinted at the angle of the sun. "Less than a hour to our appointment," came back the reply and a shrug of his shoulders. "Or thereabouts."

Thaw repeated the information down the phone then added. "Have you heard anything different reported on the police scanner than what's being released to the news crews?"

Bisset cracked an answer: "Yeah a bit. The traffic lights will be out of action for hours. The first of the local emergency services have just arrived at the funeral pyre and the body count is rising quite nicely as they search for injured. Vehicles can't move in any direction on the motorways and between the overpass we blew up, even the hard shoulders are out of commission for the ambulances and fire engines to use."

"Uh-huh," he exclaimed as he listened attentively, keeping the disgust of what he felt to himself.

"Police resources are being redeployed," the voice crackled on, "to cope with the disaster area. Additional officers are been drafted in to follow up all of the starling new leads they getting plus more police teams are en route in a bid to lessen the traffic jams behind the roadblocks by hurrying up the inspection time for each vehicle."

Thaw blinked, feeling conscious guilt and a spasm of emotional distress over his part in the murder of so many innocent people. It was for the sake of the greater good he mentally told himself but nothing he knew warranted the taking of all those lives. He swallowed but didn't let the agony he was experiencing deep down inside of the event, show outwardly on his face. "Good work Nathan!" He replied evenly. "By the way is there any report of the Caravelle being discovered yet?"

"No! Only the one we supplied them with," Bisset assured him. "I alert you otherwise if the situation changes before then."

"Understood! See you shortly," Thaw proclaimed. Abruptly ending the call, and slipping the mobile into his boiler suit pocket.

"Okay Jerome," Klugman said, eager to learn what he could from the conversation. "Let's hear it."

"You will," Thaw said, turning to stride over to where the pouches lay. "But on the way down. Adrian," he added bending to pick up his money bag, "if your ready, move us out."

* * *

"Sir! The data's finally decoded and is printing out now," the police office announced. Stepping away from the teleprinter to carry out her other duties.

"Thanks Scheider." Detective sergeant Keane replied, marching over as the machine continued to churn out the output. When it had finished typing, Keane ripped off the paper and read it quickly to himself. Canal locks and a system of sewer pipes have been blown to smithereens.

He looked up and a deep frown crossed his features as he gave the news a seconds thought. The various aspects of the two incidents urged him from the outset to think it was terrorism but his training whispered to him that there something wrong with his conjecture which he just couldn't put his finger on at the moment. He turned and sighed, listening to the noise around him. If the armed robbery and the devastation on the motorway weren't bad enough for one day then there was the strong possibility of this worry as well. The guv was gonna think this was great.

"John!" The sergeant bellowed to a young office on the phone.

"Can you wait while I check," he said, putting his hand over the mouth piece and tapped a key on the computer. He blinked and stared at the sergeant.

"Inform me the instant the investigators arrive at the crime scenes and if you receive anything like demands or messages from terrorists claiming responsibility."

John nodded, removed his hand before carrying on with his conversation. "I'm sorry Madam," he stared at the monitor and it was blank of information. "I haven't any news at this time..."

He didn't see Keane spin on his heels and dart out of the incident room.

* * *

The companions trekked down the slope in ragged, single file and when they reached a fork in the trail, Cummings turned, leading the others along the right hand split. Not to many minutes further on Sycamores and Cedars, and poplars began to crowd the spoor which then threaded along to be lost to the untrained eye in the midst of overgrown vegetation: low growing Clover, wild Pansies and six foot long knotgrass. Tendrils of Morning Glory and Crabgrass stalks popped out from behind the thick boles.

"Hey guys," Klugman exclaimed in surprise. "Listen to this, the news reader just said that all the old banknotes we stole are estimated to be worth a cool five million pounds. If only that were true eh? We would all be nearer to living on easy street if it was."

"Yeah," Cummings replied vehemently as a squirrel scurried across the tree branches above. His darting eyes continuing to comb the shade from side to side. "Bastard security firm is trying to claim more by deceiving their insurance company." He cleared his throat by hawking up some phlegm. He spat it into a collection of weeds, he passed. "They taking no risks but gaining plenty as I see it. Whatever next they gonna do? Put up a reward for out capture."

"I'm certain of it," Thaw answered, with a nod. "You know! They're almost becoming as crooked as us. Let's pick it up people."

The trio trampled on, minutes slipping by, the underbrush making their progress slow. Gradually the day slipped towards the early stages of mid-afternoon and around the walkers, prickly brambles fought for dominance with yard-high ferns while the trees became more scattered. Up above their clawing skeletal branches, the shafting rays of sunlight became softer and diffuse as dark clouds began assembling in the sky. A low gurgling sound directly ahead of them could just be faintly heard, Cummings smiled and continued forward at a steady pace, vegetation thinning until he came up to the bank of a small, fresh water stream. Liverwort and yellow-green mosses flourished along the raised land border, sunshine glittered and sparkled off the water as the brook bubbled slowly over smooth stones.

"Jerome! I just heard the blackout is in full effect," Klugman declared. Pulling off his earphones with his free hand to leave them dangling around his neck. "Odds are the water, gas and sewerage should go off line at any second."

Thaw smiled and said. "If I was still a betting man I've lay even money on it."

Cummings halted on the edge of the bank where a series of stepping stones were just visible above the water line. He cast a quick glance over his right shoulder and said. "Guys! We're cross the stream here! A few minutes and we'll be at the refuge," he smiled at his companions as they bore down on his position. His facial expression creasing in relief and pleasure. "Hundred yards! Just through that cluster of plants over there," he pointed a finger straight ahead to show them the direction. "Catch up when you can! I'm going on ahead to scope the place out." He turned his gaze forward and set off, striding out onto the first stone, leaving a muddy impression of his boot treads in his wake.

Three more measured steps brought him to the opposite bank. Thaw and Klugman followed carrying their load, exercising care in walking over the slippery path, springing over the second and third stones. Cummings drew his weapon and clinked off the safety then after letting his eyes adapt to the faint light beneath the canopy, the strident cracking sound of leaves being crushed underfoot accompanied him as he sprinted on ahead.

"Kyle!" Thaw said, reaching the bank and going onward, without a backward glance. "I want an alarm system. Leave one of your calling cards around here? It should slow the law down a bit and forwarn us if they're giving chase not to far behind."

"You got it," Klugman replied, fathoming his intention. Stepping back on dry land. "And I've got just the thing for the job too. I'll see you at the car." He watched Thaw go before he dumped the money pouch onto the bank, slipped the straps off his shoulders and knelt down. Next, Klugman opened up the rucksack, rummaged inside and finally extracted a Claymore and a length of strong, light-green twine.

CHAPTER THREE

Cummings brushed through the greenery, knocking aside the leaflets with the barrel of his gun. After ducking low under a branch, he glimpsed patches of the changing landscape beyond, between the gaps in the wall of orange and red bushes. Depositing his pouch on the ground, flattening some flowering heather, he advanced cautiously and parted the mass of foliage to gaze at a broad, flat meadow drenched in sunlight. A scattering of tree stumps were over-shadowed by tall glasses in the midst of Autumn Crocus growing wild around a large outbuilding about forty yards directly before him. Cummings' restless eyes and the flawless pattern of movement of his sweeping gun barrel finally settled upon the ramshackle construction. It was dilapidated and so neglected it looked as if it would fall to pieces if anyone sneezed at it. The sun-blenched walls of wooden planks had thinned over time and had also shrunk here and there; and in other places the overlapping boards were either warped or the edges were split and darkened where they had soaked up the damp from the ground.

With his free hand he unzipped his boiler suit to reveal his polo shirt underneath. He could see there was a window set in the one facing wall, the four panes of glass were blackened with grime. He holstered his Colt 45, took off his broad belt and let it drop to the ground before slipping both of his arms out of the sleeves of the coveralls, as he did Cummings saw higher up a small portion of the structure's roof had collapsed inward. Between himself and the building there were a couple of large rotten, bald tractor tyres plus a trio of rusted furrowing spades with different shaped cutting edges that had been broken off the frame of their plough. Elsewhere on his right, under the chipped and cracked ceramic drainpipe was a water barrel whose bulging staves had holes in the sides.

Thaw dropped his pouch beside the other bag and came forward, reaching into a small pocket of his boiler suit as he came through the thick greenery to crouch at the edge of the brushes right behind Cummings hulking frame. He was tugging down the top of his boiler suit to his waist. Withdrawing a tiny device, Thaw attached it to the muzzle of his semi-automatic and glanced furtively over the terrain with his finger on the trigger of his UZI, and asked a whispered question. "Adrian, is the coast clear?"

"So far," he announced. Not relaxing while he tied the sleeves of his boiler suit together into a makeshift knot in front of his stomach so he wouldn't trip over them when he was about his next task. "To be on the safe side, I am going to do a bit of reconnoitering and check out the building first to make sure it's only filled with friends, and not foes." He peered up once more at the sky where between the thickening gray clouds there were still patches of blue, some of which were steadily being obscured by detached, towering cumulus whose cauliflower peaks were presently an outstanding feature lit by subdued sunlight.

Thaw nodded thoughtfully. "If it's the latter, then kill them. We've come to far to have everything we've accomplished be reversed."

"That's my intention," Cummings announced, lowering his eyes. "Stay here Jerome and look after my stuff." He flipped his shirt collar up so the pointed edges stuck up, passed his ears. "If you hear anything like shots or see me return without my collar still up," he gestured towards it, "then get the hell out of here quick. Okay!"

"Yeah," Thaw confirmed with an adjoining nod.

Cummings cracked his knuckles. He pulled the knife from his boot and despite his bulk he made his way at a dash, out of the bushes, across the open ground like a graceful panther before halting at the rear facing side of the outbuilding. Behind Thaw, the rustle of leaves beneath a set of heavy footfalls preceded the arrival of Klugman carrying his pouch in the crook of his left arm whilst grasping the handle of his Magnum in his right hand.

Thaw wrenched his head around to the noise and eyed his Colt Python. He spoke in a low yet firm tone. "Shush, and get yourself down here now. You're presenting to good a target for anyone to see, stomping about up there."

Klugman's keen eyes tracked Cummings warily pass weeds growing in profusion before disappearing round the corner of the structure. Glancing at Thaw, Klugman gave him a wicked glare before stooping low beside him. "The booby's set! So where's high pockets going then?" He asked, shooting distrustful looks around him.

"Just on patrol!" Thaw explained with a sigh, speaking very softly. "He thought the place warranted a thorough, once-over."

Thaw rose and remaining low, crept around another plant and settled to peer between the branching stems of a thicket of shrubs on the pretext of watching the terrain from a different angle. It covered his real reason for putting distance between himself and Klugman in case Klugman chose this moment, now they were alone, to obtain a larger share of the money and even the score by attempting to pistol-whip him.

Out of annoyance, Klugman shook his head and made a loud clinking sound with his tongue. "Tut! If you ask me Jerome this is a complete waste of time." He said, boldly opposing this strategy. "Instead of skulking around like this, we ought to use the time to get further away while the going's good."

"Hah!" Thaw replied, glancing at him from the corner of his left eye. "Coming from you Kyle, that almost sounds comical especially when you take into account your track record to date." His limbs were close to his body, the business end of the UZI was cradled in the curve of his left arm.

With his mouth a unyielding line, Klugman stared sternly at his companion, narrowing his eyes, glittering with fury. "As I said before, I was in control of the situation Jerome." He answered with animosity in his voice. His heart then sank as his gaze finally noticed the stubby barrel of Thaw's UZI, pointing at him. The muzzle had been extended by a tiny, black silencer.

* * *

With the tip of his knife to the fore, Cummings slacked off his initial pace and went carefully with a slow and unvarying tread. He progressed through long, open shadows cast by the timber wall he traveled alongside. He passed another tractor wheel in similar condition to the other ones, yet of a smaller size lying beside more weeds. As he neared one of the front corners of the building, Cummings heard talking, reverberating upon the air. He blinked and recognised two of the voices at once as being those of his acquaintances. However the owner of the third he couldn't identify at all. Paying close attention to his surroundings, he saw a low knothole in one of the boards, and knelt down to peer into it as a temporary spy hole but alas, there were something that obscured his view.

Feeling frustrated with only the knowledge of what his ears were picked up, Cummings lowered himself onto his belly then quietly slithered forward thorough the tall grass to the corner and took a swift look around it. A pair of long ruts were cut deep into the ground and led away from the old barn's huge double-doors. From his perspective, he could just see the entrance, standing against the single, open door was a short-haired, thirty year old, heavy-set man dressed in loose-fitting coveralls, leaning with practiced ease on the long handle of a axe, resting in the tall grass, between the ruts. Cummings listened to the conversation as he judged and appraised the measure of the stranger.

"Look Miss Clark! I understand that you and your father have traveled a long way from Scotland and I can imagine your legs would be aching sir after driving such a distance." The young man said cordially, in a west country accent. His gaze flicking from face to face, seeing certain similarities in their height if not in the faces between the pair he was talking to. "I really sympathy with you but you can't rest here," he shook his head sadly. "It's private property and it's not safe. Part of the roof has fallen in and by rights my boss would have torn down this barn last year if some lousy tree-hugger hadn't convinced the National Trust it had some historical importance to British heritage and got them to save it for the nation." He swallowed. "If this was my land," he spoke on, "I would overlook the hour you asked for, and you could stop on the path outside, but it's not. I'm only a laborer and it's more than my jobs worth to let you stay."

Having heard and seen enough, Cummings pulled his head back and flicked a glance at the ground around him, he brushed his free hand between the grass until he found just what he wanted. Wetting his dry lips, he readied himself for the task ahead then quietly got to his feet. Holding a small, smooth stone in one hand, he tucked his knife back into his boot with the other, deciding before he did, that he wouldn't need to dirty his blade for this particular foe. With only one determinate aim in mind and lacking any sting of conscience, Cummings edged himself slowly around the corner as he continued to listen to the rest of what the labourer had to say. "You're trespassing pure and simple. You'll have to go now. There's a lay-by about a quarter of a mile down the road in that direction." He gestured with his thumb over his broad shoulder, towards the track, as Cummings took another step towards him and drew back his right arm. "I got to make a start on splitting some firewood. I'll be back in about twenty minutes and by then," he went on, unknowingly behind him the stone was thrown towards the open door, "I want you to be gone."

The stone banged loudly high up against the barn's door and the laborer jumped at the noise and involuntary let go of his axe as he turned around to see what had caused the impact. Before the axe had fallen, the drawn stares from the people standing on the threshold caught sight of Cummings as he surged forward into view. A flicker of recognition washed over both of their faces as they saw the hands of the tall robber lash out with incredible speed to latch around the laborer's neck and chin. Moments lengthened and a muffled struggle ensured. Cummings arm tighten its grip about the man's neck as he wrenched up the man's jawbone, tendons become prominent in the stain and the laborer's face contorted in a rictus of pain until there was a audible crack; the light fading from his eyes as his dead body slumped into Cummings arms. Gillett exhaled a dazed breathe while Bisset felt a little bit nauseous from the sight.

Nathan Bisset was six foot one in height and was thin as a rake with slim undersized shoulders and absolutely no waist to speak of. He was in his late fifties with bones jutting out of a lean, hatched-face that was lined and weathered around his sharp features. He was immaculately dressed in a suit tailor-made for his scrawny frame and rangy limbs. His pale skin was stretched tight over his sunken cheeks and narrow, nicotine-stained, fingers which again had protruding bones. Dark purple shadows from lack of sleep and work related worry were under his gray tinted eyes behind thick-lenses, horn-rimmed glasses resting beneath his shiny bald head adorned with a few wispy strands of brown and white hair pressed down behind his ears with vaseline.

Taking the laborer's frame effortlessly, Cummings stentorian voice barked an order to impel his acquaintances to action as he dragged the limp corpse inside the outbuilding and behind the wall of one of the stalls. When the pair had snapped out of their initial shock, they busied themselves by picking up the axe and closing the door behind them. Leaving the body on top of the dusty straw, Cummings heard Bisset retching in another booth when he walked out of the stall and began scrutinizing his surroundings. The interior of the barn had the appearance of being adapted for many uses by its owners over the years. A stable and a barn were the most evident. Beneath shafts of subdued sunlight lancing down through the collapsed roof and between the timber rafters adorned with whitish thread-like fungi and cobwebs, there were a number of wooden stalls that had once housed horses and livestock for the winter.

Rusted and broken machines and equipment presently lay in some of the stalls while others were either empty, or filled with ripped grain sacks, decaying fodder and a long blonde wig. The only window was covered with debris from the roof and snapped beams split asunder from their fall. Moldy straw covered the wooden floor which was eclipsed presently by a red, Mark Five, Ford Escort.

"Sophie!" He asked in a very business-like tone, speaking much more quieter on this occasion. "Did you bring Kyle's other munitions?" He breathed in, and his nose wrinkled in distaste as it detected the reek of dry rot, mustiness and dampness in the air.

Gillett hurried around the back of the vehicle. "Yes!" She nodded. The keys jangled in her hand. "The supplies are in the trunk and a few smaller bits and pieces are in the glove compartment." The lock clinked and she opening up the boot.

"Excellent!" He replied. "We're moving out of here in promptly six minutes."

Bisset finished his dry heaving and emerged from another stall on Gillett's left, wiping his mouth with an handkerchief. He had hurled up the contents of his stomach and some of the vomit had gone over the right trouser leg of his Versace suit and his expensive loafers.

"Gotcha!" She acknowledged, pulling her hairpins out and slowly her choppy crop fell free.

Noticing Bisset had visibly paled and was leaning against the wooden segregating wall of the stall he'd just left, Cummings' face adopted an unresponsive expression as he begin striding alongside the car. "What's wrong Nathan." He shouted back. "Don't tell me that killing upset you, not after you blew up all those people on the motorway?"

"it's a little bit different this close up."

"Wuss!" Gillett called before addressing Cummings. "How many bags did you get?"

"Three!" He answered. "Million in each."

"Wow! That many," she uttered. Her eyes glittering with astonishment as Cummings brushed past the front of the car and headed towards the entrance of the barn.

Tasting bile within his mouth, Bisset became more cheerful at the mere mention of the money and his face regained a hint of its former colour as he took some small delight in the reimbursement he would receive for being treated so unfairly by his firm over the years when it promoted all those younger men and women ahead of him. He pushed his glasses up to the bridge of his nose and unwaveringly he became determine to have the last laugh by ruining the company once and for all by making it pay out again and again for the countless jobs he'd conceived in his mind.

"I've going to help retrieve them, now." Cummings responded, reaching the door and pushing it slightly ajar. Taking great care he cautiously thrust his head around the door before gazing right and left on the look out for danger.

Behind him Gillett shifted a couple of holdalls to the side of the boot so there would be plenty of space for the incoming pouches. Cummings cast one more quick glance over his shoulder at the pair of them.

"Nathan!" He uttered. "Cover the door until we get back. Understand?"

The older man slowly and reluctantly straightened his posture. "You can rely on me Adrian." He smiled faintly with a slight quivering vibration in his reedy voice.

Cummings bobbed his head. He saw him reach into his jacket pocket and withdraw a small, short barreled Derringer. Cummings then turned, shoved the door open further and disappeared into the sunlight.

* * *

Klugman faulted for a moment, taking in the silencer and the deadly repercussions it meant to him particularly when the muzzle of his Colt Python directed towards the barn ahead of him. Thaw smirked. As he resumed, Klugman carried on with his subject but his voice was now carefully casual to avoid antagonising Thaw into an outright confrontation. "I consider our headway is more important than Adrian pussy-footing around here." He spoke in a whisper, seeing Thaw nod. "Look we've thrown the cops of our scent for the time being plus the Caravelle is in all likelihood still stashed under the trees," Klugman continued, stirring restlessly. "But that won't last long. Going along the spool track might have minimized our passage through the forest and took us beyond the search area, but the filth aren't stupid, they'll expand the radius eventually to also cover this area when they don't find any trace of us. That could happen at any second."

Thaw scratched his stubbed chin. "Your quite right Kyle." He replied, also talking low, with a knowing smile. "I don't think that will occur for a bit." He stole a glance and saw Klugman furrow his brow. "Not in the next fifteen minutes or thereabouts, so we can afford to cool our heels for a bit. It won't hurt us. This is a enormous region of countryside for our pursuers to scour, and they'll be far to busy dealing with the havoc we've wrought plus chasing down all the phone leads they receive about us from the general public to bother coming in this direction."

A puzzled expression crossed Klugman's already creased features.

Thaw glanced at his watch. "Quarter to three." He muttered, raising his eyes to scan the landscape again to see any sign of movement, suspicious or otherwise. "A short while ago," he revealed, "the police had an anomalous tip-off from a woman who told them she saw an identical silver Caravelle with matching plates and tyres in a Rutherwick garage twenty miles east of Cuilfield." Klugman's eyes opened wide in surprise at this revelation. "Just one of several," Thaw went on, "observations Sophie and Nathan have telephoned in at irregular times en route to the police stations in the last couple of hours to send the boys in blue on another wild goose chase, miles out of their way."

"Clever," Klugman admitted in a whisper with a mindful nod, catching sight of movement from the corner of the barn which interrupted his train of thought. "We've got activity at three o'clock! Behind the water barrel."

"I see him," Thaw confirmed. "Stay down until we can learn more. We can't afford to be complacent. Not now when one mistake could cost us dearly and," he saw Cummings step into view empty handed, "undo all of the good things the false eyewitness accounts have brought us." Cummings swiveled his head this way and that.

"Yeah!" Klugman pondered. Thaw's words influencing him to return to his previous line of thought. "Maybe so! Nevertheless it's just a shame this house of lies you constructed is built upon such bad foundations. The whole thing is going to fall apart once the filth find the other Caravelle is not in the garage. They'll know something's up with the calls when they're led to another false trail."

"Oh, but they won't be disappointed Kyle!" He stated matter-of-factly, speaking just as softly while he watched Cummings approach, in a low, running crouch. "Not on this occasion. For that's exactly what they'll get."

His companions jaws dropped. "How?" He sputtered, seeing Cummings close the distance between them.

Thaw paused to let out an audible sigh of relief when he perceived Cummings' collar was still sticking up. "We've all been keeping an eye out for some time. Nathan got wind of one while he was at work so he called us, and Adrian stole and planted it in the garage early yesterday morning along with a couple of other things to confuse the police even more."

With his face going red with rage and his eyebrows contacting into a scowl Klugman stated, "that explains the reason for his disappearance. Why on earth didn't you simply tell me this before today, Thaw?"

"You're the newcomer to this operation, Kyle," he answered honestly. "None of us had worked with you before. We only heard of you from Max who knew of your reputation. Therefore the rest of us believed it would be in all our best interest to keep some of the facts on a need to know basis until you proved we could trust you."

Smoldering with anger and resentment, Klugman swore deep down he would settle accounts with everyone, once this was all over. Then a thought flashed through his mind but before he could ask if there were any more future surprises for him, Cummings burst through the overgrown foliage, brushing passed Klugman and came within inches of almost knocking him over as he dashed between the two men, skidding to a halt. Hardly panting from his run, Cummings knelt beside Thaw.

"Report," he said peering at the taller man anxiously.

"Outside is clear Jerome," he replied, folding down his collar. "As is the inside now, that I've taken care of an unwanted visitor."

Klugman grunted in approval.

Thaw frowned. "Police?" He asked firmly, yet inside dreading the answer.

"Negative!" Came back the reply as he looked down to gather up his bandoleer in one hand and his money bag in the other. "Just the local yokel. He wouldn't swallow Sophie's cover story. Anyhow, he's stopped being a problem." He glanced up and levelled his gaze at him. "Our people are on site and are set for transit."

Klugman raised his eyebrows at the word people for it answered his unspoken question, and in a state of confusion, he interrupted his associate's conversation. "We're taking Bisset along with us?" He asked, keeping his cool, if not his counsel to himself. "I thought our little insurance salesman would be surplus to requirements once he'd delivered the goods?"

"Not quite," Thaw revealed in exasperation, breaking eye contact to probe the sky for helicopters. "Nathan is Max's uncle and even if he wasn't he remains a precious commodity because he's revealed to me that he's got access to more juicy targets his firm has only recently insured. I'll tell you more when we're heading away from here." Thaw turned back to Cummings. "Adrian lead us across."

Cummings nodded, and then without further chatter, he rose and retraced his steps towards the building. Thaw and Klugman, carrying their weapons and the canvas bags, hurried along close behind. Tense minutes slipped by inside the barn during which Gillett and Bisset stowed the cumbersome bundles of money with the other paraphernalia in the Escort's boot. And as the pair preceded to place the bandoleers carefully on top of the pouches; around the front of the car the three robbers had already removed their boiler suits and discarded them between the stalls. Thaw and Cummings then took up defensive positions about the barn door, donning coats as they did, while Klugman hunkered beside the wig, and gently placed next to it, a shoebox filled with wires connecting to sticks of dynamite and a clock timer.

Within the inconspicuous box were nails and a jam jar containing a mixture of finely granulated aluminum with an iron oxide. The stall opposite reeked of vomit.

"The Thermit in this jar is used in incendiary bombs you know." Klugman said to no one in particular as he turned some kind of mechanism inside the shoebox to balance a mercury switch. "Alone it will produce enough heat to burn the entire barn to ashes." He then picked up the lid from the ground. "Any stray finger prints or strands of hair we unintentionally leave behind will now be vaporized in the blast, have no worry about that." He gingerly lowered the lid into place. Again there was another audible distinct noise like drinking glasses striking together in a toast.

Bisset looked up from the loading and bit his lower lip. "What's that clink Kyle?" He inquired, a nervous undertone clearly evident in his voice. "You haven't armed the device yet have you not while we're still in here."

"Course I have, you old ponce," Klugman declared cruelly, slowing getting to his feet before moving back to the car. "Don't have a coronary. Everything's fine. I set the timers earlier this morning when I was double-checking all the satchels of explosives I installed. What you heard was me triggering another booby trap to go off when this," he pointed to the shoebox, "seemingly harmless looking object is lifted. Even if I don't radio remote the charges and our pursers manage to somehow get passed my hi-tech trip wire in the next twenty hours then my fail-safe padlock Jerome's holding will initiate the chain reaction and everything will still go boom."

"Another little bit of hell on earth eh?" Gillett said, slamming the boot shut. "I like it! We're done here."

"Same as us," Thaw replied, turning to address Klugman. "How long you going to be Kyle?" Seeing him slip his jacket on before pick up his rucksack from the bonnet of the car.

"No more than a minute tops," he answered. Without braking stride as he moved over to the door frame where he quickly knelt in front of the upright. In the shadow near the ground, a cylindrical piece of plastic with a helical groove cut into it, attached to some exposed wires were sticking out from the edges of a strip of masking tape. He set the rucksack down and next rummaged about inside. "All I got to do is fasten this laser targeting scope and we're be laughing." He extracted an object no larger than a cigarette lighter. It had a cylindrical piece of metal threaded evenly around its outside surface. Klugman screwed the equipment together, taking care not to scratch or damage the contacts.

Eventually both doors of the barn were opened wide by Thaw and Cummings. Mellow sunshine slanted through the gap to reflect twinkling light off the windscreen and bonnet. Then the engine of the Ford Escort roared into life. Gillett threw the gear stick into first, raised the clutch and eased the car forward at a low speed through the opening, passing Klugman's kneeling form, along the ruts until she brought it to a stop about a dozen yards from the entrance. As the car ticked over, with the hand brake on, its occupants threw open the passenger doors and waited for their associates to come to them. After taping the targeting scope to the upright, Klugman dropped the adhesive roll back into his rucksack, stood and pressed a button twice on the side of his digital watch. At ground level, just inside the threshold, a thin red beam from the scope shot directly across the barn entrance.

Stepping over the laser, Klugman said. “Close her up guys.” He sprinted for the Escort’s rear passenger door with his rucksack grasped firmly in his hand. “Get ready Sophie. I want to be out of here like we were Federal Expressed.” He clambered inside.

Gillett smirked at the Americanism. “I let you do your job Kyle. Now let me do mine.” She replied, peering into the mirror.

Behind him, Cummings and Thaw obeyed, having to use brute strength to the sound of screeching hinges as they shoved their individual doors back together, darkness fell onto the interior. A few moments later they sealed the opening. Thaw removed a padlock from his coat pocket and passed the pivoting link through a stable jutting from one of the barn doors. He fastened it cautiously with a clink and gave the lock a slight tug to see that it was secure. Satisfied, he nodded to Cummings and preceded to turn and dash for the car. Cummings shadowed him at a trot and when they’d covered the short distance, both men piled in the back, and shut the doors with an audible slam. Even before the pair had buckled up their seatbelts, the Escort rumbled down the narrow path, between hedgerows towards the country lane.

A gentle breeze blowing into the car sharpened gradually into a strong gale during the course of their journey through the declining hours of the afternoon while high above rain threatened the route they followed as thickening storm clouds filled the sky before being ultimately enveloped in the early, purple dusk.

CHAPTER FOUR

Detective inspector Hallie Sinclair pushed the tortoiseshell frames of her glasses up to the bridge of her broad nose and peered at the Nordic looking young police officer standing tensely opposite her. "So let me get this straight Keane," she repeated with a frown. Staring into his piercing blue eyes, not totally sure she heard the detective sergeant clearly the first time around. "Your saying that after four hours of searching with patrol cars and helicopters, we're no better off in our homicide investigation?"

"In a nut shell, yes guv," he spoke respectfully, in a rich Lancaster accent. Clenching his chiseled jaw as he met her gaze. "Apart from the statement we received from our painting parson, nothing new has come forward as yet but it is early days concerning the leaflets we handed out and the witness appeal boards we left at the crime scene." He swallowed. "Cameras monitoring the traffic flow on the nearby motorway junctions revealed the raiders didn't go in that direction, and the Caravelle wasn't seen either travelling along any of the A-roads or passing through the adjacent towns. The video footage from the security CCTV confirms this. To all intended purposes the vehicles done a disappearing act even Houndini would have been proud of."

Sinclair rose from her chair and tossed her ball-point pen down onto the top of the desk littered with candles, distinct photographs of ghastly post-mortem, images of two dissected corpses, a jar of pens and pencils, reports and a number of tottering files. "I'm not one for magicians myself Justin," she revealed, using his first name. She moved around the pulled-out drawers of her desk to the large map of northern England hanging on the wall. "In the end their act is just an illusion: smoke and mirrors to easily fool an audience that are unable to see the truth."

"That's precisely what I believe those murdering sods are doing now, pulling a fast one on us, lying low in an old building somewhere, evading our helicopters while awaiting the arrival of the dark so they can slip easily across a field, past our roadblocks or, my personnel favourite, they've managed to already dump the Caravelle and are travelling on foot out of the search area. it's the only way those bastards are able to move beyond the gridlock on the motorways presently."

Keane scratched one of his well defined cheek bones and followed the inspector around her desk to the left hand side of the map. They stood within her average sized office. A desk ruled the roost in the center of the room and a single small window overlooked the station's car park. A brown carpet stretched beneath her computer terminal on her right and the framed scene of a group of grazing zebra on an African grassland hung above the bank of filing cabinets along one wall.

"Off the record guv," Keane told her, "most of the relief in the incident room are of a similar opinion."

"Well it'll make a change!" She replied. Brushing aside some of her beaded plaits drooping over her face as she stared at the drawing, with a marked radius around the Lancaster village of Cuilfield, patterned like a pie chart with the circle divided into clear and darkened sections in which there were a bristling amount of small coloured flags and pins depicting among other things the relative positions of nearby towns, a caravan park and a few farmsteads. "It's not like I get second guessed all that often." She stabbed a thick finger at a red pin as she returned to a business-like tone. "Right then, let's do this before the generator in the basement runs out of fuel and I have to light those pissing candles. The village is here and there," she traced a line down to a yellow flag just below, "is the crossroads where the skid-marks were found."

Keane nodded. "Officers have already took photographs and measurements. We have a fair idea what type of belted radial tyre they were using."

While Keane spoke, she drew another invisible line across to a blue pin. "Uh-huh! And this is the place where the Clergyman saw our felons next on a heading taking them East towards an assortment of bus terminus and trains stations."

"The region might be assessable to transport guv," Keane reasoned. "But if anyone of them has an ounce of brains then they're suspect those would be the first places we were going to look for them."

"True!" Sinclair agreed with a nod. "There's nothing dumb about this lot. That's why we've drawn a blank. They would have considered we'd get their description out quick and patrol the main routes so to keep the lowest profile possible circumstances dictate the robbers would have headed down something less public like the rural lanes, barely noticeable that way, probably following someone whose connected to the region and knows every cattle shed, barn and outhouse for miles around."

"Miles is the word guv," he said with a single bob of his head, stealing a glance at the detective inspector. "Even with what we've already covered," he pointed at the darkened zones on the map. "There's still a large area of countryside out there that's wild from traditional farming going back years." He swallowed. "And to get a visual fix this late in the day with the light dwindling and the predicted storm, well is going to be very difficult at best."

"I'll accede to that Justin," Sinclair declared with a sniffle. Pulling a kleenex tissue out from the long sleeve of her cardigan and wiping her nose. "It'd be like trying to find an ant on a football pitch. But they aren't the only ones to be armed and mean business. Until the weather turns nasty I plan on keeping the manhunt going for as long as we can today then tomorrow I want to test my theory by flooding sections one and three with enough officers," she gestured at the regions of the map in question, "to flush them out of hiding. I'm going to do everything in my power to prevent this robbery from being the first in a major crime spree."

"That might make them resurface," Keane acknowledged, "and with the extra man power being drafted in from the other forces, we should finally be able to cope with the drain chewing on our resources. I've ordered files to be duplicated to bring those senior officers up to speed."

Being reminded of additional facts by his comment, Sinclair asked. "Incidentally, how are the anomalous tip-offs going?" She pushed her hanky inside her sleeve and turned back to the desk. "Have we received any more phone calls since the last one at two-twenty-five?"

"None sir," he replied, following her. "That's not saying they couldn't have tried the phone lines and failed to get through. The station's switchboard has been engaged due to being inundated with distraught people attempting to find out about family or friends caught up in the explosion on the motorway."

"Any progress in tracing the tip-offs?" Sinclair asked as an afterthought since she couldn't recall seeing the report on her desk. "Because I'm sure you haven't brought me up to speed on that."

"No! The tricksters weren't on long enough for us to trace

them, not even partially but studying the frequency and intensity of speech sound waves we audio taped of the most recent calls by putting them through the sound spectrograph has revealed the accents and the speech mannerisms of the speakers seem to be the same pair who made the other hoax calls. I wouldn't though want to prove the accuracy of a positive identification in court. Although they weren't speaking through a voice box, their utterances was still slightly muffled like their owners were speaking with handkerchiefs pressed over the mouth pieces of the phone."

Sinclair slowly lowered her bulky body down on to the chair and digested that information. "I see!" Sensing the doubt in his voice. "Duly noted! Take a seat Justin," she gesture at the chair opposite. He nodded and plonked himself down. "Any heavy background noise like a sound of a train passing by, a drill from some road works, church bell ringing, anything like that to indicate the location of where they made the tip-offs from," her flabby hand clutched a small, shot-glass while her other seized a bottle of bourbon.

"To early to say at the moment," Keane answered, watching her pour herself a drink. "The recording are still being analyzed by our team of experts."

She sipped the bourbon then lowered the glass as the strip light above her head flickered before returning to full strength. "Light the candles! Has traffic congestion eased on the roads since we replaced the roadblocks with the new roadside ANRP checks?"

"A little," he concede. Withdrawing a box of matches from his pocket, vividly recalling visual images from his eidetic memory. "From the early figures I managed to glimpse from the report before coming over here, we've also had some mixed results." He struck the match and lit the candle wicks. "Of the few thousands cars the Automatic Number Plate Recognition system scanned so far, sixteen made an impact on our database and were stopped by officers on the scene. Seven motorists were wanted on outstanding warrants, two more were supposed to be disqualified from driving until early next year, a further five had no car insurance or out dated road tax discs."

"And the last couple Justin?" Sinclair inquired, raising her glass again.

"A guy suspected of beating up his girlfriend's lover," Keane revealed, "and a van load of illegal immigrants from Iran."

"That's the second lot we're caught this week," she said with a brief shake of her head. "You know if we have anymore coming across the channel our little island will sink. Oh well, not what I wanted to hear. What about the silver Caravelle we were steered to that garage in Rutherwick? Has anything more turned up from that yet?"

Knowing there was a lot on his superior's plate right about now, Keane decided to give her a brief recap to remind her of past developments in case she forgotten them before going on with current proceedings. "Well!" He swallowed. "As you already know the Volkswagen Caravelle our lads found is the only lead we had to check that didn't end up sending us on another fool's errand. Our forensic experts have cordoned off the area and have since the last time we spoke placed the vehicle on the back of a low loader and removed it for examination."

"Concentrating on facts," he went on, "the Caravelle's definitely been stolen. The serial number on its chassis has been scratched off. Whoever the owner was must have thought a steering wheel lock and alarm would be enough to stop the theft because the vehicles proper registration number isn't etched on all the windows as it should. Apart from that it matches the description of the wanted Caravelle almost perfectly: similar model, tire type, colour and has the same false license plates as the picture of the people-carrier the speed camera captured outside Cuilfield..."

"Except the tinted windows weren't identical to the clear ones depicted in the photograph and the set of statistics we collated from the statements from the eyewitnesses on the scene." She interrupted irritably, raising her arm and extracting some more bourbon from the glass. "Yes! yes, I'm aware of all this, therefore what new?"

The young officer blinked. "Actually not a lot in this department. The map of Devon and the train timetable that were found inside the vehicle could be red herrings but we are checking them out nevertheless along with the strands of hair our people discovered on the back seats. One good piece of news though. We've surmised why the immobiliser on the Caravelle didn't work! The owner must have left his spare set of car keys in the glove compartment or hidden on the top of his sun visor."

The detective inspector bobbed her head. "Yes!" She said thoughtfully, coming to the same conclusion. "That gets my vote too. Bleeding foolish though, in all probability he left the vehicle's documentation in there too."

"You never know," he spoke on. "What's gets me guv is instead of changing plates, why didn't they simply shoot hair spray over them to stop the reflection? Our speed cameras can't read them."

"Maybe the raiders weren't leaving anything to chance. I'm just thankful the camera was one of the newer versions which has good zoom capability and it was actually working with film in, covering that precise hour of the rotation."

"Certainly is considering the crippling expense of keeping the cameras going any longer than that. Anyway as per your instructions, we're using a different team to avoid cross contamination issues. Like at the crime scene, forensic teams are continuing to conduct a gradual search for traces of DNA and fibers from articles of clothing. It's a painstakingly slow process but despite that so far we've learned that the driver of this decoy Caravelle had to be at least six foot four in height we judged this from the retracted position of the driver's seat in relation to the distance from the foot peddles."

"Interesting," Sinclair said, rubbing her double chin thoughtfully. "Several of the eyewitnesses testified at seeing a tall man among the robbers in-between diving for cover."

"Indeed," Keane admitted. "He's the one we've got footage of from the Post Office's security camera. He left us a lovely set of bloody footprints he trampled across the floor after treading on the back of one of the dead bodies. He has a size twelve foot with a tack embedded in the heel. We traced the pattern of the boot tread to a special type sold at a local sports and camping store but this brand has been on sale for over a year and the store has branch outlets more or less through out the country."

"They could have been brought as long as six months ago," he continued. "Presently uniform are delving into the shop's recorded transactions for the sake of seeing if any of those sized boots were purchased with cash or by credit card. He may have got careless and left a name or an address behind."

"Ah," the inspector expressed her delight. "First-rate as usual Justin. I don't suppose the villain did us a favor and left any fingerprints on the steering wheel or on the door handle on the driver's side?"

"Afraid not sir," he shook his head. "They were the first places we dusted and were found to be clean. He must have wore gloves and simply smudged or wiped the owner's dabs along the way to be on the safe side. Other areas are being scrutinised though even as we speak. We've already begun to run a computer check on matching vehicles to see if we can track down the registered owner's of it."

The inspector nodded, and some of the long braids tumbled down again, over her lined, dark-skinned face.

"There was no evidence of latent fingerprints either on the discarded 9mm bullet casings on the road," Keane pushed on, not hearing her mentally say consistence of them. "And from what we dug out of the woodwork, and bagged off the pavement we found evidence that there were additional and different caliber handgun and a semi-automatic gun involved in the shooting as well. A Colt 45 and an Uzi according to the second ballistics report. With the exception of the slugs discharged from the Colt Python that killed the postmaster and the security courier, there was no visible traces of blood on the other ejected cartridge casings at the scene."

"Huh!" Sinclair uttered, expressing her surprise. Brushing the braids away from her face with her free hand. "So this is where we stand in this madness thanks to a bunch of cost cutting bureaucrats." She went on feeling it was necessary to summarize events in her mind. "We have a contaminated crime scene that has due to the villagers and the paramedics had more people through it than Grand Central Station. There were three different guns belonging to three perpetrators. An Uzi, a Colt 45 and the 357 Magnum was the one used as the murder weapon. The getaway vehicle: a silver Volkswagen Caravelle with fake number plates has dissolved into thin air despite being in a selected search radius that's been patrolled by countless ground and airborne units."

"And if that's not all, we have a major disaster on our hands on the M6; explosions all over the place which points to terrorists, we quashed a riot at the bus station and almost had gridlock on every road in the county to say nothing of the power cut, several villagers suffering from severe trauma from the shock and a couple of car accident victims are in hospital being tended for their various injuries not to mention the man and woman callers who are most likely additional members of the gang, with little evidence which at present we can't trace back to an individual source." She paused for breath. "Have I missed out anything of note Justin?"

He shook his head. "Not much. Just the approaching storm which will detain us even more while piling on additional hours to the raiders head start."

The fluorescent tube above their heads sputtered anew before the light returned to normal illumination. "Maybe." She replied. Smiling in the face of adversity yet keeping her thoughts focused and on track. "By the way Justin, have you seen sergeant Giddings anywhere on your travels? I keep missing him. I wanted to catch hold of him and see how he's doing with the primary inquiries? He's away from the car radio and his mobile's switched off again. I've left messages but he hasn't gotten back to me."

"Sorry! I haven't seen him in the last couple of hours." Keane responded with a brief shake of his head before asking a question of his own. "So guv, you still feel strongly about this being an inside job?"

"You know me. Everyone's a suspect however I do as it happens." She told him frankly, taking a sip of her drink. "I generally examine a problem from all of its angles to start with but this crime reeks of being an inside job. You see I've got an inner radar screen up here," she tapped her temper with a finger, "that I just can't ignore. It doesn't take me three guesses as to who my two prime suspects are at the moment."

"The security courier Ralph Jenkins and Abraham Rutten: the post master." Keane ventured a guess.

"Oh, yes," the inspector confirmed with a grim expression. "And until proven otherwise either one of them could have blabbed on purpose or unintentionally over a drink in the local pub, and the rest of the gang decided to shut them up permanently or the employee was part of the organized group, and the others simply got greedy and didn't want to pay out another share of the booty."

"Could be both," he voiced his opinion. "At the moment though that's pure supposition."

"Well you can never tell," she admitted openly, not offended by his comments. "Ruthless I grant you but sensible to a pack of killers like these. For only a former or present employee of either organization perhaps with gambling debts or another ulterior motive based on," she shrugged her shoulders, "some real or imaginary grievance against their company would be privy to confidential information in regard to dates and times, routes and pick up points, and could have relayed that knowledge onto the robbers."

"Furthermore," Sinclair continued, barely pausing for breath, "who else besides one or two exceptions could have known that millions of pounds in old paper currency ready to be burned in the furnaces down south would have been shipped in such an insecure way from a Post Office instead of a bank, within mail pouches, loaded in the boot of a Morris Marina." She drained her glass then in one gulp. "And all because an armored car was to conspicuous and damn well to costly to run for the company just to take a short trip down to the rail depot." She set the glass down on the desk top and picked up the telephone receiver.

"I want a through background check of both suspects before you go off researching others. They both had opportunity now find me their motive. While you're at it I also want their homes searched for additional lines of inquiry. Address books, diaries to see if they were acting under the duress by threat, and if they have a computer analysis the hard drive, and any Internet sites they might have visited lately, I want to know about it. And to be prudent Justin we'll go with our version of Code B, wait until we've got the relations out of the houses then enter the premises. I don't think they frustrate the object of the search but you can never tell. Leave the Notice of Power and Rights somewhere prominent but not on the door we smash down."

"Consider it done." Keane said.

"Okay then! Is there anything else you've got to tell me before I make this call?"

"Nothing sir," Keane said, getting to his feet. "You're now up to date on my end of the investigation. However receipts for credit card transactions inside the time frame you suggested and checks upon call records from mobile phones in the area will take much longer to compile according to our SO11 intelligence squad."

"All right!" She replied, immediately knowing which of the attached specialist units he meant. "Keep your nose to the grindstone, Justin. Dismissed."

Keane turned and left, leaving Sinclair alone to dial her number. The line connected at the other end.

"Tamzin," Sinclair said. "Hallie here! How's your investigation going at all the sites. Have you discovered if it's terrorism yet?"

"Sure looks that way Hallie," the female voice replied. "We have a couple of clues and no answers but initial reports indicate that minute traces of an explosive called salt of fulminic acid were found very close to the ruptured water pipe and at the traffic lights. As you know that stuff is used in percussion caps and detonators. We've got people checking the locations of the sewerage and gas lines that blew but the areas are dark and rural, and our findings may take some time to gather before we get the big picture."

"Oh great more problems," Sinclair said, "at least the cover stories for the press are holding water for the time being. Okay Tamzin let me know when you learn more especially from the investigators at the electric substation and the construction crews at the flyover."

"You got it Hallie," the speaker replied. "Bye!"

The Detective inspector replaced her receiver and with a shake of the head became lost in a troubled reverie.

CHAPTER FIVE

Avoiding the major cities and the motorways like the plague, the Ford Escort kept to the country roads at a steady speed as it proceeded initially along a roundabout route out of the Lancaster low-land before Gillett steered the vehicle on a pre-scouted route taking them due south. Out of their windows, low dry stone walls and gaps in rows of hedges where gates resided, afforded the five associates with beautiful, fleeting views of the ever changing English scenery. There were rolling, green pastures with cattle or sheep gazing, farms and fields gave way to meadows and tracts of open land covered with white and purple heather, lavender, and grass that melted into clumps of trees.

Of these Bisset, just gave a passing interest as he sucked his minty sweet. For despite knowing they no longer matched the description of the all-points bulletin, he still nervously took a backward glance out of the rear window every so often to get a sense of ease and see for himself that no patrol cars were shadowing them. Only a M-reg, Honda Civic gave Bisset any cause for concern when it tagged along behind them for a couple of miles until the driver turned down another road and disappeared from sight. An hour and a half after leaving the barn behind, the autumn twilight had descended upon the countryside. Gillett flicked the headlamps on full and the lancing beams sliced through the gloom as she and her companions listened attentively to the goings on from the news reports on the radio.

"And to repeat the main headlines: tonight emergency workers are still frantically searching through the devastation blocking both lanes of the M6 motorway near junction ten just hours after a flyover collapsed onto a petrol tanker and caused its load of fuel to ignite into a massive fireball that engulfed people and vehicles in a hundred and fifty metre radius." The news reader announced gravely. There was a low bass tone in his voice as he continued with the report. "Survivors found on the outer edges of the explosive wave were cut out from cars by firefighters and lifted by air ambulance to awaiting burns units at nearby hospitals which are being powered by back-up generators. All the injured are in intensive care and many of them are said to be in a critical condition."

The announcer paused for breath before going on. "A grim procession of the dead have been stored in the Edinshire Leisure Centre until refrigerated trucks arrive to transport the bodies away to be identified and examined at the local morgue. As yet a list of casualty numbers hasn't been released but unofficially the estimated death toll is thought to run into the upper hundreds. Police have opened up additional inquiry phone lines so anyone who is worrying about a family member should call this number now..."

Thaw turned the radio's volume down. "Piece of luck that petrol tanker was going under the bomb at the time it exploded. It masked what really happened. Engineers might blame cheap materials being used in the construction of the overpass."

"Or the volume of traffic going across the flyover was too much weight for the span to bear, weakening the supports." Bisset declared.

"Both suggestions will be ruled out when the area's been properly sealed off and the structural engineers have underpinned what's left of the overpass," Klugman said with certainty. "It's inevitable the investigators will think of foul play once they've found there's no obvious sagging in the span and some debris fragments are blackened by an explosive blast. From the evidence though, the cops are gonna connect this and the utility locations, and attributed the blame to really any number of foreign terrorism groups around at the moment."

"Not bad." Gillett declared, peering into the blackness. "Very conceivable."

"It's nice to know you can still rely on the media to not even attempt to subdue the panic and fear people are feeling now." Cummings remarked. "I quite liked the line about the scene on the motorway had taken on the appearance of a war zone. Classic stuff."

"I welcome it," Bisset announced.

Gillett nodded. "Between the turmoil running everyone ragged and what we've heard earlier, on the police scanner, saying they don't have a clue of our whereabouts or the real Caravelle, well guys I wish we'd brought a bottle of champagne along for the ride because I reckon this calls for a celebration."

Klugman couldn't help but grin broadly at the message on the radio advertising the new Adam Sandler movie. "Yep! Those idiots keep up with progress like that," He announced with obvious delight in his voice. Speaking over the broadcast, his words reflecting the general mood of those around him, "and we're bound to make it."

Gillett's face lit up at the possibility while Bisset rubbed his hands together and a thin, semi-relaxing smile crossed his features. Cummings kept a neutral expression, Thaw however nodded but like Cummings, didn't let the infectious ambiance get to him.

"Hmmm," Thaw uttered thoughtfully, considering his statement. "It a possibility Kyle! I'm not one to count my chickens to prematurely. The police might retain only faint traces of evidence like skidmarks and witness sightings but I think I'll wait until we've put some more miles between us and the Caravelle before I jump up and down about it."

Klugman grunted derisively, but said no more on the subject. Thaw turned up the volume on the radio when the advertising ended and the music blared out a dance song from Fatboy Slim. The late afternoon turned slowly into the early evening. The temperate outside dropped considerably and a gentle breeze increased steadily to a screaming gale. Overhead in the sky, stars scattered around the dark expanse began winking out of view as storm clouds extended across the horizon. The Escort traveled ever onward, further south, past crossroads and down winding lanes that on occasion led to bumpy stretches of road that were so narrow that they were only wide enough for a single line of traffic. An old isolated, stone house located on a bend, and a reservoir were the only variety of change in the uneventful, repetitive region of fences and hedgerows.

At a point in their journey, a pending pit stop was taken beside an opening in a split-rail fence. Cummings took a couple of fuel containers from the boot to top up the petrol in the tank while three of the car's occupants swung the gate inward and progressed into the field beyond to answer the call of nature. Bisset came tramping back with the soles of his shoes stinking of cow dung.

"Shit," he bemoaned, scraping the bottom of his feet on the grass verge. "I've just trod in some."

Klugman beamed. "If nothing else we can smell you Nathan even if we can't see you very well out there."

Bisset make a face of distaste and stepped inside the vehicle. Before the car got underway again, Gillett took a break from driving, Thaw being the one to replaced her behind the wheel. The conditions outside made Thaw turn the heater up but slowly the windows began to steam as he changed gear and proceeded along a straight stretch of deserted, concrete road. In the front passenger seat, Cummings saw the mist condense on the glass and turned the heater off then using an old tissue, wiped a wide clean spot in the steam above the steering wheel before carrying on to do his side. Thaw nodded his thanks and kept his full concentration upon the road.

* * *

Danielle Huxley stood by her friends bedroom window and idly pulled aside one of the heavy drapes concealing the glass pane before peering out through the wide gap into the early evening darkness. In the daylight hours the room was afforded the view of the large back garden it overlooked. But now the triangular-shaped yard with its hedgerows had faded away in the gloom along with the adjacent gardens and the rear of the semi-detached houses beyond on the visual-horizon. Except for the distant rumble of passing traffic, all was quiet outside. No wind whipped through the branches of the trees or disturbed the limp washing, hanging on the clothes-line. No dog in the vicinity barked to suggest there were prowlers about. Danielle watched another of the diffused lights flick on from behind one of the curtain-covered rooms of the houses opposite and smiled in response to what her friend had just said.

"Ah, you're pulling my leg Lois." She announced to her companion, releasing the curtain and allowing it to fall back into place when she turned and walked over to the elegant armchair near the bedroom wall.

"No! Straight up." Lois replied, standing in front of her, neatly folding up the pair of fashionable jeans she held.

Danielle sat down and reclined against the chair's comfortably padded high back, sinking into its deep luxurious cushion.

"Trust me on this Danielle," Lois continued. "My aunt's parties are simply boring. And tomorrow nights affair on All Hallows-Eve are generally the worst of the lot because my uncle gets in on the act too." She placed the bundle carefully on top of her folded lingerie, inside the open suitcase lying on her bed.

Danielle crossed one leg over the other.

"You'll be able to see for yourself I'm not putting you on when you get there." Lois went on. "For starters my aunt Ashley is a real disco freak! She's absolutely, loves the music of the seventies and early eighties, and always hires a crap disc jockey for the night to play the stuff."

Danielle blinked. "What nothing from the clubs? Like Shah or Xenuf."

"If we're lucky we might hear a modern song from Ricky or Brittany."

Danielle groaned. "Fantastic!"

"Then it'll be YMCA or something just as old like Agadoo all night."

"Oh! Nothing like listening to repetitious lyrics for a few hours Lois. What are we doing for an encore? Bob for apples with your little cousins."

"There'll be plenty of entertainment for us to look forward to later on, I can tell you." She removed the heavy square, brown paper package from its hiding place under the trousers and showed her companion with a flourishing gesture. "And my cousins won't be attending. They visiting gran in Birmingham."

"Now your talking." Danielle admitted with a smile.

"If my Aunt isn't bad enough then there's my uncle Rob." Lois went on, replacing the package back inside her suitcase. "He's not a blood relation, thank god. He's married to my dad's sister and he ain't no oil painting You know the only reason I can figure why Ashley walked up the aisle with the idiot in the first place is because his rich. He's as hairy as an ape and he's got such a strong Scottish accent, I need subtitles just to under stand what's he has to say at times."

Danielle laughed out loud. "Yuck!" She expressed in disgust.

"Now, I wouldn't call Rob a bit eccentric but in my judgment, he's more downright loony tune. Definitely one sandwich short of a picnic."

"In what way?" Danielle asked, raising her eyebrows in puzzlement.

"Well he likes to call Halloween: Samhaim which is what the Celts appointed this time of the year to be in their calendar."

"Uh-huh!" Danielle uttered, folding her arms as she watched Lois pick up a blouse from atop of the bed and fold it.

"And no word of a lie Danielle, the prat likes to pretend he's a firm believer in the superstitions and traditional customs of the celebrations, saying that because his mother was Irish that it's part of his Celtic heritage to copy what the ancient druids enacted on the day."

"Hmmm, your right he does sound like an oddball." Danielle declared, seeing her friend agree by bobbing her head. "So what kind of ceremony does he observe then?"

"Apart from pouring good plonk on the lawn and hanging mistletoe that's supposed to bring safety, fortune and happiness as long as it doesn't make contact with the ground," Lois replied with a smile, placing the blouse into the case. "He's quite fond of lighting a big bonfire in the back garden."

"Really," Danielle said incredibly, seeing her companion continue to rearrange the contents of the suitcase to her satisfaction. "What's that suppose to achieve?"

"Rob said," Lois explained, holding up her strip of birth control pills to check she had an adequate supply. "Spirits of the dead and wicked evil forms would wander abroad upon the final October evening and the druids held certain views that lighting these bonfires as night fell, would basically frighten off these souls and the ghoulies," her smile broadened as she paused briefly for breathe, slipping the pills next to the packet of lemon favored condoms and her Tampax. "from hurting anyone they met while they visited the old houses where they used to live."

"I see," Danielle said, nodding thoughtfully. Out of habit she began to stroke one of the smooth collection of beads strung around her neck in an effort to alleviate the trepidation she was feeling at the moment. "I didn't thing the Celts were such a superstitious lot."

"A number of ancient civilisations were." Lois said, pressing down hard upon the piles of clothes. "You haven't heard the best yet because this year Rob actually outdid himself. He brought this black sheep and also had this dummy made to burn on top of the bonfire."

A puzzled expression crossed her angelic features. "I must still have water in my ears from when I went swimming this morning," Danielle announced astonishingly. "Because I thought you just said..."

"I did," Lois interrupted.

"Don't tell me, he's killing two birds with one stone and getting in early for bonfire night?"

"Not quite." Lois response, shaking her head. "The druids worshipped the sun and the effigy is suppose to represent the person sacrifice who the priests burned in the hope of requesting the sun to return in the spring of next year."

"Bit barbaric!" Danielle said. "Why did your uncle buy the sheep? He wasn't thinking of drinking the milk or using it to make cheese was he."

"If only." Lois declared, delighted in the way her efforts had paid off by making slightly more room in her case. "He was going to sacrifice the sheep too."

"Honestly?" Danielle asked with a hint of disbelief in her voice.

"Yep! He would have Danielle," Lois replied, "if my aunt hadn't put a stop to it. She threatened to call the police and the RSPCA. She even told him she was considering a divorce because she was fed up of his antics and just couldn't take the family looking like a laughing stock anymore. That put him in his place. I don't think Rob had planned on spending that much on her for Christmas."

At the mere mention of laughing stock, Danielle frowned and began to fiddle with her necklace more energetically. Danielle Huxley had a natural beauty with a flawless complexion glowing with health. She had just turned eighteen years and was about five foot three in height when she wore her favourite leather shoes with the three-inch high heels. She was slim with a splendidly proportioned figure. Pretty green eyes and full red lips shining with gloss occupied a heart-shaped face framed by curly ash-blonde that tumbled down just beyond her shoulder-blades. She wore tight, black trousers and a blue sweater beneath a hip-length, brown leather jacket.

Standing before Danielle, Lois Elmes was just as petite and lovely yet she wasn't so aesthetically pleasing on the eye as her best friend was. Lois was pretty but had to work at it with enough cosmetics on her face to give her the appearance her make-up had been applied with a trowel. She was the same age as her friend and had short lustrous black hair cut in a well-defined bob that had sharp jagged ends about the sides. The bob wreathed an elliptical face set with almond-shaped, dark brown eyes framed with lashes of purple mascara above a sapphire stud in her long straight nose. Her mouth was generous and she had a mole on the left hand side of her jaw.

She had a lean, athletic figure and was extremely attentive of it. Careful of what she ate just in case her weight ballooned and she couldn't slip into the figure-hugging suede trousers she wore presently. A pair of snakeskin boots encased her feet while around her torso she wore a ribbed-sweater.

In an attempt to take her mind of her current thoughts, Danielle threw a question at her friend. “So why was Halloween important to the Celts?”

“It was the final day of their year.” She knelt down to one of the pair of slide-out drawers set beneath the mattress. “This was an auspicious occasion to analyse the signs around as a means to giving them any clues about what their future might hold. The declining vigor of the sun was one such unfavorable omen.” She straightened and placed a dress into the suitcase.

“Lois I’m not sure I understand. How can the sun be an unfavorable omen?”

“With winter coming the druids expected the cold to produce a massive death toll in life and the land to suffer widespread devastation unless they came up with an imaginable way to counteract the conditions they were about to be faced with.”

“The bonfires.”

“Yep.” Lois grunted as she forced the piles of clothes down to made her next task a little bit easier. “They were certain it would be enough to enkindle the sun’s fading power, arousing its frame by the bonfires heat and sort of reinvigorate it for the return in the spring.”

The room was bright and compacted in size. It was modern and stylish and reflected the young brunette’s sense of taste and requirements. A sixty watt bulb illuminated the space. There was a plain light blue carpet beneath their feet, and the four walls and the ceiling itself were coated with white silk emulsion. On the walls were pictures of various country scenes. Lois’ bed dominated the room. Opposite that stood a dressing table filled with a hair-dryer and a collection of cosmetics. To the left was the picture window near the armchair and beside the bed set against one wall was a squat cabinet with two drawers. On top of this was a clock radio and a lamp.

“Do you want any help with that,” Danielle said. Seeing Lois release her free hand and finally flip the top of the case over as the clothes sprang back up again.

“Thought you would never ask,” Lois replied. “I sort of packed to much stuff.”

Danielle stood and walked over to the bed. “Nothing new there.” She said without surprise. “The only thing you didn’t cram in was the kitchen sink.” Lois blinked. “We’re going just for three days. Counting all your luggage, you’re bringing enough for a fortnights stay.”

Lois sniffed in mock disdain and pushed the suitcase lid lower. "You cheeky cow, Danielle," she displayed an amiable smile. "A girl's got to have pride in her appearance. There are women to outshine and guys to snag. Just sit on it will ya." Seeing her friend mirror her expression and do as she asked. "For the record, I'm traveling lighter than I usually do. One of the suitcases is filled up with the chalk, candles and the rest of the material we're going to use at the party."

"Oh right." Danielle frowned at the mention of the Halloween festivities and the corner of her lips twitched. All of the apprehension Danielle felt resurfaced, and her face paled slightly with nervousness. She knelt on top, applying pressure until the sides of the case were together. "I wondered where you'd put them." Lois locked it with an audible clink and noticed her friend's reply lacked the previous enthusiasm that had been so apparent in her tone. She turned towards Danielle and saw the visible discomfort etched in her features. Lois had recognised something was troubling her before when she had been fiddling with her necklace and had a fair inkling what the underlying cause might be.

"Okay," Lois uttered. "What's wrong?"

"Nothing," Danielle said in denial. "Why do you ask?" She ran one of her hands through her hair as an aftereffect to the tension she was experiencing.

"Well! You've got a face as long as a wet weekend," she declared, folding her arms in front of her. "Something's bothering you otherwise you wouldn't have been playing with those damn worry beads of yours for the last few minutes. And now, the look on your face is the last straw."

Danielle broke eye contact and glanced at the floor.

"You've got a problem on your mind." The brunette went on with sincerely. "So spit it out! We're not leaving here until I know what it is?"

Danielle sighed. "I didn't think I was being so damned obvious," she stated, after a moment of thought.

"You were," Lois nodded. "Now, come on, tell me."

"You'll only laugh," she said, looking back up, and meeting Lois' steady gaze.

"Try me." Lois replied. "Is this about your awkwardness?"

Danielle bit her lip before letting out another sigh. "In part! It's really to do with the party in general, and in particular the nobs you told me who are going to be there. You know I have two left feet don't you?"

Lois nodded. "It hasn't escaped my families' attention. Dad still has a limp to prove it."

Danielle pulled a face. "I can't dance for toffee and if one of these wealthy types asks me to walk the dinosaur or do the birdie song with him. What am I suppose to do? Tread all over him."

"Some of them deserve a good kicking."

"Lois! This is serious. If this isn't bad enough what's worse is I'm still accident-prone despite that bit of salt magic you tried to use on my behalf."

"Danielle! Magic can't be rushed. It's not an instant cure. I'll tell you what. I'll learn you some steps and with a bit of practice you come through fine. I know where this is coming from. You're scared of showing yourself up but you have to remember it wasn't your fault you tripped over the cat and elbowed the local member of parliament in the eye or you smashed mom's expensive vase. It could have happened to anyone."

"Yeah to me. I don't want to become the butt of peoples jokes as they all giggle behind my back, bringing shame on me and embarrassment to your family for asking me to come in the first place."

Lois shook her head before expressing her thoughts. "Danielle, don't be so bloody stupid. Really, you can be too self-conscious some times." She unfolded her arms. "You couldn't shame us, not when I have a crackpot like Rob already in the family." She declared in an effort to restore her confidence by convincing her that her concerns were without foundation. "No one's prefect! Don't forget we were in the middle of the routine. Dad and that MP shouldn't have been so rude by barging in to the living room without knocking."

"I look at it this way our display for the match had to be practiced somewhere and the music might have been a tad loud for dad's delicate ears," Lois continued to speak with a straight face, "but I ain't doing my cheerleading in the garage. It's freezing cold in there especially wearing a short skirt."

A ghost of a smile appeared on Danielle's features.

"And as for the rest," Lois added, "you did mom a favor because she never did like that vase, it was only a copy and it clashed horribly with the new drapes."

Danielle blinked. "You're not just saying this to make me feel better?"

"Course not," Lois lied convincingly, walking over to where her friend stood before putting her arms around her and holding her close in an affectionate hug. "Now listen okay! Rob and Ashley have insurance against such mishaps and we try another salt spell. This time we'll say the incantation, putting emphasis on every third word and sprinkle the stuff together and while that's taking effect, we gonna have a good time. There'll be some familiar faces to have a laugh with, without mixing with them freeloaders on the guest list." Lois spoke on, offering Danielle another bit of comfort as she released her and took a step back. "No one will notice you, not in the way you think they will anyway."

Danielle nodded.

Lois swallowed. "I never fraternised with posh people until a couple of years ago and to me they aren't anything special. After a while you'll wonder what you were so nervous about because your find out we're not only just as good as those people, but in fact, we're much better even if we don't own a gold card. So!" Lois pressed on. "Pull yourself together. Tomorrow we'll have a blast. Everything will go like clockwork okay. Just concentrate on enjoying yourself and what's not there to occupy us, we'll make some entertainment for ourselves later on when we get all the gang together and create a paranormal party of our very own."

She noticed Danielle's mood and expression brighten considerably. "I will." The relief and encouragement in her voice were evident to her.

"Good!" Lois replied, sharing a smile. "Let's get going." She turned back to the suitcase. She gasped the handle and grunted only to find the case was too heavy for her to carry on her own. She sighed. "Help me out with this case." Lois beseeched. "I can barely pick it up."

"Sure!" Danielle replied, still beaming as she wrapped one hand alongside her friends while she placed the other beneath the suitcase.

"On three we lift," Lois arranged.

Danielle nodded again.

"One, two, three." They echoed as they jerked the case up, off the bed.

"All we got to do now is place this next to the others in the hallway." Lois said, beginning to walk unsteadily to the bedroom doorway. “Before dad finds out I’ve brought another bag down. He’s going to have a moaning fit when he feels the weight of this. It might not have any wheels but he can drag it to the car.”

“Easier said than done Lois.” Danielle reached the entrance, releasing her hold on the bottom of the case, and opening the door to reveal the passageway beyond. “You can’t do anything secret in this house not with those creaky stairs of yours.”

“Well they can make all the noise they like,” Lois replied, crossing into the passageway, sideways like a crab. “Dad won’t hear us because he’s in the garage making sure that the car’s got enough oil and water for tonight’s trip to Hereford.”

She then waited for a moment while her companion turned off the light. “So we might just do it then.” Danielle answered, following on her heels, closing the door behind her.

* * *

The octagonal wall clock read six-thirty seven when the two women passed it, sharing the weight of the case between them as they stealthily made their way along the passageway ending at the landing adjourning the staircase. Leading, Lois cast a quick glance back and put a finger to her lips to show the need for silence. She received a friendly nod before Lois cautiously walked on tip-toes over to the banister and peered over the edge of the railing, down at the hallway below. Seeing no movement or hearing any footsteps resounding off the tiled floor, Lois waved to indicate the coast was clear and without uttering another sound, she quietly mouthed “come on!”

CHAPTER SIX

The air in the kitchen suddenly reverberated with the sound of footfalls and voices as someone slammed the back door shut. Standing at the bottom of the staircase, Lois locked eyes with Danielle. "Did you hear that?" She whispered. Danielle nodded. The faucet turned. "Shit! Dad's finished checking the car over. Hurry."

Instinctively Lois took off down the hallway at a mad dash as water began splashing into a metal container. Danielle followed her, almost dragged along by the strength of Lois' impetus. Ahead the water sounds ceased; and their footsteps echoed loudly off the tiled floor. Lois slowed and placed the suitcase next to the other pieces of luggage laying haphazardly at the nearest corner of the hall. An instant later the kitchen door swing silently inward to reveal Lois' father standing in the doorway.

"Ah," he said in delight at seeing them. "I thought I could hear the approach of your dainty feet Lois." He pushed the door against the wall and knelt, shoving the wooden wedge beneath the bottom of the door to prevent it from closing. "I was just about to call you again because your tea's getting cold and there won't be anymore." He straightened and walked over to where his cup rested on the worktop. "Except what your mom's making which is going straight into the thermos for the trip."

The companions followed him into the kitchen proper. The room was quite large in size with a door directly opposite them leading straight into the garden. Its walls were papered with floral designs, influenced by the natural setting of a country meadow. A single window overlooked part of the garage and the driveway outside. There were the usual fittings inside: washing machine, cooker, and a boxy fridge/freezer.

"We heard you dad." Lois stated. "I just wanted to finish tidying up my bedroom. I didn't want to come back to a mess."

"Oh," he uttered in surprise, raising his cup to his lips. "That's got to be a first." He frowned thoughtfully. "You feeling all right?"

"The reason of the week is more like how much do you want to accessorize something?" Vertly Elmes declared.

"Jeez!" Lois uttered, "feel the faith in here. 'Scuse me! I'm not after anything yet. Remember," she pointed to herself. "I've turned over a new leaf now."

Her father tightened his lips, and peered at her lopsided grin.

"So, Mister Elmes," Danielle inquired in curiously, to change the subject. "I was merely wondering what time are we starting off?"

He took a sip of his lukewarm tea only to be beaten to the punch as he lowered his cup when Vertly answered the question for him.

"About twenty minutes my dear." Vertly pulled one of the cupboard drawers open and stared inside. "That is, of course, if Andrew can locate his torch." She lifted up a disheveled dish cloth at the back of the draw to see if it was somehow hiding underneath. "We'd had quite a lot of trouble in finding it so far." She blinked at him. "Haven't we!"

As soon as her mother had mentioned the missing object, something abruptly registered in Lois' head that had until now completely slipped her mind.

Andrew sighed in defeat. "I can't understand where it's gone." He shook his head. "I'm certain I put it away in this draw when I finished work but it's not there now."

"Well at least we know where it isn't, in the cupboards, the garage or the garden shed." Vertly said, removing the lid of the bread box to look inside. "We could have been on the road twenty minutes ago if it wasn't for your phobia." She refitted the lid. "What a waste of time. The only thing we've got to show for it is your aching back."

"Faugh!" He exclamation of disgust. "I don't care what you think Vertly. It relaxes my mind, having a torch around for practical purposes. Anyway rush hour might be over but we can still expect delays and heavy traffic with all the road works going on. The radio said so earlier on."

Andrew Elmes was in his early forties and had a corpulent, pot-bellied frame that owned its entire existence to the man's love of junk food and his complete loathing of all forms of exercise. The nearest he ever got to exerting himself on a daily basis was when he was in the pub putting up with the strain of his right arm bending under the weight of a pint of beer. He was five foot five inches in height and had a double chin beneath a rounded clean-shaven face that looked like it was ready to burst. He was heavily-jowled and the little red veins criss-crossing his nose were sharply defined. He had short, tawny-coloured hair peppered with gray that was beginning to bald around the crown. His arms and legs had areas of pale, blotchy skin and a ruddy complexion covering the features of his broad flat nose, his beady eyes and small mouth. He wore blue jeans held up with braces and loafers beneath a white sweatshirt and over this was a hooded parka which just couldn't be zipped up past his bulging stomach how ever hard he tried.

On a sudden whim and with no real idea where else to look next, he asked the girls. "Have either of you seen my torch on your travels." He shifted his attention between their faces. "It's a long black one I use when I'm on my night watchman duties. I'd hate to go out at this hour without it when we'll be driving down county lanes just in case we conk out." He sighed heavily and saw Danielle's eyes blink beneath a brow furrowed in puzzlement. Seeing her bewilderment he felt the need to explain himself. "Has my daughter ever told you Danielle that I have a fear of breaking down? It's happened more times than I care to admit in the past. Some sort of emergency always arises on the journey if I don't take a spare petrol can or a torch along but I've found if I've got the stuff handy then I never need it."

Danielle shook her head: "I haven't seen it."

His daughter was a little more reluctant to reply.

"Okay!" Andrew smiled to hide his annoyance. "What about you Lois?" He raised his cup to his lips.

"Er!" Lois articulated, taking a deep breath and meeting her father's steady gaze. "Dad. You should have said something earlier on because I could have saved you all the trouble of looking for it." Her mother pulled a face. "I lent the torch to the neighbors up the road at number 47. They needed to borrow it to change a fuse and with all the rushing around I've done lately, helping mom with the shopping, picking up the party outfits and revising for my theory test, it just slipped my mind."

Lois smiled apologetically and shrugged her shoulders, awaiting the onset of the flak she knew should come, yet astonished when it didn't.

"Never mind." He replied, his face red as he fumed deep inside but restraining the curt return since he didn't want to show her up in front of Danielle. "Next time Lois leave us a message by the phone." Vertly arched a single eyebrow.

"Sure." Lois said through gritted teeth.

Behind him the kettle began to whistle.

"I'll get the torch back off them," he paused for breathe. "Then I'll put all the luggage in the back of the car."

The clear-shill sound grew louder.

Vertly spun around. "Don't bother! I'll pop over Andrew." She said, turning off the hob. "You get cracking on the loading. It won't take me a couple of ticks and I'll be warm enough in this." She gestured towards the coat she wore.

Vertly Elmes was just above medium height and she was quite attractive and was obsessively vain about it. Gold circle earrings dangled beneath her long, straight lustrous, black hair which framed an oval-shaped face set with tiny eyelashes surrounding dark eyes with epicanthic folds above a snub nose and strawberry-red lips. She had well-toned limbs and a lean, fit physique that had curves in all the right places. This was in recognition to her regime of going regularly to her local gym and avoiding greasy foods at all costs. She was wearing a pale blue fleece jacket over a long sleeved top over a pair of silver-gray trousers. A pair of high-heels encased her feet.

Vertly took a couple of steps and then was followed out by her husband. "I'll come out the front with you and load that way." He announced. "It'll be easier."

Vertly lingered for a moment as she reached the hallway threshold, casting a glance back over her shoulder. "Lois while I'm gone," she uttered. "Pour the water into the teapot. Its already got the bags inside. I'll fill the thermos and add the milk and sugar when I get back."

"Not a problem." Lois replied with a nod as she saw her turn and disappear around the corner. Andrew brought up the rear as the front door opened only for him next to pretend to scream – merely in fun – at the moment his wife was out of earshot. "Ahhh," when he finally saw the huge amount of suitcases on the floor. He put his hands on his hips and let his eyes wander over the luggage assembled at his feet. "My god! What have these cases been doing since I turned my back, breeding?"

"Probably dad," Lois smiled, playing along. She went up to the cooker and lifted the kettle. "Mom said you were to take it easy with the blue one because she packed the new ironing board so she can show aunt Ashley what you brought for her birthday." She crossed to the units and poured the hot water into the teapot. Next to it was the thermos flask and a quartet of cups on the wooden tray. Danielle laughed.

With a smirk, Andrew shook his head before choosing a suitcase at random. He hoisted it up with ease then selected another case which just happened to be the same one the two girls had just brought down the stairs. He grunted with surprised effort at the weight of it as he lifted it past his knees. "I think I found it," he declared, tottering through the open front doorway on his way out to the car. "Bloody hell! Hernia here I come."

Watching him go, and hearing his footfalls diminish as he went, Danielle said. "I didn't think we'd make it down with the case but we did." She walked over to Lois and took the proffered tea cup before peering out of the window to see with her own eyes where Andrew was so he couldn't hear their conversation. "We're now set for tomorrow evening."

Lois smiled, raising her cup to her lips. "Yep. I'm looking forward to it." She took a sip and tasted the tea. "It'll be a nice change of scene from the capital." She made a wry face as she stared at the cup. "I don't envy the guys going up to the estate by rail." She poured the rest of the beverage down the sink. "Sitting across from strangers on a train is crap when you're not in a window seat. If you haven't brought a paper along then throughout the journey you're trying to look every where except straight at the person in front of you. It's a right pain in the neck." She put the empty cup back on the worktop.

"Yeah," Danielle said in agreement.

"Yet I always tolerate incidents like those if I can look forward to the bonus that awaits us at uncle Robs. It's the only time when mom feels free to relax her fitness regime and actually enjoy herself. Just think for the duration of our stay we'll be able to taste some of the finest vintage wines," she sighed. Picking up a spoon, she dipped it into the teapot and began stirring. "And even eat caviar if we want to, instead of only being able to afford chips and mushy peas."

"I still can't believe your uncle is that wealthy though." Danielle said, bringing up a past piece of gossip her friend had shared with her. "And you say he earned it all from the stock market?"

"Uh-huh," she confirmed, watching her friend swallow a mouthful of the drink and wince. "After making the money he got out quick, selling everything just in case there was another stock market crash like black Monday."

"Wise decision." Danielle stated, seeing Andrew emerge into view from behind the garage wall. "Particularly when share prices fluctuate as they do."

Lois paused for a moment as her father entered the hallway and picked up more pieces of luggage. She placed the spoon on the tray. When his footsteps had again began to lessen she resumed, safe in the knowledge that the subject of their conversation was still secret. "Rob used the money to buy the Wildwood Haven estate," Lois said, smiling to her father just before he disappeared behind the brick wall. "He funded the reconstructed of the manor house and some of the outbuildings that were almost falling down round his ears. He turned one into an art studio for my aunt and another into a workshop devoted to his hobby which he now has time to pursue."

"Huh," Danielle expressed in surprise, lowering her cup. "I've seen the junk. Who'd have thought he would have had the nerve to advertise it on the Internet."

"I'll say," Lois responded. Folding her arms she caught a glimpse of an Austin Maestro roaring past, along the road beyond her house's driveway and fence. "It raised a few eyebrows. But not as many when the stuff started to attract clients to his web page and he actually managed to sell some of the pieces."

"Does he make a good living out of it?" Danielle asked.

"He doesn't have to, but according to mom he's doing all right." Lois answered. "He employees a staff of five, and makes a wide range of stuff out of wrought-iron like curtain poles, candle sticks, headboards and fencing. Rob's trying to improve his client base by targeting people who aren't connected to the web. He's produced a colour brochure to promote his merchandise and has asked us to distribute them around the capital when we return from the trip."

"What," Danielle uttered in complete shock, locking eyes with her friend. "Please say you're not serious?"

"I am," she declared truly. "I was going to tell you later but since you brought it up, there's really no time like the present. That was the condition my uncle set for picking up the gang at the train station in the morning."

"Oh flipping hell Lois. I bet we get lumbered while they do nothing and hog all the fun."

"Puh-lesze! There's an expiration date on the offer even if Rob don't know it yet. After the ritual he can hand out his own bloody pamphlets. We'll be far to busy testing our powers on the walls of the nearest bank to do his dirty work."

Danielle bobbed her head thoughtfully and shifted her attention to stare back out the window to see Andrew reappear, red faced and empty-handed from behind the garage wall. "Have you told any of the others anything more about the special activates we've got planned for the evening?" She enquired as the man's footsteps grew louder.

Lois paused and waited before the echoing had faded from the passageway. "No I haven't," Lois told her. "I'm leaving it until they'd knocked back the drinks before springing it upon them. They won't be in such a mood to disbelieve us and call us crazy then will they?"

Danielle nodded again, also mindful of Andrew's presence as he vanished into the garage, carrying another two suitcases. "Will Josh be bringing some spliffs along?"

"Plenty! By the way, you never said who or what you managed to finally go as?"

A Ford Escort sped up the street while more traffic roared unseen at the junction a dozen yards to the right of the kitchen window. The teenager stirred uneasily beside her friend. "Didn't I?" She replied innocently. "Well a lot of people are throwing fancy dress balls at the moment and because I hardly had any notice due to you forgetting to tell me I needed a masquerade costume to this little social..."

"Hey, Danielle, wait a minute. I did apologise when you told me." Lois interrupted in mock sincerely. Her eyes flashing as she glanced at her. "I know it was a mistake except," she placed her hand to her heart, "it wasn't my fault to began with but moms." Danielle nodded to accept this. "She was the one who mislaid the other box of invites only to then find and mail them four days before the party." She swallowed. "I didn't bring it up earlier because I assumed you knew the theme from the invitation and were keeping your costume secret so you could surprise us on the night. How was I to know your invitation had arrived late and you had been running around like a headless chicken trying to find something suitable to wear?"

She sighed. "I understand." Danielle replied in frustration at being interrupted in the way that she had. "What I was trying to get at was, unlike you, I didn't have the luxury to pick and choose because when I arrived at the hire shop, one had closed down while and I had to travel miles to get to the second, and there wasn't all that many variety of costumes left in my size still available or anything else for that matter. Nearly all of his best stock had been snapped up already."

"So what did you do?" Lois asked.

"What do you think? Take the best of what was on offer of course." Danielle answered truthfully, putting her cup down on the worktop. "Which wasn't much. I passed on a Scooby-Doo suit. I felt that just wasn't me. And after rejecting the gear of some comedian from the nineteen twenties I'd never heard off, all the assistant had left to offer me was either a spare back end of an horse costume or a skimpy belly-dancer outfit, consequently I choose the latter. I just hope your aunt's house has gas central heating otherwise I'm going to have goose bumps on my goose bumps."

Not showing her annoyance over this state of affairs, Lois grinned and shook her head. "You certainly went through it didn't you?" Her gaze returned to the window and saw her mother pass beneath the yellow glow of the nearest street lamp before she turned down the driveway, approaching the house. "Mom's back and she's got the torch with her." Smiling, Andrew emerged, holding a lighted-cigarette, striding towards his wife whose face grimaced with blazing eyes at the sight of what greeted her. "Thank heaven, he's got his toy back 'cause we wouldn't have heard the end of it."

Then Lois realised that there was another potential source of embarrassment heading her way if she didn't do something fast to nip it in the bud. Her gaze roamed the kitchen worktop as her parents came to a halt and spoke in a brief conversation. An idea formed in Lois' mind when she spotted an object that would serve her requirements sufficiently. "Danielle! Quick rip off some of that kitchen roll and hand it to me. I want to look busy when she comes in."

"Sure," Danielle frown, grabbing the roll and tearing a strip free. "I just know I'm going to regret asking this but why?"

"You're a guest so it doesn't apply to you." Lois replied, taking the strip and sneaking a glance out of the window to see where her mother was as she pretended to wipe the work surfaces in front of her, of imaginary-spilled tea stains with an ever widening circular motion. "But if I'm not doing something then she'll wonder why I haven't saved dad a journey by helping him load up some of the lighter cases. Only yesterday I had to load up the dishwasher with a mountain of plates and traipse down to the recycling bin on the high street with three bags of empties. I'm not going to be caught like that again in a hurry."

* * *

Andrew shivered in the chilly evening air. "Thanks honey." He said. With a quick labored breath he grabbed the torch and took in his wife's disgusted expression, knowing exactly what was causing it since he'd been subjected to enough nagging about it in the past. "I was just pacing myself, relaxing for a minute in between trips. I've got three cases to go then we can get off. And before you say it Vertly I'll only had the one," He gestured with the cigarette. "You can ask the girls if you don't believe me."

"Okay" Vertly said, not entirely convinced. "You don't need to make a song and dance out of it Andrew. I believe you, thousands wouldn't." His eyes opened wide at that comment, smoke curling upwards from the cigarette. "You know what your doing to your body," she continued superciliously. "Remember cutting down on your intake of beer won't be enough to help your ticker if you still keep puffing away on too many of those in a day," she gestured at the cigarette. "Anyway, I warned you. Made sure you keep that filthy habit outside like we agreed, not in the house. So the rest of us don't have to breathe in the smoke and you're not dirtying up my nice clean walls with it either. The same goes at your sisters house and inside the car while we're going along, is that understood?"

"Yes dear." Andrew said bitterly with an audible sigh, resentful of her demands and her marvelous black-mailing skills of withdrawing all marital favors until she forced him to comply to her wishes.

Vertly glanced at her digital watch which was on the underside of her wrist. It read ten past seven. "Right then," She said, in an attempt to motivated him into action. "I'll go and finish off my chores." She turned and walked into the house.

Instead of following in her footsteps, Andrew showed defiant by shaking his head and take a deep drag, finding the experience invigorating before expelling the smoke from his lungs and dropping the cigarette butt to the tarmac. As he began to extinguished it under the sole of his shoe, he heard someone's knuckles knocking on the pane of glass.

He peered at the kitchen window and in place of his daughter's pleasant face, he saw Vertly's scowling countenance glaring at him and jerking her chin towards the doorway. "Get a move on or else," she mouthed silently in an effort to spare his blushes.

As awareness crept in of what she meant with the last part of the sentence, Andrew's stance of bold rebellion faded under her dirty look. Depressed with his domestic lot, he inwardly cursed his weakness for his wife's flesh and then wishing for a good stiff drink, made his way into the hallway to pick up the remainder of the luggage.

CHAPTER SEVEN

Around eight-thirty-five, drizzle started to spit onto the Escort's windscreen, blown against the glass by the moaning wind. Thaw decreased speed and flicked on the wipers. As the car moved down another rural lane, nothing could spoil the jubilant mood everyone was in following radio newscasts revealing that not only hadn't the real Caravelle been sighted since the robbery but the worsening change in the weather and the lateness of the hour had forced the police to drastically scale down their manhunt until first light tomorrow morning. By the time the car had devoured well over two hundred and thirty kilometers in their indirect route, the rain around them began falling in heavier sheets. Wild flowers and weeds growing alongside the road were flatted by the intensity of the downpour which lashed the tarmac with savage fury. Progressing through the tempest, Thaw lowered the vehicle's speed before arching his back and leaning forward, closer to the steering wheel, a deepening frown developed on his forehead as he gazed out of the rain-streaked window and saw his visibility fade in front of him, to less than thirty yards.

Lightning flared across the darkened sky.

"That was a bright one," Gillett said, staring out of her window, and commenting upon the electric discharge.

Bisset nodded, unwrapping another peppermint from its tube and popping it into his mouth. "You can say that again my dear," he replied. Peering through his thick-lenses and raising his voice slightly as thunder boomed above. He offered her a sweet but she refused. "The forecaster didn't predict the weather being this bad." He shifted his attention to the rearview mirror where he saw Thaw's eyes were locked on the road ahead. "Jerome! Don't you think we should maybe stop somewhere for a bit and wait up until the storm blows itself out? There's nothing brief or local about this baby."

Feeling averse to the suggestion because it produced all kinds of problems for them, Thaw down-shifted going into a corner and floored the peddle as the car accelerated out. Gathering his wits, he devised a quick excuse as he drove the car further into the torrential rain. When he spoke, there wasn't any sign of indecision in his voice just authority. "No! The police are expecting us to take it easier in this weather Nathan, now that the hunt's been called off but I'm not going to do that." He shook his head, seeing another jagged flash of light on high. "The sooner we're off these country lanes, the better I'll like it, especially with this lightning."

The road glistened in the headlamps, the beams reflected a distorted squiggly-image on the wet tarmaced surface beneath them. A thunderclap bellowed above them.

"A good lightening bolt could bring down a tree with no difficulty straight across our path or worse right on top of us." Thaw uttered, going on with genuine concern in his voice. The tyres sloshed through widening puddles, when he steered the vehicle around a tight turn that debouched onto an intersection where three roads joined. He stared into his rearview mirror to see Bisset pushing his glasses up the bridge of his nose. "I prefer pushing our luck by being a moving target more than just a stationary one."

Cummings nodded. "Agreed!" He declared, studying the small, global positioning system on the dashboard. "Jerome! I don't know where you got this GPS from but it hasn't shown these roads were on for ages?"

"The satellite always picks up the main roads when we're in range, regretfully mine doesn't always reveal the country lanes. How's our current time comparing to the schedule of the dry run? Are we still on to reach the junction in about thirty minutes?" He crossed the intersection and proceeded down the road directly ahead.

"No," Cummings stated methodically. Thaw stole a quick glance at him. "The rain's delayed us a lot. At this rate of speed, we can add at least another thirty minutes to our arrival time, properly a little more."

Thaw averted his eyes and gazed at the clock set in the dashboard. It read 9.20 pm. Klugman clicked his tongue, and tutted to express his annoyance.

Hedges and grass verges bordering the lane gave way to long, thin ditches behind which grew tangled undergrowth hiding on one side a wide river. The surging water churned into eddies and wave crests broke into white foam along the slanting channel. Slender reeds bent and snapped against the onslaught, the flow splashed over the banks as it went around an outcropping of stone.

Bisset's brow furrowed and his eyes narrowed tensely as he gave Klugman a contemptible look. "Ahem!" He coughed, to get everyone's attention, the dissolving sweet lodged in his cheek. "Does it really matter all that much now?" He said, with evident alarm in his voice that mirrored the dread in his eyes. "When we're this far along and gained so much? Surely it not worth rushing and endangering everything we achieved." He smiled faintly. "Just for slightly more speed?"

Thaw shook his head. "Keep your hair on Nathan. We're not stupid," he declared firmly. The needle of the speed gauge decreasing inch by inch to the twenty-five mark. "I expected it might happen. And as you say it doesn't matter at this late stage in the proceedings, not when Hereford is only six miles away. Once clear of the storm we'll be able to made up that lost time on the motorway."

"Hah! That's if the maintenance crews have opened up all the south bound lanes by now." Klugman said.

About a mile ahead of the Escort, the rain was falling heavier still, saturating the sodden landscape and causing the raging torrent to swell into a massive rolling wave which flowed over the river banks. It tumbled down the steep sloping ground, with an impetus that splashed around a moss-covered tree stump, pushing rocks out of their path, uprooting saplings and washing away pebbles, clumps of coarse grass and layers of soft drenched earth, exposing dark-coloured minerals underneath. The rush of water was unfaltering, eroding more soil by degrees, several small masses formed a tilted steplike structure as they slid. A large cleft in the land appeared and the wet earth plunged over this ledge, falling about twenty feet to where the uneven stretch of the lane was at its lowest. Between the cliff walls, the muddy flow cascaded into a deepening pool gradually becoming dirtier and ascending above the road surface as it was fed by the heavy deluge and because the drains were clogged up with deposits of plants, mud and old leaves. Lightning shot from one dark cloud to another as the flood water below crept a little bit higher up the sides of the slanted road and the vertical rock faces; a deafening sharp peal of thunder reverberated with an intensity that was louder than any that had preceded it. A short distance behind the gorge, drainage ditches carried away storm-water off the road while rain drummed fiercely onto the Escort's roof, teeming down the windscreen. Wipers squealed. The passengers experienced a slight bump when their vehicle rolled over an squashed hedgehog then Thaw eased the car onto the narrow grass verge to let a Toyota Corolla pass.

Looking up from his pocket computer game, Klugman asked in surprise. "Why've we stopped?"

"Just showing some road courtesy Kyle," Thaw uttered, seeing the Corolla fade into the distance. "Nothing more."

"Good thinking my friend," Bisset commented as the Escort roared off and turned left at the junction. "Have to keep everything looking normal."

Lightning flared again and helped to define the landscape around them. Hammering rain focused in the stabbing glare of the headlamps. A sign post with the lettering 'No Road Markings', went by followed by a stile on the same side of the lane. Thunder resonated like an explosive charge and the overgrown hedges flanking the car yielded as the land formation elevated into ridges. An instant later the road dipped suddenly ahead and Thaw saw gradually that the stretch of concrete fell away, straight down into a gorge. The rain continued to fall, drowning out every other sound in the neighborhood except the loud rumble of the thunder. The terrain got considerably steeper the further the car went down the slope. Visibility worsened in the shadows of the high cliffs and the additional light provided by the lightening flashes failed to penetrate all the way down to the lower reaches of the gorge. Then abruptly, about eight yards ahead, the headlamps dispelled enough of the darkness for Thaw and Cummings to observe the road before them.

Thaw's widening eyes blinked in disbelief and Cummings cursed aloud as they saw the bottom of the gully was full with a deepening pool of muddy water which was constantly being increased by the torrential rain and the flowing volumes of brown sludge pouring steadily from the left side of the cliff. Curbing the panic swelling within him, Thaw's mind raced and his immediate reaction was to estimate the distance to the muddy overflow and apply pressure to his brakes. The brakes screeched and the tyres squealed, shooting back-spray as the Escort's wheels locked and skidded down the glistening surface of the incline. Inside the car the action catapulted the five occupants forward only to be restrained by their seatbelts. Smoke rose from the burned rubber and rain lashed the terrain as the vehicle's momentum conveyed the criminals the last few yards before ploughing into the swelling flood. A drenching wave splashed over the hood and smeared the windscreen with soggy earth while the steaming exhaust pipe became immersed when the car eventually skidded to a halt upon the bottom of the gorge.

"Fucking mudslide!" Thaw blurted out suddenly, without stopping to think. "We'll get stuck here if we don't watch it." A surge of adrenaline made his heart beat faster. He glanced into his rear view mirror to see the way behind was clear before slamming the car into reverse and his foot pressed down on the accelerator. Gillett blinked and trembled at the thought, Bisset swallowed his mint and leaned his face against the glass of the passenger window to observe the unfolding situation for himself. His breath steamed up the glass.

The wipers struggled sluggishly to clear a space through the thick slime obscuring the windscreen and below them the wheels spun wildly, rotating smoothly and unhindered when they couldn't get any traction on the muddy deposits. Water crept further up the hubcaps and slush oozed between the revolving treads while the tyres themselves sank into the mushy mass of clay and sediment as Thaw frantically gunned the engine in the hope that the additional power would free them.

"Come on, damn you," Gillett grumbled peevishly at the car, with a hint of desperation in her voice. "Come on! Don't you dare disappoint us now, not after all we've gone through to get here." She stared through the widening gap opening up in the windscreen, at the flowing mud sliding down into the pool, lit up again by the lightning. "We wouldn't have this problem if we'd used a Landrover."

Cummings kept a dignified silence but within him, he was just as anxious about their plight as she was. He had seen the temperature bulb in the dashboard go red, indicating the staining engine was beginning to overheat. Klugman saw it too from his seat, and stiffened in alarm as an appalling realisation dawned on him that if the water cooling system couldn't extract the heat fast enough then the radiator would blow.

Alas the Escort remained where it was and its wheels digging deeper into the mud, becoming stuck as the tyres finally reached the concrete surface of the lane. Finding an accumulating amount of facts increasingly hard to ignore, Klugman scowled and spoke. "Guys I think it's time we cut our losses and ran." He zipped up his funnel-necked, jacket. "We're becoming bogged down and the mud's getting dangerously high. If we don't get out of here soon, then we'll find ourselves in a whole lot of trouble."

"Kyle's right for once. The water's coming up to the chassis," Cummings warned, echoing Klugman's statement but he communicated the news with an unruffled calm that lacked the excitement of the previous speaker. He peered through his side window at the rising level of mud.

Fuming with frustration and rage but not yet ready to admit defeat, Thaw sighed irritably and opened up the throttle again, his foot thrusting the pedal to the floor. The car jerked and shuddered when the resistance of the mud offered the wheels hardly any grip on the surface of the road. An excessive amount of fuel began to flood the carburettor and at the same time the toil the engine was under caused its temperature to go up, as the mud climbed up the chassis. Above, thunder crashed anew and the wind continued insistently to wail through the bare tree limbs.

In a state of unhappiness, Klugman frowned and unfolded his baseball cap and put it on his head, with the brim projecting forward to cover his eyes. Gillett bit her lower lip in observation. "This just ain't fair," she stated with a shake of her head, hearing the rain drumming loudly above her. The restraint she normally exercised over her emotions and feelings slipped as she became afraid and overwrought from their lack of progress. "Is there any chance," she addressed to no one in particular, unfolding her arms, "we can go forward or just get out and push the car back up the slope?" Bisset glanced at her and witnessed the anguish upon her countenance.

Tense moments passed. Lightning cracked across the sky. The deluge continued to pelt down and in concert, rising cold water inundated the Escort's warm engine, producing tendrils of steam seeping upwards through the seams between the bonnet and the body work. Thaw tightened his grip on the steering wheel and as his foot pumped the pedal, and the engine whined, he directed his comments to what his girlfriend had just referred to.

"No! Sophie, both would be futile gestures." He said calmly with absolute confidence, yet beginning to breathe hard. "There's no way we could push the car back up the hill not in this weather. It's to bloody heavy and slippery for that underfoot and as for going forward, that's also out of the question. Water's flooding the engine and there's no degree of certainty we'd make it up the other slope in one piece anyway, not with that mudflow threatening to come down like an avalanche at any time and bury us if we tried to pass it."

The wheels somehow purchased some hold on the road beneath the water and the car began to insignificantly move backwards. With a resigned bob of her head, Gillett's brow furrowed and her taut face paled at her propositions were dispassionately rejected out of hand. Then the Escort's engine began to sputter, it's operation hindered by the glut of fuel inundating the carburettor. A thunderclap boomed. Simultaneously, Thaw mindful of the way the engine was malfunctioning and his current surroundings made him come to the dreadful conclusion that Klugman was right about bailing out. Not really wanting to come to terms with abandoning the car unconditionally without one more try, but knowing it was impossible to delay for too much longer, Thaw weighed up his diminishing options and finally yielded to reason by striking a balance with a decision that not only satisfied his stubborn pride but also appeased his passengers, and reduced the weight inside the Escort. It might be sufficient to stave off the probable mutiny he sensed from their glowing disquiet already boiling within their ranks.

"Jerome! Water level is up to the bottom of the doors." Cummings notified the driver, with stern undertones in his voice that reflected the forbidding expression upon his face.

Beside herself with shredded nerves and almost out of her wits, Gillett's heart pounded and her breathing was becoming more frantic and her lips trembled from all of her stress. With the worsening developments outside, inciting her to do something quick to escape this dilemma, and caught in the slowly tightening grip of an approaching panic-attack, she glanced at the doors around her and saw that sandwiched between Bisset and Klugman, she'd have to climb over either of them to get to the exits. Gillett's gaze wandered for another way out and her attention focused upon the small sunroof. But before she could explode in a fit of hysterics or even attempt to slide back the roof panel above her, Thaw acknowledged Cummings' report and issued a fresh set of instructions.

"Okay," Thaw said, his tone grim. Slipping one hand into the pocket of his coat. "We'll evacuate." He pulled out a key that opened up the Escort's boot.

"About time," Gillett responded, echoing Klugman's thoughts in a raised voice which was evidence to everyone that wide emotional cracks had developed in her composure. Thaw frowned in some concern over her well-being and his heart began to rule his head.

"Calm down, Sophie." he said, going on to reassure her, "Everything going to be fine." He slid his window down to allow in an abundance of fresh air. The wind influenced the heavy rain to slant through the opening. The engine stalled, and the car came to a standstill. Lightning flashed once more and lit up the mudflow which was streaming down faster and thicker than ever. "Damn," Thaw uttered with a brief shake of his head in disbelief, his heart sinking as the car seized up. "Adrian," stealing a glance as he passed the key to Cummings. "You and Kyle get the pouch's out of the boot," the tall man took the proffered key, "and anything else useful in there including our carry-on's. Get them back up the hill as fast as you can, under some cover."

Cummings gave a short nod, reaching behind the collar of his weather-proof jacket, and bringing up the detachable hood to cover his head while Klugman threw his door open. "You don't have to tell me twice." He said, plucking the torch from his lap and turning it on.

Launching himself out of his seat, Klugman plunged out into the deluge. The cold mud immediately engulfed his boot's and socks and crept up the baggy-legs of his trousers to just below his knees. Cummings opened his door and let his eyes briefly adjust to the gloom before stepping out into the slime, suppressing a shiver as he did. Behind him, Klugman trained the beam of the torch ahead of him, and lowered his head against the keening howl of the gnawingly cold wind and the lashing rain, huddling his face low, water streaming from the brim of his cap during his difficult walk through the scummy water, around to the back of the Escort. Bisset braced himself for his journey, buttoned up his Mackintosh then reached for the door handle. Beside him, Gillett's eyes darted at the exit where Klugman had just gone through, and slowly getting a hold of herself, she breathe in and out, and untied a square piece of cloth from, about her neck.

"Nathan!" Thaw went on, turning back and twisting the ignition key but to no avail. "Take Sophie to high ground." Cummings trudged along the side of the car, wet slime clung to his Chinos and it affected his process, offering resistance as he proceeded over to where Klugman waited. "I'll rendezvous with all of you, up there in a jiffy."

Simmering down yet the symptoms far from being abated within her, Gillett sighed inwardly with resentment as she objected to being treated like this, and wrapped the kerchief around her head. Bisset stared uncomprehendingly at the driver. "Why?" He asked in curiously. "What are you going to do Jerome?" He flung his door wide.

Gillett tied two of the corners of the kerchief together beneath her chin. "I'm going to try and get the car started," Thaw answered. "Get it out of here before the water gets any higher." He twisted the ignition key again, only to get no response. The vehicle juddered as the lid of the trunk was quickly lifted up. Gillett clutched the handle of her handbag, bringing it up to her bosom and slipped the strap over her right shoulder.

"Jerome! you're flogging a dead horse." Bisset said, peering over Thaw shoulder at the illuminated gauges flickering unsteadily in the dashboard, and the beams of the headlamps diminished in strength by the slightest degree. "The only way you're going to get the engine running now is by divine intervention."

Thaw concealed his true feelings and took another stab at starting the engine, but still, it didn't catch.

Sophie nodded. "Yeah," she announced with unwavering resolution, knowing her own mind and not about to hold back in speaking up for herself. Her voice slightly lowered in tone as she slid herself across the rear seats, heading towards the opening. "A miracle's about the only chance you'll ever have of getting to nursemaid me. Your heart's in the right place, Jerry." She continued, using the diminutive version of his name. She reached the entrance. "I'm no southern belle and I certainly don't need no gallantry from anyone." She lingered on the edge of the seat and scanned the environment unenthusiastically, saw the thick slime had ascended gradually to be about a thousandth of an inch below the door frame. "I'm perfectly able to manage on my own, lover. Clear your mind of those kind of thoughts, I'll be fine."

Wishing she had exchanged her shoes for something more suitable for this occasion like her pair of high-leg boots she'd left at home instead of the flat open-toed mules she wore now, Gillett got out of the car into the drenching expanse, stifling a "Eeeyiiick!" as her one inch heeled shoes sank without trace, beneath the mud. A thunderclap filled the air. Becoming steadily wetter, her lips pulled apart to show gritted teeth, and her cheeks stung from the cold gale. She swore under her breath, and adopted a long face, trembling as she struggled with real physical effort, using weakened muscles from her near anxiety attack to wade through the deluge and the mire. "Omigod! I'm looking at some major shrinkage here."

Once Gillett reached the rear of the car, her toes were numb. Klugman and Cummings had already removed two of the canvas packages from the boot, and both of them, she saw from the glare of the lightning were out of the slime and on their way back up the right side of the incline in single file with all the speed their legs could muster. The beam from Klugman's torch preceding them to stab the darkness, and water dripped from their apparel smeared at various places with mud. Rain ran off her saturated kerchief and beneath the long ladder in her nylons, goosebumps rose the length of her freezing legs from fear and the cold. Her clothes clung to her skin and her teeth had begun to chatter. Leaving the third money pouch lying where it was next to the spare tyre and the jack, Gillett plucked a small lightweight piece of green luggage from atop of two similar carry-on's beside a leather satchel before whirling about and prodding along, angling up the slippery uneven road.

Without delay, the mud coursed over the threshold of the Escort's open door and into the compartment, dolloping into a developing mass over three of the interior's rubber car mats. Thaw turned the key in the ignition only to fail once more while Bisset, vexed by Gillett's response kept his opinion of how obstinate she was to himself. "I hate to impair the enjoyment of such a charming Oprah moment." Bisset said uncertainly. "But do you still want me to maintain an eye on Sophie?" He emerged from cover and splashed into the slime, the experience causing him to expose his teeth in a gasping rictus.

From out of his periphery vision, Thaw saw the torrent of flowing slush descending from the cliff suddenly thickened considerably, becoming an overwhelming mass as it fed the flood more quickly still, elevating its level around the car with a surge to approximately three inches above the door line. Thaw remained speechless for a instant and his emotional stress caused him to swallow and the tensed muscles throughout his body to develop knots. Then as Bisset felt the cold and the dampness seep into his clothes, Thaw arrived at a snap decision, galvanized by the avalanche of mud and the unsuccessful attempts of getting the engine started.

"Don't bother Nathan," he said, looking briefly at the police scanner where it rested on top of the dashboard. Making up his mind about something as he flicked on the car's ceiling light to help him to see by. "I'll do it myself." He sighed as conflicting emotions raged deep inside. He slid back the unlocked sunroof and at once heavy rain fell through the opening.

Bisset nodded, turned and moved forward through the climbing mire towards the rear of the car. "I'll grab anything that's going from the boot then." He shouted, directing his head downwards against the wind and the rain which almost muffled Thaw's affirmation. Bisset's breathe, little by little grew rapid and heavy the further he labored through the filthy substance, his face darkening slightly from his energetic effort's.

Having to shove the door forcibly open due to the drag resistance of the mud which immediately gushed into his side of the compartment, splashing over his clothes and boots, Thaw scrambled out of the car and unhesitatingly landed in the liquid. He pushed forward a few paces behind Bisset, cold ooze slipped into his boots while the deluge flattened his hair and streamed down his black leather jacket.

When he reached the boot, he saw Bisset grab his satchel and one of the flight bags.

"Go," Thaw growled with a jerk of his head as he caught sight of Cummings about twenty feet away in the diminishing red glow of the tail-lamps and in the glare of another lightening flash, coming towards them, passing the receding figure of Gillett, down the slope of the hill. His destination lit up by the fading, wavering brightness of the car's ceiling light. "We'll deal with the rest." He felt his skin tingle and the hair on his back stand up from the nearness of the lightning as he plucked the third pouch out of the Escort's boot.

Not bothering to shout against the howling wind, Bisset answered with another affirmative nod, and gripped the satchel's handle in his teeth before wiping rivulets of rainwater away from his eyes. He shoved his glasses further up his nose in mid-turn and, in the falling curtain of rain, Cummings drew his attention as he approached the rising shoreline, empty handed and clomped with a splash, into the mud. Water streaming down the sides of his hood.

"Keep moving Nathan," Cummings shouted to Bisset whose head was bent against the wind and the driving rain. "Follow motor mouth." He jerked his thumb over his shoulder, the way he'd come. "She led you to a spot we found about half way up the hill." Receiving only a grunt of acknowledgment, he passed him and waded deeper into the mud as he focused his gaze on Thaw's back. "I thought I'd better get back on the double before the car gets completely submerged."

"Won't be long."

"So what's left?" He asked, taking into account what he and Klugman had taken up already plus observing the others loaded down with baggage when they'd approached him, not being able to see what was in the boot for himself due to Thaw presently standing in front of the raised lid blocking his view of the contents.

Thaw blinked and his one eye stung when salty sweat trickling into it. "Only one flight bag." He replied with the money pouch held tightly under the crook of his arm, his right hand occupied in raking back strands of hair and runnels of rain away from his face as the tall man slogged up to his side. "Fish it out Adrian, then close the lid." He cleared the vision and conceded space to allow Cummings better access to the boot. "I want whoever finds the car the impression that joy-riders were the ones who abandoned it when they got caught in the flood." Cummings complied to the instructions. Thunder rumbled.

"Neat treat if you can. How though is another matter?" He enquired out of curiously, a deep frown creasing his forehead. His free hand slamming the lid of the boot shut with a bang before turning and following Thaw as he hoisted the pouch atop of his left shoulder and withdrew out of the still, ascending mire.

"By leaving the police scanner inside the car on purpose," he announced, quickening his pace through the slashing rain as he headed up the slippery slope. With disbelief etched on his shadowed features, Cummings kept up. His trousers feeling heavy and clinging damply to his legs as he ran alongside him, continuing to listen to what Thaw had to say. "It'll lend some credibility to that assumption and it's not like we need it anymore not when we're so far beyond the search area."

Another flash of lightening fleetingly lit up a place less than thirty yards ahead of them where only two of their party were having a respite beside the cliff, beneath the cluster of lofty, overhanging branches of an evergreen tree. Rain water coursed down the road from higher ground and round the pouches and flight bags dumped unceremoniously at their feet. Shivering, Thaw took a quick look at the scene and noticed that Klugman was missing. Wondering where it was, yet preoccupied with thoughts in regard to their present surroundings, he suppressed his inquisitiveness and filed it away for future reference when he wasn't so wet and he'd had the chance to catch his breath.

"Until someone does a check," Cummings answered, casting doubt on the idea, slightly laboring for breath from his exertion, "and spots no one's reported it nicked."

"That's Klugman's problem sometime tomorrow." Thaw grasped, soaked to the skin. His trousers like Cummings were smeared with muck and felt heavy thanks to the dripping water, some of which was in their pockets. "By then we'll have acquired another car and be down the motorway with most of the physical evidence we left behind, hopefully eliminated by the rainwater," he panted, "which I made sure I let in when I threw open the sunroof before getting out of there."

The road fell away behind their echoing boots, the tail lights dulled in intensity beneath the slime as the car slowly vanished, melting into the darkness when it was finally submerged by the rising mud.

CHAPTER EIGHT

The familiar male voice shouted "Inspector Sinclair!" as she came out of her office and turned to see the person it belonged to. "Have you got minute guv?

The fifty-four year old detective peered at Giddings, dressed in a suit and clasping a small memorandum book as he approached along the corridor towards her. The lens of her glasses magnified her brown eyes to twice the size of what they normally were. "Aw! Sergeant," she glanced at her wristwatch illuminated in sharp relief beneath the section of strip lighting. "I can't speak long, I've got to get rolling, I got another appointment with my superiors in thirty minutes to discuss the possible reconstruction of the crime and my chariot awaits." She looked back up and caught movement from her edge of her vision. "Have you replaced the battery in your mobile yet?" She asked as a burly constable emerged through the doorway of the office opposite.

"I have sir." Giddings replied, picking up the pretend question and playing along with it. His dark and blooding looks were not apparent in his chirpy disposition as he drew to a halt, his height easily towering a foot over her medium stature, eyeing the traffic cop close the door and walk down the corridor behind them, stealing a glance in his direction to make sure he was out of earshot. "I wanted to thank you, Hallie for covering up for me today especially after the alleged claim I was diddling the overtime figures." He whispered with a smile, halting his speech when a couple of the stations full-time civilian staff passed by. "Nothing personal but that ex-wife of mine is a right royal pain. I'm bloody sure she's got my number on speed dial," he resumed, his voice a little bit louder in tone. "I didn't think she'd have the nerve to tie up my mobile number and even bother me at work just because my lousy alimony check is late arriving through the post. If it's the last thing I do, I'm gotta sort out my financial problems."

She sighed sorrowfully. "There wasn't an ounce of proof in those allegations and like I said before I'm not taking sides here but if you've got an shred of decency inside you then you'll make sure you will Bryan." She said sincerely. Seeing a middle-aged cleaner appear from around the corner, carrying a upright vacuum in a two-handed grip. "I know what your wife is going through for while being a widower myself, I've still raised a daughter on my own too and it isn't easy for her living from hand to mouth so get your act together understand? Otherwise I'll see to it personally that you're directing traffic on the busiest stretch of road I can find."

Giddings blinked and swallowed.

Sinclair's voice rose slightly with a definite edge emerging as she continued the lecture, peering around her as their conversation became on the verge of being eavesdropped. "I'll always support you as a friend," she added, communicating her deepest feelings, in an attempt to stoke his bruised ego. "However remember as your boss, this is the last time I'm going out on a limb for you and that's a promise, do you hear me, Bryan."

Emotionally as sullen now as he looked, Giddings nodded almost forlornly, and forced a thin smile when the cleaning woman closed upon their position and put the vacuum down on the carpet. She started uncoiling the flex behind the handle.

"Now! Come on. Walk with me." Sinclair ordered sternly. Shutting her office door with a clink, she shoved her handbag strap over the shoulder of her jacket and set off down the corridor with the detective half a stride behind her. "What's the situation at your end? Any new developments at the security firm that I can inform the superintendent about?"

"Well inspector," Giddings began. Promptly becoming more professional and hiding his petulance, organizing his thoughts as the pair turned left into another passageway and strode down its entire length. "The problem with their computer crash has been resolved."

"Uh-huh!" Sinclair exclaimed affirmatively. Listening attentively to what he had to say, feeling her fleshy thighs rubbing against the legs of her trousers.

"It was some error in the program according to the chief executive of Sentinel Enterprises: A mister Kenneth Dickenson," he went on. Diverting his attention between where he was going and his memorandum book as he glanced at the record of events and his observations to refresh his memory. "In keeping with his guarantee to give us his full collaboration, Dickenson has already started faxing us lists of current company timetables, names of employees, apprentices and managing personal along with each of their work assignments detailing the responsibility involved."

The inspector bid good evening to one of the computer analysts in passing from their intelligence branch, and Giddings pushed open a fire door and walked through alongside Sinclair to come out in another stretch of corridor: the walls decorated like the other in pastel colours, hung with an occasional picture of a cityscape in-between the intervening office doors.

"Do those references include all the administrative staff and auxiliaries?" Sinclair inquired calmly.

"Yeah!" Giddings reported. Licking the tip of his plastered-thumb prior to sliding over a page on his book and consulting what he'd written underneath. "Secretaries, the receptionist, department manager's past and present plus names of courier's, mechanics, security guards and even the janitor of the building." His lip twitched. "Though at the moment we're still awaiting information in regard to who of those individuals had the authority to access the company files."

"Hmmm," the inspector mused. "Very public minded of Dickenson. To be on the safe side I'll start the ball rolling on obtaining a warrant and a wire tap from an amiable judge just in case he or his superiors at headquarters have a sudden change of heart and not want their files, contacts and accounts looked at." She paused to swallow.

"What about probable cause sir?"

Sinclair smiled thinned but lingered. "Huh," she uttered, expressing her contempt of the question. "Sodding bureaucratic red tape. Always ties my hands up. Oh, I'll tell the judge something half believable. It's never stopped me before now has it Bryan?" She saw him then break into a grin too. "Incidentally are there any back-up files to the ones on the computer's mainframe? I want them checked to see if any have been purged from the system."

"Funny you should say that sir." He answered assuredly. "I'll got two of our expects already on it to determine if everything is as it should be."

"Hmmm, good." She uttered thoughtfully. "At least we're making progress of a kind Bryan. Only if we are dealing with it, item by bloody item. The news elsewhere is pretty bleak. As a side effect of the storm and the lateness of the day, the assistant commissioner has ordered us to break off the search for the Caravelle until dawn tomorrow."

"I heard guv," Giddings replied, detecting the annoyance and irritation in her voice. "I expected as much when I caught the forecast on the evening news. I have something else you won't be too ecstatic about either."

They went beyond a fire extinguisher and rounded a corner. In the distance the detectives saw the corridor ended at a pair of double doors which concealed the interior of a lift.

"Go on!"

"To complicate matters further," he announced evenly. "I've just finished running the checks on the whereabouts of suspects whose previous crimes bore certain similarities to the one upon this Post Office."

"And?" Sinclair said. Breaking into the sentence as she came to a halt before the lift doors and jabbed a thumb hard against the down button.

"I found out that most of the mob's are still in prison," he replied. Stopping in his tracks and turning his book over to view the writing on the reverse side of the page. "While those remaining on the outside had rock solid alibis at the time of the heist."

The doors of the lift slid open with a chime to expose an empty space and the pair entered the car proper.

"Okay how about their cell mates?" She said, pressing the button marked G then watched the doors shut. "Maybe a member of the mob got bored and decided to pass the time by blabbing about his exploits to another inmate."

The lift begun to descend. Above their heads the indicator countered off the floors in reverse order. Giddings frowned and signed, grabbing hold of his long dark hair at the back and giving it a squeeze in apparent frustration. "You mean we might not have to look for a mastermind, just a copy-cat instead."

Sinclair exchanged glances and nodded.

"I overlooked that sir." He confessed grudgingly. "I'll take care of it personally and I'll keep you informed of my findings when I've assembled all of the facts."

The car slowed and came to a sudden stop on the ground floor.

"Fine!" Sinclair said. "You know Bryan, it could be an obvious answer like that which provides us with a way forward in this case."

The doors parted again to reveal a slender uniformed, female standing, ready to enter the car to go up. The inspector stepped out while the young Bangladeshi officer slipped into the vacant space.

"I'll see you later." Sinclair added in parting, without glancing back before he'd had the chance to move a muscle. "Duty calls and all that."

Giddings punched his button and it lit up just a floor below the level where the woman wanted to go to. Then, contemplating on all of his misfortunes, he observed his boss walk across the lobby and bump into a soggy looking Keane who approached her through the front entrance before the lift doors closed once more on the car blocking his view, and he started his ride back up to the sixth floor.

* * *

"Keane!" The inspector nodded in greeting, mirroring his movements as they both came to a standstill about an arms length away from each other. "Got anything for me?" She added, taking in his strapping appearance at a glance.

His short blond hair was plastered wetly to his head but his rain-proof jacket had managed to keep dry some of the denim he was wearing underneath it. "Yeah! a little guv," he responded. Trying to talk with a mouthful of food as he used the edge of his sleeve to rake rain water and his fringe off his face.

"Spit it out, but nothing long-winded, just a quick summery if you please for I've places to go and people to see."

"Right-o!" He began pausing fleetingly to swallow. "We're still awaiting test results from forensics on just about everything. James Stacey is in charge down at the village and he says they're going to maintain their search throughout the night if need be. His got the tent up and the portable floodlights are on."

"Items of clothing from the first aiders have been sealed up in bags and taken away for scientific examination to determinate if certain fibers that Stacey's team found can be eliminated from the investigation. Some of their findings, including the results of the strands of hair found in the impounded people-carrier, will on its way to us by tomorrow evening at the latest."

"Continue!" The inspector began tapping her foot on the pea-green carpet covering the lobby floor.

"Up to now we've managed to trace the present location of a quarter of the Caravelles to their registered owners and in accordance with your suspicion of the dead men. I'm about half way through compiling a detailed report of the life style and personal lives of both suspects."

"Anything of note in your finding so far sergeant?"

"Not really! From the fingerprints we took off them in the morgue, not one of the victims had any real form to shout about. Rutten was a bachelor but was by far from being celibate according to a work colleague of his who claimed they frequented a brothel quite regularly but he wasn't sure if being middle aged, the post master wasn't trying to relive his youth or simply rebelling against his strict religious upbringing. Rutten had no arrest record but he did have one outstanding parking ticket."

"Uh-huh!"

"Jenkins was in his sixties, married with a daughter and kept pretty much to himself. He had been arrested for criminal damage a few years ago, having to pay a fine and court costs when he scratched a neighbor's car because she kept leaving it parked outside his driveway. But you're gonna love this, his wife Rosalind said he'd been awful depressed of late and was inclined to hitting the bottle due to the worry of an overdraft and declining physical health. He had been a diabetic for a long time and that condition had caused him to suffer from failing eyesight and poor bladder control."

"Hmmm," Sinclair uttered with a sigh, briefly putting aside her urgency to be somewhere else. "I hate to cast suspicion without proof yet it's sticking out a mile that Jenkins wasn't satisfied with his lot in life. And who could blame him with the problems he had? That could have made him go towards a particular direction."

"In anticipation of attaining more contrasting information, of whether Jenkins or Rutten were in league with the raiders I want you to delegate someone to dig deeper Keane, find out about their past movements. Were they members of a trade union or what are their religious views. Does the courier own any more money? Check his payroll and look through his garbage if it's necessary then talk to his daughter and visit his hangouts and interview the people he mixed with. Tell them that it's only routine enquires. The same procedure goes for Rutten! He isn't as squeaky clean as he appeared on the surface either."

"It was the next thing to do on my list." The young detective announced evenly. "The search is still going on at both of the suspect's properties. No diaries, though we did pick up an address book from Jenkins' place and his wife has been very helpful by confirming that only yesterday they had a plumber in to repair a pipe and unblock their toilet. I've got the name and I'll question him tomorrow morning. Jenkins didn't have a computer, Rutten did and had Internet access. He'd been hitting a Russian dating agency site for weeks and has been interested in one young woman from Vladivostok.."

"Foreign brides! That's muddied up the waters quite nicely. Good work sergeant." Sinclair answered, remembering something that had almost completely slipped from her mind. "Er," she expressed in hesitation but decided quickly to press on and mentioned it nevertheless. "Keep that tradesmen number handy, I need someone to maintain a few of my fittings at home. Good plumbers are harder to find than gold dust."

"Will do sir." he said in a deadpan manner.

"Oh, before I forget, did Jenkins or Rutten have a mobile upon them?" She asked, returning to her businesslike tone.

"Only Jenkins," he replied. "We contacted his phone service provider and they furnished us with a bill of his past calls and a log of which masts he used this morning. Jenkins made just one call fifteen minutes before he was killed to his boss, a mister Gary Welsh in shipping and distribution, to double check the route to the second pick-up point. Welsh stated as much in an affidavit. Jenkins re-dial and the phone bill confirms this with the firm's number and the time it took place."

Sinclair scowled and bit her lower lip in frustration.

"Rutten on the other hand had a land line in his shop." He proclaimed. "He had two incoming calls which we traced back to residents in the village. One was off a close relative to remind him that it was his mother's birthday coming up soon, and the second was from a wrong number made by an old biddy who claimed she was trying to get in touch with the local cats home."

"How is constable Kitridge's investigation going at the boarding houses in the area? Any strangers fitting the description of our man-mountain? Or anyone else walking their dog or acting suspiciously."

"She's checked out three B and Bs, so far guv." The sergeant replied. "Being October it's the start of the off-season for the businesses and most of them are empty save for a few regulars but that doesn't prove anything not when one of the regulars could be the individual who guided the felons out of the area."

"To true, Justin," Sinclair answered with a nod.

"No one fitted the man's description. I think it's a dead end there."

"Maybe! Get her to do a background check on proprietors,

their families and the regulars plus their whereabouts at the time of the robbery."

"Will do sir," Keane confirmed. "It will take time."

"Doesn't it always? What about the parked cars in the area at the time of the robbery? Any joy there?"

"Thanks to the local neighborhood watch scheme, we traced a few of the license plates to residents and another to a white bakery van whose driver was late with his delivers due to having to change a blown tyre. Also we're checking out the milkman, postman and dustbin men to see if anyone could remember seeing a big man or any other stranger loitering in the region."

"Outstanding! Right while Kitridge continues to poke around, this is what I want you to do Keane." She stated thoughtfully. "Join forces with Giddings, and check Welsh and everyone else on the lists the chief executive of Sentinel enterprises faxed over to us. Put everyone in the spotlight then go back over there and scrutinize their E-mails, do a background check to learn if anyone's got a criminal record or an outstanding warrant against them, and if anyone's screwing around behind their partner's back, I want to know about that too."

"You got it sir!"

"Okey-dokey," Sinclair replied. "I'm out of here. Let me know when you have anything else that has a bearing on the case."

The inspector nodded a farewell then flashed past him, out of the doors of the building to emerge into the pouring rain, getting slightly wet as she hurried over to the curb where her car and driver awaited her.

CHAPTER NINE

Staring sullenly down the hill, with her back towards the aggressive gale which was shoving against her, Gillett uttered, "here they come." Her breath was ragged from her exhaustion and her hands trembled from the cold and the after-effects of her adrenaline rush.

Bisset was out of breath too, but unlike Sophie he maintained control over his emotions, just staying non-committal as he cleaned the rain off the thick-lenses of his glasses with a silk handkerchief and fixing his blinking gaze upon the approaching pair.

Cummings and Thaw reached the inadequate shelter provided by the high overhanging branches and the full, almost overlapping foliage of the evergreen tree. A single, exposed root curled out of the cliff's steep broad-face. Perched approximately twelve feet above them, atop of the bluff, the branches of the tree swayed in the wailing wind and rain water leaked through gaps in the leaves, falling into the expanding stream coursing down the sloping road, along the edge of the rock wall.

"Get out from under there you two." Cummings ordered as he and Thaw pulled up just outside the canopy and took it in turns to fling down what they carried. Water poured down their clothes. "Haven't you got any sense? That's one of the tallest structures around." He gazed nervously at the night sky, the growing despair was evident in his voice. "It is one of the most dangerous places to occupy in this kind of weather."

Gillett blinked in the gloomy atmosphere, standing in a spot under the oscillating green canopy where rain wasn't dribbling down from above. "So if we don't get struck by lightning here," she grumbled irritably above the wind and pointed at the curtain of rain. "We risk getting more wet and catching colds and pneumonia out there."

Having heard enough, Bisset sighed and put on his glasses before picking up a pair of flight bags and walking out to join them. Still shaken from the ordeal, Gillett's breathing eased little by little until it became comparatively regular. A torrent of cold water washed over her dirty mules, numbing her feet and causing her to become more annoyed and peer down to see a stone being gently pushed towards her. Succumbing to a fit of temper she moodily delivered a sideswiped kick as an outlet for her frustration. The pebble sailed through the air and disappeared into the darkness.

"God this is just terrific isn't it?" Gillett said, not waiting for a reply. She seized some baggage and moved out of the shelter. "So what are we going to now? We're in the middle of nowhere at the mercy of the elements." Her voice crackling under the strain and raising somewhat in scale but not to the near hysterical level as it was before. "I for one won't be diving flat in the open in this storm. I'm damp enough as it is."

"Oh, for Pete's sake Sophie," Thaw growled sharply with a slight indication of impatience and a tough unfeeling steel edge developing in his tone. "Just knock it off and stay cool will you? I'm trying to think of something."

Forked lightning flashed above, but the time between it and the preceding electrical discharge had lengthened moderately. Gillett flinched at the flash, not noticing the duration as she gaped at him, anger blazed at being spoken to like that.

Bisset nodded in assent, his glasses beginning to slightly fog up again from his pluming breath.

"If we crouch down and make ourselves as small as possible." Cummings stated. "We can move out that way."

"Where to?" Bisset asked. "I don't see a house nearby."

"Not sure." Cummings remarked. "I'm fresh out of ideas."

"I can't see of any other way but to hike back-up to the last junction with all the gear and see if we can flag down a passing car or find some refuge like a bus shelter or something."

"All that way Jerry?" Gillett declared.

"Better than nothing." Cummings conceded, squaring his shoulders. "I'll guide us back."

"Before you do Adrian." Thaw turned to address his girlfriend laconically. "I want Sophie to tell us where's Kyle gone to?"

"Eh!" she uttered, snapping out of her reverie, as she stooped. "He went to investigate something he spotted before we entered the gully."

"Hmmm," Thaw expressed while kneeling like the others around him. "Did he take one of the walkie-talkie's?" He enquired in the same tone, not feeling any remorse for what he'd said to her.

"No, Jerome!" Bisset declared, raising his voice to cut into the conversation. "Once we got here Kyle told us to look after things."

He pointed. "After that he headed up the slope, a.s.a.p!"

Thaw nodded, following his finger, his eyes squinting against the force of the gale and seeing a single cone of unsteady torch-light cresting the top of the hill ahead of him, heralding the approach of Klugman. "Well it look's like he's coming now. Let's hope he's bringing some good news with him, otherwise if none of you have got a better alternative." He shouted above the gale. "We go with my plan."

The beam penetrated the darkness and swayed to and fro as Klugman ran down the incline. His footsteps would have normally echoed loudly off the concrete road and the steep walls of the surrounding cliffs; yet the sound of his footfalls were muffled by the noise of the elements and the constant, yet now slightly less audible, crash of thunder. As the cold begun to seep into their bones, and the wind influenced the rain to slant into them, Klugman breathing hard, steam rising from the heat of his body, splashed through the descending water flow and slowed his pace. A stitch gave him a dull yet steady pain in his side and the air he drew into his lungs burned as he covered the final few yards that separated him from the rest of the party.

"What did you find Kyle?" Gillett enquired. Her face pale and taut with tension at their sole prospect filled her with reluctant dread.

"A stile!" Klugman gasped breathlessly. Coming to a halt in front of Thaw who frowned pensively before waiting until Klugman had finished speaking to throw a question of his own. "About two hundred yards on the right as we go up, probably a little less from where the road dips."

"What's on the other side," Thaw asked loudly, seeing him bend at the waist and place both of his hands on the filthy trouser knees while continuing to struggle with short quick breaths, his mouth agape.

"A hiking trail!" He wheezed, tilting his head back to look up, his heart still throbbed quite rapidly but his breath eased ever so slightly as it slowly returned to normal. "Only a beaten path. I followed it for a few yards into a thick growth of trees before turning back." Rain dripped steadily off the peak of his baseball cap as he straightened up. "I don't know where it leads or how far it goes on for," he panted, his voice barely audible. "But I'm betting there's an inn or some other hostel further on for ramblers to crash for the night."

Thaw nodded in agreement, quietly applauding his initiate. And by degrees the information caused the nervous strain to suddenly trickle out of Gillett's dour face.

"Possible." Cummings confirmed. Increasing the volume of his voice, tossing his thoughts into the conversation. "We could head that way and see where it takes us Jerome," he adjoined, reinforcing Thaw's unspoken, snap decision.

"I concur!" Bisset declared, making himself heard. One more lightning flash broke the longest gap yet and shot between the clouds to brighten up their surroundings. "Both routes will be hard going for us especially trudging through this rain, in the dark carrying all the equipment." He swallowed. "The trail is a much more preferable option than having to lug our gear back up to the junction before being able to hijack a passing car if there's one about while trying at the same time to find some shelter."

In the midst of Bisset's discourse, thunder reverberated anew, though the peal had lost a lot of its amplification. Klugman lifted a single bushy eyebrow in scepticism. His sense of optimism reflecting the views and the lack of confidence, the rest of the gang had in Thaw's hastily thought-up plan. The intervening break separating the lightning flashes again extended, peering up at the sky, Bisset discerned this and pressed on.

"We might even come across a hostel with a car park." Cummings nodded while the prospect of some place warm and dry loaned Gillett's aching leg tendons and arm muscles fresh strength and a modest amount of comfort. "If the worst does come to the worst and we don't find anything." He lowered his gaze and shrugged his shoulders. "Then we're going in the right direction towards Hereford and the motorway. From the looks of it we won't have to endure the rest of the storm because it's moving on."

Clapping her hands together and rubbing them in an effort to stimulate some warmth and get the feeling of numbness from her fingers, Gillett tilted her face skyward only to have rain funnel into her eyes. Pulling a small pocket compass out his Mackintosh, Bisset raised it to Thaw's face who saw the needle highlighted by the luminous dial, point to an easterly bearing. A speck of water dabbed the lucent face of the compass.

"Enough talk people, let's just do it." She shrilled, struggling to be heard over the wind and the rustling foliage above them, if not the decreasing sound of a thunder clap. Her cheeks still numb from the cold, Sophie picked up one of the carry-alls and slipped the strap over her left shoulder. "I'm to tired and wet to care anymore. Anywhere that leads me to a warm drink and to some cover out from this wretched weather for the night will get my vote."

"I'll get you your drink sugar." Thaw proclaimed affably with unashamed affection. A ghost of a smile developed across Gillett's features when she moved closer to her associates. "Okay then," he added business-like. Glancing away from her to the stern male faces around him. "It's settled. We'll wait until Kyle has a breather then my friend," he said politely, locking eyes with Klugman, "You can show us the way there."

* * *

Once Klugman had got his breath back, he grabbed a money pouch from the pile and with the beam of the torch lancing ahead of him, retraced his steps back up the incline. Loaded down with baggage, of one sort or another, the rest of the party followed close on his heels. High cliff walls and the sloping road soon yielded around them to scrub-covered ridges gradually decreasing in elevation while the concrete surface beneath their feet levelled out. Above the travelers, the thunder and the lightning became less frequent but the wind kept on moaning and its chilly current ripped through them like a knife.

Farther along the lane, rows of dense, towering hedges abruptly sprouted up to flank both sides of the drenched procession. Klugman trained the torch-light upon one of the lines of closely-planted trees, and mottled shades of darkness gave way under the dazzling glare to reveal plenty of overgrown leafy stalks swaying in the gale. Eventually, the dilapidated stile came into view on their right, inserted tightly inbetween a split within the foliage. When the five companions reached it, they found a set of loose and rickety stairs arched over a low, mended stretch of wooden fence edged in by the hedges.

"Blimey. This looks older than me and that's saying something." Bisset remarked.

"Okay guys," Cummings said over the wind, thinking on his feet. Rain tumbling down the sides of his hood. "It's going to be awkward getting over the stile carrying all this baggage so dump it here. Kyle and I will bring it across when you're all over."

Bisset bent his head close to the tall man and in a raised voice remarked: "Capital idea, Adrian!" He unslung his flight bag from his shoulder and placed it in the gathering pile beside a widening puddle on the road side.

With adequate light to see by, the bedraggled band climbed over the stile, the gale again tousled Thaw's hair, dripping wet with sweat and rain as he arrived at the top of it. Clambering on down to the other side to join Bisset, he used his fingers to brush away the water trickling down his face and his eyes wandered over the terrain ahead of him. The torch beam illuminated the arrangement of steps behind him and silhouetted the rear half of Thaw's frame, and some of the light filtered past him to stab the gloom, exposing a glimpse of fronds and saplings flourishing wildly along the edge of the beaten trail ahead. His boots made a squishing sound and sank a couple of inches into the muddy soil as Thaw turned about and blinked, then squinted his watery eyes, sensitive against the brilliant glare of the torch which dipped immediately to the ground when Thaw complained about it. "Get that bloody light out of my eyes."

A rebuke died on his lips after he bore the brunt of Thaw's acrimony, and burning rage again flamed within Klugman as he added another account to the accumulating mass of others which he would settle later on in blood when he considered the time was ripe. Picking up one of the carry-ons with his free hand, he pretended to take the remark in his stride and watched as Thaw came up to the side of the stile, almost directly below his girlfriend's high left elbow before he raised his hand to grasp her arm in order to help her get down, but Gillett shifted her weight, supporting herself so she wouldn't slip by holding onto the top of the steps, just shook her head and vocally rejected his assistance.

"No thanks, Jerry!" She replied tensely, in a tone that was flat from tiredness. "Sometimes, you're like a dog with a bone, you know that. Just leave me alone and don't fuss over me okay. I can cope quite fine by myself." He sighed and watched her gingerly descend towards the sodden ground, the mud clinging to her legs almost hid the ladder in her tights, and he absolutely knew with certainty that tonight he wasn't going to be allowed to tread those steps to heaven.

Behind the wall, Cummings came alongside Klugman, holding two of the flight bags. There was an annoying expression upon his crumpled features as he waited impatiently at the steps to pass the bags across while Gillett took her time reaching the opposite end of the stile. "All right, I'll leave it to you." Thaw said briskly. Getting extremely pissed off with her stubborn attitude when she plopped into the saturated path and winced wryly, to express her glowing distaste. "We need room to move around in so clear out of our way." He extended his hands across the fence and snatched the carry-ons from Cummings. "And while you're at it, take these with you." He trudged up to her while she was in the act of turning to see what he meant. He then shoved the bags into her arms.

Looking daggers at him, Gillett began muttering obscene language under her breath, around the word 'men' as she diverted her attention and laboriously headed for the thick clumps of flattened coarse grass hemming in the path in the hopeless search for some firmer ground. During the next few minutes the fierceness of the rain lessened slightly but it was hardly noticeable to the criminals as Cummings stepped from the stile. Thaw relinquish his grip of one of the money pouches to Klugman who took it and hoisted it in one fluid motion atop of a shoulder.

"Kyle," Thaw shouted against the shrieking wind. Catching out of his periphery vision, Cummings grab another canvas package and stick it under the crook of his arm. "You seem to be more sharp-eyed than the rest of us are especially with spotting the stile, so take the point!" He saw a flicker of surprise at the faith he had for him and a tiny amount of eagerness darted into his eyes while Thaw sensed more than saw Cummings' silent gaze drill into him from the side. "Sophie, you and Nathan go after." He glanced from one member to the next, making sure that they were all carrying something. "Adrian and I will bring up the rear." His eyes then wandered across the muddy ground to see that they hadn't left anything behind. "We all ready?" He paused for a moment while he turned back and received nods. "Okay then, let's go!"

The procession set off with Klugman leading the way, directing the torch in front of him, raking the terrain with the beam, sweeping it from left to right. Clusters of ferns, their fronds drooping under the deluges slowly decreasing onslaught, dripped rainwater off the leafy offshoots. Saplings and wild pansies yielded to tussocks of ribbon-bladed grass and densely growing scrub. The mud in the beaten trail squelched beneath the pressure and suction of moving feet trampling over leaves. These oaks had thick trunks and their wide-spreading rustling boughs soared over a hundred feet above the criminal's heads. They progressed slowly onward. Then, as the small company traversed through the diminishing rainfall, along the degenerating trail that began to narrow and coil through the woodland, the wind died abruptly and their trek became more arduous when the land became steeper. Cummings saw Thaw in front suddenly dump his pouch onto the moist soil and crouch down to tie up his boot laces. Thaw lingered for a second or two, shifting his attention between his task and the dwindling figures in front of him, casting one backways glance at Cummings' position, until he was close to drawing level at which point Thaw finished tying the laces before he scooped up his parcel and straightened alongside Cummings.

"I suppose your wondering Adrian," Thaw looked askance at the man as he walked beside him, "why I sent Klugman out at point when you've the best woodcraft between us, and should be up there, guiding us in his place?"

The elevating path they slogged along, again became intermittent, broken by a carpet of leaves shed by the closely packed trees, the bark of these shimmered wetly with moisture before the trail reappeared once more. "It did cross my mind." Cummings replied dryly. Shivering in the diminishing rainfall, passing the slender truck of a tall birch. Its white bark was barely visible beneath the vivid scarlet leaves and the tendril-strand's of a climbing plant.

"Well," Thaw said, his gaze returning back to the trail, "I'd rather have him in front of us where we can both keep an eye on him, than at our back ready at any time to put a knife into us." The infrequent knotted and twisted bole and branches of an old oak loomed ahead, he swept a low branch out of his way.

"I wouldn't put it past him, not after today's run-in." Cummings uttered, seeing Gillett was becoming gradually heavy-footed as he peered around and strained his eyes against the gloom. "Look if we don't find the hostel in the next half an hour, we better make camp for the night otherwise Sophie and Nathan will drop from exhaustion if this slope gets any steeper." Thaw nodded in agreement, his heart beating a little faster in the course of toiling non-stop through the rain and the mud.

"We'll have to endure the cold for a few hours until first light," Cummings went on, "because I ain't risking starting a fire in case it gives us away, but what I can do is fashion us a crude shelter of sorts under a tree from what's around so at least the ground won't be that wet and we'll be able to dry ourselves off and change clothes."

"That's something I suppose. I've got a couple of chocolate bars in my bag so shared out that will go a little towards taking the edge off everyone's hunger." Thaw revealed.

"And I'll set up a snare and catch us a rabbit for breakfast." Cummings said, prodding across an expanse of ground ivy, not commenting upon the fact that his legs were becoming as heavy as lead. "We'll have to eat it raw."

"Fine by me!" Thaw announced, "if not Sophie. She can have my share of the chocolate. When we make camp you take the first watch Adrian then wake me up a couple of hours before dawn. That way, you and I will be the only ones doing the guard-shift. My gut instinct tells me that will be the time Kyle will try and get the drop on us. It's something I would do."

"And me." Cummings stated in harmony. "Most assuredly."

The quantity of trees around the bedraggled party began to progressively thin as they tramped along the treacherous trail to the rounded top of the rise. With their strength flagging from each energy sapping step, Klugman guided his companions down the reverse side of the hill. Before them, the path deteriorated into deep slush and straightened. On the way down, Bisset slid in the mud, almost losing his footing a couple of times while Gillett stumbled over a tree root and fell forward, face down into the turgid muck which cushioned her fall. She sputtered then the air turned blue with language as she screamed in anger and hauled herself up to her knees. Thaw smirked and sauntered over and saw her wipe the mud away from her eyes before flinging it from her fingers at arms length. The rain was no more than drizzling presently but the water still cut narrow channels into her filthy countenance.

"You haven't injured himself, have you?" Thaw inquired brusquely, the rough and harsh matter of his speech was not typified by the genuine concern he felt for her deep down inside, offering her a handkerchief.

"No I'm all right," she snapped, snatching the tissue and removing more of the mud from her face. "Just give me a hand to get up Jerry."

"Dear me our little damsel's in distress again." Klugman laughed.

"Shaddap!" The American grumbled with a scowl.

Despite their exhaustion the rest of the party were smiling. Hearing her plea, Bisset dropped his burdens and totted unsteadily up to them to extend a hand in assistance while Thaw, knelt and slipped his free arm around her waist. He adopted a rigid stare and focused it on her. "Oh," he responded sarcastically, a huge slice of amusement and triumph entering into his tone. "Now, you want my help."

After she was pulled to her feet and the bags were scooped up again, the companions proceeded downward passed marsh rushes to where the torch-beam exposed a cluster of willow oaks intermixed with a thicket overgrowing the path. Klugman surveyed the dense nearly impenetrable wall of vegetation with the light, seeing a small sharply contrasting gap against the paler backdrop of other kinds of greenery in the underbrush not far from where the path vanished. He headed towards it. Klugman set foot into the thicket with the torch to the fore. Thaw gestured for Cummings to go next. He moved off, forcing his way with difficulty through the tall undergrowth. Gillett and Bisset slipped in behind him and finally Thaw brought up the rear. Pine cones and a few catkins littered the ground as they threaded their way between the foliage to level ground.

Klugman cursed, tugged his arm free from a prickly bush only to wince in discomfort when he took another step, the soles of his boots squishing and sliding in the soil around him, his right cheek was grazed by a bramble in passing. His companions followed in the drizzle and didn't get away unscathed either. They felt sharp pain, their hands were stung by stinging nettles and the thickening briar patch scratched them as they groped about in the dimness. Coming to a stop and directing the beam back and forth ahead, Klugman managed to see the brambles and a couple of swamp maples blocking their way. Slopping through the slush, Cummings felt a line of hooked thorns catch on his hood and he tilted his head away from the arched stem before coming to a standstill.

"What's the hold up Kyle?" He asked.

"It's the briar!" Klugman replied, casting a quick glance over his shoulder. "It's preventing us from going any further." He panned the torch again to the right, the length of light unveiling the narrow boundary between the tough, rambling stems of the briar and the tangled undergrowth of high grasses, ferns and clumps of shrubs. "It's blocking our left but there's a narrow channel separating the vegetation running parallel from the look of things over there," he jerked his head to where the beam shone down the boundary line.

"We could use that as a path and try to circumvent the brambles at another spot."

Gazing in that direction with his experienced eye, Cummings signed. "Worth a try, I suppose." he said unenthusiastically, hearing voices and footsteps splashing through the mud behind him. "Go on!"

Turning onto the slender boundary strip, gaps began opening up in the procession, widening here and there to almost the length of a car as the wayfarers drew upon sapping strength and headstrong determination. One or two, with their heads hunched forward, slogged laterally across the face of the tangled briar, working laboriously through the mud, muscles in the back of their legs ached from the soils suction. Thorns still clung to clothing, inflicting cuts to their exposed fresh. Huffing and puffing in the drizzle, they attempted to avoid the thorns by keeping to the right side of the boundary line, their legs then brushed aside fronds and treaded down high grasses.

After ninety-five yards of trudging cautiously down this makeshift path, the torch detected the gnarled truck of an old tree lying diagonally across the briar in front of them. Klugman immediately stopped dead in his tracks at the sight, his mud-caked legs trembling with weariness, and moved the beam in an unbroken line along the visible misshapen length of the bole, illuminating the knobby lumps and the splotches of coloured lichen adorning it until it vanished on his left into the entwining mass of brambles. Then, not unnoticed from behind him, he raised the light higher and accompanied it with an appraising gaze, traced how far back the tree went into the tangled depths by following the receding series of twisted branches spouting up at various places, which stood out starkly against the arching tendrils of thorns. An idea occurred to him when he heard Cummings moving closer to him.

"Hey, Adrian!" He said, whirling around and lowering the beam to the ground. "I've got a hunch I want to follow." Cummings stubbed his toe against a branch and then pulled up. His eyes narrowing in suspicion and distrust. Grasping the meaning of the look and acting upon it, eyeing Cummings maliciously as he deposited his money pouch directly on top of the drooping stems of a shrub beside him. "Tell the others I won't be long. Incidentally lend me your knife. I'm sure to need it where I'm going."

With his chest heaving, and his keen senses aware of everything surrounding him, Cummings blinked, threw down his cargo and stooped to pull the knife free from his boot. "Has it anything to do with that old tree?" He enquired with a frown, reaching the obvious conclusion after observing the fallen oak and Klugman's ensuing actions with the torch.

"Yeah," Klugman answered tersely as Cummings straightened and with practiced ease flipped the knife up and caught the blade in his hand before proffering him the hilt first. Catching sight of Gillett approaching and a tiny pool of flicking, sputtering light behind her, outlining a portion of Bisset's mackintosh. Klugman grasped the handle, turned and brought up the torch to shine at the terrain ahead, as he climbed up onto the gnarled trunk. Gillett squelched to a stop and peered nonplussed at Klugman actions, while the naked flame from Bisset's lighter wavered and sputtered in the drizzle.

"The tree goes across the briar like a bridge," Klugman explained, beginning with one boot then the other to scrape the soles against the edge of a lump to gain a degree of purchase on the bark, freeing the treads of some of the mud filling them. "Whether it spans the complete patch or not is something I've got to check out. I'll be back before you know it."

He stamped his feet hard to get rid of any remaining wet earth still clinging to his boots before moving with deliberate caution along the trunk towards the bramble patch. Behind him, Thaw jostled past Gillett and Bisset who vocalize their surprise with "Hey," and "Watch it," which he ignored, and braked at Cummings elbow.

"Where the hell is he going with our only dependable source of light?" His voice had a slight edge, his gaze fixed upon the moving beam.

"To test a hunch," replied Cummings watching the light fade disappearing into the tangled gloom. "The tree extends at an angle into the briar and he's gone to see if it can furnish us with a possible route across,"

"Hmmm," Thaw expressed thoughtfully, furrowing his forehead. Casting a furtive glance over his shoulder at the two people behind him, glimpsing in the flickering lighter flame Bisset's face which mirrored everyone's by being drawn and tired from their fatiguing hike. "If it does, it'll be a well spent effort on his part." He turned back, coming up with a course of action to resolve the situation. "Because it'll mean we can start looking for a place to camp over there."

"You mean sleep rough in the open air with all the creepy crawlys?" The young American asked in shock, behind him. "Out here, on the wet ground, in the back of beyond! Together!"

"Yes!" Her boyfriend replied with a deep breath, not about to tolerate another of her emotional outbursts. Thaw whirled to face her and was just ready to give her a piece of his mind when Gillett beat him to the punch by airing her concerns.

"But Jerome! I'm a city girl. I panic when the sidewalk runs out."

"Tough!"

Fuming she went on, her words almost tripping over themselves in their haste to come out. "We haven't got any camping equipment with us – such as sleeping bags. We'll suffer from cramp or rheumatics if we just sleep on the damp earth."

Thaw sighed and saw the worried expression etched in Gillett's visage and his tone immediately softened like snow melting in the spring sunshine.

"God! Sophie you wail like a baby! And I thought you yanks were supposed to come from strong pioneering stock." Cummings said with a shake of his head. "Yours must have been diluted along the way. You'll be afraid to dig your own toilet next."

The American's eyebrows ascended to her hairline at the comment. "I've slogged my guts out on his trip, you bastard."

"Actually my parents are married." Cummings replied in good humor.

"Cool it guys!" Thaw smirked. "Has Kyle been training you Adrian?"

"Naw! Just had plenty of practice with my ex-mother-in-law."

"Look Sophie, how's this," Thaw said, adopting a practical and serious tone in a bid to defuse tension. "We'll rig up some kind of groundsheet to keep you dry so you can sleep through the night. I've got an extra jumper in my bag you can lie on and the others have possibly brought along the odd item of clothing or a newspaper we can use to spread across the grass. Bisset and Cummings nodded. "Then in the morning, we'll get cracking very early to find our way back to the trail Okay?" Gillett sniffed and gave a nod.

* * *

In the interim, Klugman proceeded along the gnarled truck, its misshapen length was generous in breadth with sufficient space for two people to walk abreast but despite that he kept to the centre whenever possible. Ahead the torch beam revealed a rising curve in the trunk about Cummings' height which he agilely scrambled up and over. Another bough approached him, about half way across, and this one rose almost vertically. Again it was contorted and knotty and Klugman had to move along the edge of it to get to the other side. The beam next captured tendrils of intertwining thorns arching across the tree to block his progress. Using the knife in his other hand, he swept the blade out in front of him, receiving a few more scratches on his arms and hands, his breathing became slightly more rapid and heavier as he sliced apart braids of thorns which fell away like wheat before a scythe. Pressing on, he jumped over a broad gap where the trunk bent below him through the arches of thorns growing over it before the length of bole curved back up and straightened. Klugman circumvented two more branches without any trouble then as a mild putrid smell assailed his nostrils, several deep water-filled hollows appeared in the trunk where the slick bark had been removed, the wood underneath had long since rotted away. The trunk split asunder after that, and diverted into a fork. The first branch he saw went left and descended into the brambles while the second smaller fork went straight on. The latter he followed, finding it became narrower until he saw the limb clear the briar and its taping end vanish into a massive clump of coarse bracken.

Resting up for a moment prior to returning to his associates with the good news, Klugman wrinkled his nose in distaste at the fetid stink of decomposing vegetable matter, and once more, albeit awkwardly, swept the torch beam back and forth to survey the terrain around him. On his left he observed the range of the briar spread out almost endlessly, further than the eye could perceive, revolving his torso in the opposite direction revealed an area of the briar stretching for several yards before yielding to sundews and bladderworts which fringed a basin of liquid that had a partial floating lid of plants beginning to cover it. Approximately seven feet beyond the brambles, a crescent-shaped expanse of muddy soil stretched away from the taping bough that Klugman was standing on, unto it melted into the tall wall of bracken whose depths ahead of him extended across the face of the visible horizon. Here and there behind the weedy ferns, dank trees loomed up indistinctly out of the shadowy night.

By this time, the drizzle was only sprinkling down yet it still dripped steadily off the peak of his cap as he moved off again, cautiously reversing his direction, his torch whipping around to probe the increasing width of the trunk.

CHAPTER TEN

The rain had begun almost three hours before as no more than a light drizzle as Andrew Elmes guided his five-door hatchback through the traffic and out of the busy London streets, but the further his vehicle headed out along the glistening highway into the English countryside, the thicker the downpour became. Back-lit by the lights stationed at the junctions and caught in the high beams of approaching cars, the rain pelted down in forceful sheets, drumming loudly on the roof of the hatchback and flowed down the windscreen in a steady stream. The squeegee blades squeaked and groaned clearing the back-spray shooting up from the tyres belonging to the car moving slowly ahead. Inside the vehicle, sitting in the front passenger seat, Vertly Elmes was humming to the song 'Oklahoma' that was blasting out of the car's stereo as she traced the beam of her penlight along the various coloured lines decorating the folded AA road map lying on her lap. Andrew downshifted and reduced speed to thirty miles per hour as the song on the tape finished its rip-roaring melody.

"Where are we now," Vertly asked.

"Oh that's comforting," Lois replied with a groan. "Mom's got the map in front of her and we're still lost."

"I know where we are." Andrew remarked sternly, reaching down to switch off the stereo. They were a yard behind a blue Landrover. "It's not easy to tell in this weather."

Andrew decreased his speed further, and steadily a larger gap opened up between the vehicles. Then the car bounced in and out of a deep pothole, the sudden jolt made Vertly look up and through the poor visibility and rain streaking the side window, she saw a sign post indicating there were major road works only four miles ahead. Vertly sniffed in disdain and with her head thumping from all of the travelling, returned her gaze to the map where she traced the route of another, lower-volume road heading away from the one they were on.

"Great." Lois said, seeing the blurry, lit-up sign from the rear of the car. "More delays coming up. I ain't seen so many road cones in one journey in my entire life." She sighed and shook her head. "I've been counting the numbers on the junction signs and ours is next. What do you think dad? Will we be able to miss those roadworks or have to go through it all again?"

"We should be lucky this time," Andrew remarked. "Our junction's only about a mile or so ahead of us." He checked his rear-view mirror and as he did, he switched it to anti-glare then shifted his gaze towards the road. It began to gradually climb. He yawned. "I can always tell when we getting close to our exit once we've passed that last service station." He explained, steering the car up the incline, the glare from a pair of headlights shone in his wing-mirror. "There should be a gantry just over the rise of this hill and that'll tell us for sure." He changed to a higher gear. "We'll make it before Eleven tonight."

A fork of lightening illuminated the sky and the swirling wind seemed to scream.

Lois nodded thoughtfully while Danielle continued to chew her gum loudly.

The sound of a thunderclap rumbled overhead.

Before long they cleared the crest of the hill and it quickly fell away behind the car to dwindle into the distance. Lois had begun to stir uneasily in her seat as she spotted the large illuminated sign mounted on the gantry above the roadway. Hereford, one mile was written on the sign. A white arrow pointing down at their lane. Torrential rain continued to pour and after several minutes Andrew with absolute relief flicked his left indicator on as the blue markers counted down to their junction. He steered the vehicle off the motorway and onto the slip road, keeping just under the speed limit as Vertly gave instructions where to go next. Sets of signal lights and traffic islands came and went, only delaying the travelers briefly as the hatchback rolled down a stretch of wet road bypassing the town's centre. The beams of Andrew's headlamps stabbed the darkness ahead, reflecting off the cats-eyes. Street lamps illuminated the surrounding houses until the lampposts disappeared along the side of the road and the suburbs yielded to the natural landscape of the countryside.

Danielle winced as a sudden and painful spasm flared up from having her legs bent up and restricted in one position for to long. "Eh, Mr Elmes," she began, leaning down and rubbing her lower muscles. "How far is it before we reached your sister's place?" A bolt of lightning arched across the sky.

Andrew yawned, showing more evidence of his drowsiness and a sudden chilly breeze blew into the car when he pushed a button and his electric window slid down further. "Another two miles, why Danielle?" He replied, looking into his rearview mirror at her. The strong rain occasionally blew in through the window and dotted his seat and steering wheel with wet droplets. Thunder clashed on high.

"I've got cramp. I need to stand and stretch my legs a bit. They're hurting."

"Actually dad I was about to say the same," Lois piped in as well. "Except I'm sitting on mine and it's bloody sore."

"Okay," he nodded. Glancing back to the road ahead, and despite his eyelids feeling heavy, he suppressed a smile for his daughter's difficulty. "Can you both hold on for the next ten minutes or so? We'll be there by then."

Danielle nodded. "Sure!"

"I suppose," Lois answered, with a painful grimace.

"How are you faring Andrew?" Vertly asked in concern at seeing the fatigue he was under. "Do you want to take a rest now we're off the motorway? Lois can take over and drive us the rest of the way if you're feeling tired."

"No thanks hon," he replied, glancing at her with a smile before reinstating his eyes to the road. "Nice thought, but I'm okay." He affirmed, hearing the gale wailing outside. "I can handle it until we get there."

Content with his genial disposition yet not with his answer, Vertly nodded thoughtfully as she saw him breathe in another lung-full of air. "Lois pour out the last drop of tea from the thermos, into one of the cups and pass it over for your father."

"Sure mom! But it will be cold," Lois announced, doing as she was bid.

"It doesn't matter," Vertly admitted, "so long as it's wet." She heard the liquid sloshing into the cup behind her. "It's to help him keep awake."

Andrew sighed then scowled at her. "I said I can manage dear." He stated softly, remembering the company they had with them.

"Thanks Lois!" said Vertly taking the proffered cup prior to addressing her husband. "Yeah, well, just humour me okay. Drink up so you can give me some piece of mind."

Andrew sighed again. On this occasion the audible breath was longer and deeper. "Oh, all right!" He answered a little to sharply, with a strained smile. Surrendering to Vertly's wishes as he struggled to keep his temper in check and the bitter disagreeableness out of his voice. Still fuming deep inside, he took the cup. He looked back at the windscreen wipers swishing back and forth, and drained the cup in three steady gulps.

Vertly nodded in approval. Creases of careful thought lined his forehead as he reconsidered the wisdom of her words. Vertly retrieved the cup then passed it back to Lois. Andrew glanced in his wing-mirror to check the car behind wasn't too close while hiding his reddening face, yet the blush was not out of anger but instead of embarrassment. His attitude started to soften and he was presently ashamed of letting his emotions get the better of him as he could finally see the sense of what she'd said. He diverted his attention between her and the road. "I'm feeling slightly better," he said in a low tone. "More awake."

Vertly sniffed. "A drop of tea or lemonade will do that." Her head still thumped maddeningly.

He breathe in another whiff of air blowing in from outside and whispered to his wife. "I sorry for snapping hon. I'm stubborn and everything that's happened tonight has just made me very weary. I don't know what I would do without you sometimes."

Vertly studied him for a moment. "Yes I know. Let's hope you never have to find out," she replied cryptically. "Apology accepted." Then, without another word on the subject, she returned her gaze to the map on her lap.

Behind him the two friends heard everything. They exchanged looks and while Danielle rolled her eyes to the roof of the car and shook her head, Lois make a wry face of what she thought of her father's sickeningly-sweet, sentiment, and leaned across the seat to whisper in Danielle's ear. "Ugh! Pass me the sick bucket quick. I'm going to puke." She smiled which was reflected in Danielle's expression. Having heard snatches of the conversation, Vertly glanced back and glared daggers at her daughter as the pair giggled.

Lightning flashed again. Following Vertly's instruction Lois saw her father change direction a couple of more times then cross an old stone bridge spanning the upsurging, fast flowing river before another turn found the hatchback on a much narrower road with hardly any markings and flanked on both sides of the secluded lane with trees, telephone poles and high hedges.

"Almost there!" Andrew said reassuringly to everyone in general but to the girls in particular. "About a hundred and fifty yards up this road."

Another deafening wave thunder boomed. The car splashed through rain water which was accumulating around a blocked drain before abruptly a distant, yellowy glare cut into the darkness. The light parted when the car progressed nearer. Within seconds the vegetation gave way on the right to a tarmaced-driveway flanked by a pair of granite gate posts each one had a heavy ball of iron resting on top. A single outdoor lantern was mounted on the exterior side of each of the uprights and the lights shone through the decorative casings. The rain maintained its drenching fury as Andrew flicked his indicator on and turned into the driveway, passing the intercom box and through the pair of open wrought-iron gates.

Andrew frowned, and making a mental note, forged onward, along the path lit up at various places by a number of light fittings in the form of far eastern pagodas. A streak of lightning was succeed by thunder crashing. From behind a corner dominated by a collection of tall evergreens, the facade of the manor house came into sight as the driveway ended at a curving loop. The house was lit up like a Christmas tree against the darkness and the rain, and the spectacle absolutely took Danielle's breath away for it was not what she'd expected in the least. The mansion itself was massive and imposing not only in size but also in its overall design that was an assortment of architectural styles that ranged from 16th century Tudor to Victorian-Gothic to the artistic style of the Georgian period.

From her vantage point she saw a pair of towers looming before her topped with soaring slender spires flanking a turret and half a dozen chimneys two of which were ornate; one of these had smoke climbing from the top. Under the eaves were guttering troughs filled with torrents of flowing water and projecting from these were carved rainspouts in the form of gargoyles, harpies and other grotesque animals of myth and legend. Elsewhere adorning the structure were the odd balconies and walls of asymmetrical bricks, pointed arches with large tracery windows and a gothic bay window jutting out from the wall on the first floor. Wood-panelled, folding shutters adorned the upper floors and ceramic drainpipes were busy conveying water away from the mansion. Across the front entrance of the house was a portico. The roof of this rested upon thick Corinthian columns extending from the arched doorway to cover a portion of the driveway.

Lois glanced at Danielle's rubbernecking, engrossed face and saw that her cramp had been temporarily forgotten as she took in the style of the house. Lois grinned and gave Danielle a gentle nudge in the side with her elbow. "It leaves you with a real impression, doesn't it? I bet you haven't seen anything quite like it before. This is the only piece of real estate without a Starbucks."

Danielle grinned. "I can honestly say I haven't. It's like nothing I ever thought I would come across on this trip." She returned her attention back to the front of the car.

"If you thought the house was impressive now." Lois said, shifting in her seat once again. "Then you just wait, it'll knock you speechless because it looks even better in the daylight. There are sixty bedrooms, three reception rooms and one breakfast and living room apiece." Danielle raised her eyebrows in mild surprise. "Plus the ballroom which is about two hundred feet across and almost that again in width."

The hatchback roared round the looping section of the driveway and triggered a series of motion detectors. Security-lighting provided sudden illumination as Andrew drew up under the portico.

"And tomorrow, I'll take you around the grounds and show you some of the sights." Lois spoke on, not the only one having to blink and squint her eyes against the glare as more halogen bulbs flashed on. An instant later the windscreen wipers ceased as Andrew turned the engine off and put on his hand brake. Through partly narrowed eyes, Danielle noticed an adjoining gravel path ahead now visible in the strong light. It was wide and looked solid enough for light traffic. It veered to the right, from the macadam bend in the driveway, winding around to the side of the manor where it disappeared from sight.

"As long as you two don't go anywhere near the bog." Vertly cautioned them in an austere manner. Undoing her seatbelt and peering over her shoulder, giving the girls a stern look through the space between the headrests. "It's right by the archeological dig and knowing you that'll be the first place you'll head to find something valuable after borrowing your uncle's metal detectors." Her headache pounded as she saw Lois and Danielle undo the buckles and remove the straps from across their hips.

Lois raised her eyebrows in mock innocence as her eyes slowly adjusted to the light. "We wouldn't do that mom." She uttered, failing to suppress a ghost of a smile as she joined Danielle in getting out.

"Yes, you would." Vertly replied with a sigh at the girl's early exit yet understanding it due to the constriction of the rear seats. She opened up her own door and slipped out. "Look I don't care what you get up to with Rob's detectors or what you may come across, come to that." She came to stand directly in front of Lois who was rubbing her buttocks behind the door while Danielle walked around the other side of the vehicle, flexing her joints and muscles in an attempt to get the stiffness out of them. "Just please be careful with the bog okay. I know the region is almost fenced off over here but the owner of the adjoining estate isn't so safety conscience and hasn't got any barricade on his side at all."

"His land approaches extremely close hereabouts, and it would be very easy to lose yourselves," Vertly continued, "in the midst of all those shrubs and trees and accidentally stroll behind the fence. There's some buoyant vegetation back there that won't support your weight. Remember that rambler who drowned a while back?"

Andrew got out and turned his gaze to Lois, about to put his two penny-worth in when he saw her nod and her face turn deadly serious. "All right mom!" Lois spoke, noticing Danielle from the corner of her eye, still in earshot, ambling about. "I promised we won't go beyond the dig. I never liked that area of the estate much anyway. The place gives me the creeps. I'm surprised you brought this back up again mom, you've drummed that warning speech into me that many times I can almost recite it from memory."

"Yeah well," her mother replied calmly, not getting angry by her comments. Turning away to close her passenger door with a thump. "I thought I'd better mention it again because the archeologists have recently found a gold belt and a silver brooch from the ancient battle field." Her eyes made contact with her daughter's. "And I didn't want the lure of other Saxon relics to cloud your judgment and tempt you into going treasure hunting somewhere you shouldn't."

"Ah," Lois said in comprehension, mirroring her mom's actions with the car door. "It won't mom. I might have been naughty on occasion but that was in the past. I've reformed. I'm not putting my life in jeopardy for anything. Not even treasure. It's not worth it." Her features broke into a broad friendly smile. "We've got to much sense for that. We're here simply for a good time. So don't fuss!

Trust us okay mom? We won't do anything untoward."

Vertly frowned then nodded thoughtfully. "Okay!" She said finally with reserved scepticism. "That's relieved my mind. Why don't you and Danielle see why Anderson hasn't met us?" She frowned. "He should've know we've arrived by now. Your dad and I will start unloading the suitcases."

"Sure mom!" Lois replied in sheer delight of escaping that most boring and arduous of tasks. "Come on Danielle." Seeing her companion had finally shaken off the effects of her cramp, jerking her head towards the manor house's arched doorway as she walked around to the front of the car. "Let's go and see where our welcome committee is."

Full of thoughts over Lois' comments in the discussion with her mother, and her curiously aroused by a number of the things referred to, Danielle nodded and fell into step alongside Lois and walked between the columns, up to the huge wooden portal. "So who's Anderson?" Danielle begun to ask, unable to wait until they got together someplace alone to appease her inquisitiveness.

"Oh, he's only the butler." Lois explained as they came to a halt before the door. "He's a real piece of work, in change of seven servants all together and they do all the household chores." On the door there was a bronzed grizzly-bear with a thick metal ring hanging down from its closed mouth. "Like chauffeur, cook, maid and so on." Lois seized the knocker and banged it hard a couple of times.

* * *

The rain had finally subsided when Klugman eventually emerged from the bramble line. A calm and reassuring smile decorated his features as he came forward along the visible segment of the tree trunk and dipped his torch at the moment his companions blinked and raised a hand to shield their eyes against the glaring light.

"Well, Kyle? Did your hunch pay off?" Thaw enquired. Not seeing his expression until he advanced and cleared the moistness from his eyes, leading the others as they converged onto his position, vegetation dripping all around them. Bisset snapped shut his lighter lid to save on fuel.

"It certainly did," he replied, taking another step over the gnarled stem before seeing the members of his party gather around.

"The tree goes straight across the entire patch like this," he dropped down to one knee on top of the bark and pointed the edge of the knife to a knobby lump covered with scraped mud. "This is where we are and," his audience crowded closer into the light, "here represents the other side of the briar," Klugman traced the tip of the blade directly across the wet bark to a splotch of lichen endowed with colour, before going on to explain among other things the path he cleared through the thorns, plus mark the locations of what else he'd seen in his travels.

* * *

Behind them, Vertly stood by the back of the car and watched the friends chatting as they made their way forward. Andrew had already unlocked the car's tailgate and was presently swinging it up to is maximum height.

"I don't know what to really think Andrew," Vertly replied with a brief shake of her head. "I'd like to give Lois the benefit of the doubt, believe she's telling us the truth that she's done with the whole teen rebellion thing." She saw him duck underneath the door to began unloading. "After all it's been over a year since she caused all the trouble with the drug taking and joyriding." Andrew removed the first two cases and placed them on the driveway. "But with all her friends coming up in the morning including that layabout boyfriend of hers..." Andrew nodded in understanding, "and the possibility of picking up those artifacts with the metal detector, is more than enough of an inducement for Josh or one of the others to urge her to fall back into her old ways."

"I see your point," Andrew conceded with a frown as he kept his head low and withdrew another pair of suitcases. "I wouldn't put it past him." He pursed his lips in disapproval, "this is all news to me because I didn't even know he'd been invited."

The knocker banged against the door again.

"I hadn't planned on it." Vertly answered. "However our precious daughter invited the bum behind my back and god only knows who else out of that crowd she hangs out with at college. It was him that make her so wild and abusive. I've never liked Josh. He drives to fast and I'm sure she got the stuff off him. I've still haven't lived down the fact that Lois received those Probation and Community Orders."

He let out a long, deep breath and set the cases down. "Undergoing treatment for her drug abuse was the best thing that happened to her. She clean now and determined to stay that way."

"Indeed. it's just a shame she was made to paint her old school and me being head of our branch of the Parent-Teacher Association."

"It hurt her more working eight hours on a Saturday without pay and being barred from the mall. I'll have a word with Rob, about the detector and check this little undertaking of theirs at its earliest stage." He clasped his hands together and extended his arms into an arch above his head to straighten out his back, his spine lengthening as he stretched, grunting with effort, his face wincing at the pain. "Mind you," he resumed after a moment, "the more I think about it," he lowered his arms, "Lois is certainly not stupid. She's aware that her friend's reputation is going to proceed him. You made sure of that."

"Damn right I have," she agreed.

"And if anything goes missing then you're the one pointing the finger of blame at him." His wife nodded vigorously. "So if I were you Vertly I wouldn't get too het up over this. I'm confident she and the rest of her gang will be on their best behavior throughout their stay here. None of them will want to jeopardise their new found respectability not in front of those toffs even Russel, Josh's crony isn't that dumb to know which side his bread's buttered on."

Vertly frowned and gave him a questioning look. "What do you mean Andrew? You don't think Russel's coming too."

"Among others under the guise of her student buddies."

"Hell that's all I need."

"Most of the gang are all self-seeking opportunists." He stated from his own observation, ducking his head anew beneath the raised door as he started to unload more of the suitcases. "Favorable circumstances such as this to mix with celebrities and the upper crust of society won't come along again in a hurry and one thing I've learned from watching them is that they like to take advantage of a situation." He deposited the two cases besides the others. "There's plenty networking to be made by a bright person who wants to make a good first impression." His wife nodded as she pondered this. "There will be quite a few rich men's daughters at the party who could be easily charmed by a man such as Josh who I've always found to have that most annoying quality to attract and delight people like moths to a flame."

"Hmmm," she uttered, "Maybe you're right. Nevertheless to be on the safe side I'm still going to keep an eye on them all."

"Off course!" Andrew uttered in agreement. "Do so and with a little bit of luck Josh will pick up with someone else at the party and drop Lois like a hot potato. I know it will hurt her, but at least we can wash our hands of him once and for all. And afterwards she can move on and date someone better who we feel is right for her."

* * *

When there was still no response to the resounding blows, Lois sighed and told Danielle to ring the doorbell. She pushed the button and a loud orchestral rendition of Wagner's 'The Valkyrie' blared out of hidden speakers to finally alert the residents they had visitors waiting at the front door. "That should wake them up a bit." Lois declared with a smile.

"Certainly will." Danielle bobbed her head and without making it obvious that she was keeping an eye on the whereabouts of Lois' parents, she pretended to look at one of the thick Corinthian columns which had the car and Andrew and Vertly as a backdrop. "It's got to be another one of your uncles' ideas? A simple chime wouldn't do."

"Actually no!" The brunette revealed, glancing at her. "It's my aunts in fact. She likes opera and that composer in particular. She thought that piece of music would be great as a doorbell because it's loud enough to reach all the parts of the house. It does too!" She knelt down to the letter box and lifted up the copper lid covering the hole before peering into the hallway beyond. "We should find that out in a minute or two. For myself though, I feel she's lived with Rob for far to long and picked up on his eccentric habits."

"I've heard somewhere that you can become like the company you keep." Danielle said. Satisfied that no one was close enough to eavesdrop on their conversation, Danielle let a ghost of a smile fade and moved nearer to her companion. Then tilting her head back, she began studying the pillar higher up like some tourist while minimizing the risk of being heard by whispering what she had to say. "You've got some bare-faced brass you know that," she shook her head. "But I love it, telling your mom we won't be doing anything untoward."

"Well we won't! Outside." Lois announced honestly. "We won't be putting our lives in danger either, not with the conjuring spell taking place within the pentacle. And as for the Saxon treasure, why get dirty and look for it ourselves when it can easily be one of the first things I bid Bartok to bring me after we meet the price of its fee."

From the other side of the teakwood portal, tumultuous footsteps could be heard increasing in volume over the sound of the rain, advancing towards the girl's location along with the odd creaking floorboard and a woman's voice shouting. "I'm coming! I'm coming!"

"Shush now!" Lois told her companion. "I see my aunt approaching. It's only us, aunt Ashley." She bellowed through the gap in the letterbox. "We finally made it."

"Oh," Ashley expressed in surprise, moving towards the door. Lois released the lid and stood up. "Danielle, tell mom we've got in."

"Okay!" Came the reply before Danielle hurried back along the colonnade to deliver her welcome news.

Behind her, the huge portal swung inward and standing in the doorway was a woman in her late thirties with anxiety etched upon her sharp-featured face. "What on earth happened to you Lois?" She asked with apparent concern in her voice, taking a couple of steps back and to the side to allow her space to pass. Her left heel striking against the case of wine laying on the floor, near the wall. "Come on in out of this weather. I've been worried to death about you all. I thought something had happened because we expected you ages ago." She watched her niece wipe her feet on the doormat and enter. "You didn't break down did you?" Ashley added, peering out through the doorway to see where the rest of her family might be. The paler light from the hallway penetrated outside to be lost in the whitish brightness of the security beams. "I know what my brother's luck is with cars."

Ashley Crowe was five foot four inches in height and upon the bathroom scales she weighed in at eight and a half stone. She had a small bust and a pear-shaped frame with a wide waist that merged into her hips and the extra body fat stored in her rounded, pulpy stomach. She was well groomed with pale skin that resembled white porcelain and shoulder-length, lustrous auburn hair in a long-layered style with a soft sweeping fringe framing an oval face that showed laughter lines around her wide mouth and sky blue eyes.

One or two gray hairs resided near her temple which she hadn't spotted to pluck out as yet. She was wearing a gold wedding ring and an analogue watch with matching bracelet alongside on the same wrist. She wore slim-fitting, dark suede trousers, spike-heeled crocodile boots and a fluffy off-the-shoulder sweater.

Ashley saw another young woman approach her whom she didn't recognize. Some paces behind her, Vertly was carrying an travel case while Andrew was hoisting up a pair of blue suitcases from where he'd previously placed them.

"No just delays!" Lois revealed, answering the last question first. "We were subjected to traffic jams, rain, and a number of roadworks." As she walked across the patterned carpet a thought came to her when she saw something was out of the ordinary: "Eh, aunt," she inquired curiously, "where's your butler? Opening doors is suppose to be in his job description."

Ashley broke into a smile. "I gave Anderson and the remainder of the household staff the day off." She took her eyes off the advancing stranger for a second to peer at her niece, "we thought we'd do that considering tomorrow is going to be a busy day for them. They're going to be rushed off their feet attending to the needs of the guests and helping out the caterers with all the food and the wine." Lois nodded in understanding.

"I just wish though," Ashley remarked with a sigh as she pointed at a high pile of wooden boxes, "the wholesaler had managed to come earlier when the staff were still here so we could have shifted these cases to where I wanted them stored out back."

At length Danielle set a foot into the hallway. "Aunt Ashley! This is my friend Danielle." Lois introduced and after formal greeting was exchanged between the two women, Lois spoke on. "The rest of my mates will be coming up on tomorrow's eleven o'clock train."

Danielle threaded her way between a collection of items and moved over to stand beside Lois near the staircase. "I know," Ashley said, locking eyes with her niece. "You're uncle informed me of their arrival and I'm sure they'll find themselves quite comfortable in the rooms we put aside for them in the guest quarters."

"Oh!" Lois said, arching an eyebrow in surprise. "The cottages out back."

"That right my dear," Ashley declared, before going on to explain herself. "We've got that many people coming from afar that some of them have asked to stay the night so they could have a drink and not worry about driving home afterwards. Therefore on a first come, first served basis, I'm afraid they get the rooms in the main house."

"Huh! And all because I asked last, if my pals could come up." Lois remarked in annoyance. "They get the leavings." Vertly walked along the portico. Andrew staggered after her.

Her aunt took a deep breath. "It's not as bad as you think." Ashley said calmly, seeing her niece scowl in dissatisfaction as she tried to convince Lois that she wasn't unfeeling in her actions. "I admit that the cottages haven't been used in a while but the servants have given the rooms a good dust and vacuum plus the maid told me, she personally opened up all the upstairs windows to air the interior. It's true your friends will be separated from the main house yet the cottages don't lack in amenities and they won't have to share with anyone else like some of the others will."

"After the news of your bombshell, I had enquires about stopovers from another dozen latecomers who had visited us before and knew about the accommodation down there, but when I told them those quarters were reserved for your mob, some of them immediately agreed to double up and sleep on camp beds or cots, just happy to partake of our hospitality and have a roof over their heads for the night."

"Ah," Lois said in comprehension. "I see!" The harshness in her voice mellowing. "I didn't think you had been put out so much."

"Well I have," her aunt replied calmly. "It's been a real juggle for me. Anyway," Ashley pressed on, "the library is yours completely; and your friends will find that the cottages are prefect. They'll be able to play their garage music as loud as they like without disturbing us in the day, and if exploring the estate isn't their cup of tea, well there's always a television they can watch with plenty to eat until the party begins. They won't be bored not by a long shot."

"I suppose not," Lois replied. Her boiling temper abating and her current mood brightening a little as she came to the conclusion that her aunt wasn't being unfriendly at all, instead she was just using cold logic to solve a very awkward problem fate had dealt her.

Ashley shifted her gaze towards the front doorway when she heard more footsteps approaching and as she did, Danielle took the opportunity to let her eyes wander casually over the splendid decor within the hallway. The reception area was bright and airy. It was generous in size and Danielle believed the chamber was as large as her parents living and front rooms combined. There was a vaulted ceiling that would look more at home in a cathedral with two skylights between a colourful single stained-glass window depicting a fierce fire-breathing dragon with massive bat-like wings and sharp extended claws. Beneath these were a number of rooms whose doors of finest red oak opened onto handrailed-galleries projecting from the upper floor along the length of three of the wood paneled walls above the hallway.

Here and there, bathed in light from several bulbs and naked candle flames, hung tapestries of pictures and designs dangling down from just below the platforms. At the heart of the hallway was a grand oak staircase rising until it reached the curved landing above. It gave access to the first floor and a long passageway whose mouth was situated off to the right of the landing. Around the reception area there were boxes of Halloween decorations waiting to be put up; and cases of wine and beer placed where they'd been delivered and not yet removed by the servants. Amongst this mess was a hat stand and an assortment of strategically placed wrought iron candle holders. Behind the girls there was a second yawning mouth of a passageway that mirrored the one high over it. With similar doors and junctions, this corridor also led further into the interior of the manor.

"Hi Vertly!" Ashley welcomed her warmly seeing her cross the threshold and drop the traveling case. "Lois says you had some problems on your way up here?"

"Yeah," Vertly uttered, "you can say that again." She progressed over to the two girls, her husband followed her in a few seconds later. "We must have hit every snag for miles."

"We did." He replied. Breathing heavily as he put the luggage down. Ashley itched her thin pointed nose. "Normally it's quieter driving at night. I checked the travel reports on the radio and the announcer said there would be delays but he didn't say that what seemed like every maintenance crew in Britain was out there." He exaggerated the number somewhat, "in places it was worst than peak hour, crawling along almost bumper to bumper and my engine was heating up. We started out around 7:30," his sister nodded as he took a brief look at the watch, "and now it's almost eleven." He shook his head. "Wherever we went we hit jams or detours sending us miles out of our way. Flooding from a blocked culvert on one stretch while crews decided tonight was the ideal time to fix damaged guardrails and paint over faint road markings. The bloody rain didn't help either reducing visibility down to mere feet."

"Phew," Ashley said. "Sounds awful."

"Exhausting journey and I'm knackered." Her brother stated.

"I bet you all are!" Ashley said. Frowning in sympathy as she saw the evident fatigue in his eyes.

"That's why when I saw your gates already open for us, I was glad to just drive on through and not have to wait for you to buzz us in."

"Hmmm," Ashley declared thoughtfully, "Rob must have forgot to close the gates in his haste to get out. That would explain why you used the doorbell instead of the intercom to alert me to your presence."

During his sister's reply, Andrew took the opportunity to slip his hand into his coat pocket and pull out a small, flat flask. He unscrewed the top and glanced out through the open doorway. The rain he saw backlit against the glare of the security lighting continued to fall heavily. "So where's Rob gone anyway?" He lifted the flask to his lips. "A business meeting?" He sipped the liquid then shuddered at the taste. Instead of malt whiskey, he found that it was some sort of soft drink Vertly had substituted before the journey.

"I reckon!" Ashley said, "if down the pub qualifies."

Andrew smiled weary as he stared daggers at his wife who smirked knowingly back. "Ah a man after my own heart," he uttered calmly. Returning his gaze to his sister as he screwed the top back on his flask and returned to his pocket. "Oh well, I've had my little rest, now all I have to do is bring in the rest of the baggage and park the car in the garage then I've finally finished for the night." He then waited for a moment or two, letting his eyes roam from face to face for an offer of assistance from his family. Vertly and Ashley volunteered immediately but it wasn't as forthcoming as he would have liked from the others present, he raised an eyebrow. Danielle submitted herself more out of guilt than anything else. Andrew next turned towards his daughter and put his hands on his hips, "have you gone on strike Lois or what?"

"Oh," Lois said in mock innocence, fluttering her eyelashes at him, accompanied with an intentional smirk. "Of course not dad. I'll help. I didn't want to get under your feet."

"I should think so too," he said, turning towards the front door. "Considering half of the baggage out there is your stuff. I did wonder if the tyres would last when we were going along the road because I surprised the car didn't break down under all of that load." He headed outside.

"Dad!" Lois said, above the rain dripping from the roof. "A girl has to look her best at all times."

"I don't doubt that," Andrew replied in mid-stride. "It's just a shame we have to take the entire department store along with us for the ride."

"I can't help it if I'm a shoe-aholic dad," his daughter said.

"Well I just wish you could get patches for kind of thing," Andrew answered her back.

Behind him Lois exhaled, pulled a face and followed in a huff. Danielle went next, extremely amused. Ashley came after and Vertly brought up the rear.

"Tell you what Andrew," Ashley suggested, hearing her sister-in-law yawn loudly. "We'll all have a nice cup of herbal tea in the kitchen after this. I've got some honey too."

Ahead of her, Andrew stopped by the luggage pile and bent his knees. "Something to look forward too," he answered. Keeping the sarcasm out of his tone as he picked two of the suitcases up, his right knee creaking when he straightened up. "Any soda crackers?"

"As many as you can eat," came back the reply.

"Can't wait," Lois remarked in a veiled sneer, also lifting a suitcase up.

"Then I'll show you all to your rooms," Ashley spoke on, "and once you've had a good nights sleep, you'll be back to your old selves again in the morning which is just as well because I may have to be cheeky and ask you all to do me a very small favour by helping me put up the decorations." She hoisted up a heavy suitcase with both hands. "I'm down to a skeleton crew with less than half the number of staff I originally hired from the agency because some fool double-booked my ball with a midnight wedding."

"We'll help in any way we can." Vertly said, carrying a holdall with ease. "And I sure Lois' friends will be glad to pitch in as well seeing as how they're getting everything free of charge."

Lois groaned in disapproval and muttered something filthy under her breath.

“That would be fantastic Vertly,” Ashley declared with a laugh of absolute relief as the pair walked back towards the house with their burdens. “It won’t be much work but any weight taken from my shoulders will be much appreciated.”

“Sounds like you having a hard time coping.” Vertly inquired with a frown.

“Yes! To be quite truthful I am,” Ashley admitted in a lower tone. “I thought I wouldn’t hire a party planner this year, just have the joy of doing everything myself. But nothing is going as it should and all Rob seems to want to do is swan off somewhere and leave me to deal with it all. You know among other things the extra tables and chairs I ordered weeks ago are late arriving so too are the flowers. I haven’t seen the carpenters all day. They were supposed to come and repair the decking outside and finish the closet in one of the guest bedrooms. The wrong fish dishes have been delivered, my tumble dryer has broken down so I’m having to air some of my unmentionables on the clotheshorse in front of the cooker by myself, and the marquee the workman erected first thing this morning has a leaky roof and the coloured strips don’t match with my wallpaper...”

Danielle shook her head and went after them.

Loaded down with bags, Andrew exchanged glances with his daughter and said with a sigh to express his contempt: “Huh! Even on holiday I can’t get out of doing extra work your mom arranges for me. It does my head in. I must be the sap of this family tree.”

He lumbered forward, bearing the heftiest of the luggage.

“You and me both dad,” she echoed loudly with a grumble then setting off, she quietly uttered. “However tomorrow it’s a habit that ends, bloodily if need be.”

CHAPTER ELEVEN

Nothing compared to the bog, Gillett thought, unable to remain silent after hearing about the few other little hindrances he'd encountered along the length of the bole. "You mean as in quicksand?" She asked with a question, directing it at Klugman yet getting a response from someone else instead. Her lips tightening shut into a firm white line.

"Could be," Cummings replied with a frown. "They're generally found along stretches of river or on beaches but you can never tell. There is a danger I do know about, and it's the buoyant vegetation Kyle saw growing over the scummy pool. Sometimes a mat like this can completely cover the top of the basin and when that occurs it goes by the name of a quaking bog."

"Very nice Adrian," Gillet sneered. "I'd like to hear something more useful though."

"They won't hold your weight. If any of you happen to wander upon one especially when we're strung out in the dark where they're almost undetectable then you'll sink like a stone and easily drown in the water underneath. How's that Sophie?"

"Oh fucking great!" Gillett said, feeling distraught and shivering at the thought but trying desperately to exhibit nerves of steel. "Talk about being caught between a rock and a hard place," she sighed heavily, not really relishing the idea of going through there. "This whole situation continues to get worse and worse by the minute." She swallowed hard, her throat immediately becoming quite dry. "Well this is about as welcome as being audited by the I.R.S. How on earth are we going to get pass that?" She observed Klugman release the hilt of the knife and leave it embedded in the bark.

"Well I believe I can solve that problem," Cummings said, looking up. "Kyle shine the torch over there for a second will you?" He jerked with his thumb, over his right shoulder to a place very near to the spot where all the bags had been again dumped atop of the money pouches. "By chance I stuck my foot against something not long ago." He detached himself from the group and went over to a clump of shrubs as Thaw and Gillett moved aside so the beam could pass between them. "I only got a glimpse of it when it caught my eye but if it's as long as it appeared then it could fit the requirements for what I have in mind."

His companions watched with interest as Cummings bent down in the torch light. He groped beneath some low drooping stems. "Found it." He bellowed, quickly straightening up beside the fringe of tangled underbrush, clutching a slender bough about the size of a walking stick. One end thinned out while the other was jagged with a wider end that showed it had been ripped from a nearby tree. "We'll use this branch to prod the ground in front of us." He trudged back towards his associates. "If it sinks, we'll have to circumvent the wetland until we find a safe path we can use to get across."

"Ingenious in it's simplicity!" Bisset said in approval, echoing the silent thought of those around him.

Cummings nodded in gratitude just as he reached the bole. Leaning the bough against the trunk, he plucked his knife from the bark and sheathed it within his boot. "Once we enter the mire I'll take point. I've got the woodcraft skills and even in unfamiliar terrain such as what's over there," he gestured with his head towards the other side of the briar, "I'll have the healthier chance of plotting us safely through the bog, while hopefully not bungling into anything awkward. You can still bring up the rear Jerome and keep a watchful eye out for any stragglers."

Thaw saw the wisdom in his words and finding a limited degree of consolation from Cummings' hidden meaning in regard to Klugman. He nodded, "sounds like a plan to me." He slapped his hands together. "Load up!"

Remaining atop of the bole Klugman directed the torch light to illuminate the baggage-heap as the remainder of the party followed Thaw who crouched beside them. "Kyle!" He said in a no-nonsense tone, "take the branch and guide us to the bracken." He caught a flicker of movement from the corner of his eye, preceded by the loud sound of the mud being squealed beneath booted feet as he scooped up a couple of the carry-on's and released them to Bisset's custody. "Then Adrian will switch places and take us through till we either get clear of it or you," he addressed the taller man who crouched to help distribute the pieces of baggage, "locate us some relatively firmer ground so we can make camp for the night."

Thaw saw his jaded girlfriend supersede Bisset at the front of the line, and grab hold of the last two bags. Drying mud clung to her face.

"I think camping is the likelier choice." Cummings spoke, not noticing Gillett pale some more at the prospect of staying over night in the marsh, "but I can't be certain of that until we get under way." He stood up with a bag shoved under each arm.

"Agreed!" Thaw answered, shooting up to his full height with the final pouch clutched tightly to his chest. "All right! Are we good to go?" He glanced about to check everyone's readiness and received assured nods. "Remember we still have a lot of treacherous ground to cover tonight. So watch where you step. One mistake will be fatal. Same positions as last time. Keep close and scrape your feet on the log. It might prevent you from slipping. Kyle start off."

The light flitted about as Klugman helped first Bisset and then Gillett to sluggishly climb up onto the bark before he picked up the branch and headed towards the bramble line. Behind them, Cummings and Thaw ascended, left mud on the roughened bark and brought up the rear.

* * *

Leading the way, Klugman progressed along the gnarled trunk at a regular unhurried pace. He frowned in concentration and navigated them around the three thick, twisted branches before going on to reach the rising curve in the trunk. Most of the party succeeded without to much difficulty to clamber up and over the elevated bend and hand the baggage up afterwards. Yet for the less nimble and more exhausted among them, Gillett and Bisset had to wait until they could began their ascent for Thaw to form a stirrup with his hands so he could give them a leg up. Once everyone was hauled up over the crest by Cummings, they were guided unerringly along the bark past additional hazards, Klugman directing the beam down and back to light the way for his companions. Then something fluttered past them into the darkness, a thin membrane wing which brushed into the torch beam for a second before the creature rapidly flew out of the light and vanished.

"What was that?" Gillett asked in startled surprise. She glanced in the direction of where the animal had departed, straining her eyes against the blackness to see if she could get another glimpse of it.

"Only a bat, Sophie," Cummings revealed. "There's sure to be more around here somewhere chasing insects."

As cracks began to gradually emerge in the rolling clouds in the sky, the companions bore down upon the diversion in the trunk, their nostrils suddenly detected a whiff of putrid stench which slowly became fouler the further forward they progressed.

"Phew!" Gillett voiced, with a sniff. Flinching and pulling a face, expressing her disgust and surprise at the decaying odor. "What a horrible stink. Smells like rotten eggs. We must be almost near the bog, then?"

"Yeah!" Klugman confirmed, with a brief nod. Inhaling and exhaling through his mouth, leaving the final hole in the trunk behind. The torch light lancing the direct line of his course. "What your smelling is swamp gas. It's just a little farther on."

Seconds later the bole split into two. Without hesitating Klugman took the straighter and thinner of the branches and in the light, he saw the width of the bough gradually begin to shrink by degrees. He then began edging to his left crab-like along the trunk, taking one step sideways then another. Thaw peered around Gillett, and smiled tiredly at what Klugman advocated while the American sighed heavily at the ridiculous procedure, but despite this she realised there was method behind his madness.

"Whatever works is all right with me." Cummings said, falling in behind Klugman, moving laterally over the trunk.

"Same here," Bisset said with a slight wheeze, echoing his companions sentiments, his voice unyielding and decisive as he assumed the posture and took the first in a series of sidelong steps. With a brief shake of her head, Gillett clutched her belongings and went next, gently following suit. Beads of sweat established themselves upon her mucky brow as she shuffled her feet along the branch to catch up with the rest. Thaw came last and maneuvered, with a determinate face, closer and closer, towards the bracken.

* * *

Muddy soil sucked at their feet when each of them stepped down from the bough and moved out of the way to make some room for the next person along. Once all the companions were standing together, Klugman and Cummings traded places, with the taller man leading to penetrate the tall thicket of coarse ferns and advancing to delve further into its shadowy depths. From somewhere nearby, a frog croaked as the companions were slowly steered warily through the bracken, the quagmire yielding beneath their feet as they went beyond maple and willow trees. Poking the slushy earth in front of him with the branch he now held, Cummings pushed aside foliage. They hadn't gone far when another weedy frond gave away before Cummings' impetus and the end of the twig sloshed into a stagnant pool.

He blinked and immediately stopped the procession. Withdrawing the dripping twig, Cummings encompassed the area with his flashlight, only to discover that the deepness and the circumference of this sphagnum bog couldn't be clearly defined due to the veil of darkness and the dense growth of foliage surrounding them. Water lilies plus dirty brown leaves and a greenish layer of scum atop of the putrid water were slowly being immersed by the floating mat of mosses and bushy heath-shrubs. In the glare of the torch, Cummings lunged the branch repeatedly into the terrain below him to explore where the marshy-land ended and the bog began. More often than not the branch slipped unhindered through the vegetation and parted the floating film but gradually as minutes flew by he established, by prodding along through the thinning bracken, that there was an evident route across the concealed wash. Stretches of the squashy ground offered some relatively firm resistance in places to the pressure of the branch and it was these narrow occasionally, bush-dwelling areas he traversed. He did not force the pace because he knew that they could come unstuck. Saving his breath for the trek ahead, except when he indicated a bearing change by shouting for them to go right or left as he guided the way for the others, Klugman was almost breathing down Cummings' neck as their course took short, sharp-angled turns in alternate directions, gaining ground only to then lose a fraction of it when they had to go back and circumvent an additional swale.

"Oh jeeez," Gillett bemoaned with a shiver. "Two steps forward and one step back. The fun never stops for us does it?"

Having had enough of her by this stage, the others kept quiet and focused their concentration upon not losing their footing on the marshy ground all around them. Aquatic vegetation appeared on their left and in the shifting torchlight began spreading across the spongy terrain. Before long, the enormous girth of a bald cypress became visible on their right. The tree was perched almost atop of a small, quite broad natural elevation rising up several yards above the surrounding geography. The lay of the land forced Cummings to execute another abrupt turn and head directly for the mound. Beneath the soaring sixty-foot branches they ventured, passing in the vicinity of a flimsy, gossamer cobweb draped across the branches, specked with snared water droplets that made it look like a discarded necklace, and between driblets of rainwater falling from the spreaded boughs above. Tiredness now started gradually taking its toll upon everyone whose bent-backs and aching calf muscles protested as grim courage and determination urged them all on. Steering slightly left of the cypress to avoid some treacherously soft earth, Cummings continued upon that bearing for a couple more yards to ascend up the slope, feeling firmer ground beneath his boots as he climbed through a gap in a thicket, tramping down tufts of long grass and sedges marking the beginnings of a fen upon the other side. At the uppermost portion of the mound, the branch uncovered another depression in the darkness. However instead of detecting the splash of foul bog water being disturbed, the tall thief heard the wood contact with unyielding stone. With a thoughtful frown, Cummings hesitantly put one foot in front of the other until he crested the summit of the knoll then paused, and his gaze followed the light shearing downward to see a deep vee-shaped cleft, flanked by ivy drooping over both rims, extending and sinking from the point of the angle, the steepening, vertical sides dividing and lengthening outward, cutting through the ground, deepening and widening slowly to about seventy inches, from left to right diagonally across his path until the split vanished beneath a dark, arching breach in the supporting roots of the bald cypress.

Inserted and sunk about sixteen centimeters from the surface, within the depths of the cleft, there was a set of broad, heavy stairs, extending from the walls and dropping down into the bowels of the earth. Here and there a fallen sprinkling of needle-like leaves and a fine crust of moss coated the steps and, where patches of gray rock could still be perceived in the light, Cummings saw the stairs appeared to have been chiseled out of granite and were deeply indented as if damaged by the elements and constant use by generations of people.

"Huh!" Cummings expressed in surprise, with a brief shake of his head. "Hell of a place to find something like this in a bog. Jerome!" He shouted, glancing over his right shoulder. "Get yourself up here. It's important you see this."

"What is it Adrian?" Klugman asked. Pressing close with a money pouch under the crook of each of his arms and despite the load, he swayed around Cummings torso in the hope of getting a look for himself. The rest of the party dragged themselves up the incline and arrived a few seconds later.

"Only a damn well staircase of all things," he revealed. On a hunch he shifted his gaze and trained the beam around at the encompassing environment to see if there were any more man-made objects about. "Hewed out of the very stone below us. It's gotta be as old as the hills." Not seeing from his vantage point anything visible to suggest an abandoned trail leading away from the knoll in the midst of the usual physical features of the wash but having an inkling that there might be one nevertheless, lurking somewhere around the other lonely island-hummocks beyond, jutting up past the scummy surface at various places, though inundated now, beneath the water-logged marsh.

Thaw dumped the burdens atop of the ground he'd just worked his way up, knowing it to be comparative firm before going forward and squeezing past Gillett and Bisset so he wouldn't stray off the slender path Cummings had visibly traced through the knee-high greenery. Whirling about at the sucking sound of approaching footsteps, Cummings brought the beam of the flashlight with him and lowered it into a slanting dip to shine down the staircase as Thaw finally fell in beside him.

"Blimey," he exclaimed, his face registering the astonishment he felt as he took in the illuminated sight of the stairway below him. "That's a turn up for the books." He scratched the side of his forehead in puzzlement as a dull thud of something being dropped onto a soft surface could be heard before Klugman advanced empty handed and filled the place on the left of the hulking figure. "You're right! They're ancient. They could possibly show us the way to a cavern or an old mine tunnel of some sort," He declared, thinking things through properly, "whose course has got to run under the water table of this bog."

"That's my opinion too," Cummings stated. "This was originally an outlet like a vent or a sinkhole. Then the steps were probably added later. It also stands to reason that if there's an underground passage beneath us, it must be of a similar age and not very stable at that." He paused for breath. "Not with the earth level above it saturated with water. It's bound to have drained downward over the years and caused some kind of erosion to occur in the rock. We could be looking at cracks or anything, particularly if the deepest recesses have been shaped out of limestone."

There was a brief scuff of feet upon the grass behind him as Bisset and Gillett's lack of energy showed in their limps when they progressed over to the cleft. Thaw nodded while Cummings paused to swallow. "I hope I'm wrong and just worrying unduly about this but," he resumed, putting it mildly, "even supposing we're not immediately greeted by rubble then the passageway could easily cave in at any moment and squash us under tones of debris like insects."

"God! You paint a wonderful picture of doom, Adrian you know that?" Klugman declared with a shake of his head. "Remind me to ask you over to my place for Christmas so you can sour the eggnog."

Cummings' features smirked. Ignoring the comment and staring at the staircase, Thaw said. "High stakes to go down there," he nodded, mulling over everything. "Still I think it's worth the risk, just to satisfy our curiosity as to where the tunnel itself leads to?"

"Well, now you're talking Jerome but we won't learn anything just waiting here for it to come to us," Klugman declared impetuously. Having heard enough of the chatter, again showing a sense of responsibility he hadn't exhibited too much in the past as he moved forward to grab a handful of the climbing ivy at the side of the cleft for support and put his left foot gingerly into space over the deep opening before dropping it down upon the first, distant slippery, wide tread. "We've got to get down there and find out what's what. I'll made good time if I go on my own."

"My thoughts precisely!" Thaw acceded. "But for the present, you can hold your horses. It's been a long hard day that doesn't seem to be drawing to a close for us any time soon," he saw Klugman stiffen and shift his attention upwards to fix the speaker with his steady gaze. "And I don't want you rushing down below particularly solo before I've had the chance to setup your lifeline."

At his side, Cummings shot him a nonplussed look whilst Klugman furrowed his brow and spoke: "Lifeline! What do you mean?" To tired and fatigued like the remainder of the party to grasp the significance behind the concept.

"Exactly what I said Kyle," Thaw pressed on in a sharp no-nonsense manner. "Now, Take off your belt. You too Adrian," he glanced at the taller man. "Because for my plan to work it's going to be necessity for you, to accompany Kyle down those stairs like you're his shadow."

"You what?" Klugman commented. Cummings nodded thoughtfully.

"Your job Adrian is to linger behind at a distance when you reach the bottom, and maintain a cautious eye out for him, both for mutual help and his protection should Kyle require an extra pair of hands to maybe clear some rubble obstructing the passage or simply pull Kyle and the torch out of harms way if a cave in seems to be imminent." Thaw gazed at Klugman, meeting his eyes with a steely glare, spurring him into action when it seemed to him for the briefest of moments that Klugman was averse to following the orders.

"All right!" He answered, without arguing on the subject. "I get the picture. You better take these for a bit then," he passed over the stick and torch to Thaw so he could free his hands for the task. "I take it Jerome," his mind worked furiously, shrewdly sussing out what Thaw intended to do as he unbuckled his belt, "that the belts are going to be attached next to make up this lifeline?"

"Yeah," Thaw replied, dipping the flashlight. Picking up on the disquieting feeling in the tone of his voice, as he watched Klugman blink and unthread his leather band. "Fasten the buckle of the one belt together with the holes in the strap of the other then wind and clasp the remaining ends of the belts tightly in your dominant hand. It hasn't got the strength of a good rope and it could unravel. However, if push comes to shove it might also save a life down there."

Remaining slightly winded, their shoulders slumped from physical exhaustion, Bisset and Gillett rubbed their hands together, and seeing that Thaw wasn't uncoiling his belt, they exchanged puzzled glances with each other.

"Your concern for my well-being is really touching and gratifying, Jerome." Klugman replied sarcastically. In a voice oozing with venom yet cautiously softened to regulate an outward calm. He drew out the final segment of the strap from the trousers. His features cracked into a broad, humorless smile. "I didn't know you cared." He stapled on the end of the sentence with a ironic taunt. He extended his belt up to Cummings who took it. "Here you go Adrian, you can do the honours. I'll hook up with you once we get to the bottom of the stairs."

"We've no room for complacency, Kyle," Thaw began after a heavy sigh. "We can ill afford to lose anyone we don't have to especially weighted down with the burden of all this baggage. We might have successfully crossed that section of the bog but we were lucky." He glanced at Cummings, observing him fixing the belts together then put his strength behind a good tug in order to test if both attachments were fastened securely. They held firmly. "And with things as they are," Thaw added, twisting his gaze back to Klugman, "we still haven't escaped just yet for we'll have to navigate our way through the rest of the swamp if this underground passage is heavily blocked off." He squatted beside the rim of the cleft and handed the torch over. "Just watch yourself okay, and on the outside chance you find the tunnel is clear then one of you'll have to come back and fetch us. I'm not sure if the walkie-talkie will work below the surface."

"Noted!" Klugman replied gruffly. Perceiving the wisdom finally behind Thaw's words. He took the torch in his right hand and immediately shone the beam down at his feet to see the section of stone stretch out and down beneath them. Moving off warily across the slippery moss, to where the dense vine obscured the left side of the wall, he grasped a fistful in an effort to keep himself from slipping and unhurriedly lowered his boot to the next step.

Gillett enquired. "Don't you want our belts as well Jerry?"

"No Sophie!" He straightened. Bisset pulled out his lighter and send a frame erupting forth to illuminate their surroundings. "We'll manage with the one's the lads have."

Thaw's concentration wavered as he caught sight of motion from the corner of his left eye. He turned and spoke to Cummings who had progressed to the top of the sunken staircase. "Considering how unsteady he is on his feet and at the pace he's setting, you better count to ten, Adrian before you start following him."

"Gotcha!" The man announced, dropping into a crouch to seize a handful of the ivy. The connected belts were wrapped around his other hand. Gillett stifled a yawn.

"Eh, Adrian!" Bisset enquired as Klugman descended another step. "I was wondering are we going to proceed through the tunnel when you return? For I think I can speak for both Sophie and myself," he darted a quick glance at her and saw her nod, "when I say we're both knackered from all the trekking and desperately need a rest that won't be so temporary."

"I know you do, who isn't though? It all depends on what we discover below." Cummings addressed the question as honestly as he could. Staring down and watching the slowly dwindling light and

Klugman's silhouette captured therein. "Before the stairs I was gonna make camp here for the remainder of the night then in the morning try and glimpse a pylon or some smoke from a distance chimney that might tell us there was a farmstead nearby." His knuckles shone white as he tightened his grip on the ivy and descended to the first step. The sight of the torch light faded as Klugman descended further, his presence disappearing beneath the tree. "This spot is quite high up and offers us a better view of the area ahead of us but I just took a quick gander and as far as I could see, the region is almost awash." He came down upon another stone tread and then a third, caution controlling his movements, each foot he set down was on a clear space devoid of moss as Bisset and Gillett traded looks with one another in the tiny, flicking pool of the lighter frame.

"But these stairs have made me postpone that decision until we've gained some knowledge of where the tunnel comes out. Just make the best of a bad situation Nathan," he added, lowering, his head which was now merely inches above the rim of the cleft, "and pray we manage to find a way through. Otherwise we'll be crossing the rest of this fen at first light, and we'll be doing much more than a doggy paddle and that's a certainty."

Without a further word, Cummings proceeded further down. His dwindling footsteps continued to reverberate quite loudly for awhile, on the troubled quiet he left behind.

* * *

The darkness receded before the penetrating glare of the torch and the footfalls upon granite echoed back off the confining walls as the two men moved sluggishly down the slippery stone staircase. The ceiling became vaulted and lost in the gloom as they proceeded steadily, Klugman uttering a sprinkling of words from time to time to point out the potential problems along the way, their foreheads furrowing in concentration as they took one agonising step after another, occasionally sliding when a tread was entirely covered with the mossy growth but mostly they swerved to circumvent the green patches where they could while groping about in the near blackness for handholds among the tendrils of ivy.

"I keep thinking I'm gonna see a white rabbit with a silver pocket watch down here at any minute," Cummings remarked, placing his weight gently atop of the next tread.

"I'm more a Lord of the Rings fan myself," Klugman answered quietly. "But I'll be surprised if anything comes within fifty feet of us after they get a reek of that bad aftershave you got on ya."

He smirked while Cummings said nothing, his pulse edged up yet his cool head exercised strict control over his bubbling emotions.

At a certain depth the length of ivy ended abruptly and Cummings, to his increasing discomfort, began to shiver as the temperature dropped gradually the deeper they went. Averse to letting go of the leafy-vine yet having no choice, Cummings released his grip and edged closer to the wall, straining his eyes in the dim light to detect and stride in the trail Klugman's footprints made in the thin layer of dust beginning to cover the risers below him. Simultaneously he outstretched his trembling, calloused hand to search with his uncertain fingertips the now, exposed wall of cold bricks and flaking mortar for an occasional niche that could furnish him with just a fraction of aid in his descent. Cummings inhaled and his fingers sank a few inches when they came across a shallow pit in the wall where the face of one of the bricks had partly crumbled away then, a little further down the staircase, he heard a surprised grunt from Klugman's position before his companion informed him of what he'd detected in the stabbing light.

"Hey, Adrian I've found us a handhold," Klugman announced jubilantly. Despite the cold which was seeping into his bones, he clutched the iron projection securely with a one handed grip while directing the torch with the other, swinging across the wall to see if there were any more fixtures hiding in the darkness. There were, at regular intervals, sloping down the length of both sides of the brick enclosure. "It's no 'jug' that I'm use to," he said, employing the mountaineering term for a much larger handhold as he descended onto another step. His breath began to be visible as it steamed in the chilling air, "But the bracket is firm enough when I tugged it and there seems to be quite a number of them on the wall, lower down."

With a puzzled frown, Cummings passed a few more steps, through stirred up dust, still planting his boots where the trail exposed visible stone for surer footing, and as he emerged from a vaporous gray cloud of his own breath, out of the darkness came the developing shape of a sconce jutting out from the wall. He gladly wrapped his hand tightly around the ornate bracket and held onto it when he went past, curiously peering into the spiked-holder for a moment, only just making out that it contained the remains of a dusty old candle stub at the bottom. He blinked and kept going, leaving behind half a dozen more sconces on his way down, clutching each succeeding fixture, noticing again that the brackets were corroded with rust. He breathed in the air which was gradually becoming staler due to the lessening in oxygen content. By the time, sixty worn-treads had passed under their boots, the blackness below divided at the periphery of the torch's beam to finally reveal the foot of the staircase.

"Adrian," Klugman pronounced, going down another step, "the bottom coming into view. I thought our little excursion would never end."

"Nor me." Cummings replied, after a cough. Progressing downward he adhered to Klugman's footprints. "It felt like I've endured an eternity in this darkness," his voice trembled from the cold as he glimpsed his companion blazing a trail as he went down the last three steps to the floor. "And this lousy fall in temperature isn't helping matters either. I still can't feel my feet very well."

"I know what you mean. It's fucking unpleasant." Klugman said, seeing his breath plume out in front of him. "I expected it to be warmer down here than outside in the open air, yet instead it's exactly the opposite."

"With good reason Kyle, because we've got to be right under the bog by now." Cummings explained, descending into one of the last footprints left in Klugman's wake. "And this far down, the cold's gotta be kept shut in by the water plus the tens of thousands of pounds of rock and earth suspended above our heads."

Klugman nodded thoughtfully and only moments later Cummings reached the base of the staircase. He commenced to unwind the leather belts as he came to a halt alongside his partner whose gaze followed the sweeping torch around their current environment in an attempt to get his bearings. A large cobweb confronted them, partly obstructing a yawning tunnel mouth composed of thick masonry blocks. It was topped with an arch which was as high as Cummings' shoulders and easily had the width for two men to walk abreast. The air had lost it freshness, it was musty and stale: smells from damp and decay mingled with the foul odor of prolonged disuse, but drawing the air into his nostrils, Klugman found it to be still quite suitable for breathing.

"Judging by the dust on the floor and the moldiness in the air," Klugman announced, crinkling his nose in distaste, "it's been a hell of a while since someone was here."

"Yeah!" Cummings replied, glancing around as he finished uncoiling the belts. "Certainly looks that's way."

"I wonder what the tunnel was used for?" Klugman said, taking strides towards the yawning opening and shining the beam between the arch, the light filtering through the cobwebs revealed a dim impression of the length of curved, shadowed-patterned brickwork beyond, extending into the darkness. "Some kind of smugglers route perhaps?" he speculated, parting the cobweb.

"Maybe," Cummings replied. Advancing and letting the leather-loop fall away to dangle at his feet, "or it's simply a bolt-hole going back to the 16th century, meant to hide the Roman Catholic priests when the penal laws were made to persecute them. This might have given them another path of escape if they believed it to be too dangerous to return the way they came."

Klugman's eyebrows shot up as a flicker of surprise crossed his countenance. The possibility hadn't even occurred to him. "Hmmm, I've heard about that before," he admitted, warming to the subject as it began to arouse his curiosity, "I thought priest holes were only a secret room in a house somewhere."

"Yeah, they are generally. I read once there are also other places of concealment," Cummings replied, "so why can't this be one of them that goes straight under a house?"

His companion executed a turn towards him, "well, you've sold me the idea." Klugman answered attentively, "hook-me up Adrian and we'll go and see if you're right."

CHAPTER TWELVE

The red D-reg Audi drew to a squealing halt between the bay's white lines across the floor of the underground parking garage and, behind the steering wheel, Dawn Blye switched off the ignition as requested and employed her hand brake.

"Well this is the time and place where the E-mail said you had to meet," her short, thickset companion commented in a preoccupied voice across from her. Releasing his door lock, his beady eyes roamed the recess, noticing the lettered sign above him, taking in the crudely drawn graffiti-slogans and scribbled inscriptions on the walls, the deserted parking spaces filled, in one case with an abandoned shopping trolley. He noted the shadows cast by the pillars where the glare of the strip lighting couldn't penetrate. "There there doesn't seem to be any sign of this snitch as yet."

"We could have scared him off Fletcher," Blye answered her slightly older colleague dryly, using his first name with familiarity. She eyed the exit of the stairwell in the concrete wall, concealed partly behind more of the red and white pillars holding up the roof. "The message did say I had to arrive here at the garage alone without a tape recorder or a camera."

"Yeah! Well I'm not letting you go on your own," Fletcher replied remonstratively. Giving her a quick peeved look, observing again the gold ring piercing her lip as it stood out against her olive-hued complexion. "This might be a safe environment for whoever sent the address but not for you. There's too many weirdos out here for my liking and that big sister of yours wouldn't let me hear the end of it." He went on, about to dismiss any element of doubt that had introduced itself to her. "He'll come. He isn't gotta back out of the deal no matter what the circumstances are if there's a chance he can get his hands on all of this cash." He patted a small suitcase on his lap.

The thirty year old nodded to Fletcher's blemished face where severe scarring had left pits around his cheeks and forehead from the results of deep infected acne. "I've got to wondering, you know, what the scoop is and if it relates to any of the news stories being broadcast at present..." Blye speculated curiously. Staring into her rearview mirror to see what might be behind her, yet seeing nothing at first but her reflection in the glass. Her own distinguishing Mediterranean features exemplified by her brown eyes and brown hair worn in a roll at the back of her broad head.

"Hmmm," he uttered thoughtfully. "Could be anything home or aboard. The motorway explosion, the robbery or the prime minister's speech." His fingers began drumming upon the lid of the case, showing his slight annoyance at the delay as his gaze wandered around the parking lot afresh. "I don't mind so long as it's something good we can use to our advantage over our competitors."

Tilting the mirror to get a better range of vision at her rear, Blye observed a tall figure emerge from behind one of the pillars and slipping his hand in an outside pocket as he walked slowly towards the boot of the car. He wore a long trenchcoat that stretched to his knees and a broad brimmed hat with a dented crown which was pulled down to his eyes, concealing most of his features. In one hand he carried a bulging Manila folder and his footsteps echoed loudly, his eyes sweeping the empty area to make sure that those in the car were the only ones to see his approach.

"It's show time!" She wrenched her gaze away from the mirror and quietly alerted her companion. "Our source has arrived looking like he's something straight out of one of those old B-movies from the nineteen forties with the gear he'd got on."

"Okay!" Fletcher announced cautiously, ceasing his devil's tattoo. "Let's both get out simultaneously, nice and easy and above all play it cool."

"Right!" Blye said, opening the car door wide on her side. "Let me do all the talking okay?" She threw out her right leg, "I'm gonna have to explain your presence to him and to defuse any tension, it's best that it comes only from me."

"Knock yourself out," Fletcher replied, holding the handle of the case as he mirrored her movements and stepped out into the chilly habitat. "I'm here if you need me."

Staying where he was, he watched as Blye went forward, and then stopped dead in her tracks when the pair finally came together a few feet from the car.

"Hello! I'm Dawn Blye. Are you the guy responsible for sending me that very interesting bit of electronic mail?" She asked politely, looking at his smoothly shaven face and his long dark hair stretching from under the hat to well down passed his ears.

"I am," he acknowledged with a nod and a thin smile. Peering down at her petite figure while he pulled out a black and white photograph from his coat pocket and held it up for her to see . "You may call me Alexander for the duration of our meeting. And according to this you're the journalist I've been waiting for." Blye stared at the picture and lifted her eyebrows as she surveyed the detailed image of her rounded face.

"Huh! Where on earth did you that close-up of me?" She said suddenly in surprise. Narrowing her eyes as she peered up at his gloomy countenance again. "I haven't seen it before. If I didn't know any better I swear you've had me under surveillance?"

"No I haven't Miss Blye," Alexander replied defensively. Lowering the picture and tucking it away back into his coat pocket. "But I do have ways of obtaining things like this," he said cryptically, gesturing with his other hand to indicate the folder before going on the offensive and shifting his attention to the pony-tailed man standing behind her. "I see that against my wishes you brought someone along for the ride."

"Yes! This is Fletcher Everett." She glanced over her shoulder and gestured her head in introduction. "He's my brother-in-law and writing partner on *The Daily Clarion*."

Both men nodded to each other.

"Fletcher!" Alexander said thoughtfully. "Unusual first name."

"It was my mom's maiden name." Fletcher answered. "She didn't want it dying out altogether when my grandad finally passed away."

"Ah," the informer uttered smoothly. "I understand."

Returning to their previous topic, she said: "And I hope you do too when I say Marcus Yates, my editor thought it would only make sense to assign someone to protect our cargo and myself from harm especially considering I was to meet a complete stranger in a deserted garage at this late hour of the night."

Alexander sniffed with contempt and when he spoke again, his manner had become aloof. "Fair enough Miss Blye. it's appropriate under the circumstances. Now let's get down to business. I hope what I've heard is true and that your newspaper has deep pockets."

"It has, Alexander!" Fletcher declared, striding around the back of the car towards them, carrying the suitcase and hearing Blye tut with her tongue in annoyance. "So what have you got for us. Remember this mister," he spoke on, using the title loosely with a hint of coarseness in his voice. "Your information had better be good. We won't be swayed to pay out by just anything you show us."

Alexander grinned and flipped up the folder's flap and exposed an array of papers with all sorts of printed matter, separated here and there by colour-coded dividers. "I can guarantee this will provide you with plenty to think about. I assume you know all about the robbery this morning in that Lancaster village?" He reached inside and quickly withdrew four unpublished Polaroid pictures which showed two similar standpoints that had obviously been taken from different angles by the photographer. Both shots were close-ups and depicted the graphic setting of the murdered remains of the two dead men sprawled on the pavement and inside the post office.

"Cuilfield?" Fletcher ventured with a frown, coming to a halt beside the others and putting the suitcase down on the concrete floor. "Yeah it's been lodged within the second story slot on the television news for most of the day. Why? You got something pertaining to that crime we haven't seen yet?"

"Enough and some to spare. And that's putting it mildly." The informer announced matter-of-factly. "Exclusive and sensational stuff I know will beat all of your rival tabloids by miles because none of the data I have has been officially released to the media."

The man saw the pair of reporters swap dumbfounded glances for a moment then Fletcher turned back to lock eyes with him and said: "In the interest of curiosity, why don't you proceed to give us all of the facts?" He struggled to keep the excitement out of his voice. "We can assess afterwards if it serves as justification for the amount of money you asked for in the beginning."

"That's acceptable to me," replied Alexander with a nod as a prelude to handing out the photographs. "These snaps were taken at the crime scene just after the raid. It's a bit grisly with all the blood if you've got a weak stomach." He watched their reactions and saw that the newshounds had quite strong dispositions; Blye paled and shivered involuntarily at the images of the bodies against the backdrop, Fletcher grimaced a wry face to express his distaste. "The bullets drilled through Jenkins' chest, shoving him back with the momentum and exploding his heart. Rutten the postmaster was shot in the head, from behind. Both deaths were instantaneous. From the diameter of the entry wounds and the blood pattern, forensics say the hand gun was a big caliber pistol."

"Jesus! This was brutal and senseless work," Blye said. Shaking her head and making a cross in the air in front of her chest with her free hand. She then saw Alexander remove a thick document from the interior of the crammed envelope.

"It could have easily turned out to be a massacre though with all the bullets the witnesses say the robbers fired," Alexander observed.

"What did they use on the poor victims: a cannon?" Blye asked.

"No just a 357 Magnum!" Alexander revealed calmly before going on. "The shooter blew them both away from a killing range that was gauged to be point-blank then his companion broke some bones as he trod on Rutten's body in his haste to get inside the premises and seize the money on the counter top."

"Hey Dawn!" Fletcher called her name to attract her attention, "take this will you."

"Sure!" She said, taking the proffered snap off her companion before addressing Alexander, "Inspector Sinclair stated in the press conference that the raiders got away with about five million pounds in old, used paper notes that were going to be incinerated down in London, is that right or wrong?"

Alexander handed the document and directed his first words to Fletcher. "Take this Mister Everett. Please browse! It will show you what's on offer."

He nodded silently.

"As to answer your query Miss Blye," Alexander spoke on, "I have evidence in my folder from the royal mint that confirms her remark is accurate. The currency was all in English pounds notes and had been amassed in bundles of large denominations: Fifties and twenties mainly with a few tenners thrown in for good measure." He dug his hand inside the manila folder once more.

"What about dye packs?" Blye asked, throwing him another question, "surely there were a few inside the pouches to explode and stain the money?"

"Generally there are," Alexander told her, "yet not on this occasion. The powers that be didn't reckon they were needed on such a low-profile job like this."

"Huh," the woman expressed her astonishment.

"By any chance did you take those Polaroids," Fletcher asked. Flipping over the cover and scanning the photocopied pages beneath, his mind working furiously as he came to a pretty shrewd suspicion over who this man was, "or did the forensic team?"

Not suiting his mood or purpose to volunteer an answer, Alexander kept his face firm and sidestepped the question. "You'll find all manner of goodies among the things in the document like authentic ballistic reports, audio tapes," he withdrew a small cassette and showed them before slipping it back inside the folder, "facts about the victims, more photographs of the crime scene to make up your very own calendar and even the autopsies of Jenkins and Rutten that were carried out in the local morgue a couple of hours after the event."

"I'll be damned!" Blye swore and blinked. Fletcher raised his eyebrows and turned one page after another in quick succession with a mixture of shock and delight in regard to the material. "You don't do things by half do you Alexander?"

"I promised you a scoop Miss Blye," he said, "and that's precisely what you've got."

Fletcher looked up and shook his head. "You've got to have a look at this Dawn! it's all insider data. There's a Pathological report, statement's from eye witnesses..."

Something flashed through her mind from what he'd just said and she mentally snapped her fingers in recognition as she moved across to her brother-in-law, and saw him turn back over several pages to reveal the wealth of information therein.

"Write-ups from officers, graphics and official statistics," Fletcher continued. Stopping at a page with an image of a HOLMES 2 enquiry system. "The SO11 intelligence unit has got its hands on a distinctive home office computer to sort through all the leads which," he traced a finger down to the opposite page of text, "in keeping with this progress report has already eliminated from their enquires a number of suspects on the evidence of them having an alibi elsewhere in the country at the time."

"Yes," the informer announced, without having to consult from his notes, "the known facts are detailed in there. Basically a mob carried out raids on Post Offices about five years ago, not dissimilar to the one at Cuilfield. Most of them, including previous cell mates are either still in jail or have proven excuses. One man was a cabby who was taking a fare to the airport, another was with her parole officer when the heist was going on and the last one released was miles away, employed making tent pegs in a factory in Torquay."

Blye frowned. "So your saying Alexander, there could be another organizer out there who's the brains behind the theft?"

"I'm not implying anything," the stranger replied, "but from what I've seen, the facts seem to speak for themselves."

Then suddenly, a beeping sound emitted from under his clothes. Alexander groaned and, in annoyance, reached under his trenchcoat and switched off his pager. He stared at the text page. "She would have to pick now of all times to need of me," he sighed deeply. "I've got to go something's come up. I'm sorry to rush you into a decision like this but I have to have your answer now. Is the information I've shown you both agreeable to the sum I requested?"

Blye and Fletcher exchanged glances.

"I wasn't born yesterday. You're taking the Mickey out of us aren't you?" Fletcher said. His voice like his temper was raising slightly, sharing his thoughts as he gave the stranger a hard stare. "You've got someone to page you so you could make us come to a quick conclusion before we're ready to do so."

"That's nonsense and the furthest thing from the truth!" Alexander declared calmly. "I have no intention of narrowing your choices and just hemming you into one. However you think what you like Mister Everett. You're absolutely under no obligation to purchase my material. I must go though. I'm certain there are other news organizations out there who will be more than happy to make a deal."

"You're buggering us about." Fletcher said, shutting the document. His face ruddy from the anger boiling inside him. "Wanting more money off us than we brought along."

"My settlement stands." The stranger replied without emotion. "No more, no less. So what's it to be? Do we have a bargain or not?"

Fletcher frowned in confusion and stood there for a moment, completely speechless.

"We do Alexander." Blye said gently, offering a voice of reason to the overall proceedings. "You dealt fairly with us, it only right we return the complement." She glanced across at her writing partner and addressed him in a firm tone. "Fletcher! Give him the money. He's earned it for what he brought us."

Fletcher grunted as he stooped to pick up the suitcase from the floor. He straightened and went forward a couple of steps and then exchanged the case for the rest of the contents in the folder.

"And that brings our transaction to an end," Alexander announced, gripping the handle of the case tightly.

"Good night all!" He grinned at Fletcher, then whirled about and strode off, heading towards another stairwell, partly concealed in the shadows. Fletcher and Blye watched him recede into the pool of blackness before turning and making their way back towards their Audi.

"You can be such a Neanderthal sometimes Fletcher you know that," she said. They detached from one another and went around to their own sides of the car. "With a mouth on you like a skip. Ever thought of taking charm lessons."

"Yeah well," Fletcher commented. His temper abating as he came to a halt by his door and peered across at her, shoving the document back into the crammed file as he did. "The prick really rubbed me up the wrong way with that pager routine." He threw open his door, climbed in and the deposited the folder inside the glove compartment. "It was just too much of a coincidence for it to be an emergency or something."

"Maybe it was to him," Blye answered, hearing his door bang shut as she clambered into the vehicle and slam the door shut behind her with a similar boom. "He sounded pretty sincere from where I stood. I think the signal was as much as a surprise to him as it was to us. Anyhow! What's it matter? We got the information we came for." She heaved her shoulders indifferently. "That's all that's counts in my opinion."

Fletcher nodded as he finally saw sense. "Yeah," he said grudgingly, loathe to admit such a thing. "I suppose!" He fastened his seat belt as Blye buckled hers across her hips. "But there's no way we'll be going to press with this tonight. There's to much to sort through and examine." Blye turned the key and the Audi's engine roared into life. "It's a probability though we'll made the next addition of the *Clarion*. Front page for sure. The story is too bleeding important and sensational to go anywhere else."

Blye smiled broadly and released the hand brake. "We're going have a field day with this, I just know it. It'll be the first time I've had my by-line on the front page." She wheeled the car left, out of the parking space and drove it steadily through a set of cones towards the other side of the divided ramp they'd came down earlier on. Suddenly something, harsh occurred to her. "Oh shit! Hey Fletcher I've just had a thought." She added. The tyres hit the ramp, and she changed gear and pressed her foot down on the accelerator. Progressing up the slope, she followed the arrowed wall signs directing them up towards the exit. "What if Yates isn't courageous enough to print our articles without the name of our source to back up the data?"

"Not a problem Dawn," Fletcher replied evenly. The car turned right and nosed into the road, bathed in the light of a lamppost. "When Marcus sees the material and notices that it's all reproductions of original paperwork like the authentic autopsy reports that the average member of the public can't get their hands on, to say nothing of the probation officers client index, then he'd know someone with clout gave us this and that will be good enough for him. He'll consign the lot to the typesetter before you can say Jack Robinson. Take us to my place Dawn, it's nearer. This could turn out to be an all nighter."

"Right! Who do you think Alexander really was?" Blye inquired, steering the Audi left. The road and pavements were moist from the downpour, reflecting the wavy light-lines of lampposts and neon signs advertising a pizzeria and a local health club. "I was initially going to say a hacker? Easy to gain access to all the files in the different systems and download them yet he would have risked being traced if he stayed on the telephone lines to long. Consequently I go for a senior detective."

"Perceptive! It could very well be," he replied. "Myself I'm inclined towards the Pathologist but it could easily be anyone with high ranking security clearance. We'll soon see anyway, as a matter of procedure the police are sure to do an interior probe once they find they have a mole in their midst. The office where our E-mail originally came from will be the first target but you know what? If I'm any judge of character, my reporter's intuition tells me Alexander was already astutely aware of that fact and I wouldn't put it past him to fix it so he loaded the message in a terminal in the very last place anyone would ever think of looking for it."

A ghost of a smile crossed her features as she drove straight across an intersection into an avenue, going past a waste bin and a bottle bank. "Providing that the police don't catch anybody specific tomorrow or the next day from their investigation," Blye said, expressing her thoughts in soft and mellow voice, "we could actually see this story run and run nationwide. It would certainly benefit our careers no end."

"Yep!" He nodded. "Bottom feeders no more. We'll leak the information out a bit at a time in each addition, cheaply sensationalizing the stuff. I've always fancied doing a bit of yellow journalism, now here is our chance. We might not win a Pulitzer but at least I can dream."

Blye's smile broadened considerably and said. "Can't we all!"

Another block fell behind as she changed gear once more and the Audi sped on along the street.

* * *

"I really see little sense in travelling all the way up to Hereford just to publicise my new film, Alice when I could do a better job doing all the rounds of the radio and television stations back here in Birmingham..." Kalvinder Kapoor announced, signing her scrawly signature at the bottom of the picture of herself, the lamp light spilling across the top of the desk littered with piles of the same photograph.

"Well Kal, your film is called the *Jewel box of India*," her personal assistant stated matter-of-factly. Seeing her employer pick up another picture from the pile and began scribbling her name and an inscription again. "Your agent did think it was very apt and even I think it's a good idea. They've got a supermodel to wear some of the pieces the archeologists have found, and if you're there then maybe the press will ask you to get in on the act as well. Whatever happens there's going to be plenty of exposure for you and that can only help your career here and across the Atlantic."

"I suppose," Kapoor sniffed. Not looking forward to shuttling back and forth to America, putting her pen down when she felt the painful, spasmodic contractions of the muscles of her right hand. "I just don't want the reporters asking me about my drunken incident on the train."

"You're an actress. People expect stars to act like that. Just say to them it will all be in your autobiography when you write it one of these days. You'll have to consider then if you want the press and your fans to discover your philandering ways. I never know if that's the correct term for a woman whose playing away."

"That's it for the autographs for a while Alice, my hand is hurting me," Kapoor went on. Curling her fingers as she stopped the subject of the conversation in its tracks before Snodgress asked something else of her. "Anyone else wanting a memento will have to wait until I get back."

"Aw," Alice Snodgress uttered nonchalantly, meeting her gaze squarely. "You'll be fine. it's only tension and writing cramp," she took a sip of her Scotch, the swirling ice cubes had almost dissolved in the glass. "Nothing you haven't had before."

"If only that were the case," Kapoor said, raising her hand to the light of the desk lamp and seeing her little finger shake. "This is just one of the signs of Parkinson's disease and it doesn't discriminate against age Alice." She looked down at her picture on the top of the pile. The image showed an attractive young face which looked fit and healthy. "I'm thirty-three years of age and this morning for the first time I felt seventy. My muscles were stiff and my movements were, to say the least, slow. That isn't good, not when you sing and dance for a living like I do."

Kalvinder Kapoor had lived all of her young life in India. From humble beginnings in Delhi, working in the resale trade, she swapped her old life when she was discovered almost over night by her film director and ex-lover. She had never once looked back to see whom she had trodden on or slept with to get to the top of her career. She now owned a large mansion in New Delhi not far from the Presidential Palace and to her gall, spent most of her wages paying bills to pay for its running costs. She was single, kept her friends close but her enemies closer and trusted no one including her Personal Assistant Alice Snodgress who had written daily records of the star's sexual adventures plus other experiences and thoughts in a diary and planned one day to publish it to the highest bidder if she was ever unfortunate enough to get the sack or not get the pay rise she desperately wanted.

Kapoor was five foot six in height and had a quite neat, lean figure. She was attractive in an unconventional way. Her face was sharply-boned with dark eyes set above wide cheeks, a small hooked nose and plump lips. Long black hair, the colour of night fell just below her smooth, slim shoulders. A silken, blue sari was wrapped around her body.

"My dear Kal," Snodgress said, in a low and even voice, "I know your diagnosis was a complete shock for all of us closest to you but the doctor has prescribed you some drugs to relieve the symptoms and you must remember that not all cases of the disease are the same. There is every chance that it could go so far and not get any worse. Believe me when I say you can still lead a full and rich life."

Opposite her, sitting comfortingly in a straight backed chair, Alice Snodgress finished off her drink then lowered the glass to the padded arm, her eyes glancing slyly towards the drinks cabinet standing against the wall of the hotel room. Shrew and capable of anything her job had thrown at her over the last five years,

Snodgress was dumpy and had such a bland face that it was almost forgettable to anyone who meet, except when she opened her generous mouth and added sardonic words to her quick temper. Short curly brown hair sprinkled with white sprouted around her full face seamed with crows feet and frown lines. In her mid-forties, a good stone overweight and way below medium height with skin that could scour pans, Snodgress' eyes had gone slightly paler blue with age and the bags under them were beginning to bulge more, but there was a steely spark in her that when fixed set many a persons teeth on edge. She wore jeans and a warm woollen blouse under a denim jacket. Moccasins with a hard heel and sole encased her feet.

Kapoor sighed then smiled sourly. "Oh the rigors that try my stamina. Okay! Let's change the subject Alice. This one is leaving me with a bitter taste in my mouth. What time do we have to get to the airport in the morning?"

Snodgress replied quickly: "Before eight. The bags are packed and the taxi will pick us up outside here at six."

"Competent as ever Alice."

"I try Kal." Snodgress said with a narrow smile. "After all I do have to earn the liposuction you promise me, now don't I."

* * *

After taking his leave from the reporters, Giddings took the concrete steps two at a time as he climbed to ground level, clutching the suitcase of money in his left hand. Upon reaching the landing where a metal fire exit door was set in the wall directly in front of him, the sergeant paused and while his heart pounded from the effort of his ascent, he cast a swift glance up the next flight of steps leading to the higher stories of the parking lot then back down the stairway he'd just come up to see if anyone had followed him up from the basement floor.

Once he was completely satisfied that no one was hanging around to identify him, he pulled off Alexander's old felt hat, scarcely containing his excitement, and shoved it deep down into the pocket of his trenchcoat. He felt like celebrating, and this was easily mirrored in the jauntiness in his step as he went up to the fire exit and pushed up the locking bar to open up the heavy door. The sergeant emerged into a short, dark alley just off the high street, and with quitting the scene being uppermost in his thoughts, he began walking unhurriedly in the other direction between the high brick walls, avoiding a stack of cardboard boxes and some broken glass.

Giddings then heard a sudden roar of a car engine. He tensed, hesitating and a rush of adrenaline flooded his body. He choose a strategy and immediately crouched for a moment or two in the gloom, while the red Audi sped past the mouth of the alley before vanishing from sight. He sighed with relief at seeing it was not what he thought it was. A police car. Generally his nerves were like steel, nothing disturbed him, but even out here in this small borough in the middle of West Yorkshire where none of the locals or the out of town journalists would ever recogonise him, Giddings knew he could ill afford to be caught with a suitcase full of cash when he reckoned he was still under suspicion by internal affairs for fiddling the figures of his overtime sheets.

When he made the crucial decision back in the lift to sell his evidence to the newshounds, Giddings was in a wretched mood, looking into an abyss of financial problems that were crying out for solutions. His rank had enabled him free access to view all the data and be above suspicion when he duplicated an extra copy of it for himself. By the time the sergeant had gathered the information, he sent the E-mail via Sinclair's computer terminal and modem to involve the inspector in the deception, leaving text in the memory for anyone in the know to retrieve while demonstrating he wasn't the only one with a possible track record. Giddings straightened and moved cautiously off again, out of the alley and along the narrow side street, glancing at anything that moved around.

About half a mile on, Giddings arrived at an old traditional red telephone kiosk; a couple of the small panes were smashed but the glass within the other frames around the booth were intact. He flung open the door and in the vivid light of a neon sign from the liquor store across the street, entered the kiosk, noticing with satisfaction that nothing was vandalized inside as he put the suitcase down on the floor between his feet. He picked up the receiver and began dialing the rotating disk on the phone. A connection was made and a woman's voice answered the other end.

"Speak!" She said gruffly, down the line with some authority in her voice.

Giddings inserted a couple of coins into the slender slot. "Bryan here guv," he responded, "you paged me?"

"Yep." Sinclair affirmed. "Where are you?"

"On my way up to my flat." Giddings lied, feeling his solid plans loosening slightly. "I was just grabbing myself a take-away but it'll be touch and go if I finish it without falling to sleep in-between. Why! What's up?"

"Oh!" Sinclair said in surprise, forgetting the lateness of the hour and his established shift that had ended some time ago. "I had something I wanted stringently checked out that's relevant to the case. As you're aware Bryan, earlier I granted an interview to the media, and among other things I released details of the Caravelle the raiders drove to get away from the village."

"Uh-huh."

"Well since then sections of my press conference have been repeated on the news bulletins every hour and in response to the last airing," the inspector continued, "our hotline received a call from a Mrs Victoria O'Donnell in Barnsely, about one of the people carriers we haven't tracked down yet."

"Really!" He said, emphasizing the word. "What did she say?"

"Just that she'd came back off holiday with her two sons twenty minutes ago and found as they got off the airport shuttle that their Caravelle was missing from the driveway outside her home."

"Any margin for error?" Giddings asked thoughtfully. "Like her husband borrowing it while she was away to go to work?"

"Nope!" Sinclair replied, "Graham O'Donnell, her husband is currently staying in France. For a living he's a traveling salesman and he went over there to sell farm machinery."

"So!" Giddings replied cautiously, "this vehicle could be one of those stolen for the raid?"

"The evidence seems to point in that general direction, yes." Sinclair agreed with an unseen nod. "I know it's late but what I'm going to do now is send Higginson down there in your place and get him to take down some details of any distinguishing characteristics of the vehicle then tomorrow you can take time out from the investigation over at Sentinel Enterprises, and visit Mrs O'Donnell to get her statement."

"Suits me guv," he said in harmony as a stray thought occurred to him. "You still at the station?"

"Yep. Burning the midnight oil." She confirmed, about to give him a brief progress report. "Whilst you've been finished for the day, the officers in the incident room have managed up to this very moment to identify and place over half of the Caravelles in the country plus begin to chase down other leads which can't be ignored from the Internet."

"Great news guv," Giddings declared ecstatically, "we really are making headway. What about the other incidents that happened today? The traffic lights and the locks on the canal that blew up. Anything on those?"

"Some! Investigators have spent the whole of today sifting through the still-smoldering remains of the blast sites. They found explosive residues there. Tamzin believes all the devastation is connected. So do I, but no one is claiming responsibility for this. I have a theory which I won't tell you over the phone. Tomorrow will do."

"Okay! Remember to go home and get some rest okay Hallie? You're no good to any one if your wasted."

"I will," she returned, thankful to the concern in his voice. "Same to you. See you in the morning."

"Right," he answered, "bye."

The connection ended as Giddings replaced the receiver into its cradle. Upon leaving the kiosk, he furtively looked around once more then started off along the road, the sounds of distant traffic rumbled behind him as he strode on, turning into the shadows of another dark backstreet, halting temporarily to let his eyes adjust to the gloom ahead before proceeding onward towards the rear of the nearest dumpster where his powerful and cherished Harley Davidson was parked.

DAY TWO

OCTOBER THE THIRY FIRST

STRANGE BEDFELLOWS

CHAPTER THIRTEEN

No sooner had Klugman wrapped the belts around his hand, then he strode down the subterranean passage. Behind him, Cummings paused fleetingly, letting the slack of the lifeline play-out until it was almost taut before he ducked beneath the arch and followed his associate with slower strides to accommodate his guide and to maintain the distance between them. Klugman sneezed as they pressed on. From the archway the brickwork opened out alongside them, giving ground and providing about a yard of extra width upon either side of the passageway. Water dripped from a narrow crack in the ceiling to splash into a shallow cavity eating into the limestone floor. An empty sconce came and went, and although it was cold, the drop in temperature wasn't bitter enough to freeze the moisture flowing down the slippery, curved walls. They had gone about forty-two paces, additional wall brackets falling away behind them as their footfalls rang hollow in the motionless air, when the torch revealed the tunnel turned to the right. They carried on, a distant trickling sound at the very edge of their hearing suddenly became audible and increased gradually in rumbling resonance the nearer they came to the source. Cummings listened to the amplifying noise and considered the ramifications should the reflecting sound waves, not be the exaggerated effects of their close surroundings.

"Hear that," Klugman said, getting a mental impression of the conditions ahead. He directed the torch beam forward.

"Yeah, running water!"

"Sounds like we're going towards it," Klugman remarked, panning the light to catch sight of any sudden flow of water rushing down the corridor towards them. "Let's hope the seepage isn't much and it allows us to pass. There's nothing around here to shore it up with."

"It might not come to that, Kyle." Cummings answered, tightening his grasp upon the belts as a precaution. "Vibrations always sound louder underground," he progressed forward. "Hard to say how bad it is until we get there and see for ourselves. Though for all we know we could be listening to just magnified echos thrown back off the floor and walls, and they're not dissipating because there might be not one big flow but several smaller ones, similar to the one we passed earlier on, dripping constantly to strengthen the volume."

"Interesting!" Klugman replied. Arching a single eyebrow as he grudgingly conceded to himself that there could be a grain of truth in this because although the rumbling ahead of him was growing louder still, no torrent had so far appeared out of the blackness to sweep them away. "Well we'll find out soon enough, for if that increasing roar is any indication, then we've almost reached the source."

The companions walked the next few yards in complete silence and in due course they came upon more water trickling from the roof of the corridor. Klugman wended his way past the green slime adorning the walls, between the seepage drops and slender streams fell slowly into perforated depressions worn into the stone floor. Klugman briefly trained the torch back and down to enable Cummings to follow, and the towering figure in a passing glance saw that some of the depressions were not deep enough to float a match while a couple of the others had depth, with their bottom not in plain sight. Swiveling the beam back out ahead of him, Klugman walked on, the roaring noise continued to fill their ears like thunder. The tunnel twisted again to the left, and when the men ventured around this corner, they encountered fine droplets of spray and discovered what was producing the clamor. The torch beam reflected off the brackets and the glistening walls were dotted with moisture as water was thrown onto them from the miniature brownish waterfall which plunged from a widening ceiling cleft, filling just over half of the tunnel. Klugman came to a halt and his face registered surprise. He squinted and shook his head to clear his vision as water splashed into his eyes while behind him, Cummings blinked and gasped at the spectacle which greeted him. When his perception returned, Klugman guided the beam methodically to-and-fro ahead of him to trace the movement of the waterfall, judging not only if there were any loose bricks ready to fall on their heads but also see if there was a sufficient gap for them to get by. To his relief, no bricks dangled precariously from the edges of the crevice splitting the ceiling. The dirty cascade, fell freely until it splashed loudly, draining away into a saucer-shaped sink-hole indenting all but two feet of the smooth floor near the right hand side of the tunnel.

After a quick appraisal, Klugman cast a glance over his shoulder and shouted at the top of his voice over the roar. "I've seen enough," he waved his free hand back towards him. "Come on! This is no challenge. Let's get going." Cummings mouthed the word "okay!" He bobbed his head in agreement.

Klugman grinned headed onward, treading upon the crumbled, ancient remains of wet clay, the pieces disintegrated under his boots, slowing only to turn sideways and edge himself past the waterfall before moving off again. Cummings followed. As they continued upon their way they noticed a thickening layer of dust returned gradually to carpet the floor. In addition they saw further patches of algae decorating the brickwork and the row of sconces disappeared from the wall on their left while the ones opposite suddenly developed spiked-holder's that were slightly larger in diameter.

Thirty paces beyond, dust topped flambeaus started to come irregularly into view in some of the brackets. Klugman passed without sparing a second glance at them, yet Cummings took a quick thoughtful look at each of them in turn. They were no more than just sticks of wood with a bundle of stiff twigs bound to the end of the long handle. At first he past a couple that had minor flaws like having little or no sprigs, a third had a broken shaft that was directly beneath another bit of leakage. When he came to the next flambeau, he expect to see similar decay but only the bindings were slightly disentangled.

"I wonder," he muttered, coming up to the flambeau. He peered closely at the heavy dark, substance smearing the sprigs and began unwrapping the belt from his hand. "Kyle! Hold-up for a second and swing the torch around. I want to try something."

Klugman frowned and skidded to a stop, muddling up his tracks in the dust when he turned and returned the way he'd come. He lowered the torch: "Sure! What are you intending to do?"

"Grab this and I'll show you." Cummings replied, handing him the lifeline before shifting his gaze back to the wall sconce and pulling up his trousers which were beginning to slide down his waist. Klugman's frown deepened, took the proffered buckle, and watched.

"This torch," Cummings said slipping his hand in his trouser pocket. "Has been down here a couple of hundred years and despite that it's withstood the onset of decay and deterioration quite well."

"I suppose," Klugman agreed indifferently, viewing him pull out a cotton handkerchief.

"The twigs in the head are dry and brittle," Cummings spoke on, catching the absence of interest in Klugman's voice. He screwed up the handkerchief. "The bindings are fraying here and there." Dust and pieces of the dark substance flaked off as he grabbed hold of some of the sprigs, parted them then shoved the crumbled handkerchief into the gap until he left just the one wedged-shaped corner protruding out about an inch and a half from the top of the bundle. "But a kind of resin is coating the twigs. Maybe its pitch from the conifers nearby. It appears to be still pretty solid at this temperature so," he patted the outside of his coat pockets randomly until he found the familiar bulge he'd been looking for, "let's see if I can conjure up another source of light."

Klugman eyed him dubiously. "It'd be handy. The batteries in this torch might not hold up forever." He tried to suppress a bemused smile and keep the sceptical tone out of his voice. "But I won't hold my breath." Cummings freed a match box.

He slid it open, took out a match and struck it. He carefully extended the flame and lit the corner of the hankie. Taking hold, the cloth smoldered; dense curls of smoke rose from diminutive flames. Cummings blew lightly upon the fire which steadily grew brighter and hotter. In time, the flames thrived, sprouting up fiercely in the draught towards the sprigs.

"The torch should flare up if it's going to at any second now." Cummings warned, backpedaling a couple of paces, down the tunnel. Indulging his whim, only out of humor, Klugman retreated a step in the opposite direction. Then suddenly the flambeau ignited, acquiring sustenance from the musty air, the flames violently burst, leaping up around the twigs with a roar, generating a great amount of heat and light which cast bright, quivering, reddish-orange shadows upon the tunnel walls.

"Yes!" Cummings whooped in utter delight. Klugman blinked and jumped involuntary in surprise. The loud cracking of the fire echoed and fought to drown out the fainter noise of the miniature waterfall behind them.

Klugman shook his head. "Never thought you'd actually get it lit."

Cummings advanced and curled his thick fingers around the shaft of the burning brand, hefting it free from the sconce, with a flourish. "I believe you can't discount anything until you've given it a go and I've been quite fortuitous tonight to prove myself twice.

Now!" he locked eyes with Klugman, "we better be getting on. I'll keep hold of the back-up."

"Right!" Klugman announced, stretching out his left hand to present him with the lifeline.

Cummings took it and gestured a sweeping movement with his torch hand towards the darkness behind Klugman. "After you!"

* * *

They traipsed for another twenty metres in a straight line as a prelude to discovering a kink in the tunnel itself, instead of bending right or left, it suddenly begin to elevate at an eight-degree angle.

"Looks like we're getting out of here. We're about to head up." Klugman said in his normal tone. The echo of the running water had reduced in volume, the crackling flames of the firebrand gave Cummings a ruddy complexion as they danced and reflected off the walls.

"Excellent!" Cummings replied. "We've finally cleared the bog."

"You said it," Klugman declared with a weary smile. His tired legs allowing him to slightly pick up the pace, as he begun to rise, eager to get to the top more quickly. "How far do you reckon we've come?" He struggled further up the incline, almost reaching the limit of his strength and stamina.

From the moment Cummings walked up the sloping stone floor, he stretched up his hand to feel above him and eyed the ceiling expecting the complication of having to bend his body at any time to avoid banging his head against the lowering roof of the passageway but, as he ascended, his suspicion proved to be unfounded for the ceiling just duplicated the inclination of the floor and tilted upwards by a relative amount.

"By my estimate," Cummings answered, lengthening his stride to match his companions, "we've covered well over a mile. That should please little miss personality up above no end."

"You ain't kidding." Klugman puffed, as the slope elevated a couple of more degrees, "talk about a pain the arse. I know she's a good looker and all, but she's only good for one thing. I don't see how Thaw puts up with her, not with all the ear bashing she's given him of late. Bisset might not be dead wood at the moment but in my opinion she is. I wouldn't tolerate her behavior and if I had my way, once we reach journey's end, the only talking she would ever do afterwards is through a medium."

Cummings smiled thinly and sighed. "Uh-huh!" He was having no difficulty in reading Klugman's train of thought as he strung along behind him. "Well, between you and me, I feel like I could strangle her, me bleedin' self. But Jerome has a lot of affection for the girl and he trusts her implicitly so what can we do?" He cautioned, speaking firmly, "except be patient and just grin and bear her for the time being until we divide up the money then go our separate ways."

"Yeah!" Klugman answered innocently. His persuasive rejoinder came across perfectly natural in an effort to diffuse any tension, yet his passion deep inside him was already dictating his future responses. "I can put up with her for a little bit longer. She's not even a priority compared to the other problems we still face." He played the torch beam upon the brickwork and strode on upwards while at his rear, the blazing flambeau loudly crackled beside Cummings whose eyes glinted with slight unease and his forehead creased with a deepening frown as he walked on, wondering vaguely if Klugman was really saying what he truly thought.

* * *

For the next couple of minutes they silently climbed up the arduous incline, their breath ragged and their feet becoming harder to lift as they felt they were gradually developing the heaviness of lead. Exceeding the limit of his endurance, Klugman was just about to call a breather so he could gather his strength for the ultimate, upward leg of their journey when the beam of the torch suddenly revealed the top of the slope above them. Postponing his decision until he reached the higher ground, he concentrated on just putting one foot before the other as he trudged up the remaining distance to the top where a wide flat landing led into the darkness.

"We've made it! There's no rockfall blocking our path." Klugman panted. His breathing heavy and his heart was hammering in his chest as he pulled up for breath, he still managed to play the beam along the surroundings forward of his position.

"Not quite the place we thought we'd end up in either," Cummings replied. Less than delighted with the view, his mind more than a little plagued by identical thoughts as he drew alongside and stole a glance at his firebrand which continued to crackle loudly yet was now burning fitfully. “We still don’t seem to be any closer to finding a way out of here.”

Within the panning beam the smooth texture of their surroundings suddenly became rougher in appearance as the masonry gave way to the bumpy rock surface. The floor of the passageway opened into a natural, roofed-over limestone cavern, haphazardly scattered with a small number of tapering stalagmites and stalactites whose shape and colour were diverse.

“Maybe it’s just beyond this chamber?” Klugman suggested. His heart rate gradually slowing and his breathing easing a little as he began to acquire his second wind. “I’m too tired to go on for a bit. The climb took a lot out of me.”

“I thought you army types kept in trim Kyle?”

“I’m fit. But even I have my limits and I’ve reached mine. If you’re up to it Cummings why don’t you check it out. I’ll wait here until you return.”

“No can do Kyle,” he said, glancing at him. The tongues of frame flickered around the firebrand, smoke rising to the ceiling. “For safety reasons we stay together, come what may. We can lengthen our visual range if you take your breather where that column of stone is.” He pointed at the object twenty feet ahead.

Klugman scratched his lip and nodded. “Okay, works for me.” His breathing becoming less harsh and ragged. “We better swap lights before we go on though,” he gestured with the torch. “This torch will be more suitable to your needs than that relic your holding.”

Unbidden a series of images flashed within Cummings mind. “Not worth it. There could be a crevice or a sinkhole punctuating the cavern floor just outside the lights. I only have to stumble down one and it’d be instinctive for me to lose the torch trying to find a handhold to halt my fall. But this old thing, is beginning to gutter. It won’t be long before it goes out altogether. So I’ll take point. Come on! Follow where I tread. Water could have weakened the stone under us and made it as thin as tissue paper.”

“Gotcha!” Klugman replied, watching him set off. “I don’t fancy doing a freefall from this high up.” He weaved a little on his feet from his weariness as he brought up the rear. “I did enough of that before I was cashiered out and at least then I had the luxury of having a parachute strapped to my back.”

Grimacing, Cummings proceeded with the barest pressure of his heel preceding by the rest of his foot to test the floor ahead for his weight, he slowly lead at a careful walk. Echoes resounded off the cavern walls from the cracking flames and Cummings' footfalls as he kicked up more dust, sneezing involuntary, his eyes beginning to sting from the smoke while the impressions of his boots left a trail of footprints in his wake. Klugman stopped alongside the merged column of a joined stalactite and stalagmite. By the ruddy glow of his flambeau, Cummings navigated passed water trickling from above, between a pair of conical-shaped stalagmites wrinkled with ring marks rising from the chamber floor, a fossilized Ammonite embedded in the nearest rock wall, without encountering any of the dangers he envisaged along the way. Then he caught sight of a low indistinct object just about a metre in front of him but before he could proceed to get a closer look, he was forced to stop when the life line snapped taut, having reached the limit of its range.

"Shit!" He swore, casting a quick glance back towards his companion. "Give me some slack on the belts. I'll seen something I can't made out from here."

With blood roaring in his ears, he wearily sighed yet the mere prospect of Cummings spotting some undetermined thing in the shadows beyond the flambeau gave him reason to hope that their bad luck was on the verge of a bit of an upswing. "You got it," Klugman wheezed, his face remaining drawn. He pushed himself away from the wall and making an effort to shake off the fatigue he was still experiencing inside, he proceeded along the trail. "What is it?" The belts dropped to become a loop.

When he heard Krugman approaching from behind, Cummings resumed onward, the weakening flame causing him to strain his eyes to pierce the gloom in front of him. "We got ourselves some Brewers casks." He came up to a littered arrangement of old barrels amassed in various sizes: rusty metal hoops held bulging wooden staves that were either rotten from the damp and decorated with dry rot or just infested with countless woodworm holes. "This gives credence to your idea of a smuggler's route, Kyle."

Klugman's footsteps reverberated and magnified again off the surrounding walls. Cummings stepped in among the barrels, the blackness inched back around the sickly glow slowly shrinking as the guttering flame consumed the remainder of the bundle of twigs.

"Certainly does!" Klugman announced tersely, approaching to

drew level. "Then perhaps the house you spoke off might not be all that way off either. Let's see how much further this bleeding cave goes on for." He levelled the torch at his waist, directing the length ahead of them. Beyond the barrels the opposite side of the cavern appeared. A dark, contoured shape of a silhouetted-stalactite hung down from the ceiling to mar the perfect light disc at the edge of the beam.

"We've hit the cave wall," he frowned. Panning the light to the right, he only outlined another column of stone and a curtain of calcite. "Now! To prevent this trip from being a total washout I'll settle for a natural opening leading us to anything which passes for civilization."

"There doesn't seem to be any sign at the moment, not from where we are anyway," Cummings answered, his gaze following the sweeping beam. "Try left, Kyle." He pointed with a finger. "There's got to be an entry point concealed over in that direction. Those barrels didn't come down here on their own."

"Oh the entrance is here somewhere." He replied, playing the torch light to the left. "Blocked up with debris or behind one of these damn stalagmites."

After a few seconds, Klugman blinked in surprised recognition when the light gradually exposed an opening in the bare rock. It was filled with a thick, heavy door that gleamed dully. The beam flashed upon the paneled-wood and the verdigris-coated copper handle. The door was flanked by a pair of iron brackets, and dropped in place across these, was a great locking bar. This vision caused a rush of strength to sweep through their weary muscles.

"Well! This is getting just curiouser and curiouser." Klugman declared with a taut smile, studying it carefully. Particles of stirred up dust floated in the air in front of the buckled doorframe. "First the steps hewed out of the bedrock and now this doors appeared. It makes you wonder what we're gonna come across next."

"It does a little," Cummings said with a nod. "What's made me curious is why is the door locked from this side?"

"Good question," Klugman muttered, focusing upon more practical matters. "We'll know in a couple of minutes." Without being told, he aimed his torch downward to sweep the remaining few feet that separated them from the doorway ahead. Nothing was revealed in the glare except the same irregular projections and the odd depression in the cavern floor. "No sinkholes but don't step on that dip over there," he pointed unnecessarily at the directed area. "Could be a pitfall."

"I see it," Cummings acknowledged, taking a tentative footstep forward. "I'll go first Kyle and get the door open. You light my way from here." The beam became smudged when he walked into it. Three measured steps led him past the depression and to the door. "Apart from the bolt," he surveyed, "I don't see another lock but the frame's warped. it's gonna be stuck." In one fluid motion, he dropped his end of the lifeline and lifted up the bar from the brackets with his free hand like it was weightless. "Couple of good tugs should take care of it."

Once he'd placed the bar against the bare stone wall, Cummings switched hands with his firebrand and clasped the copper doorknob. With a grunted effort he succeeded in twisting the handle clockwise to release the latch which produced a harsh, rasping sound as it groaned in distress from being moved for the first time in over a century. Then his right arm wrenched, sweat beaded his forehead as the wooden slab trembled violently under the applied pressure until he pulled the door open with a sudden jerk. The distinctive sound of protesting hinges briefly drowned out Cummings' heavier breathing as they squealed shrilly in motion, the removal of the door created a vacuum until he shoved the guttering flambeau through the opening and trailed on after it.

Inside of a few seconds, Cummings re-emerged and beckoned Klugman over.

"What you find?" He asked curiously. Lowering the torch and walking across to him. "Someone's cellar?" Intense anxiety knotting the pit of his stomach.

"Not quite," he responded. Turning and vanishing again from view. Klugman neared the doorframe and saw the flambeau's ruddy glow continued to faintly illuminate the curving wall beyond. "But it's a way out nevertheless. Be careful where you put your feet. The ground abruptly ends in here at a lip with some water beneath."

Klugman's forehead wrinkled with interest as he entered and paused to take in his current surroundings on the rim of a ledge. He raked the beam around the length of the wall and saw the shaft was composed of blocks of granite, sandwiching crumpling mortar and decorated with patches of lichen. The shaft was ten feet in height and was about a metre and a half in diameter with a wooden lid covering the top of the cylinder. From the top, the rungs of a slender yet rusty metal ladder descended to the thick ledge encircling the circumference of the shaft, above a dark tranquil pool of water. Cummings stood at the base of the ladder, the crackling flambeau was burning extremely low now.

"A well." Klugman expressed in surprise, glancing to his right over to where Cummings stood.

"Uh-huh!" Cummings responded, peering up at the ladder. "Absolute perfect isn't it?" He reached up and pulled on a rung to test if it was secure. It held firmly. "What better way of hiding the entrance to those tunnels from the custom's officers than in plain sight." He took a quick look at Klugman. "This way," he pointed at the curving section of ledge he had just traversed along. "It's safe. Just hug the wall and come around."

Suppressing his apprehension, Klugman nodded and edged slowly towards his destination. Cummings thrust his hand into his coat and fished out the walkie-talkie. "This is Scout calling to cohort, do you copy? Over." He heard nothing but static. His voice echoed off the walls along with the scuff of Klugman's boots as he came nearer. "I repeat this is Scout, cohort. Do you receive? Over." Again only noise issued forth from the walkie-talkie.

"Any luck?" Klugman inquired, stopping beside him.

"No!" He answered, slipping the walkie-talkie back inside his pocket. "Jerome's right. Our current depth is blocking the signal. I'll try again up top once I've seen what's about. Keep the light trained on the ladder so I can see what I'm climbing." He tossed the flambeau over his shoulder and it plunged into the water, dousing the frame with a sizzle.

Then he grasped the ladder and started on up. He ascended gradually and when the top came into reach, he pushed up to find that the cover was moveable. Lifting the lid, he slid it quietly off the well's stone rim before clambering up the last couple of rungs to emerge into the open air which stank of banana, curry and other strong smells. He breathed in and noticed his surrounding were still draped with the night shadows, but the waning of the odd star visible through clouds indicated that daybreak was only a few hours from showing itself on the eastern horizon.

Cummings noiselessly clambered over the rim and immediately, through a gap in the fence, caught sight of an encouraging radiant light blink on in the distance, etching roofs and chimneys in sharp relief. Recognising it for what it was and adding it together with the other marvelous reasons he suddenly felt elated at this second, Cummings calmly leaned back over the stone opening, and waved his companion up.

He whispered. "Come on up and be as quiet as you can. There are locals close by."

Pushing himself off the well, Cummings straightened, turned and weaved between a number of garbage cans and wheelie bins filled to the brim with black bags as he bore down on a bamboo fence. It was high in places and merged on his left with a row of yew trees whose leaves ruffled slightly in the cool breeze. Climbing vines were trained on trellis encircling the well on two sides while the forth partly formed an entrance he presumed to allow the dustbin men to collect the trash whilst screening the offensive blot on the landscape from the nearby residents. Behind him there was a metallic sound as Klugman climbed the ladder. He popped his head up through the opening but failed to see the distance brightness. It had already winked out of view to let the darkness reclaim the scene. Klugman wrinkled in nose in disgust at the cabbage and fishy smell coming from the nearest wheelie bin. "Phew!" He complained softly, hauling himself out of the well. "The air's not any better up here than it was down below. Where are we anyway?" Eyeing the amount of rubbish and recalling similar images from his youth as he swept the light around the contained area in an attempt to get his own bearings. "Near a housing estate?"

"No! I can see how you might think that from all this refuse," Cummings replied. "Where then?" Klugman demanded. A little bit of restless eagerness creeping into his voice as he made his way through the bins, his torch preceding him, towards where Cummings stood.

"Something equally as good," Cummings remarked. Staring through the small gap within the packed bamboo fence at a couple of small bedroom lights shining through the distance skeletal branches of a deciduous tree. "A house! Quite a big one from what I can see with the most usual architecture I've ever seen. I imagine it has all that we'll need and served on a silver platter!"

* * *

Inside the house, Robert J. Crowe barfed over the cat, a meal he couldn't remember eating. He shook his head and weaved drunkenly up the staircase, across the gallery and along the corridor stretching out before him. His tall distorted reflection drifted passed the polished suits of armour lining the wood-paneled walls. His heavy footsteps, squelching with water, echoed loudly off the tongue and groove flooring. The sound of his passage blended with his spasmodic hiccuping and sharp braking of wind. Approximately six foot one in height, Robert was forty-eight years of age but looked considerably older with his weather-beaten features and a shock of short, wiry hair that had been prematurely white since his early twenties. He had broad shoulders topping a lean sinewy frame and a non-discript face showing five o'clock shadow around his mustache. He wore a heavy lumberjack shirt and faded denim jeans, wet up to his knees, above a pair of scuffed boots.

A long, unbuttoned trench-coat dripping with water bellowed out behind him as he swayed slightly in his progress. Faltering in his step to avoid a chair set against the nearest wall, he failed to keep his stride and lost his balance, his weak knee giving way under him causing him to topple over sideways with an almighty crash into another suit of armour on his right. Ahead a massive oak door swung inward as the helmet rolled off in that direction, while the large handled axe-head sliced down to embed itself deeply into the floor, coming precariously close to his face and severing half of his mustache in the process.

"Bastard football injury," Robert cursed loudly, trembling as he grunted to push aside the heavy plate corselet that had fallen on top of him. "Who's the pissing idiot who put armor there of all places?" He added incoherently, his speech slurred from the amount of alcohol he downed earlier on in the evening.

A short pear-shaped shadow emerged out of the doorway preceded by Ashley as she marched into the corridor and up to the prone form of her husband who was presently balancing himself up onto one trembling arm, his heavily-lidded, bloodshot eyes watering from the pain of the pressure he was enduring, while his other hand quickly removed a pair of armored greaves that were beginning to squash his testicles.

"That would be you, you drunken pig," she replied, her voice stern and rising in anger as she came to a halt in front of him. Smelling the stink of alcohol on his breath from a distance of three feet, she squinted her eyes and frowned, cracks appearing in the mud pack concealing her face. "So you've finally come home have you?"

She folded her arms across her breasts and began tapping her slippered foot as he pushed himself up to a kneeling position and saw the nightgown didn't extend past her bum, revealing corn beef legs from sitting in front of the fire for to long. "I don't know how you can stand to drink so much."

"I don't generally. I sit on a bar stool. Anyway I'm not all that drunk my love," he ventured sheepishly, looking up and blinking at his wife who saw his eyes were glazed. "Umm..I...Er suffered from a bit of vertigo then," he smiled lamely, her glowering gaze told him that his excuse had not worked.

"No that's your cousin Ruth who has Meniere's disease not you," his wife said angrily, an note of scepticism in her voice, "and in case you thinking of coming down with anything else, I really don't want to hear it okay!"

He thought cloudily for a moment about telling her how he had driven his Mercedes Benz through a pool of flood water down the road where it was still stalled but decided this wasn't the time to bring it up. "Okay I'm pissed. Your female intuition is good."

"You hurt me tonight Robert, did you know that?" Ashley spoke on. "I had to entertain my family alone. Do you have any idea what time it is?"

He exhaled a tense breath. "No Ash! But I'm sure you going to tell me anyway," he replied, continuing to pronounce his words rapidly and indistinctly as he found some backbone from somewhere.

"It will be morning soon and from the noise you've just made, the only ones in the entire house who didn't hear you come in are the cockroaches in the cellar." She watched her husband rise and stab his index fingers into his ears to try and prevent hearing the lecture. "I think I need to see a therapist after putting up with what you've put me through over the past few years. Oh the sacrifices I've made. If it wasn't for the kids and the amount of love I have for your bank balance, I would have divorced you long ago."

"One of these days your gonna come up for air and then I might be able to get a word in edgeways," Robert declared, the beer relaxing him so much that it allowed him to speak his mind as he walked towards her.

"Oh shut up. You're getting on my nerves, you're not in the pub now with your boozy mates or that tart behind the bar," Ashley answered, turning back to their bedroom. "You can sleep on the couch for the rest of the night, I don't want you all over me not in the state you're in." Robert followed with a long face. "Now get in and shut the door. I just hope it was all worth it that's all."

"It was," Robert said proudly, heading through the doorway. "It took ten pints of lager but I finally got the local butcher to agree to put my posters up in his shop window. You never know what orders and clientele I might acquire because of this."

"Yes," Ashley said sarcastically as the door closed behind him. "We'll really have the vegans queuing up outside when they find out about this."

"You never can tell," Robert answered. He went forward and swayed again, in his current state the sneering remark failed to penetrate his inebriated skull, and was completely lost on him.

* * *

Lois Elmes grinned as she lowered the glass tumbler from her ear and stepped away from the bedroom wall. She turned, her curvy figure concealed beneath the baggy red top and shorts she wore for bed, and with a weary yawn, weaved between the furniture, crossing back over the thick-pile carpet where one of her suitcases lay, wide open on the floor. After placing the tumbler on top of her bedside cabinet, she knelt to pick up the highlighter pen and notebook, the page filled with a written list. Then peering inside the case, she continued to verify the checklist against the items tidily contained there.

In spite of being extremely fatigued from the journey, Lois had been determined to check off the list tonight to see if there was nothing amiss after packing the case this morning. She knew her entire future rested on it. She could never see herself employed in a clothing factory like her mom or working hard in an office shuffling paperwork from 9-5 every day of the week. It just wasn't her. Nor did she ever want to run foul of the police again.

Special community penalties were one thing, but she knew if she'd carried on committing more serious crimes she could have been locked up in a young offenders' center. She wanted fame and fortune without the risk of going to jail afterwards, especially when she considered her next possible stay over would be at an adult prison. Lois shuddered at the prospect and yawned, breathing in deeply, wishing she hadn't stopped to eavesdrop on her aunt's conversation but the gossip had been too tasty an opportunity to ignore.

"Salt-container. Check," Lois muttered, marking off the object by colouring it with an orange strip. "Candle sticks, coloured candles and chalk," she blinked and fought to stay awake just long enough to finish the task. "Ouija board and Tarot cards to get the suckers into the party mood," she moved the broad felt tip across the capital letters. "*The Grimorie*, incense, the gong," her eyes fixing upon the metallic disk and its accompanying small hammer. "Ingredients and last but not least the crystals."

Lois crossed off the item with a sweep of the pen then tossed the notebook and pen into the case. She closed the lid, locked it and shoved it out of sight under the mattress. Satisfied, Lois switched off the lamp and slid beneath the duvet, rolling it tightly around her to keep warm and in the hope of drowning out the loud snoring emitting from next door.

* * *

Klugman frowned and when he halted beside Cummings, dipping his torch and brushing aside the broad leaves of one of the Yews, only to squint and observe nothing but the twin glows of electric lights seeping through the pair of faraway curtained-windows. "Huh!" He expressed his doubt. "Can't see a bloody thing out there. How can you be so sure?"

Cummings smiled and faced him. "There are security lamps fixed to the walls of the house. As you were coming up the ladder, a cat crossed the lawn, triggering the motion detectors, illuminating the place as bright as Blackpool's golden mile."

He sighed audibly. "Oh great. Another fly in the ointment. Of all the things we could have come across, we end up with a fucking fortress on our doorstep. We're right back to square one. We ain't going to get any nearer to the house if those damn security systems light up every time something moving is detected."

One of the bedroom lights in the house switched off.

Cummings smile broadened. "That might be true Kyle, but they won't work when the dawn comes. It isn't all that far off now."

Klugman digested this piece of news. He furrowed his brow thoughtfully, grasping the gist behind the information. "So, you're saying we could lie low here until it gets light then pounce on the house?"

"Not the house!" Cummings answered quickly. "When I was studying the lay out of the property, I noticed only trees and bushes on the right but several outbuildings on the left of the lawn."

"That so!" Klugman replied attentively, his eyes roaming up into that direction to try and perceive the tantalising outline of a roof, without the torch to accompany them though, for he kept it dipped to the flagstones for fear of the light giving their presence away. "We still gonna have the same problem with the security systems?" He asked with slight unease, seeing absolutely nothing, except darkness, beyond the height of the hedges.

"I didn't see a halogen lamp flick on over there so either there aren't any in the vicinity or the mechanism operates on some kind of timer. One way or another we'll find out which it is!" Cummings declared, pulling up the waist of his trousers again to conceal the blue rim of his underpants. "There's enough shrubbery in front to hide behind when I creep over to investigate. If the light does comes on, I'll stay concealed and the lack of movement will make it look like some bat or owl had flown past before vanishing back into the night."

"Like the encounter when we were crossing the log." Klugman said, nodding in understanding. "That'll explain the lack of visual contact."

"Exactly!" Cummings answered. "This is the countryside and anyone staying up late at this god forsaken hour, looking out of those windows will assume that to be the case, expecting it from time to time especially when they check their other security systems and find nothing's wrong. We're undetected here Kyle because we came under the walls of the grounds, not over them."

"Not bad," Klugman grudgingly admitted, a thin smile twisting his lips which eased some of the tension in his dirty face. "As solutions go."

"I'll do that after we lead the others back through the tunnels." Cummings announced, turning around and taking Klugman's exhaustion into account. "We'll leave in ten when we're fresher. It's gonna take all of us to hump those bags all that way back." His voice displayed his lack of enthusiasm for the task ahead. "I want to avoid spending any longer than I have to down there. There's still the probability of the ceiling collapsing on our heads."

"You'll get no argument from me on that score," Klugman agreed candidly, glancing at his companion. "I'm just as concerned.

The news of us escaping the bog will be enough motivation to get the others moving and if we split the slog up into legs, pick the places in our journey where the tunnels are relatively solid like say the bottom of the stairs and past the waterfall, then we should make it through in one piece."

"Yeah," Cummings conceded with a nod. "Okay! Who could have anticipated the car getting stuck in that flashflood and the tortuous trail."

"No one could," Klugman said honestly. "If I knew what the future held for me this morning, I would've asked Thaw for danger money on top."

The second bedroom light winked out of view.

Cummings' face mirrored Klugman's thin smile. "You said it. When we go Kyle, you continue to lead."

"Fine!"

"And along the way," Cummings added. "I just want to stop off briefly in the cave."

"Yeah now that you mention it I'll join you," Klugman replied.

"No not that," Cummings remarked with a sigh. "I've got to retrieve my belt before my damn trousers fall down altogether."

CHAPTER FOURTEEN

Back along the subterranean passageway the pair went; their lungs laboring in the stale air and the ache of their tightening hamstrings protesting as Klugman and Cummings cautiously led the way, toting their share of the baggage back up the slope with the remainder of the bedraggled group in tow, listening to the muttered grumblings of Gillett who limped after her boyfriend.

The American grimaced as her new mules rubbed her feet with every step she took. "Ow, ow," She complained, "bastard shoes! I'm looking at loads of blisters at the rate I'm going on. Can't we stop for a moment so I can pull out my other pair from the holdall?"

Lips parted in a humorous smile. "Not down here. I'm carrying some plasters in my bag Sophie," Cummings wheezed, arriving at the top of the incline, "I'll give you the pack when we get outside.

Klugman thought she should save one of the plasters to cover her big gob. It would be whole lot quieter that way. The procession headed along the short tunnel in single file and proceeded into the cavern.

"Save one for me too," Klugman announced gruffly. "Thorns cut me up a bit back there." He peered at his hands and saw in the feeble light the blood had already began to coagulate."

"Likewise!" Thaw agreed, scratching his arm. His voice blending with the scuff of his boots to echo off the cave walls as he saw the torch shine upon the breathtaking sight of the stalagmites and stalactites around them. "I also went through some stinging nettles. It's itchy as hell. It's a good job my arms were covered otherwise I'd be red raw by now."

"I've got something for that in my pocket Jerome," Cummings remarked, "which I managed to pick up near the brier. Dock leaves. All you do is rub the leaf on where you're stung until it breaks up with wear and tear. It'll stop the stinging and will leave a green mark on your skin but you'll be able to wash it off in time."

With the torch to the fore, Klugman make a brief comment to the rest of his party upon what to expect ahead of them then he passed through the old doorway illuminated in the beam. Cummings closely succeeded him. Thaw and Gillett came next, and

Bisset brought up the rear. Klugman circled the wall and clambered up the ladder first. The others went up without difficulty, Thaw the last to ascend after handing up the cases to Cummings who took them one at a time and tossed them out of sight. Thaw stepped off the rim and saw that the outline of the surrounding features were becoming slightly clearer as the night shadows continued to dilute some more with the scheduled arrival of dawn.

Waving her hand in front of her in an attempt to drive some of the smell of the rubbish away, Gillett whispered: "So where are these outbuildings you mentioned back in the bog, Adrian? I could just curl up in a nice corner and fall fast asleep." Bisset nodded slightly in agreement.

"Over to our left," Cummings returned very softly. Breathing quickly in a labored manner, noticing the dissolving darkness with a concerned scowl as he pointed. "Screened off beyond those yew trees. If we're lucky there might be a stable or a woodshed, we can hide in till morning then find the nearest car and head on out. Just hold here a spell while I give those buildings the once over. Jerome!" He glanced at Thaw. "I want you along to find us a way in without making to much noise to alert anyone that may be about."

"Fine," Thaw proclaimed softly with a nod. "I've got just the tool for the job in my bag." He whirled and knelt by his flight bag.

Bisset pursed his lips and carefully thought about what Cummings had said. "Didn't you mention in the tunnels that you saw no one about when the security lights came on earlier?"

"Sure!" Cummings confirmed. "That doesn't mean that there isn't someone out there though." Thaw unzipped his carry-on.

"If I have to force a door or window open and there is a security guard close by," Thaw produced a short steel jimmy before shoving some clothing back inside the interior and zipping the bag back up. "He'll come running to investigate because there's not enough wind blowing now to mask the sound I gotta make."

"Let's cross that bridge when it happens shall we?" Cummings replied. His heart rate slowing a little, seeing his companion rise from his crouch as he tried to soothe the building tenseness lifting around them. "You follow me and when we reach our destination, I'll act as lookout as you do your thing. And between us," he blinked and grinned maliciously, "we should be able to do quite a bit of bodily harm to anyone that comes along."

“True,” Thaw remarked, circumventing a wheelie bin, “I’m ready to go when you are. it’s getting lighter so we won’t need to use the torch.”

“Yeah!” Cummings answered, his face clouding as he was reminded by what was troubling him. “I know. Come on!” He beckoned in urgently, refusing to dwell upon it any longer then he had to. He spun and loped to the opening in the screen. “Let’s do this while there’s still some darkness around to cover our movements.”

* * *

Barely daring to breath, Cummings turned left and to avoid detection, broke into a low, running crouch as he quickly glided from one untidy evergreen shrub to the next, snatching up along the way, a fallen egg-shaped cone from a nearby Norwegian pine. Thaw crept after him, glancing furtively about as he trailed behind at a slower yet equally steady pace, the dull sound of his footfalls signaled to Cummings that despite a recent stretch in prison, his friend had lost none of the stealth he’d acquired from his burglary days. Several steps across the long grass, Cummings acted upon instinct and hunkered down behind a bushy, full-sized daphne where he gnawed on his lower lip and hurled the cone forward, a few feet in front of the wall of one of the visible outbuildings he estimated to be just inside the possible perimeter of a concealed lamp up above. When the cone landed with a muffled sound, and no light flicked on, he grinned at the prospect of having no electric beams to deal with, and set off again through a couple of more bushes until he was beside the wall.

In seconds, Thaw caught up with him only to see Cummings waste no time in summoning him by a silent gesture over to a window on their left. Co-operating, Thaw came across to one of the panes, peered into the building’s interior and in the available light, could just make out the vague shape of a massive workbench littered with a collection of objects to small for his eyes to discern in the diluted darkness beyond.

Thaw leaned over to whisper in the other man’s ear. “Looks like a workshop. Probably where the owner does his DIY?”

“Maybe!” Cummings remarked, shifting his gaze back again to the window. “Or this is the manufacturing site of some kind to a business venture the owners have got going here.”

"Relatively small scale operation if it is," Thaw whispered. Hoisting the jimmy easily as he eyed the window frame to see where he could best find a place to pry it open. "From what I can see it doesn't appear to be anything more than a carpentry shop or a smithy. We can always come back later and check it out. This window will be a piece of cake to open but first I want to snoop around just in case there are easier pickings elsewhere."

"Agreed!" Cummings softly spoke. "We'll go this way." He gestured with his head towards the corner of the workshop. "We'll go right at the corner and see where that takes us. This building will conceal us from the people in the house."

Without saying another word, Cummings moved off, striding over to the corner and then rounding it. Thaw follow closely behind and when he passed the bend he saw the uneven white walls of an adjacent structure come into sight. Recognising the house for what it was, Thaw frowned and stole a glance upwards just above the second story and found the chalk walls were topped with an angled-edged roof of straw thatch. A short narrow alleyway separated both buildings and down this passage the pair went, the only sounds was their breathing and the scuff of the odd boot scraping against the dry, packed earth protected from the recent rain by the overhanging eaves of the workshop roof.

Before long Cummings slowed as he came up to the mouth of the alleyway. On his left, ivy flourished, spreading around the corner of the side wall, growing to almost reach the roof. Beside the ivy was a stoneware drainpipe that shot up to the second floor. Cummings raised his hand above his shoulder to halt. Thaw did as Cummings shrank down into the shadows against the workshop wall and crept forward alone, until he crouched on the threshold of the alley. Still having to strain his eyes to perceive through the thinning gloom, he saw beyond that the passageway opened onto a massive open air courtyard where more structures stood at interval's around the paving, three of which were roughly opposite him. He could just discern they were in differing states of repair from the amount of scaffolding erected around the exterior walls.

Edging further out from the wall, his ears straining for the slightest sound, Cummings quickly glanced about, his keen eyes picking out the outline of a large skip filled with builders rubbish and the drum of a cement mixer among the other smaller objects scattered about the courtyard, but what caught his eye the most were the three country cottages located on his left. They were each two-storied dwellings with white walls and a frontage dominated by a pair of dormer windows partially protruding from a neat, decorative yet functional sculpturesque form of a thatched roof. Another smaller pair of latticed windows flanked the doorway at ground level but ivy in different stages of growth and thickness climbed up the walls here, offering Cummings the only distinction between the buildings.

Not wanting to hang about any more than he had to, Cummings cast a glance back and beckoned Thaw forward. He then went left, smoothly around the curved perimeter of the flagstoned courtyard, stopping at the first of the cottage doors. He pulled down on the handle hard but to his disappointment the door was locked. Then as something occurred to him, Cummings took a step back and knelt down low beside the doormat, only to find when he lifted it up and swept his hand over the floor there was no spare house key underneath. Approaching from behind the hulking figure, Thaw showed a passing interest in his surroundings before he observed something from the edge of his peripheral vision and craned his neck up at the dormer windows above. His eyes wandered and he frowned thoughtfully for each one of the windows were wide open to the chilly night air; their interior latch bars were visible and fastened to the last notch in the bar.

As Thaw strode over, Cummings sighed and stood, glancing around at the courtyard again to check there wasn't any perceptible movement among the stationary outlines in the hope that their footfalls hadn't split the quiet around them.

"No joy, I see," Thaw whispered. The ivy attracted his notice and out of curiosity he sneaked a peek inside one of the windows. A plain net curtain covered the glass but he could still see into the depths of the interior. Beneath a draped-collection of dust sheet's, there was an assortment of bulky shapes, resembling furniture laid out functionally in the middle of the room.

"Naw!" Cummings replied just as softly, turning back, after his gaze had failed to resister any signs of life. "At any rate there's still nobody around to bother us. That's a plus."

"And from here it seems the cottages are pretty much deserted too." Thaw committed cautiously. Basing his assumption on what he was able to see inside the little building, He stepped back and glanced up at the ivy covering the frontage of the properties, his eyes studying the exposed white patches of the wall and the tendrils skirting the smaller latticed windows. "I bet upstairs is the same," he added, these and previous observations running quickly through his mind. "Anyone trying to sleep would find it quite nippy with those windows open wide, all night."

Cummings nodded at his astute observation. "Yeah! Let's try to get into one of the cottages. I'll take the middle, Jerome you go to the next one along. If you find you can't open the door then give it a nudge with your crowbar. That'll do the trick."

Cummings moved off closely followed by Thaw who said. "As much as it would make a nice change for me to go through a door. It's not very practical here, not when the damaged wood will be on full view for all the builders to see in the morning. I intend to keep as low a profile as possible."

"Where then?" Cummings asked softly, just a few steps later. "Up the ivy and through the upstairs window?" He frowned, slowing in front of the second cottage door and tried the handle. He grimaced when he tugged for that too was locked. "I saw you browse over it."

"Perhaps!" Thaw conceded, gliding passed him to pause only briefly while he crouched to tilt over a nearby flower pot and peer underneath, "providing the ivy will support my weight." There was nothing below it except a small broken flagstone. He replaced the pot in disgust to exactly. "It's critical we get indoors. But we can't go off half cocked on this either. Any luck your end?" He set off again.

"Only bad." Cummings declared, turning to walk over to where his associate was going. He watched Thaw arrive at the door, grab the handle and give it a yank but the door obstinately refused to budge one inch. Coming nearer with his long swinging stride, Cummings caught a backward glance from his partner and a shake of the head to confirm what he had already witnessed. "What now?" He enquired, falling in alongside Thaw. "Back to the workshop I suppose?"

"Not yet! You wait here." Thaw instructed after reaching a fast decision. "I'm going to check around the back and see whether I can enter from there. Keep a sharp eye out and give me one of your special calls if you spot anything. We can deal with the patrol together."

A nearby fox from the darkness emitted a yapping bark.

“Check!” Cummings answered. His muscles tightening as he glanced in the direction of the house. “I’ll do a hoot.”

The other nodded.

“Be careful.” Cummings advised, stooping low and pulling his limbs close to his body so he would make a smaller target to view from a distance.

“It goes without saying my friend.” Thaw replied in mid turn. “See you in a bit.”

He scurried off with all possible urgency, his pace quick and stealthy, taking him from sight around the corner of one of the small houses.

* * *

Suddenly there was the unmistakable noise of breaking glass which sounded awfully loud in the quiet dawn. Before the disturbance had faded, a fainter commotion split the air at the back of one of the cottages. Thaw squinted his eyes and jabbed his jimmy again and again at the damaged pane to remove the remaining jagged shards of glass sticking out of the frame so he didn’t cut his arm when he eventually pushed his hand through the opening. Fumbling slightly with the catch before unfastening it, the former burglar then withdrew his arm, and with his fingers around the short steel bar, shoved the business end of the jimmy into a seam at the base of the sash where the window was set against the frame of the sill. Putting strength behind the thrust, the flattened wedge dug deep into the wood, splintering it as he grunted and applied force by leaning on the metal bar, influencing it down until with a audible crack of painted-over wood and a squeak, Thaw prized up the window.

With his adrenaline pumping, he lifted the lower half of the sash as far as it would go, the weight attached to one of the cords inside the cottage slid down towards the darkened floor. The diffused light from outside penetrated a few yards into the interior as Thaw clambered over the window sill, ducking below the drawn blinds, into the room proper, and it was there where he paused momentarily to let his eyes adjust to the gloom before glancing left and right in the attempt to survey his surroundings. There were exposed beams on the ceiling above the kitchen units set in one corner with a number of stools standing below a dinning counter along the other part of the wall adjacent to the appliance area.

Advancing across the cork flooring towards the entrance set within the dividing wall, Thaw noticed the room became slightly gloomier the further he went away from the window but he still had enough light to see the door. He pushed it open wide, to emerge into a lounge littered with an arrangement of furniture mostly covered with dust sheets. As Thaw headed towards the diffused light seeping in through the flowery net curtains covering the windows before him, he took a quick look around in passing at a large inglenook fireplace on his left with a bench set in the alcove, on the other side of the room was a narrow staircase going up to the second floor. Exposed beams spanned the ceiling while an expanse of seagrass carpet fell away behind his strides. Thaw arrived at the front door and unlocked it, throwing the paneled slab wide to reveal his friend who quickly whirled around a hundred and eighty degrees on the balls of his feet and rose in one fluid motion.

"See anything?" Thaw asked anxiously.

"Nothing to suggest we've invited trouble!" Cummings answered calmly. "It appears the coast is clear for now. Either they are asleep or they've got some double-glazing up there at the main house that prevented them from hearing us. You find anyone inside?"

"Not at the moment," Thaw replied with a barely audible whisper, his face flushing with relief at the implications of the news. "Ground floor is empty but I haven't had time to carry out a full interior sweep. It's not as deserted as I first thought," he frowned, "someone's been in recently because there's no dust around on the mantelpiece or on the worktops in the kitchen."

"You want some company?" Cummings enquired, "your buddy-buddy system worked once and after all two can search more quickly than one."

"Nah!" Thaw uttered with a shake of his head. "Go and fetch the others. I still think it's uninhabited for now at least. But if not then I'll take care of any trouble I find upstairs personally with this." He hoisted up the jimmy and then brought the metal bar down to slam gently into the palm of his other hand. "I'll leave this door ajar. Just come on though to the kitchen at the back."

"Gotcha!" Cummings said with a nod, seeing him disappear back inside the cottage, before setting off himself to retrace his steps. Very soon he too had melted into the shadows, his departure marked by his dwindling footfalls.

* * *

Thaw was toweling his face dry in the kitchen, the cold water beginning to clear his head somewhat, when he heard a thud of something heavy repeatedly fall onto the carpet in the next room. Suspecting the disturbance to be his companions entering, but not taking any chances he tensed his muscles and he dropped the towel quietly onto the dining counter. Leaving the coffee maker to simmer, he picked up his jimmy and cautiously make his way over to the door, eased it open a little, and peered inside. The lounge was still draped in gloom but the dim light coming through the windows was enough to reveal the rest of his bedraggled party. With a sigh of relief and a lengthening grin, he pushed the door open and stepped through the gap.

"Is the area secure Jerome?" Cummings whispered. Seeing Thaw approaching and giving him the thumbs up. "Excellent!" He glanced behind him when he heard Bisset enter the cottage puffing and panting as he fought fatigue, clutching more than his fair share of the flight bags. "Put your load down beside the pouches Nathan," he told the older man before turning around to address Thaw. "I thought we'd stash our belongings behind this sofa then take them upstairs and shove them in a cupboard or something so they won't be on show when the builders show up for work."

Bisset collapsed in exhaustion onto the seat of a dust-sheeted armchair.

"We're thinking along similar lines Adrian!" Thaw nodded with approval. "But I've got a better place to store the pouches."

"Where?" Cummings asked with a frown. Gillett and Klugman finally set foot into the lounge, hauling the last of the baggage between them.

"Under the floorboards in the kitchen." Thaw revealed, going towards the front door. "I looked under the carpet and saw it was concrete in here but it's prefect out back, just floorboards. Rip them up then replace them after. Better than a cupboard which could be searched."

Cummings beckoned the last of the party over, his brows contracted in concentrated thought. "True!"

"I'll get the door," Thaw said.

"Sophie! Kyle! Dump the gear here with the rest." Cummings pointed behind the side of the sofa where a large pile of baggage was assembling quite nicely.

"I'm bastard glad this traveling lark is over with for a bit." Gillett declared softly in between labored breaths. Coming to a halt, she threw her load down upon the top of the growing pile. "Talk about a frustrating day, I'm done in and I thought I had plenty of zip when I worked as a holiday rep in Ibiza."

"Well," Bisset gasped, his eyelids feeling heavy as he stared around him. "That's makes two of us Sophie. I've been running on pure adrenaline since the tunnels and I didn't think I'd make it this far. We hiked further than I believed we would after we entered the bog. This place may not be our planned hideaway, at least for now we've got a dry roof over our heads."

Thaw locked the front door and heard a satisfactory click then peered out the windows to see if it was still quiet outside. It was. The only movement he observed was the foliage in the nearby plant pot ruffling in the breeze.

"I've been in a lot worse in my time," Klugman said gruffly, tossing down his pouch. "This will do for me to rest up in until we see what the morning brings."

"Agreed!" Cummings declared, bobbing his head.

"I don't suppose Jerry," Gillett asked, proceeding towards him. "You've had the time to check if this cottage has any plumping? I could kill for a hot shower."

"I'll settle for some paracetamol tablets myself," Klugman said. Glancing at Gillett, with slightly different priorities, careful to bury the aversion he felt for her deep down by keeping his expression neutral. "Something warm to eat wouldn't go amiss either right about now, that's if there are any facilities."

Thaw smiled. "Astonishing enough, Kyle. There is." He said, passing between them and heading towards the rear of the lounge. "I've already got something brewing. Follow me!" He beckoned over his shoulder. "The kitchen's this way. We must be in someone's holiday home because we've got electrically, gas and cabinets stocked with food. Upstairs has even got a water heater. I already flicked it on but it may take about half an hour or so for it to warm up."

"Well I never," Gillett exclaimed in surprise, more than a little curious as regards to what he was boiling. "Things are looking up. First dibs on the warm water." Hurrying after him with Klugman close on her heels, pondering the future repercussions of what the available power supply could mean to them. Bisset grunted and applied the last of his energy as he struggled to heave himself up, out of the chair.

"Here! Nathan." Cummings said, extending an arm, seeing the tiredness and stress on his face. "Let me give you a hand up."

The older man nodded his thanks and took Cummings up on his kind offer. Then together, they crossed over to the kitchen door illuminated feebly underneath the threshold, their nostrils flared at the aromatic wafts of the coffee through the cracks from the other side.

* * *

In the kitchen, Klugman sighed and set about cracking free the cylinder of his Colt Python. "We may have hidden the pouches out of sight but we're still in a right old pickle, Jerome," he proclaimed in exasperation, about to dampen their spirits. He sat on one of the stools beside the counter, turning his revolver upside down and shaking loose the empty shells which clattered and bounced on the counter beside his sugary coffee, the jimmy, and a half eaten Mars bar. "The power's on for a reason and when you add in to the equation the open windows and that someone's been here doing the dusting then we can assume the cottage is going to be occupied very soon." He plucked fresh cartridges from the loops on his bandoleer and thumbed each in turn into the chamber's of the Magnum.

"I'll second that Kyle." Thaw agreed, failing to keep the frustration and despondence out of his voice. He glanced down when slices of crispy, browned bread sprung up from the toaster. "I'm getting a headache just thinking about it." He snatched up one of the slices from the slot before spreading plenty of butter on his toast, "but we can't do anything except wait and see who turns up in a few hours time."

Klugman closed the cylinder with a clink and holstered the Colt Python and then began picking up the spent bullets from the counter, shoving them into his jacket pocket so he wouldn't leave any incriminating evidence behind.

"We're all too knackered to go on Kyle. In our present state we're prone to making mistakes and faulty judgment could still get us all banged up or bring us head on with the Met's SO19 firearms unit." He folded the toast in half and his teeth tore a big bite out of it.

Flames licked around the hob's on the cooker, bestowing a degree of heat to warm them. Illumination was provided by a ceramic table lamp in the corner Thaw had brought down from the biggest bedroom upstairs. Venetian blinds covered the sash window and a pair of tea towels lay like draught excluders across the bottom of the door preventing light from filtering through the gap underneath.

Klugman took a sip of his coffee, the caffeine in his second cup was beginning to slightly ease his tiredness and cultivate the acceleration and clarity of his thoughts while Bisset spoke.

"There's something else we may have to consider guys," he tilted the bottle of pasteurized milk and poured it over the bowl of cereal in front of him. "We might not be able to go anywhere because we could be cut off here."

Seeing where Bisset was going with this, Klugman lowered his mug and addressed him: "You're referring to the flash flood we got caught in?"

Bisset nodded. He pulled the cutlery draw open wide. "None other Kyle. Until learning otherwise, we ought to consider that it may not be an isolated incident." He pulled out a spoon and closed the draw with a clatter. "We traveled through enough torrential rain to burst the banks of the River Wye which if I'm not mistaken passes through Hereford not all that far from here?"

Thaw swallowed. "You ain't wrong. I saw it on the road map before we crashed into the pond."

Bisset spooned some cereal into his mouth while Klugman took another sip of his drink and listened attentively to the rest of what Thaw had to say.

"Whether or not there's a road open we'll know for sure in a little while," he added, a little bit of confidence returning to his tone. "That's pending the arrival of the builders. If they're able to get through then not all of the surrounding lanes are under water. They'll come early to accomplish what they can especially with the night drawing in around four in the afternoon. Adrian will alert us via the walkie-talkie should he see any movement beforehand." He bite off more of his toast.

"Makes sense," Klugman admitted. "Be wise to exchange our look-out with someone fresher before it gets light so Adrian can get a bit of shut eye," he yawned, reacting to his fatigue. "I'm too tired to sleep. I'll just huddle up to my insomnia, to much stress and worry over things I guess, so I could take over the next stint after his, if you want?"

Alarm bells rang in Thaw's head and he forced himself to grin. "Way ahead of you Kyle," Thaw announced, after he'd finished chewing his food. "I was gonna relieve him myself in about an hour's time." He glanced up at the wall clock. "You aren't the only one that's going to have trouble getting some rest with this in our systems." He lowered his eyes and gestured with the coffee cup in his free hand as something occurred which made him have a change of heart, "but since you're volunteering, be my guest." He bit off more toast, and tossed the remaining crust onto the plate, rubbing the grease off his hands with a torn strip of kitchen roll. "It'll give me the time to finish freshening up," he added in-between chews, "and clean up my guns."

"Well, if nothing else I do think we can cheer up a tiny bit because it's not all gloom and doom here for there are a few crumbs of comfort we can take from this situation we find ourselves in," Bisset said, talking thickly around another mouthful of cereal. His bowl emptying quickly as Thaw snatched up his Uzi from another stool and pulled out the cartridge clip to check the load, only to see that the magazine was severely depleted with just the vestiges of a few rounds lying inside.

"Oh it appears Nathan's put on his practical hat Jerome," Klugman announced in a sneering manner. Picking up his Mars bar, he yanked the wrapper down to reveal more of the chocolate inside, "this should be good. Go on then! Like what?"

"Firstly, we have the element of surprise over whoever barges in on us," he answered. His gaze wandering to each of them in turn, trying to hearten his companions and brighten the mood in the room. "Secondly, it's gonna take a detective the caliber of Columbo himself to ferret out any trace of evidence and track us down here with all the country lanes we traveled down I can tell you."

Thaw slammed in a new clip into his Uzi and slotted the almost empty magazine under the spare loop in his bandoleer belt before flipping the selector switch from full automatic to single shot.

"The police can't issue a photofit of any of you for example," Bisset reminded them, "because the witnesses in the village not ducking the bullets wouldn't have recognised you on account of your masks. The same goes for the CCTV cameras that were about. If that doesn't drive the law nuts then to make matters worse their forensic specialists won't discover any fingerprints on the discarded bullet casings since you all wore gloves when you loaded your weapons and as for what other physical clues like hair strands, dandruff or shreds of fibre, we unwittingly left behind," he struggled his shoulders, "will be incinerated to ashes along with the bones, flesh and everything else when the time bombs planted in the barn and the Caravelle explode in several hours time."

Klugman swallowed. "The carrier could go off earlier than this afternoon if the filth find it and turn the harmless looking key I must have forgotten in our apparent haste to get away." He lowered the remainder of his chocolate bar. "Those poor officers," he grinned, speaking with mock sympathy, "what a rotten day they've had, frustrated at every turn by our call box shenanigans, the decoy in the garage, the fake map and the stuff from the barbers we left inside while being under all that pressure to catch us before we do anymore damage. It's enough to make anyone careless and naturally curious to see if they've finally come across the genuine article now isn't it?"

"How much Semtex and C-4 do you reckon you crammed in both places?" Bisset asked, his own inquisitiveness aroused.

"In kilogram's I'm not sure," Klugman replied. "Two hundred pounds is plenty to flatten a building and there's more in there than that. I also managed to put in some accelerants I had lying around. All in all, the blast will leave hardly anything of the victim to fill an ashtray."

"Phew!" Bisset breathed in surprise, "that'll please the Pathologist."

"That's all very well," Thaw countered in opposition, "but we shouldn't be too damn complacent about things either. The police have launched a murder inquiry and it'll be a full blown nationwide man hunt for us once they find the Caravelle. They've found the skid marks and while that's not a significant lead, there's nothing preventing them from matching ballistics on file to find the kind of guns we're carrying. In addition, the rain won't have completely washed away all of our tracks. There'll still be signs for them to follow. It won't be easy but it's not gonna stop the cops from detecting the direction we took or doing a fingertip search for clues. The detective in charge..."

"Sinclair," Bisset cut in.

He nodded, "will take plaster casts of any footprints we left in the woods."

"Let them," Klugman said indifferently, putting his chocolate bar down on the counter, "they'll still have their work cut out for them." He went on in a firm voice, underlined with confidence as he was about to state the pros of the matter. "I read somewhere Jerome that at this stage of the game, all the filth can do is carry out some forensic tests to learn if our guns were used in other crime scenes. Big fucking deal!"

Thaw blinked as Klugman extending out the digits on his one hands and began tapping them one at a time in sequence with the index finger of his other. "They won't get the chance to examine the fire arms residue on our boiler suits because the furnace of the second explosion in the barn will see to that." Klugman went on, striking a second finger lightly as he explained, "they don't know where we obtained the weapons from nor can they prove we killed Jerkins and Rutten until they catch us with these beauties upon us." He patted his holstered Colt Python before returning to count on his fingers, "and as for the tracks, we were bound to leave some deep ones the rain couldn't wipe out completely. There was enough damp vegetation around to drop down on some of them but since we followed each other in single file don't you think we might have smudged most of the tracks anyway? Remember Jerome, we were also carrying the pouches. They acted like ballast, causing us to sink deeper in the mud than we should have, making us appear to pursuers that we weigh more than we really are," he grinned and picked up his coffee cup.

"Hmmm," Thaw uttered hesitatingly. Screwing up his face thoughtfully, he was not altogether convinced of the logic behind some of Klugman's facts yet he was too tired at this late in proceedings to argue the point. "You may have something there Kyle..."

Before he could say anything else, Thaw was interrupted by Cummings' loud voice crackling out of the receiver of the walkie-talkie.

"Cohort! Amber alert," he proclaimed, using a set of signals to get a certain warning across. "I repeat Amber alert!"

Knowing it wasn't of prime importance but urgent nevertheless, Thaw still grabbed the compact radio transmitter from the counter and thrust it to his ear, "I hear you Oracle!" He spoke with concern. "What's up? Over?"

"Your girlfriend's approaching. I thought you'd want to make arrangements for her visit, over."

Footsteps began to echo around the kitchenette in response to prearranged instructions.

"That's a copy," Thaw returned, "out!" He turned to see that Bisset had gone across to the lamp on his right while Klugman was presently kneeling by the entrance and quickly removed the first of the tea towels from under the door when there came a knocking at the door. "Just hold it a second Sophie," he said to her as Klugman rose to his full height again.

"All done!" He nodded, seizing the knob, ready to turn it.

Bisset killed the lamp with a flick of a switch and the kitchen plunged into semi-darkness due to the early hour of the new day. A second later the door was flung open to reveal a willowy figure, drying her hair with a filthy looking towel. Gillett appeared an awful lot cleaner, and now wore a man's dressing gown which was really a size too big for her. The sleeves were rolled up to her forearms. A cord about her waist was tied tightly to keep the sides of the garment together so she didn't expose her leopard print underwired bra and a matching thong briefs underneath.

Klugman stepped back, eyeing her rumpled appearance. Rubbing her hair some more, she entered the kitchen. "God damn it! I feel like a new woman. That was just what the doctor ordered. I got dirt out of places you wouldn't believe and I'm red raw from the scrubbing. All I need now is a nice cup of joe."

I can well imagine Bisset thought to himself with tongue firmly in cheek, his finger hovering above the lamp switch, ready to flick it back on.

"Incidentally," she said, glancing around, "there's plenty of warm water and bubble bath left up there for whoever's next."

"I won the toss so that'll be me." Klugman revealed and preceded to frown, glancing at her as he left the door ajar. "Just out of curiously Sophie, where did you get the robe?"

"In a wardrobe in one of the bedrooms upstairs." She advanced towards the counter and began to wrap the towel around her head in a neat bundle. "I found all manner of interesting stuff up there including this in my pocket here."

"Kyle!" Thaw said.

"I read you," Klugman responded, shutting the door as if he'd read his thoughts beforehand.

"Don't bother with the towel's Kyle," Thaw declared. "We'll risk it for the moment."

Bisset flicked on the lamp and Gillett squinted in the sudden brightness before producing a folded sheet of paper and a small pamphlet from the dressing gown pocket. She handed the items over one at a time to Thaw who took the sheet of paper first and unfolded it. The others crowded around and saw the paper was blank except for a message printed in capital letters and a personal letterhead at the top of the page which Thaw read aloud. "Robert and Ashley Crowe! Wildwood Haven!" He went through the rest of the address then his eyes scanned the message below it in blue ink. "Party starts at seven o'clock on the dot! Remember your costumes and don't be late! The exhibit will be on display within the trophy room until midnight."

"Wildwood Haven!" Thaw repeated, pondering the possible significance behind the name, "I've heard of this estate before somewhere but I just can't put my finger on it." He pursed his lip, disappointed. "Oh well. It'll come eventually."

"Of course it will," Bisset encouraged, stoking his chin thoughtfully, "I observed the Crowes don't go into the specific nature of their get together but it seems it can only be a Halloween party, given tomorrow's," he shook his head briefly, "I mean today's date."

"Yeah, very interesting especially about the exhibit. What's the pamphlet say Jerome? Does it have anything about what the display might be? These kind of people always act genteel and flaunt their belongings to impress their friends and neighbors."

"Er," he paused, "let's see! Hold this Sophie!" He handed the paper to Gillett who took it with one hand while surrendering the colour brochure from the other.

He glanced at the front cover and scanned the title surrounded by a ring of frames above an image of a wrought iron candle stick-holder. "Vulcan Project's!" He said, then flipped through the pages. "That's some sort of old god isn't it?" He saw a number of products the company made inside.

"Just so," Bisset confirmed with a nod, leaning beside Thaw to get a better view of the brochure. "Vulcan was the Roman deity of metal working and fire." A wrought-iron coat stand shaped like a tree took the place of a many branched candle stick-holders which in turn yielded to curtain-poles, a wine bucket, headboards, a dining suite consisting of iron-framed chairs and a table with a glass top, a coat rack and scrolled-tiered, corner shelving units.

"We passed an out-building that must have been their workshop where they made all this junk," Thaw surmised with a nod.

"Indeed," Bisset agreed, "it appears that the Crowes are trying to encourage sales by drumming up some business with pleasure."

"Could be! They also might be after someone famous to endorse what they make," Gillett said blandly. Cocking her head slightly and seeing another page flick over to expose more merchandise, on this occasion for the garden, as she stood at Thaw's elbow. "Either way it doesn't look as if any part of the exhibit is featured here."

"Probably at the back," Klugman spoke his thoughts aloud.

"Yes," Bisset agreed with a nod, "isn't that always the way?"

Sure enough, Thaw turned another couple of pages, an ornate garden gate and a bird-table came and went, and then the group were greeted with the first of two gatefolds at the rear of the pamphlet. He unfolded one immediately and the over-sized page opened to reveal a picture of a treasure trove of artifacts from diverse cultures, laying neatly in line on a long table top: primitive tools like tree axes and farm ploughs, ceramic jars and water vessels of stoneware, diminutive strings of bone and beads, broad-bladed iron swords and axes of differing lengths with bronze scabbards richly adorned with oval-shaped spirals and flowing curves; horse harnesses and trappings.

He then turned the page and the picture continued in close up of an assortment of gold and silver jewellry such as heavy torques, bracelets, anklets, Roman Aureus and denaroius were embedded within pendants, triangular belt buckles, and gold rings ornately checkered here and there with green, blue and red enamel.

Gillett gaped and Klugman's eyes widened covetously at the sight in general and two of the articles in particular. "God almighty," he blurted out in amazement, his eyes falling on emeralds and opals, sapphires and rubies, "its a bleeding kings' ransom. I've never seen anything quite like it, not even when I went on school trips as a kid to the local museum."

"The Crowes are using this discovery as a publicity stunt for their business," Gillett said, "it must be worth a small fortune? A million at least."

"Perhaps!" Thaw said calmly, remembering something he'd seen in his past. "This lot has been unearthed from graves around the scene of an ancient battle ground."

"How can you be so sure?" Bisset asked, his eyebrows knitting as he stifled a yawn.

"I've seen some of this haul on the Internet a couple of months ago," he answered, "that's why Wildwood Haven rang so many bells in my head. You see unusual things always catch my eye and those triangular belt buckles are what brought it all back to me now. Yet that was only part of a small discovery according to the guy who wrote the article, nothing though of this magnitude we see here. Presumably, the buckles were from an Anglo-Saxon freeman: a Thegn. There were also Celtic pieces from the 7th century, a bit of silver and the odd jewel dug out from an archeological excavation in the middle of an old site where a battle was fought around here."

Gillett pondered something for a moment. "If it's anywhere it has to be near the bog. Watery and deep. Perfect place to drop offerings. Celts did that a lot with offerings to the deities they worshipped. Is there any catalogue information on the second gatefold about the exhibit?" She pointed, "a descriptive comment would be nice to confirm the authentically of the metal?."

"Or a price?" Bisset said, piping in for good measure.

"I'll take a look," Thaw replied, having a horrible feeling about where this was going. He caught the edge of the second large page and unfolded it to reveal a scaled illustration of a floor plan depicting the layout of a number of rooms and corridors on the ground floor of the manor house. A red line traced a route from the trophy room via a few passageways to the huge ballroom. "Well if this don't beat it all. No list! But we've got ourselves a map of all things."

"Yeah! Nice of them." Klugman uttered, smiling excitedly as he stared at the uneven course. "Containing directions that'll guide us from the front door, straight to the trophy room and out again."

Thaw narrowed his eyes and exhaled, giving Klugman an irritated look, "and why run the risk of being caught inside the house by the same security guys who are guarding those riches Kyle? Come on! Don't you think matters are complicated enough already without searching for treasure as well... Under normal circumstances I wouldn't hesitate to jump at the chance but we've got our three million from the heist. Let's just leave it at that. If the Crowes are using the artifacts to gain free publicity, there's going be a load of TV crews after this scoop."

"I can see why," Bisset said. "It's quite a distinctive achievement to find such a varied collection at one particular site."

Klugman smiled. "Hah! That remains to be seen with the flooding, as does everything else you've mentioned. Whether you like it or not, I'm gonna cut over there and do a bit of reconnoitering when it gets lighter. The floor plan of the house might give us the exits but we're still in the dark concerning the plan of the grounds. I want to try and find the garages and have a look for another possible hideout in case we have to relocate quickly. We'll have guests to contend with and not every one will be arriving by road."

"Uh!" Gillett uttered the prolonged sound as she collected her thoughts. "You mean by air?"

"None other," replied Klugman. "We're talking about people with class and position to uphold who get a slipped disc just by carrying their wallet around. A house that size could easily boast its own helicopter landing pad somewhere in the darkness, and one thing being in the military has taught me is never dismiss the unexpected wherever you go."

"Jerome! There's sense to what Kyle says," Bisset remarked calmly, "it wouldn't hurt to explore a little."

Thaw pursed his lips and in a split second decision he said: "All right! How are you going to do it though?"

"I don't have all the answers right now," Klugman replied truthfully. "I'll just have to act as the situation demands, hopefully with a minimum of fuss and heroics."

Thaw nodded. "Your a regular Rommel, Kyle! Okay! Get yourself cleaned up then at your first opportunity take a gander inside the airing cupboard and the wardrobes and see what you can come across in there. Any baggage or clothes with pockets search them too."

"Right!" Klugman acknowledged. Throwing open the kitchen door, light spilled into the lounge before his silhouette blocked the brightness as he stepped through the doorway.

"Kyle! You'll find a laundry basket in the bathroom, upstairs." Gillett told him. "That's where I dumped my old clothes but I'm not really sure when the time comes if we should fumigate them or just burn them?"

Thaw clenched his jaw firmly and with authority, spoke. "The latter, Sophie. Absolutely nothing else will do."

CHAPTER FIFTEEN

The ensuring hours brought forth the dawn, the day brightening yet not becoming as light as it should due to the overcast sky. Dim, slanting sunshine broke through gaps in the cloud, creating a mild mist as the warming rays heated up the dew but a cold biting wind accompanied the gloom, dispersing the gray haze while ruffling the overgrown bushes and, cutting into the warmish coats worn by the employees arriving at the Wildwood Haven Estate.

Sleepy-eyed, Danielle Huxley yawned, awakened by the crunching roar of the passing traffic outside. She turned to scoop up her wrist watch from the top of the bedside table and glanced at the white dial. It read: 8:50 am. The noise piquing her curiosity, Danielle pushed her bed covers away before slipping out of bed, shoving her feet into her fluffy green slippers and making her way to the curtained window. Parting the heavy drapes, she poked her head through the gap so her bright red pyjamas wouldn't be seen, and peered down at the access road below where a column of vehicles were slowly proceeding, their tyres agitating the gravel and causing pebbles to shoot out like bullets to hit the nearby brickwork or the occasional first-floor window.

Danielle scowled. "Mental note," she said to herself as she pulled away from the window, not seeing or hearing a section of the wood-paneled wall behind her swing open on quiet counterweights, "next time be cheeky and ask your host for a room that has double-glazing that doesn't overlook the road to the tradesman entrance."

"Ah but if you did," Lois' voice suddenly boomed out of nowhere, causing her friend to almost jump out of her skin from fright, "our rooms wouldn't be linked by this secret passageway. Nice getup by the way," she added, giving the young blonde the once over. "I didn't know you were a Manchester United supporter."

Hand on heart, Danielle span around and saw Lois step out of a yawning gap in the wall. She wore a cream-coloured rhinestone top above a tight pair of jeans. Tennis-shoes encased her feet while her face was more visible this morning because her hair was raked back from her face.

"My god Lois!" She gushed in shock, the comments on her bedclothes not immediately registering in her mind, "your stunt nearly scared me to death."

"What's new," Lois remarked casually, "You're like that anytime girl. You're as calm as a Buddhist on prozac."

Danielle let the comment slide while she stared at her companion steadily, her eyes filled with suspicion as she went on to ask in a reproachful tone, "how long you been there, watching me?"

"Haven't," Lois replied, beginning to massage her temples, "only got here a few seconds ago. Saw you up and about from the peephole up there and thought I'd let myself in," she pointed at the portrait of an Elizabethan sailor hanging above the bed. He had long hair and a greasy beard, and wore clothes that were fashionable for his day.

Danielle's gaze followed the finger to see that in the picture both of the man's painted eyes had been removed and now a pair of gloomy, hole-sockets dominated the rawboned face. "I wouldn't have disturbed you otherwise. You're lucky you slept for so long. I've been up for about forty minutes and wide awake well before that. Those sodding carpenters my aunt talked about last night finally arrived at 7 o'clock and have been extremely busy hammering and sawing next door to me ever since."

"Hmmm! So tell me what's wrong with the door?" Danielle asked. "Couldn't you have used it like anyone else?" She bent to pick up her clothes from the floor where she'd discarded them the night before and tossed them on the bed.

"What," Lois replied incredibly. Her face distorting into a grimace, horrified at the mere mention of it. "And get ourselves press-ganged by Ashley into help arrange the silver service and the after dinner mints, I don't think so. That's the servant's job. They can shove the Chinese lanterns where the sun don't shine. I've got much more pressing matters that demand our attention."

Outside, a distant rumble not from the access road began to build audibly in strength the nearer it came to the house.

"Like what?" Danielle enquired with a frown, beginning to unbutton her top of her red pyjamas. "Look for a proper place to hold the ritual."

Lois smiled: "Actually I think I've already found the right spot. It fits with the criteria of the book. Really nice and quiet and very out of the way. Finish dressing then I'll show you where it is."

* * *

"...Hospital visits are still denied. For more on this story tune in to our next broadcast at ten," the radio presenter announced, audibly shuffling papers on the air. "Now turning to other news. A month of rain fell in just a few short hours last night around Hereford causing many road closures and traffic congestion in the area. Environment Agency spokesman Larry Bowen warned last night that due to the swollen waterway many families will be waking up in flooded homes..."

Having heard enough, Kyle Klugman walked out of the kitchen and used a toothpick to get rid of the bits of food from between his teeth. Suddenly he picked up his pace and dashed across the lounge when he heard the unmistakable deep, rhythmic rumble of a helicopter outside. He skidded to a stop and peered upward through the window to glimpse the big-bellied Sikorsky skim low overhead.

"Shit!" He expressed in annoyance. A deep scowl wrinkled his brow as he urgently raised his voice while glancing back over his shoulder. "Jerome! Turn the radio down. We got trouble. An eggbeater just flew by loaded down with what must be the first of the party guests."

The response was instantaneous. Bisset's jaw tightened and Gillett clinked off the radio. Thaw lowered his watch and strode forward out of the kitchen almost at a gallop, followed more slowly by Gillett and Bisset. "Just gone ten to nine," he loudly remarked, arching a single eyebrow. Seeing Klugman stay low and slowly back away from the window. "Those freeloaders certainly like to get down here early don't they."

"While there's still not many people about, this could be the prefect time for Kyle to practice what he preaches and do a bit of poking around," Bisset said. He went over to stand by the large inglenook fireplace as Thaw dropped into a crouch as he neared the window before looking through the glass.

Gillett fell in close behind him before sitting down on the bench in the alcove.

"Okay by me," Klugman answered, abruptly cracking his knuckles loudly. "I'll go out the kitchen window and make my way round from there."

"Hold that thought Kyle," Cummings warned as he quickly descended the staircase. "I just saw some workmen from the bedroom window coming down the path in this direction. They might know these cottages are empty and wonder what you're doing here."

Bisset butted in. "We could say we're guests."

Gillett's eyes dilated and the littlest amount of sweat broke out on her forehead as she peered out from her position. "Nice try but only if we're wearing clothes from designers like Versace."

"Fantastic," Klugman uttered venomously. "We've finally found out that not all the roads around here are impassable only to have waited too long, and now we're stuck here. Damn it all to hell."

"Not necessarily Kyle," Thaw said, his brain racing as it came up with something. "I've a idea how Nathan ought to be able to get inside the house and as for scouting out the grounds, all we have to do is steal a disguise to blend in and to do that," he turned and locked eyes with his girlfriend, "we use our little temptress to distract one of the crew and lure him in here."

Bisset steeped his fingers together, wondering what Thaw had in mind for him. "It could work Jerome. But remember no witnesses."

"I hear you Nathan," Thaw agreed with a bob of his head.

"To save on any mess," Bisset pronounced. "We could use some of those sheets of newspaper in the bins out back to cover the carpet up then we can dump the lot under the kitchen floor."

"Might as well! Everything else is down there," Klugman said with a shrug. "What's the rest of it?"

Thaw went on to explain his idea. Cummings sucked his hollowed-out tooth. "As plans go I like it! Nathan's part is simple. Why didn't I think of it."

Gillett blinked and smiled. "Humph! Who cares about that, I've got promotion. From lookout to harlot in one day," she mused aloud, standing up and planting her fists on her hips. "My career prospects are looking up."

* * *

"I just don't understand Yates you know Flether." Dawn Blye proclaimed, driving her Audi along the narrow country lane towards Hereford. "We got this great story and he wants us to sit on it for one day while we cover the discoveries of this archeological expedition. Boring. The only relic I like is my tapedeck."

Everett smiled as he studied the road map. "Not my idea of fun either but Marcus did pay for the *Clarion* to have the sole publishing rights for the whole of Lancaster, and he's not going to be put off by having his top photo-journalist go down with Neuralgia."

"Fair enough but why send us on this job?" She asked, reducing speed and changing down to second gear as a swollen ford approached. "Bahrami is doing nothing except writing a piece about invading, garden worms and Marcus thinks that article will be more important to our readers."

"I like to think we're the next best in line," Everett said, seeing the car's front wheels wading into the stream. The water was running fast and crashing against the bodywork. "In reality everyone else is on assignment and we were simply unlucky to be around at the right time and the right place. it's not all bad Dawn."

"Do tell," she said, the car eventually crossing the ford and clambering up the opposite slope. Water trickled from the tyres as the vehicle sped on.

"We're going head to head with the big boys. We'll be able to do plenty of networking and we might even get to take few discreet pictures of the guests and sell them to Now or Hello Magazine."

"I said it before and I'll say it again Flet," Blye observed with a broad grin, "I do like the way your mind works."

The Audi roared round a mini-island and went straight on.

* * *

Hallie Sinclair was pushing her shopping trolley down the frozen food section of the supermarket when her mobile rang. She fished it out of her handbag and glanced as Giddings' name registered in the display. She pressed a button and spoke.

"Hi Bryan," she paused in mid stride and seized a packet of peas from the fridge. Cold surged up her fat arm and she shivered as she shoved the trolley forward, "how are you doing at Sentinel Enterprises?"

"Not much to go on my end Hallie. I've been down here for two hours and so far we'll done dozens of background checks and everyone's come up clean. Did you get the fax from Stacey?"

"Yes this morning at home," Sinclair declared, going down the next aisle. "I can't believe the amount of different human hair his forensic team found in the people carrier. Surely it has to be a mistake or the evidence has been contaminated in some way? If I didn't know better I would swear all that hair is out of a barber's shop."

"That's what I said," Giddings uttered calmly, "but Stacey denied it. According to him the vehicle's been in the impound yard under twenty four hour guard touched only by his forensic team. I put the samples through the DNA national database and we came up with the name and address of one convicted criminal. Warren Byrne but he doesn't fit any matching profile due to being a fifty-three year old pick pocket and shoplifter."

The inspector plucked some tubes of toothpaste and a bar of soap from the shelves. "Send someone down to Byrne's address and see where he was at the time of the robbery," She nodded to a neighbor in passing.

"Will do," Giddings remarked, "Mrs O'Donnel's Caravelle is the one that was stolen Hallie. She came in to identify it earlier on and told us it was hers. She pointed out the loose exhaust pipe and we can confirm that the hand brake light doesn't come on when you apply it."

"Excellent! Anything else?" Sinclair said, dropping toilet rolls into the trolley.

"Mrs O'Donnel has the same insurance company as Sentinel Enterprises. We're already checking out Prestridge, Secombe and Woodgate, and now we're seeing if the same broker has handed both cases."

"Really," the inspector reflected. The news invoked her interest as she walked. "Keep me posted about that and when the sweat evidence has finally been analysed."

"All right. What are you now?"

"Shopping. I'll be in office shortly. Phone me there. Bye."

* * *

"I wouldn't have known there was a concealed door there in a million years," Danielle said, shaking her head as she trailed her friend into the gloomy tunnel, thrusting her right arm into the sleeve of her jacket before it finally went over her shoulder. "How did you find it?"

Lois grinned. "I found it by accident while I was on a visit. I always liked to explore even back then and most often than not get myself into lots of trouble." She came to a halt about a yard inside the passageway and pushed a button on the wall. "I was a real cow. Breaking windows, pinching money out of mom's purse, getting kicked out of school." The door suddenly swung back in. The tunnel darkened around them as the feeble daylight was steadily shut out.

"Stealing cars and vandalism! Nothings changed then," Danielle replied with a wry smile, which began to fade when she glanced about her. The walls and ceiling dissolved into gloom, her high-heels clicking as she walked. "I hope you brought your dad's torch along Lois. I'm not too fond of enclosed places like this. Too many spiders for my liking, falling on my head."

Lois sighed and remarked. "Actually the tunnel fixtures work like when you open a fridge door, only in reverse."

As if her words were a signal of some kind, strip lighting above their heads flickered on first in an alternating sequence, every second one down the length of the tunnel. The lights exuded a mellow white brightness and revealed to Danielle's gaze that they were sandwiched between a pair of metal pipes stretching across the ceiling. Within moments the other strip lighting staggered on to shine unsteadily before gaining strength to eventually equal the intensity in the neighboring fixtures.

"I thought for a moment the lights were on the blink," Danielle admitted.

"Likewise," Lois agreed. "Must be a short in the circuit somewhere. Mind you I'm not really surprised, not with the damp in the walls. We're too near the bog and the wiring has almost got to be as old as this tunnel. This way." Lois turned on her heel and strode down the passageway, Danielle fell in behind her just as one light went bang, a tinkle of glass hit the ground, plunging that small section of the tunnel into blackness.

* * *

"Ridiculous!" Andrew Elmes moaned loudly to himself with a shake of his head. His thumbs tucked behind his braces as he stood by his parked car on the gravelled access road, observing the big-bellied Sikorsky skim across the roof tops of the cottages directly ahead of him. The tips of the trees wavered in the fast-flowing crosswind. "Get over to the helipad indeed. I'm suppose to be on holiday, taking it easy with my feet up, instead I playing chauffeur and baggage handler to a bunch of pissing ingrates."

He blinked and sighed deeply as the helicopter slowed to a hover several feet above a wide X; lights winked from each of the ends, the pilot using a blend of power and the pitch to make the craft carry out the maneuver. Suddenly the force of the wind worsened, slamming into the fuselage and tail boom, causing the Sikorsky to veer sideways to the right. Hearing the frightening screams of his passengers and luggage tumbling about behind the cockpit, the pilot hurriedly pressed down hard on his foot pedals and regulated the craft's direction.

"Keep yourselves strapped in," he shouted, after flicking a switch on his intercom in a bid to alleviate some of the panic he'd heard from the other compartment. "I have everything under control." Little by little, the pilot made a few adjustments to compensate for the strength of the wind until he arrived right on top of the helipad. Satisfied, he then shoved down on the collective pitch stick. The Sikorsky descended with reduced throttle, struggling against the gale as the fuselage became buffeted once more. The backwash from the propellers nudged the peddles to the edge of the gravel road. Inside a few seconds the helicopter's landing skids touched down with a thump.

* * *

Inspector Sinclair stared at the reflection of herself in the mirror and was busy applying colour to her lips with purple lipstick when Sergeant Keane burst forth into the ladies and laughed with relief instead of humour at the sight of her standing there before him.

"Ah guv," he exclaimed in delight, "glad your decent. Uh," he made the prolonged sound while he collected his thoughts.

"You and me both, Keane," Sinclair replied with a sigh. Not batting an eyelid as she slipped the top back onto her lipstick and dropped it into her handbag. "Even in here I can't get a bleeding moment to myself. So to what do I owe this unexpected interruption? Are you here to see me or are you of a different persuasion that I'm unaware of?"

Keane sputtered out a reply. "You guv. There were no female officers available and this message couldn't wait."

"Joke son," Sinclair smiled mischievously. "Report!"

From one of the cubicles behind Sinclair, a toilet flushed and another woman opened the door with one hand while she was pulling down her tight skirt with the other. Her eyes immediately went wide and her face became bright red from embarrassment when she locked eyes with Keane. She quickly withdrew into the cubicle and shut the door.

He swallowed. "Sorry Monica," he shouted sincerely. His gaze swung and he turned more businesslike to address his superior in a lower tone. "A rambler has just reported seeing a Volkswagen Caravelle draped in camouflage netting within a field about fourteen miles from Cuilfield. The field is filled with cattle. One of them must have accidentally disturbed the netting. I've already dispatched several units and they're en route to cordon off the area."

"Good work Justin!" Sinclair said with a nod of approval.

"Guv I was going through old reports this morning and I came across a file detailing information about a black Caravelle that was stolen in Ireland six months ago and never found. I know it's further afield but I do feel it's a lead we should make some enquires about. What do you reckon?"

"Bit of a long shot, still I'll think about it. First get my car ready I'm going along to personally supervise the operation. You're coming along too. And I want Stacey's best forensic team to met us out there."

"On it guv," the sergeant announced, about to turn towards the front door of the ladies when he remembered something. "Oh, Warren Byrne has an alibi for the time of the robbery. He was in the bookies placing a bet. I also finally got in touch with Perratt. Do you want him at the scene as well as the others?"

"Yes!" The inspector answered. "He can come in our car. We'll need his particular talents once we've scoured the surrounding area for clues." She followed Keane out into the corridor.

"I hear guv that Superintendent Lowther is dishing out more of her cherished in-house directives," the sergeant said, "in bright yellow paper so they can't get lost on your desk."

"Yes," Sinclair admitted as she walked alongside him. "Very intelligent of her. I can hardly wait to read them. The last three were don't chew gum, don't smoke and don't wear flip-flops in the office. You know I get more directives than logsheets nowadays. I've never shredded so much paper in my entire life even when I was receiving a load of junk mail through my door." She shook her head, "the next thing I know she'll want me to sing the prisoners to sleep."

Keane smiled as they both pushed open the double doors of the incident room and went inside to the constant noise of raised voices, the tapping of computer keyboards and ringing telephones.

* * *

When the rotors of the Sikorsky finally slowed to a halt, inside seatbelts were removed and the compartment door was thrown open by a rangy man sporting stubble and wearing an overall covered in oil strains.

"Okay everyone out," the mechanic said, seizing the handle of a travel bag knocked loose by the turbulence. "Transport has been provided by the estate," he straightened to peer out the door expecting to see a luxurious, stretch limousine parked outside but instead he saw only a rusty five-door hatchback. Footsteps approached behind him. "Hmmm," he muttered to himself, "cut-backs! The new council tax bill probably come through the post."

Someone behind him cleared his throat and a deep voice, radiating power and strength, uttered. "You gonna stand there all day fellow admiring the view," Oliver Wendell Homes the III said in a Northern America accent, "or are you gonna move to let myself and the others pass, sir."

"Sorry mush," the mechanic said apologetically, sidestepping to give the passengers room to leave. "Watch where you tread, please."

The big American nodded, his black coiffed hair was concealed as he donned his Stetson. His broad chin and jaw were the only features escaping the shade of the brim before he disembarked, ducking his head beneath the blades. He wore a shirt, riding boots, a jacket and high-waisted trousers. "Thanks I won't insult you bub by giving you a tip." Homes then addressed his much younger secretary, "come on darling. Leave the luggage. The porter can bring it up to us later on when we're settled into our rooms. That's what they get paid for."

"Okay," the feminine voice replied, her accent betraying her roots to be further down south in the American state of Georgia. "The files too Mr Homes?"

"Yeah," he shouted back over his shoulder, "those two."

As the burly form of her employer walked towards the car,

Sissy Lynskey wiggled confidently into the opening, oozing with sex appeal. Of medium height, the twenty-two year old had perfectly symmetrical features framed with long blonde hair that tumbled down to the shoulders. The mechanic gulped when his gaze openly wandered to take in her green, low-cut, figure hugging dress, molded around her narrow waist, curvy breasts and wide hips.

Lynskey caught his appreciative gaze in passing, arching her elegant eyebrows and smiling, "only in your best dreams Mack, and only then if you were a millionaire ten-times over like my dear sugar daddy there." Her hazel eyes sparkled while she gave him the once over. "Never forget it."

The mechanic blinked. His cheeks reddening, his mouth stood agape in shock at being spoken too in such a manner. He scowled but held his temper in check, knowing that jobs like this didn't grow on trees. With that, her smile broadened, she pulled her shoulders back and shoved her boobs out as she ambled down the steps after her rugged employer, her hips again began juggling from side to side, dancing sensually to music only she could hear. More passengers got off the helicopter including a tall woman with the longest legs and the shortest mini-skirt the mechanic had ever seen. The pilot came out from the cockpit and opened a bottle of coke, before he could take a sip, a dumpy woman in her mid-forties marched over to him and complained bitterly.

"I want you to know pilot that we have never been on a worst flight in our entire lives." She raised her voice as she became slightly distracted by the noise of the builders carried in their direction by the wind. "The ride over here was bumpy," she resumed, "and your customer care is non-existent. I thought we might have gotten a Danish and an Espresso but we were even denied that. We are VIPs young man, and we didn't wish to be transported by airfreight like chickens and pigs." A wiry Asian woman came to stand behind her, dressed immaculately in a trouser suit as the other passengers gathered around the car. "My employer, Miss Kapoor, is a Bollywood actress, a movie star no less, and she is not accustomed to having bags almost fall on her head."

The pilot sighed and replied: "In my defense Miss..." he awaited for the dumpy woman to disclose her name before continuing.

Her left eye twitched. "Mrs Snodgress," the woman said with an steel edge. Drawing herself up to her full height of five foot one, her neck tilting up as she stared at him.

"You haven't caught us at our best."

"I'm sure I have," Snodgress replied bitterly.

His eyes opened wider. "I can't do anything about the weather," he replied smoothly, "and most of our cabin staff are away from work with colds, maternity leave or had to take the last of their floating holidays before they lose them due to new company policy starting next month. Ben is my mechanic and is the only person available to carry out the duties inside. It was that or no flight today. I hope you understand?"

"Be that as it may," Mrs Snodgress answered, "your company shall still be receiving a letter of complaint from my employer's solicitor Silk and Silk in the not to distant future. Good day to you. Come Miss Kapoor, Your business with this individual is at an end."

* * *

The tunnel turned to the left at about twenty paces. Lois rounded the corner and set off towards another sharp bend ahead. Danielle swept after her friend, noticing that the walls of the passageway were always changing from sections of powdery brickwork to stud-partitioned walls nailed with laths. Occasionally lengths of forked wiring snaked out of holes.

"You know Danielle," Lois said, her voice increasing in volume over their footfalls echoing off the wooden floor which stretched away beneath them. "If only these tunnels could talk, the stories they could tell."

"Oh yeah," she replied with a frown, passing a severely corroded water pipe and sheets of plasterboard leaning against the wall. "Like what?"

"Well many years ago," Lois explained evenly, "the son of a rich shipowner built the manor and had these secret passageways incorporated into the design so he could not only illegally import goods like tea, tobacco, gold and lace from various coastal regions but he also used them to keep an eye on his beautiful yet very unfaithful wife who, according to uncle Rob, had a passion for a bit of rough stuff like the son of the head-gardener and a number of the stable hands."

Danielle grinned as her companion disappeared behind the second corner. "Fashions and architecture may change over the years Lois but good old human nature never will." Danielle rounded the bend and saw the floor and ceiling slant down to become a ramp as the tunnel extended to eventually end several yards ahead at a T-junction. Both of the pipes above their heads curved to the left. "Did your uncle ever find any of that smuggled gold in here?"

"Not yet," Lois conceded, passing another ventilation grille embedded in the wall. "The nearest thing is what the archaeologists have found in their excavations. Saying that you can never tell what will turn up because Rob employs a part time maintenance crew to keep up the property. They use these tunnels to keep out of sight of the guests so they're able to change bulbs, keep an eye on fuse boxes, sprinklers, the security systems and replace any defective old cables the rats have been chewing like that one," she pointed at the levelling floor where a length of wiring stuck up from a gap in the floorboards, teeth marks adorned the cable in places. "The crew are also reconstructing places in the walls so there'll be more concealed doors for easy access should there be need for another fire escape route."

Lois reached the T-junction and turned right into a narrower tunnel, fire extinguishers at intervals along the wall glinted in the lights mellow glare. A stool stood against the wall directly below one more peephole.

"Ah," Danielle expressed in recognition. "That explains the plasterboard."

"Yep!" Lois declared smoothly, the passageway widening slightly before her. "It's a maze in here but soon there'll be signs painted everywhere pointing the way out to the grounds, except of course in this direction."

Lois then came to a halt where a section of bare English bond brickwork showed on her left, she reached up to the sixth layer extending down from the ceiling and pushed a short-sided header above a crumpling stretcher. A barely audible clink echoed inside the tunnel and before the sound had completely died away altogether thin cracks became visible in the wall. Little by little they broadened, close bricks parted, the notches began to resemble vertical crenellated battlements. After a few moments, illumination from the ceiling lights spilled into the widening gap, driving the blackness sufficiently back to reveal another wall in which was embedded a rounded opening the size of a man-hole cover. Something wide and rounded projected from the opening and when Danielle had taken a couple of steps forward to satisfy her curiosity, she discovered that the object was the rim of a ceramic trough that descended into darkness. Deep wrinkle-like cracks from the passage decorated the grimy, terracotta in a zigzag pattern.

"Huh," Danielle blinked, "a chute! Don't tell me... we're going down that aren't we?"

Lois nodded. "Sure are!" She moved up to the rim of the chute, scrambled up to sit on the trough.

"Where does it lead?" Danielle asked. Her brow furrowing as she tugged at her left ear thoughtfully.

"You'll see," Lois looked back over her shoulder, "once I've gone, follow me down quickly okay? This wall works on a kind of timer mechanism and it will close back-up again in a little bit."

"Understood!" She replied, watching Lois let go of the brickwork. She slid out of sight with a whoosh and the sound of her passage echoed and receded in a matter of heartbeats. The blonde had only began to step up to the hole when she heard an audible click and the sections of the wall on either of her, begun to shudder then creep slowly sideways back towards each other. "Ah sugar," she exclaimed with a sigh, "that's faster than I would have liked. Look out below."

With that Danielle threw her arms over her head, contracted her leg muscles and leaped, plunging head first down the hole. She landed hard on the chute, squashing her breasts as she commenced her descent. More echoes resounded in her dwindling wake while pieces of mortar continued to peel from the walls which proceeded to edge across the face of the darkening hole until the bricks interlocked and slammed together perfectly, like dove-tail joints.

* * *

"Hello! My name is Andrew." he said. "Welcome all of you to Wildwood Haven."

"Hey, what is this felleh?" Homes asked with a frown. Taking no notice of the greeting as he stared at the hatchback, his secretary wiggling to a halt beside him. "The transport that's been laid on for us? Well back where I come from, I've seen bath tubs bigger than this pile of junk and that's no lie."

Sissy Lynskey glanced back at the gathering crowd of guests and then at the seating space inside the car.

"Yeah!" Andrew answered, catching the disbelief in the

undertone of his voice as he held one of the rear passenger doors open for the people to enter. "A combination of unforeseen events," he spoke on, with the speech he'd rehearsed with his sister, "has caused the estate to accumulate a backlog of miscellaneous duties that still need to be addressed."

"And I thought you Brits were prepared for wet weather," Homes said with a shake of his head. He took off his hat and stepped inside, sliding along the back seat until he came to the other door.

"Mr Crowe is apologetic," Andrew went on, "but states he's sure you don't mind roughing it for the few hundred yards to the house."

"I hope your not going to cram us in like sardines in a can," Lynskey uttered, slipping through the doorway and eventually sitting next to her boss. "I like my elbow room."

"I know that I got the bruises in my ribs to prove it," Homes remarked quietly to her ears alone. Lynskey giggled and put her hand on his knee.

"No," Andrew said. A gorgeous redhead nodded and folded herself almost in half to fill the last seat. "I shall be making two journeys." He slammed the door shut to the groans of the men in dark suits and the dumpy woman who had just approached behind them. "One more in front." He opened the other car door. A man in his late-twenties with a feminine-looking face, unbuttoned his suit jacket and then climbed aboard. "Okay that's it."

Andrew closed the door. "If you could just wait here," he spoke on, his gaze wandering from face to face of those left gathered. "I'll be back for you and your bags shortly."

"As if we had a choice," Snodgress grumbled loudly as she glared at Andrew's back.

CHAPTER SIXTEEN

Andrew threw the gear stick in reverse and gently touched the accelerator as he carried out the second stage of the three point turn across the narrow gravel road, the rear bumper inching close to the bark of a tree.

"Noisy around here isn't it," Biljana Isaaces said, with a trout pout, winding the window up to keep out the sound of a crosscut saw and the stone cutting machine, the car curved backwards as the driver started spinning the steering wheel to the right. "I find it quite distracting."

"I live near railway tracks," Connor Hannon butted in from the front seat, "and my friends say exactly the same thing when they visit me. Yet I rarely notice it myself."

Biljana Isaaces was twenty-three years old and had earned a large fortune as a catwalk supermodel for the last eight years by not picking and choosing what she did. Her face had been on wrappings advertising products ranging from computers to baby food and as yet she hadn't the effect, like so many in her profession, of her being overexposed in the public eye. She was quite aware that popularity was a fickle thing, and she was determined to milk it for everything she could. A record contract was on the cards, so was a film role. All she had to do to sign on the dotted line was to remain the favor of the month.

Isaaces was a ravishing belle who could turn heads up to a mile away and knew it. Delicate black brows hung above a pair of deep, mahogany-hued eyes framed with drooping lashes. Her nose was straight, her jaw narrow and her chin was small. Long, wavy, russet coloured hair seemed to take on the appearance of spun gold in the slanting sunlight as it tumbled down to a slender neck and a lithe figure. Jewellry decorated lean muscular arms and the ankles of her long, firm legs. Isaaces wore a skin tight leather mini skirt and a blue blouse. Mules covered her almost perfect feet.

"Driver," Isaaces asked, "what are the builders working on?"

"They renovating an old stable block," he replied, shoving his gear stick into first. "The cottages you flew over have been blocking out some of the din but the wind must be directing it this way." The hatchback trundled slowly forward, the cottages standing out against the manor house in the background..

"So we're not stopping there then bub?" Homes asked, "because there was some concern there might not be enough rooms to go around and we may have to share. That's why we got here nice and earlier just in case."

Bushes and more trees appeared spreading into a dense wood that stretched to the left. Evergreens towered over the other trees, abruptly blocking out the view of the rest of the ancient manor.

"I didn't hear nothing about that," Isaaces said with a frown, "I'm glad I came when I did now. The food at my hotel was awful and the service was a real joke."

"I don't mind sharing with you Wendell," Lynskey said with another giggle, her long-nailed hand slipping down his leg towards his crotch, "I mean Mr Homes." She corrected the slip of the tongue, her hand feeling a sudden stirring down there to her delight.

"I can assure you that all your rooms are in the main house." Andrew revealed, "but with all the torrential rain causing mayhem on the roads and the railways, I don't believe we'll have much of a problem with sharing quarters even if we do get an influx of late arrivals by this evening."

Andrew drove on and the passengers observed the trees thin out as the road widened into a large parking lot filled with a diverse array of vehicles including delivery vans, catering trucks, minibuses that could carry between five and ten passengers, a refrigerated truck supplying fresh fruit, vegetables, meat and fish to the party, a skip carrier, pickups emblazoned with contractor's names and a six-wheeled lorry with a trailer hauling timber. A four-car garage dominated the lines of parked vehicles. It sheltered two motorcycles, a red mini cooper and a sleek looking sports car. There was an empty space inside the garage which was usually occupied by Crowe's missing Mercedes Benz. The corner of the manor overlooked the parking area while another graveled path wound from the garage to join a driveway leading to the road outside of the estate.

Hannon stared at the mansion and blinked. "You know, this is a snug looking home the Crowes got here, in a kind of Addams Family sort of way."

"You ain't kidding bub," Homes remarked as the hatchback pulled up behind a garbage truck. The driver and his burly work colleague were standing in front of the refreshments wagon, eating turkey burgers while hot coffee streamed from styrofoam cups on the counter top. "Their architect must have been fascinated by Transylvania."

"Must be a hell of a place to heat in the winter time," Isaaces said, peering at the row of grotesquely carved stone gargoyles projecting from the gutter of the building.

"This is as far as I can drive you ladies and gentle men," Andrew announced, applying the hand brake and turning off the ignition. "If you would like to follow me," he threw open his door, "I take you inside and then leave you in the capable hands of Anderson."

Homes leaned over to his secretary and said: "Typical! We got lumbered with a buck-passer."

* * *

"I'd like to do this while we're still young," Klugman uttered impatiently, staring out through the cottage window at the hive of activity outside.

Directly opposite from where the other single-storey buildings were being renovated, he watched workmen wearing hard-hats and coveralls in the scaffolding, busy mixing cement, clambering up ladders carrying hods loaded down with bricks, hammering and sawing, plastering walls and using power tools.

"Me too," Thaw conceded, standing alongside him. "I don't want to stay here any longer than I have too either but we need an opportunity to get one of them over here without his colleagues spotting us do it."

Wearing jeans and an anorak, pacing across the lounge between the furnishings, the sheets of newspaper crackling and rustling under her feet, her hands clasped behind her back, Gillett's head tilted and her face suddenly sported an acute smirk. "You'll get it Jerry," she said, whirling around to face them as the pair briefly looked back at her slightly in puzzlement. "There's sure to be a break in a bit. After all, you Brits just adore that cat-piss you lovingly call tea."

Klugman nodded noncommittally and returned his gaze to the window. Thaw smiled and did the same.

* * *

Danielle slid down the chute, in the feeble light the echoes of her screams and the scuff of her heels reverberated loudly as her soles occasionally scraped the surface of the trough. Before long she glimpsed a pair of small swing doors which were still slightly quivering from Lois' passage. These she easily pushed aside, sliding on through to the other side, the hinges of the doors squeaked in loud protest. The slide abruptly vanished beneath her and Danielle found herself falling for a second in empty air before she landed with a soft thump not on cushions but inside a lidless, wicker-basket, about the side of a luggage trunk, on top of a batch of crumpled-up clothes, towels and household linens ready for washing.

"Ooh!" She uttered with a sharp intake of breath as the wheels at the base of the laundry basket begun to roll forward from the result of her momentum. "What the hell," Danielle declared in astonishment, her heart pounding. She pushed herself up on all fours before she heard a rustle of cloth and glanced up over the rim of the wickerwork to see Lois suddenly loom over her and shoved her hands out to stop the basket from traveling any further across the hard-packed, earthen floor.

"Enjoy your trip," Lois asked with a grin. Letting go of the basket she ran her hands over her dusty clothing and smoothed out the creases. Her knee rested against the basket so it wouldn't wobble again under her friend's shifting weight.

"Terrific!" Danielle replied. Making a face and sniffing as her nose began to detect the subtle whiff of damp and beeswax. She leaned back and with careful examination, tugged the heels of her shoes one at a time to see that they were still secure before testing them more by putting her whole weight upon them. "So where are we? Coal cellar?"

"Might have been used for one once but now," Lois said with a gesture, "It reverted to an chapel. Mind you I can't see why anyone would want to meditate or pray down here. It's horrible." Danielle got to her feet and climbed out of the basket and blinked as she regarded Lois for a moment before slowly letting her gaze survey the room they were in. The odors around her started to slowly become more potent as she took in the number of cone-shaped candles casting light across the scattered remains of objects resting in a disordered heap. The underground room was about the size of a badminton court with walls of crumbling bricks in the pattern of Flemish Bond. Black woolly mold formed where the damp was at its worst and a couple of snails had left wet shiny, silver trails across the darker sections of the brickwork. Cobwebs stretched across corners and between one of the walls and a rickety table.

Withered weeds sprouted up here and there about the floor choked with rubble from a stained glass window, broken wood once belonging to several pews and an ornamental brass font was almost hidden beneath a coat of green verdigris. Dusty objects littered the long altar stone along one wall. The tongues of flame flickered causing reflections to dance against the walls. Directly ahead of the pair, at the end of the room, was a simple but very narrow flight of stairs with no handrail leading up to a trapdoor set in the planks above.

"Ewwww," Danielle uttered with a grimace at the sight. "Look at the state of it. I know you've been busy setting up everything but you can't be serious about this being a proper site to hold the ritual?" She met Lois' gaze evenly. "It's too cluttered. Where are we going to put all this junk by tonight where it won't be found? In the basket you nicked from the laundry."

Lois rolled her eyes up in exasperation and sighed. "Hardly. This isn't the place I was talking about earlier." Lois replied. "It's the library above us."

"Oh thank goodness for that," Danielle returned. "I bet you thought about it?"

"Course I did, for about a second," Lois admitted, "this is still probably consecrated land though, and I didn't think the spell would work in here even on All Hallows Eve, but up there," she pointed to the trapdoor, "I believe it will. Come on! I've already made a start on the proceedings."

* * *

"You left your lady shave in the bathroom Sophie," Bisset remarked as he came down the staircase. "It was still sharp from doing your legs so I used it on my stubble." His yellow nicotined-fingers stoked his smooth chin. Smoke curled from a cigarette dangling limply from the corner of his mouth, his suit remained caked with mud. "Hope you don't mind? I needed a clean cut image to carry off my performance. I didn't bring my own shaver along with me since we weren't exactly planning on spending the night away from the hotel."

"Sure but it wasn't my legs I was shaving," Gillett said.

"What!" Bisset blurted out indignantly. "You mean..."

"This could be it," Cummings called down from the bedroom.

"Shut up the pair of you," Klugman shouted at Bisset and Gillett in a bass growl, his tone like iron as he gaze shifted back to stare out of the window once more. "Something's happening outside."

The others immediately crowded around him. Through the glass, leaves drifted between the clouds of wood dust to settle on the paving as the shrill note of the foreman's whistle blew loudly. In a low, ambled crouch, Thaw went over to the front door and opened it partially to hear what was being said.

"Down tools!" The foreman ordered, in a voice that was slightly nasal. Gripping his whistle in one hand while he made a slicing motion under his throat with the other as he surveyed his surroundings. One by one he saw the machines be switched off by the workers, drills and hammers put down, goggles were removed with sighs of relief and face masks were lowered from mouths. "Tea break lads!" He spoke on in a quieter tone, breathing in the frosty air. "Take twenty. The refreshment van is parked by the garages. This way."

With that he spun on his heels and ushered his workforce at a good sharp angle towards the right of the house.

"Okay," Thaw said, watching a few of the work force jam their hands into their coverall pockets. "This is it Sophie! Time to win your Oscar. Everyone else get to your positions."

Gillett nodded. "I'm on it." She rushed towards the front door as her companions ran for cover. Klugman dived behind the front of the settee, Cummings' knees cracked as he descended half way down the tight staircase, out of sight from any window, flexing his hands as he did. Thaw and Bisset proceeded quickly into the kitchen and pushed the door slowly until it was slightly ajar. Gillett looked about the lounge once to make certain the coast was clear then pulled the door wider and saw a couple of stragglers talking behind the rest of the receding workers as they left the paving to walk across the lawn.

"Excuse me," Gillett shouted with a wave only to get no response from the men. "Oh crap! They can't have heard me." She remarked to anyone in earshot. "I'm going out to get them. Stand ready."

With a shiver from a mixture of the cold and fear, Gillett advanced outside, moving alone after the men with long, sweeping strides. Ahead, trees began sprouting into view and the paving gave way to an untidy carpet of grass. The young American quickened her pace and heard the roaring sound of a petrol engine as she closed the gap between herself and the two stragglers. When she reached the lawn and entered into the midst of a number of gardeners loping off tree branches, pruning shrubs, plucking weeds and mowing the grass.

Gillett weaved between the obstructions, hearing snatches of conversation from a pair of gardeners as she passed. "...Wrong time of year I told him," she informed her colleague in a Somerset accent, "said the lawn should have been cut back in September when it stopped growing but he just wouldn't listen to me."

The other lopped off a twig to get the desired length and shape of the swan's wing. "Oh yeah," he muttered acknowledging the point.

"Now our lord and master wants topiary designs of..."

Gillett dodged past one of the hand-propelled lawn mowers and in a huff, finally caught up to the workmen.

"Excuse me guys," Gillett uttered with an expulsion of breath as the pair came to a halt and spun around to see what she wanted. The remainder of the crew headed off through the thickening clump of trees. "I do apologize for disturbing you especially on your tea break but I need some help." She blinked. "I'm a guest of the Crowes, and there's no power on in my cottage. I can't get anyone to answer the phone so I was wondering do you think one of you could perhaps help me out?" She smiled, "see what's wrong. I'm not very technological minded like you gentleman. I'll be ever so obliged and I'll make it worth your while."

The men exchanged glances. The leaner of the two addressed his swarthy companion. "I don't know about you Spencer," he said, taking his hard hat off and raking his hand through his crewcut, "but I could never resist a charming lady."

Spencer gave an expressive shrug of his shoulders as he pulled his gloves from his belt and began slipping them back on. "Fine with me Bruce," he replied evenly, "as long as it's clear that we get time and a half for this little bit of overtime?"

"Er," Bruce expressed his hesitation briefly, replacing his hard hat onto his tousled hair before following suit with his gloves.

"I'll see to it that you both get your just deserts," the woman said with an agreeable smile and a nod.

"Well then," Spencer answered, slapping his massive hands and rubbing them together, "now your talking miss. Let's go and see what the problem is."

* * *

Four minutes later Gillett arrived back at the cottage. "Here we are," she said, raising her voice slightly to alert the others of her presence. She pushed the door inward and stepped inside. "Home sweet home. I think the trouble's in the kitchen. This way guys," she beckoned them both to follow, "do you fancy a beer while you work, I've got some cans in the fridge."

Spencer nodded. "I never refuse anything that's going love," he replied, stomping across the lounge first without wiping his feet. He looked carefully about him as he walked along the slender line of newspaper.

"Not yet anyway," Bruce said. He closed the door behind him then went after his friend, keeping to the muddy set of tracks leading off ahead. Cummings tensed and exhaled quietly when he watched the workmen pass the staircase.

"Think nothing of it," Gillett remarked easily before addressing those inside the kitchen. "Honey! I found us some help."

The kitchen door swing open and Thaw strode in, with his right hand slightly concealed behind his hip. "Brilliant," he responded as his girlfriend sidestepped to the left to reveal the two men steadily approaching him. "it's just a shame that we don't need your services, only your clothes."

Genuine puzzlement crossed Spencer's face as he paused in mid-stride. "I don't understand?"

Thaw brought his hand out of concealment and levelled his UZI with the black silencer at the face of the swarthy workman who blinked as the shooter triggered several rounds. Words died in the man's throat as bullets stitched across Spencer's countenance, his features disintegrating into scarlet ruin. He was flung backwards, dead before he hit the ground. With his eyes wide from shock, Bruce took an involuntary step back, turned and was about to make a dash for the front door when Klugman appeared like a ghost in front of him.

"Your not going anywhere fellow," Klugman said with a broad grin, holding his sidearm by the barrel. He immediately delivered a short, swinging blow to the lower half of the workman's face, the pistol's grip smashing a couple of his teeth right out. Blood poured from his mouth as Bruce's head whipped up, his legs staggering back.

Behind the fray Cummings reached the bottom of the staircase and drawing his knife, advanced up to the retreating workman. Klugman went forward and suddenly whirled around, lashing out, the heel of his boot driving into the man's face. Bruce grunted in pain as his nose broke. Saliva and blood spewed out smearing the leather and the laces.

"Come on you fruit," Klugman sneered with a sigh at the reeling man. "Can't you bleeding well put up more of a fight than this."

Bruce totted back in agony, unable to speak as he continued to swallow blood from his bitten tongue. He collided into the barrel chest of Cummings.

"Mind if I cut in," Cummings said, reaching over the workman's shoulders. Grabbing his jaw with one hand while with the other he placed the sharp edge of his knife blade directly under Bruce's throat.

Horrified, Klugman shouted as Bruce tried to struggle free from the iron grip, tentacles of blood flowing down his face and onto the shoulder of his coveralls. "Hold it Adrian this one's mine."

"Not any more." Cummings replied, his voice hardening. He tilted the man's jaw up before he jerked his arm and slit Bruce's throat. "Don't fucking play around. Just get the job done." Cummings released the workman, and the body dropped like a sack to the carpet. A crimson pool began spreading around the workman's head, staining the newspaper underneath.

"Hah! Every rule has an exception," Klugman smiled, "I was trying to see if I still had what it takes. Lighten up a bit! There are times for business and this wasn't one of them. With my training I could've taken both of those illegitimate donkeys out with one hand tied behind me back. And I don't need any help especially from you farm boy."

Thaw saw Cummings face go red and his fingers curl into fists as he glared at Klugman. "I ain't afraid of you half-pint."

"You're probably too stupid that's why."

"Enough. We need each other Kyle. Every time you show your potential, you're damned ego gets in the way. Adrian's right! Don't made rash mistakes. It could cost all of us dearly. You're a team player now, act the part for the duration."

"Yes mother," Klugman said, his grin broadening. "I'll

remember next time."

"Sophie lock the front door," Thaw ordered, ignoring the comment. Shoving his UZI into his belt and kneeling beside Spencer's twitching carcass. "Then check the window to see that there's no one around."

"Gotcha," she nodded, weaving around the bodies as she proceeded over to the door.

"Nathan," Thaw said, flicking a glance at the older man. "Give me a hand in dragging this bastard out of sight." He hauled the torso of the body up with a grunt as Bisset went over to the other side and seized the legs. "He must weight a ton."

"Yeah," Bisset snorted. His face becoming bright red as he lifted up his share of the burden and began following Thaw slowly back into the kitchen. "I'm finding that out for myself."

"All clear outside," Gillett exhaled, peering through the window.

Behind her, Cummings knelt and picked up Bruce's body easily in a firemans lift. "I got this sorted Klugman. What won't be so easy are the coveralls. I've seen less blood on the clothes my dad wore working in a slaughter house up north." He straightened. "I suppose we could try scrubbing out the stains with soap or detergent."

"Ain't bothering," Klugman said, sitting back on his heels to pick up the nearest sheet of newspaper and crumble it up into a ball. "Simply wait until the stain's dry then just turn the coverall's inside-out and I'll wear them like that."

"How you can be so relaxed Kyle," Gillett said, putting her three cents into the conversation. Stooping low while Cummings set off towards the kitchen doorway. "Having so much blood near you." She wrung her hands in anguish and misery as she pulled a face and then gripped a corner of the crimson spotted editorial page. "I'm going to have a hard time as it is just washing my hands after this because I don't think I'll ever be able to get them clean enough again."

"Get used to it Sophie," Klugman responded, locking eyes with her. There wasn't an ounce of compassion within his voice as he squeezed the business page he'd just grabbed off the carpet, into an equally tiny ball. "You'll see more blood spilled before we're get away from here and that's a fact. Just put it out of your mind, I always do. After a few hundred, you'll adapt."

"Oh great," She stated unhappily, "that something to look forward too."

CHAPTER SEVENTEEN

Lois heaved up the trapdoor and holding onto the hinged slab with one hand so it wouldn't fall with a heavy thump, hearing the Oriental rug slide off the sloping surface, she clambered up the last few steps to emerge into the library proper and then quickly moved aside to let her companion pass. Danielle followed, taking the steps two at a time and when she came out of the hole she examined her surroundings with a glance. A fireplace and a solid oak door stood in front of her while shelves groaning under the weight of large quantities of books stretched from floor to ceiling, taking up two of the walls of the library, the fourth held a number of aquariums and terrariums. In some of the receptacles tropical fish swam over filter-boxes and between aquatic plants whose leaves they nipped at. Fluorescent lights and incandescent lamps brightened the tank walls revealing other creatures like reptiles and amphibians in the midst of rocks, sand, air pumps and heaters.

In a corner was a desk topped with a laptop, a scanner and a printer. Not far from that were chairs scattered about two tables, a globe of the world, a narrow ladder, arching at the top, leaned against one wall and a red carpet covered the floor.

"Hey Lois I would hate to see the electric bills for that lot," Danielle said, pointing a finger towards the collection of tanks. "Must keep your uncle's accountants busy."

"More than likely," Lois replied with a smile, "he can afford it." She knelt and lowered the trapdoor into place. "Well this is it – what do you think?"

Danielle looked down at a slightly smudged, blue, circle-encased, five-star pentagram upon the opposite side of the trapdoor. "You couldn't have picked a worst place Lois. For starters the fish need to be fed daily, people with this many books in the house are likely to want to read them or just show them off. This is the prefect place to hold a private meeting – which is sure to happen with all the dignitaries about today."

"Possible," Lois said, straightening and going over to the nearest shelf. She grabbed a dictionary and retraced her steps back to the pentagram, "but Rob gave us the run of the library when he heard we had to finish revising for our end of term exams. He made this room off limits to everyone working or staying here, just so long as we feed his creatures and we don't spent too many hours on the Internet."

Danielle frowned at the mention of exams because she didn't know anything about them, then her eyes lit up in sudden recognition. "Crafty!" she said with a slow nod, "so what are we suppose to be doing?"

"RSA Word Processing Stage 3," Lois remarked, flipping up the front cover to reveal the interior of the book was damaged. A hollow rectangular space had been cut out in the center of all the pages. Danielle peered inside and saw a sprig of wormwood and a pill box she knew contained the powdery toadstool. "It'll be the day when we pass Text 2."

The blonde blinked. "You're not doing what I think your doing are you?" She gulped as she heard someone in the corridor outside, pushing a rattling tea cart, "summoning Bartok right now?"

"Why not" Lois said, taking the items from the hole before dropping the dictionary to the floor. "Good a time as any. We're not going to be disturbed while the guests are arriving and the staff are attending to their needs. We can get a head start on the others by finding out what are his terms for the gifts."

"But I thought you weren't going to do the calling until this afternoon when you'd arranged the crystals and the candles in their proper setting." Danielle sputtered. Watching the spring of wormwood snap in half before her friend tossed the pieces onto the pentacle. "What about the spell of protection?"

"I'm impatient," Lois said. Twisting the lid of the pill box and leaning over to sprinkle the powdery toadstool across the chalk lines. "Anyway I found a passage in another chapter of *The Grimorie* stating we could conjure up Bartok here for five minutes on the same day and still be safe while it's inside the pentacle."

Placing the lid back on the box Lois slipped the item into the pocket of her jeans. "Remember he can't use any power directly against the living while trapped," she went on, "nor is he able to take back the gifts after they've been bestowed to us." Danielle nodded thoughtfully. "Now take a seat girl, this is where things start getting really exciting."

Recalling sacred words she'd memorised by heart from a dead language, Lois began uttering the incantation: "Kauala, Sigori, Balpera, Djehuanic, Zorth."

Danielle took a step back from the pentacle as the chalk lines suddenly sparkled like sunlit water. Glowing with pride Lois continued speaking as a narrow beam of soft, white light shot up from the center of the marked figure and extended until it reached the ceiling.

"Claabu, Warada, Xokti," Lois proclaimed loudly. Then to Danielle's startled gasp, dark dense fog flowed and rolled from the column, spreading upwards and expanding across the trapdoor, the visibility of the glittering lines faded, steadily losing distinction and colour, rapidly disappearing altogether as the billowing gray cloud enveloped the whole of the enclosed area. "Vanti, Talprim, Ferourthy!" She added, finishing the spell with emphasis upon the last three words.

An instant later, phosphorescent spots the hue of silver manifested themselves and immediately widened, their touch dispelling the fog which continued to stir as it broke up and moved in different directions, revealing a roughly hewn figure, a six foot six naked vision of a sculpted torso and what could easily have been gym obsessed biceps. Legs as thick as tree trunks appeared next, followed by massive shoulders topped by a square-featured face more rugged than attractive in appearance. Long, thick green hair stretched down his muscular back.

Lois' gaze wandered down to his crotch and her eyes widened in appreciation at the sight. "My word! You're a handsome lad," she grinned, reluctantly looking up to his beefy face.

Speechless, Danielle thought at first that she was imagining things but then she heard the vision speak in a voice that was full, deep and mellow.

"Who calls great Bartok away from the uncharted realm?" The giant bellowed. Focusing his attention on the two women before striding across the pentagram towards them, the pieces of wormwood crunched under his bare feet. Danielle drew back and cowered from fear while Lois' grin remained intact as she stood her ground, seeing the huge being suddenly halt as he crashed against an invisible energy field emitting from the chalked circle.

Bartok was shoved back a step by the powerful force, the revolting smell of his singed hair filled the companions nostrils almost making them choke as the colossal figure grimaced and screamed from the pain lancing through every muscle of his being. The girls coughed and through watery eyes, Lois approached the trapdoor while Danielle straightened.

“It is I, Lois Elmes and my friend Danielle Huxley who summon you to this place Bartok.” She said, wiping her right eye with the heel of her hand. “We request a boon from you. What are your terms for bestowing the four elements.”

The demon blinked and didn’t answer straight away as he looked around the library, seeing the books, the aquariums and the light bulb above his head. “I need slaves Mistress,” he said finally, lowering his gaze to met Lois’ eyes squarely, whirling his left index finger anti-clock wise behind his back, “to ease my confinement on the plains of fire.”

Unbeknown to the girls, vaporous tentacles began to glide from Bartok’s fingertips and swiftly extend outwards to flow through the walls and doors of the manor house.

“The more captives you deliver to me,” he spoke on, his perceptions registering sensor readings from the gaseous, mapping steam as it swept outside, across the lawns to the trees beyond. “The more control over the elements will be yours to command.”

Then he detected something in the bog, a site of slaughter followed by another and another stretching out and blending together throughout the ages. The extensive and brutal killing of thousands of warriors, the butchering of animals popped into his mind accompanied by other images of how the battles had played to their conclusion. “Do we have an agreement?” He added, “speak now or lose your chance forever.” Bartok smiled evilly as he determined its direction and distance, promptly navigating a route from the site back to the house.

“We have an agreement,” Lois replied quickly. “There will be a house full of people by tonight. You will be able to take your pick from them.”

Bartok smile broadened. “Your words are the contract Mistress, and that is exactly the payment I expect three hours before the witching hour. You have tied yourselves to me therefore I shall now undertake what you ask.” He gestured with one hand, and a blue beam shot from his palm, through the energy barrier and hit Lois directly in the chest. She felt something akin to a tickling sensation as she become enveloped in an aura which floated about her figure for another second as a prelude to sinking into her skin. Next, Bartok moved the beam across and aimed it at Danielle. It altered to a brown colour and again a nimbus covered her from head to toe. Danielle felt a cold sensation run down her back before the feeling along with the beam faded when the demon clapped his hands loudly together.

"There! As a show of good faith I have granted a fourth of the gift to both of you," he stated evenly. "You have a different power to master. They will gain in strength the more you use them. By the end of the gathering you will receive the remaining abilities." A stiffness slowly began to creep along his body as his feet and ankles dissolved from view. "My time is up. I am being summoned back to my realm. Invoke the scared words when everything is in place Mistress and know this by heart," his knees and hips vanished, "I have a very long reach if crossed." Danielle swallowed.

"Failure to do so will be dangerous to your health." He laughed, loud and wicked, a harsh, screeching which sounded like fingernails being scratched down a blackboard. His torso and his neck followed before his head glowed dim and indistinct eventually disappearing into thin air.

"You said he couldn't touch us Lois," Danielle said. Biting her lip, her hands still shaking from the ordeal as she knelt to pick up the dictionary.

"*The Grimorie* says he can't while he's in the pentacle," Lois replied calmly, going over to where the rug was. "Come on! Where he is, he can't even threaten us by text." She picked the rug up and kneeling, replaced it over the trapdoor. "Bartok is just playing mind games with us. Nothing more. He can't take our powers away either, only if we consent to it and I'm not doing that now am I?"

"What about the slaves he wanted," Danielle enquired, raising to her full height. "Just to be on the safe side, should you get your family out of here before the ceremony gets going?"

There was a abrupt knock on the library door.

"No!" Lois said, with a shake of her head. "I hate all of them. They can take their chances like everyone else. Come in!"

The door swung inward and Anderson came marching through, bold as brass. Danielle gave him the once over as he neared them. Geof Anderson was in his late sixties with a receding white hairline, a curved aquiline nose, pale blue eyes; the whites of which were yellowy with red veins; eyelashes, eyebrows and sideburns which were a light gray. His wrinkled skin was covered here and there with liver spots. A thick mustache grew on his upper lip. There was a redness to his hollow cheeks and his earlobes. A dark suit covered his slender frame and a bow tie wrapped around his turkey neck. He came to a halt a couple of steps from the companions and adopted a supercilious expression when he noticed the library's tables were empty of paperwork.

"Hard at work I see Miss Lois," the butler glanced down at her, his pinched mouth stern.

"Not so loud Anderson," Lois said, "you're disturbing the Fung Shui of the place."

The butler saw her smirk. He arched an eyebrow and continued: "Your uncle's been told that all trains are running behind schedule by an hour or two at the very least. According to the weather hotline six inches of rain fell in less than an hour last night causing chaos on roads and the railways. Engineers are apparently clearing flood water from a tunnel several stations down the line."

"I don't suppose there's any chance that the helicopter I saw earlier could pick up our guests?" Danielle asked, having an idea what the answer would be.

"No Miss Danielle," Anderson said, peering straight at her. "There's to much of a waiting list for seats and this company has only a few choppers flying anyway, the rest are grounded due to staff illness. The wind is another factor. The pilot said it's quite strong at the moment and he won't be able take off until it dies down a bit. And that could be minutes or hours."

"Okay," Lois said with a nod, unperturbed by the news, "thanks for the info."

The butler bowed politely then whirled about and left, closing the door behind him.

"No surprise there," Danielle said with a frown, flexing her fingers and feeling nothing amiss. "What's surprising is I don't feel any different considering we've got powers, do you?"

"No!" Lois replied, also staring at her hands. "However we've got them. Bartok always delivers."

"Damn he didn't say which powers he gave us," Danielle shook her head. "Or how to invoke them."

"The book says we just have to concentrate on an element. It will happen or it won't." Lois remarked calmly. "Let's go outside and experiment well away from prying eyes. First of all though I need to get my matches, an old jam jar from the kitchen and a glass of water.

* * *

Bartok reappeared on a dais of obsidian and he breathed in the ash and brimstone from the fire plains just beyond. Acid rain lashed down fiercely from the pitch black of day as he briefly stared out over his domain, a scene he'd witnessed a thousand times in the past but hoped he wouldn't have to see for too much more longer. A sea of flames stretched for miles across the barren waste, the orange tongues hissing in the rain and flickering around the base of various sized, rock intrusions from only a few centimeters across to many metres, sticking up like tabular shaped islands.

On the horizon volcanoes scattered individually and in small groups erupted in different ways. Pyroclastic material broke free from a cone-shaped mountain and fell back down to the ground. Lava seeped from fissures and ran down the side of one volcano, absorbing everything in its path. Crimson light above the volcanoes smeared a rich deep red across the dark sky.

"Damodar," Bartok bellowed, descending a step. His green hair began shrinking as two protuberances on his forehead burst through his skin at an alarming rate. Hard, bony horns grew upward and twisted to the side like a rams. Then the external top of both ears swelled to a point and the stubble on his elongating chin lengthened to a mature beard. "Where are you worm? Answer your master."

Bartok went down two more steps, and as he did his skin faded to be replaced by scales, breasts domed outwards, his mouth widened as more teeth grew, his eyes filled with blood, fingers and toes thickened until there were only three and long claws burst free from the tips. A heavy tail appeared from behind as his legs became stronger and stouter in appearance. When the demon reached the bottom of the dais, a short ghoulish figure with a humped back and five arms emerged from behind a column of a black geyser that gushed intermittently.

"You called Master," Damodar said. His necklace of bells jangled as he threw himself at the demon's feet.

"The veil has thinned between the realms. We've been summoned. Gather the legions," Bartok intoned, staring at his trembling vassal, "and bring me the alter stone. Tonight we leave this damnable dimension forever via a river of blood."

"At once Master," Damodar replied with a toothy grin. He jumped to his feet and hurried off through spreading flames to do his bidding.

Bartok nodded and folded his massive arms, peering at another distant volcano erupting rocks a hundred feet into the air. "The fools," he spoke to himself with a broadening smile, "they don't know what they're about to unleash." He then felt a tug of the vapor tentacles connecting him to the other realm. "Awaken fallen ones. Awaken I say." He shouted. His grin widening further as his summons received a slow but steady response. "Good! Now wait there my loyal army, wait until the time is right to reclaim what you lost once again."

* * *

"Right then!" Ashley Crowe declared at the employees and workmen crowding around her. "Jill, Meryl, Annette I want the glitter balls, the rubber spiders and bats plus the rest of the jack-o'-lanterns used to decorate the ballroom."

The three maids nodded and left, passing through the gap between the open French doors. A barber, a photographer loaded down with all her equipment and a carpenter surged forward next.

Directing her gaze from one to another in turn, Ashley issued orders first to the barber over the sawing of wood. "You'll find my husband upstairs second door on the left. Cut his hair and give him a shave. Don't let him give you no for an answer."

"Certainly madam," the tall man said with a grin before whirling about and shoving through the decreasing throng.

"You!" She spoke on to the thickset woman with the cameras, her face dominated by big eyes and a wide mouth, "can go straight to the trophy room and set up your equipment there. Just follow the route in the colour brochure. You can't miss it."

"Okay," she said, disappearing like the others.

"And what it is this time Mister Berkoff?" Ashley inquired. The last two people moved in on either side of him.

"Just want you to double check these measurements Mrs Crowe," the carpenter revealed with a grin, proffering her a clipboard holding a sheet of paper, "so my mate and I can finish off your decking."

She looked at the dimensions and after a moment. "When would that be exactly?"

"An hour and half tops."

"These are fine. Carry on." She handed the board back to Berkoff who took it and swiftly departed. Progressing forward for Ashley's attention came the Estates head chef.

“Mrs Crowe,” the lean cook announced, rubbing his hands on his apron, “the caterers haven’t brought us enough appetizers and the ice sculpture has arrived but we got ourselves a tiger instead of a swam as you wanted.”

Ashley signed: “Ian! Make up the short fall from what you have in the pantries. Give them a salad and some pickled vegetables, anything will do. Are we well stocked for our guests sweet teeth?”

“Yes madam. Your husband’s toffee apples have arrived too. The kitchen will have the meals prepared by seven.”

“Everything seems to be running smoothly. As for the sculpture we’ll kept it but remind both firms that I’ll want a discount for the poor service if they want me to recommend them for any of my friend’s forthcoming shindigs.”

He smiled. “I’ll convey your answer to them.”

Ashley subsequently turned her gaze towards the window cleaner, wishing for a very large Tom and Jerry, and muttering under her breath that the place was a bloody mad house.

“Joel! Nice of you to finally come,” she said, frowning, “you should have been here two days ago. What was it? The job center giving you grief.”

“Not at all! I’m a respectable business man. I just had my ladder and all my tools nicked. I had a lock on my garage door but someone unscrewed the hinges and got in that way. It put me back a bit.” Joel explained, “so I had to borrow my mate’s stuff and I had other clients to see ahead of you. But no worries we’re here now. Where do you want us to start?”

“The back windows,” she informed him directly, “we’re having a fireworks display here and I want everything to be perfect for the proceedings. Understand?”

“Say no more,” the window cleaner uttered. “We’ll get right to it.” He went to get his bucket and ladder from his van. For one moment Ashley swore she could almost hear his cowboy spurs clinking into the distance.

While there was a brief lull Ashley glanced at the lawn being mowed beyond the patio and saw a number of gazebos were springing up like mushrooms. The workmen were erecting steel frames capable of accommodating a hundred people, stretching water resistant canopies over the poles, and securing ropes to ground hooks they had only hammered in minutes before. Gardeners continued to trim bushes, scythe-away at the longer grass and pluck weeds in the mild sunshine while the builders sauntered back to work, holding cups of coffee and chatting among themselves.

Approaching from behind, a delivery driver asked, "Are you the lady in charge because I got a shipment of table top heaters I need signing for."

Ashley faced him and as she did, she failed to notice two workmen walking towards the house wearing hard hats and coveralls, one towered over the other, the legs of his trousers were a little short, the hem of his turn ups had risen to about half way up his calves. The boots of the second man looked as if their owner had put his feet into buckets of paint because the leather and laces were strained and had dried a maroon colour. Behind the pair, a lean, hatched-face man emerged from the same cottage doorway and holding a pen and note book, followed in the footsteps of the workmen, stopping occasionally to write down a hodgepodge of things that caught his passing eye. The door of the cottage slid shut as a face appeared a mere inch from the window. Thaw stayed there briefly before he faded into the depths of the interior when the builders re-entered the courtyard to resume work.

Ashley seized the invoice and pen from the driver prior to signing. "What about the bigger patio heaters I ordered? And the garden torches, when do I get those?" She asked in mid scrawl.

"In about an hour," the driver announced. Taking the proffered items and slipping them into his overall pocket. "The propane gas cylinders are on the same truck. So where do you want me to put this load?"

Klugman and Cummings veered away towards the garages but Bisset kept on going heading for the house.

"Beside the wall for the time being," she replied. Gesturing at a place beside the French doors as she caught sight of a slender man clutching a note book, drawing nearer. "I'll leave that in your capable hands while I deal with something else." Ashley turned and glanced at the individual's suit caked with dry mud. "And you are?" She asked wearily, meeting his gaze squarely. The delivery driver stomped off.

"Nathan Bisset!" He replied producing his identity badge to show her before pocketing it again. "I'm an insurance agent – representative of Prestridge, Secombe and Woodgate. My agency offers to lower premiums better than any other firm can. Are you Mrs Crowe?"

"Yeah to my misfortune," she answered with a nod, "but I don't believe we need insurance right now. I'm only trying to deal with one crisis at a time."

"Oh well I have an 11.00 o'clock appointment," Bisset declared, giving her an easy smile and a bigger white lie. "Either that or someone is playing a prank on both of us."

"I don't doubt it," she replied, thinking of one young woman in particular who could be behind this, "I haven't seen the appointment in my husband's diary but that doesn't mean Rob didn't call you in one of his less sober moments." Bisset blinked and arched his eyebrows. "He's a very busy man so I'll have to do. What happened to your suit by the way?"

"My hire car broke down coming up here from London. Then I tripped over and fell in some mud when I was waiting for the tow truck. Some how I made it here on time."

"You've come all that way?" Ashley declared. "Your prices must be low if my husband is enquiring for insurance so far a field when we have a few nearby firms. Why don't you come this way and we'll discuss it over a cup of tea."

"Okay," he nodded. He followed her as she led him into the house. Bisset glanced this way and that at the furnishings in the living room. Pictures adorned the walls while arm chairs and tables cluttered the carpeted floor. A big screen television dominated one corner of the room with a video recorder and a CD player.

"So tell me Mr Bisset," she started to say before being interrupted.

"Nathan please," he said.

"Nathan!" She corrected calmly. "What do we have to do to acquire these lower premiums?"

"Before we commit any coverage my firm would like me to inspect and test your security system, check the fuse boxes, see what type of fire and burglar alarms you have. How many guards are protecting the jewellry, blueprints, window locks. Things like that really."

"Uh-huh," Ashley uttered, heading out into a wide corridor. Staff walked by, carrying suitcases, tea trays and snacks on plates for the guests. "Some of that information is confidential."

"I understand Mrs Crowe," Bisset announced smoothly, falling in step beside her. "Surely though I can't see any harm in you showing me your prime generator, heating systems, pipes. Just to let me get a feel of the place you know?"

"Er...No I can't see that request hurting us," she replied after a second or two of thought. "All right Nathan. I'll give you a brief tour later but first we going to the kitchen. There's a drink in there with my name on it."

* * *

"This week will see the completion of your work in the field Mick," Professor Keniry said to his goat-faced student. He was sweeping the soil away from the exposing hock joint with an artist's brush, small fragments of bone flaked away beneath the thick bristles. "You couldn't have gained your experience at a better fossil site than this." His knees ached as he slowly got to his feet; the student stood behind him, holding an expensive camera. "The best find Britain's had in years. It'll set you up for when you acquire your PH.D. He moved away before adding. "Can you tell me what this fossil is?"

"From the joint Professor, this is another horse skeleton," Mick Fulford replied, crouching and raising the view-finder to his eye.

"Excellent as always my boy," Keniry said with a nod. His stringy, greasy, gray ponytail jerked with the motion when the camera flashed. The sturdy, twenty-five year old walked around to gain another perspective. "I want a shot taken from every angle then we'll chisel out these bones and the other horse and rider from the matrix."

Keniry turned to address another member of his archaeology team who was on her knees scraping bits of rock from a human arm bone with her fingers and a small pointed instrument. "Ginger! Get me some glue for the cracks and a length of burlap so I can wrap up the exposed end of this bone when I'm ready."

"On it," The woman replied, setting off briskly towards a group of tents and a caravan at the rear of the site.

"Have you got your thesis worked out yet Mick?" Keniry inquired. Glancing around the dig, observing in the background wooden packing crates, scattered tools, the holes where the other four members of his staff were busy, cataloguing artifacts, brushing or applying a coating of shellac or hot paraffin to various bones to carefully preserve them.

Behind them, rock cracked as skeletal fingers wrapped around the hilt of a rusty short-sword and a skull turned its empty eye sockets in the direction of the talking pair. Teeth clenching together.

"Not quite Professor but it's coming along," Fulford uttered, snapping a third photograph. "Just got a bit more laboratory work to do then I can start looking around for a job in a university or something," He sighed, "a holiday first though. I'm tired. The work has really done me in."

"Off course! I remember it like it was yesterday. Well don't get over doing it now you hear," Keniry remarked. Looking at the student squarely, the older man's beard was messy like an overgrown bush. "All work and no play is not good for anybody lad. You get yourself down to that party tonight at the Estate and have some fun with Ginger and the rest. I certainly am anyway. It'll be my last chance to view the entire treasure before the collection is broken up and they're shipped off to half a dozen museums around the world."

The skeleton relaxed its grip upon the hilt of the weapon and quickly returned to its original position.

"Oh I'm going to the party Professor," Fulford grinned, lowering his camera. "I heard there was a super model and a film star attending the press conference so if I can I'm gonna try and get their phone numbers."

"Yeah!" Keniry mirrored the expression, eyeing him dubiously. "And I've got more chance of seeing clod-dancing pigs flying overhead at any minute."

* * *

The tractor rumbled slowly along the country lane, the quiet disturbed by the constant blare of the car horn behind it. Hedges and flood ditches lined the narrow road. Inside the Rover 75, Hallie Sinclair sighed as she flipped over the page of the file and looked up at the rear view mirror reflecting the driver's face.

"Keane," she said with a frown,"the way we're going Stacey's forensic team will be at the site long before us. Use the siren on him and the loud hailer if you must."

"Right guv," the sergeant said before addressing the officer next to him: "Put it up Cheney."

Cheney slid his window down, reached out and stuck the portable, domed-siren onto the roof of the car then plugged the end of the trailing wire into the cigarette lighter. Keane threw a switch on the dashboard. The siren wailed loudly and a blue light flashed as

Cheney picked up the microphone and prepared to speak into it. The farmer immediately glanced over his shoulder. "We've got his attention," he added, turning the siren off,. "go to it."

"This is a police emergency," Chency announced with a slight stammer, depressing the button on the mike, "when room emerges, please move aside." He replaced the microphone as the farmer gestured with his hand to indicate his response.

The narrow lane wound around a bend, the hedges continued yet the flood ditches yielded to grass verges on both side of the car. Keane followed the road and didn't bother changing down.

"According to this report Cheney," Sinclair declared, turning another page of the document, "there were no traces of radiation emitting from the explosion on the motorway just a barely perceptible amount of C-4 but despite that and the other blast sites we still can't rule out this being the work of terrorists."

"No sir," the officer said with another involuntary pause, pulling down his sun visor, "we are currently assembling evidence and questioning eye-witnesses. It's early days. If you go to page eighteen you'll find what the civil engineers have to say."

"Express it in a few words," Sinclair asked, not really wanting to wade through the pages of the document.

"Okay," Cheney stated, "there's that much damage the engineer couldn't put a firm date on when the motorway will open again."

Sitting next to the inspector, Kris Perratt withdrew a small box from his coat pocket and took off the lid. "How about casualties," he asked calmly and without emotion. Squeezing a small amount of scented snuff between his thumb and finger before rubbing it on his teeth and gums, "the condensed version if you please office."

"Many hundreds are dead," Cheney revealed. His anger was aroused by the incident, but he didn't let anything show on his pale, sharp-featured face, "including lots of children and the elderly. Dental records and personal pieces that somehow survived the flames are the only means we have at present to identify some of them."

Ahead the lane curved to the right and the tractor driver saw the road widen as he rounded the bend. Thick, tall hedgerows stretched onward. He reduced speed and edged over to the grass verge. Keane swung out and passed the vehicle. Perratt took another pinch of snuff and on this occasion sniffed it. An instant later he dropped the box in shock and Keane slammed on his brakes as the road shuddered under the effects of the tremors two miles away. Flames erupted from the distant horizon.

The windows of a nearby farmhouse were blown out and part of the roof was ripped off in the blast. The owners ran from their home.

"Fuck!" Cheney blurted out. "What was that? It felt like a plane crash."

Sinclair shook her head. "That's no Jet. It's got to be the Caravelle. They must have booby-trapped it. I knew they were behind this somehow. It's just too much of a coincidence otherwise. Keane get us there now. God this is gonna be messy."

"And so it begins," Perratt said cryptically.

* * *

"Well we finally found a secluded place to try our experiments," Danielle announced staring around the glade. A damp looking, broken tree house was built within the branches of one of the oaks while overgrown bushes and tall grasses encroached over the ground, "not an easy thing with all the builders and gardeners about."

"It is when you grew up around here," Lois replied, placing the glass of water and the jar filled with earth among the grass, "I'll go first."

Taking a deep breath Lois focused upon the glass of water, with all her energy and enthusiasm, willing it with her mind to do something, bubble or ripple, anything just to show she had a small measure of control over the substance. Nothing happened. Unperturbed Lois concentrated next on the dirt in the jar. Again though after a minute of frowning she found she didn't make it act in the way that she wanted it too.

"Two down. Two to go for me," Lois announced more for her own comfort than anyone else. "Your turn."

Danielle nodded, fixed her attention on the water and immediately felt an undetermined thing inside of her push with force at the liquid. Tiny bubbles formed in the center of the glass, like the water was simmering just below boiling point then it began to stir violently, sloping over the sides of the glass.

"You're doing it," her friend said with widening eyes. "Make it do something else."

“I’ll try,” Danielle answered. Perspiration unexpectedly appeared on her hands and face. “What the hell...I am beginning to perspire but the weather is too cold for that.”

“It’s not that Danielle.” Lois said with genuine excitement in her voice, seeing the larger picture as she produced a box of matches from her pocket. “It’s your powers. They’re manifesting themselves in ways I didn’t think they would.” She watched as the beads of perspiration joined together then flowed off Danielle’s face down her arms to her hands.

“This is crazy. I’m sensing I should aim at that tree over there,” Danielle said, pointing both of her hands at a cluster of elms on her right. A column of water speared from her fingers as if it were coming from a hose, striking the tree a third of the way up. The bark cracked and disintegrated under the impact, the wood turned soft and pulpy. Unbidden, water from the glass shot up into the air, curved and joined the column as it made the tree tremble, the force of the blast pushing the trunk steadily back, tearing up a root.

“Enough!” Danielle shouted to herself. The water decreased in strength and lowered from the target in a receding arch, inching down the bark to the ground, the column retreating, slowly abating until the flow dribbled to a halt from her fingertips. “I’m getting a vague idea that I can do more than this.”

“Wouldn’t surprise me,” Lois replied, striking a match and seeing the flame flicker into life. Danielle rubbed her hands dry on the legs of her trousers as she observed Lois direct her gaze towards the fire but all it did was blacken the match as it crept down the stick. All of a sudden the blaze sputtered when a yellow sphere came into sight and wrapped itself around her right hand, cutting off the flow of oxygen. The flame died and smoke blackened the inside of the globe.

“Looks like I’ve got the power of air,” she experienced a strange sensation surge over her entire body before she began to slowly lift a foot into the air. “Wow! I’m weightless,” Lois said, floating up a little higher. The sphere popped like a bubble. “This is intoxicating, so alien to me. It’s like I’m high without the effects of drugs and glue.” She was enjoying herself so much with this new ability that she didn’t realise she was continuing to climb unchecked easily surpassing her friend’s height.

Danielle glanced up at her. “Talking about high. Don’t you think you ought to get down before someone sees you and wonders how you’re doing a Peter Pan impersonation without the wires.”

"Aw too true," Lois said with a nod. "Descend. Not the ability I would have liked off Bartok," she lowered and alighted on the glass, "but it'll do for our purpose tonight. Come on! I fancy some breakfast after that."

Danielle peered at her watch. "It'll be more like brunch now."

"Whatever," Lois said, walking out of the glade with Danielle in pursuit. "I could eat a horse but probably end up murdering a lettuce leaf. I wish I had your fast metabolism."

Danielle smiled. "Yeah it's great. I eat what I want and never diet."

Lois groaned, "don't I know it."

CHAPTER EIGHTEEN

A fleet of ambulances, squad cars and fire engines from different communities rushed along the county lanes to the scene where the column of dense smoke still spiralled over the bomb site. From their safe vantage point in a field at the cordon line some distance away, inspector Hallie Sinclair, Keane and Kris Perratt in the midst of other police officers watched the line of pumps and other trucks as the big, destructive fire grew worse, igniting what remained of the hedges lining the narrow road. Fire fighters, wearing breathing apparatus and carrying hoses, carefully advanced towards the conflagration, directing water at the fragments of burning debris which had been thrown and scattered over hundreds of yards; and at the huge mass of flames whisking across the ground fuelled by acceleratants and dry vegetation. Rolling smoke obscured the full scale of the devastation.

* * *

"Thanks Cheney," Sinclair said. Taking the proffered binoculars off the officer to view the activity, watching a team of firefighters train their lengths of hose and shoot hundreds of litres of water on to the blaze. "Looks like those firemen have got their work cut out for them." She lowered the glasses and handed them over to Perratt, "I hate to think of all that evidence going up in smoke while we wait here and do nothing until the fire's extinguished."

Perratt blinked, his nose wrinkling as he smelled the strong odor of gas and scanned the scene. Sinclair studied Perratt's square pleasant face beneath a short, darkened mane flecked with silver. He was in his late forties with an average build and broad shoulders. He smelt of chalk and wore a pocket protector on the jacket of his brown suit. Perratt didn't look like anything special and the detective inspector would have sworn he wasn't as threatening as he appeared, but she noticed that when he moved he carried himself well and his eyes were icy and sharp with intelligence. His reputation was shrouded in mystery and that excited her curiosity.

Perratt's mouth tightened as he let his gaze roam to the woods behind the fires as he made a tactical judgment. "It is a shame but there's nothing stopping me from searching outside the cordon line to see if I can find any car tracks. I doubt I'll discover any though because my best educated guess would be that the raiders walked through the forest and in all probability picked up a vehicle on the opposite side."

Sinclair nodded, his words mirroring her own thoughts.

"The whole place could catch fire from a spark. You don't want to be in there when that happens?" Keane said with a shake of his head.

Perratt grinned at the younger man's concern. "I've been in the Special Air Service for twenty years son. I've been trained to cope and adapt in every theater of war and if the wind does blow the fire my way then I've got skills to see me through."

"I wouldn't mind coming along to see you in action granting that you don't object to the company?" Cheney asked evenly. "I'll be surprised if you spot any tracks after all the rain we had here yesterday."

"Glad to have you aboard," Perratt said, folding his arms. "As for the weather it doesn't cover everything. If I've a mind I could find mouse shit in a field of raisins. Just stay behind me when I'm tracking and keep that cake hole of yours shut when I tell you too."

The inspector cleared her throat and regarded both of them seriously. "Harumphed. I can't sanction this mission guys. Kris you're a civilian and I can't order you in either Cheney so you'll be on your own in the woods understood? If you're caught I have to deny responsibility for all of your movements. Privately I think you're both doing the right thing. When you've found anything let me know at once."

"Heard it all before Sinclair off people with a lot less balls than you," Perratt replied with a grin. "I'll find your fugitives trail even if they've swing from tree to tree." Looking unconcerned, he addressed the lower ranked officer, "come on Cheney, let's go. Hope you bought some marshmallows along mate because I'm fresh out."

* * *

In the center of the action Fire Chief Owen Rydal was issuing orders to his personal. "Kulkami, Sweeney get the Elevating platforms up and rotated then man the monitor nozzles and douse those hedges. Radio me when either of you can see through the haze and tell me what we're facing." The firemen departed as Rydal turned his attention elsewhere to address his fire officers. "Marshall, Lynch! Front and center."

The man and woman hastened to the Chief's side as they felt the heat of the flames.

"Yes sir," Lynch said, staring into his rugged brown eyes and permanent frown, her respirator mask muffling her voice.

"Take some of the crews and go to the fire's borders. I want all possible fuel removed or moistened to minimize the fire spreading so we can isolate it. Cut branches off trees and if you run out of water apply extinguishing agents or shovel good old fashion sand and dirt on any burning vegetation. And do it as fast as you're able to. The wind could rise at any time and we don't want it fanning the flames."

Behind the Fire Chief the booms of the Elevating platforms extended. "Consider it done sir," Marshall said with a nod before his short, powerful bulldog body turned and disappeared into the darkness to fetch tools and equipment with Lynch in tow.

Another firefighter came dashing forward. "Sir! Some of the blaze is made up from flammable liquids. Petrol, oil whatever it is, it's floating and spreading when we use water on the fire."

"Class A and B, must be my lucky day. Okay Dalton. Break out the Foam extinguishers. Assuming we can't put the flames out then we'll smother the bugger instead."

Just then the flames in front of Rydal surged out and engulfed one of the firefighters on the hoses. In seconds she was a human torch but her quick-thinking colleagues smothered her with blankets to put out the flames.

"Findlay! Get up here and tell me some good news about the Gas company. When they going to turn off the supply so we can start winning this battle?"

"A few minutes boss," the radio operator calmly announced coming up to him, "they're shutting down half the power in Lancaster though."

"I don't care if it's all of England as long as I get this blaze extinguished and none of my crew are put in any further danger. This is more fun than I care to have right now."

"Gravin reported in from the farmstead," Findlay said, "the owners have been evacuated and are safe and sound but in shock. There's also a bulldozer over there he said we could borrow?"

"Say yes," the Fire Chief declared, "then get in touch with the airbase about a water drop just in case we can't get the fire under control in the next half hour or so."

"Will do," Findlay replied, as the Fire Chief glanced at the fire around him. "A Detective wants to talk to you boss after all this is over. Probably going to ask you what you think caused the explosion." He went on to guess.

"Hmmm well the police can keep asking. I haven't got a clue. It's not a normal gas blast not with accelerants involved."

"Do you think this has anything to do with what happened yesterday on the motorway?"

"We live in a crazy world with terrorists Findlay. Anything is possible. Now get me Marshall on the radio. I want to hear how he's doing."

The radio operator bobbed his head and returned to his station. Solid jets of water from the elevating platforms lanced down and began drowning out the fire which consumed the hedgerows. Smoke dissipated under the effects of the onslaught on the ground and the frames withered and died as the firefighters panned their hoses and progressed forward. Before long a call came down to the Fire Chief from Sweeney on the platform.

"Chief Rydal!" The voice paused as its owner swallowed, "a section of the road ahead is gone. There's nothing there now except a massive crater. The explosion much have ruptured other pipes as well for the cavity is filled with water."

"Roger that Sweeney," Rydal replied with a nod. "Findlay! did you hear that?"

"Clearly Boss."

"Good dispatched the message through to the crews then repeat it on the loudhailer just in case there's to much background noise for the radios."

* * *

"What did you find out Adrian," Sophie Gillett asked, glancing this way and that as she opened the door and beckoned the men to enter. Other workmen were extremely busy and too preoccupied carrying out their jobs to really notice Cummings and Klugman go into the cottage.

"A lot," Cummings remarked. Taking off the helmet and carrying it towards the kitchen. "And none of it is looking good to us."

Gillett blinked, shut the door and bolted it behind Klugman. "And where's Nathan?"

"Bisset went into the house and that was the last we saw of him." Klugman answered the second question on reflex.

Inside the kitchen Thaw was pouring himself a cup of tea when Cummings came in looking dejected. "Jerome! This place has everything except a way out of here."

"Explain." Thaw asked with a frown as Klugman dropped onto one of the stools.

"The entire house is surrounded by a swamp." Klugman said before Cummings could answer. "Posing as workmen we had no trouble in getting around or asking decreet questions from the drivers and the guy in the refreshment van." He picked up an apple from a fruit bowl. "From what they all said there's one road that leads off the grounds to a country lane outside the gates..."

"One direction takes you further into the middle of nowhere," Cummings broke in, Gillett walked in and Klugman's teeth crunched into the apple, "while the other route would take us across a bridge and back towards Hereford."

"That's not so bad," Gillett said with a shake of her head, "all we've got to do is steal a car and we can wave this place good-bye."

"If only it was that simple Sophie," Cummings said with a heavy sigh, "this piece of land we're on top of is high ground. The bridge isn't. It's passable now but the river is swollen. Any more rain and it won't be." Klugman took another big bite out of the fruit. "The means out of here is also a major pain in the ass."

"How come?" Thaw said, lowering his cup. "Aren't there enough trucks and cars in the garage so we just nick one?"

"Plenty," Klugman said after swallowing a mouthful. "None of them though are left alone for too long. When chauffeurs aren't watching then the guy in the refreshment van is. Plus you're got workmen collecting stuff from their vans and pickups, the builders on tea breaks and guests being dropped off in the parking lot before they head into the house."

"Don't forget the security lights on at night making life even more difficult for us." Klugman added.

"What about another place to hide. Did you find one?" Thaw asked.

"We split up to cover more ground." Cummings revealed gloomily, "but neither of us could see anything apart from a children's play house build in the branches of a tree."

"Kyle you said the guests were being dropped off in the parking lot," Thaw inquired, "were those from the helicopter because I've only heard it pass by once since you were gone."

"Yeah!" Klugman replied. "The eggbeater managed to bring in a load of passengers after being grounded for a while due to the wind. A couple of cars arrived as well. It appears as though it's only a trickle at the moment. The weather might have put a lot of people off."

"I hope you're right Kyle," Thaw said with a nod, "because it means we'll be able to stay here a little bit longer. Adrian! I know this sounds stupid but when Nathan returns, go and check out the tree house. See if it'll offer a possible refuge in case we need it."

"Okay."

"Kyle you ever flown a helicopter?" Gillett inquired thoughtfully.

"Yeah," Klugman uttered, "not as big as that Sikorsky but I reckon I could pilot the thing as a last resort if the police were breathing down our necks."

"If it isn't beyond you why at a last resort?" Gillett said, going over to the fruit bowl.

"I didn't see a fuel truck by the landing pad so we could have a limited supply which wouldn't get us very far, and secondly it's to do with flight plans," He replied sullenly, "every aircraft pilot has to make one to and from the destination. I don't know for sure but I bet helicopters work on the same principal."

"Just supposing we did hijack the thing and veered off the route?" Cummings said with interest. "What then?"

Klugman replied. "Air traffic control could be keeping track of us and know where we're eventually going to touch down again. I can bluff our way though on the radio, say we got engine trouble or something but we'd need wheels as soon as we hit the ground to escape otherwise it's gonna get messy if we're stranded and rescue crews come out to see if we need assistance. We would have to fight our way to freedom."

"Don't appear to me like we got an awful lot of options," Gillett commented at length, peering at a banana. "We can't travel out of here by foot in just any old direction because of the bog and it's miles by country lanes to Hereford anyway, carrying all the bags. Flying is possible if we're able to find a landing space big enough that's not to close to civilization."

Cummings raised his eyebrows as a idea flashed through his mind. "There may be a solution to one obstacle we face. Klugman remember when we were coming back and we saw a number of propane gas cylinders being delivered."

Klugman nodded silently.

"Could you create a distraction by rigging one of those things to explode," he continued, "say on the other side of the house at a predetermined time? It'll lead everybody away of the parking lot then when the coast is clear, we break in and hot-wire one of the cars. There's a lovely wire coat hanger in the wardrobe upstairs prefect for the job."

"Won't be a problem. I've got some pencil timers, C4 and grenades, enough for three distractions."

"Three," Cummings echoed, contracting his brows in concentrated thought, "you still going after the jewellry?"

"Off course," Klugman answered smoothly. "Nothing changed. The residents will think it's an earthquake by the time I've finished. I've got the plan of the ground floor of the house and ten minutes before we go, I'm going to use it."

"You'll need a hand gathering all the stuff up so I'll come too Kyle," Gillett said, in mid chew, greed blazing in her eyes.

"Before you finish making your plans," Cummings said, "I'll need someone as a look out while I'm busy crossing the ignition wires to say nothing of helping me load up the money pouches."

"Nathan can be your lookout," Thaw commented grimly. "I'm heading into the house as Kyle's back-up." He turned to address Klugman, "there's no way the trophy room will be completely empty. You're gonna require another gun in there to hold up a room full of guests, security guards and journalists."

"I wondered how long it would take before you suggested that," Klugman remarked with a grin. "Split timing with the explosion after dark will pull people away from the trophy room too. A minute later we grab the jewellry." He saw Thaw and Cummings nod. "The press conference was supposed to be scheduled for eight o'clock sharp but according to one of the columnists I talked to earlier it's been put back to ten o'clock for some reason, so I could set the charges to go off about twenty past eight or before by remote then we do the deed and we met you outside, where Adrian? Front or back."

"Front!" He answered at length. "I'll park around the side of the house and you signal me to come round. Afterwards we've a clear road which will get us out of here all the sooner."

* * *

Geof Anderson knocked on the bedroom door with a loud rap and waited dutifully until the voice inside called him in.

"Enter," Robert J. Crowe said. Sitting in front of an oak desk, typing away on his laptop. A line of text scrolled on the screen underneath a pie chart. He turned his attention to the door as the butler marched in. A brown pile carpet stretched under his feet and there was a large window overlooking the garden. A dressing table littered with cosmetics stood against one wall while wardrobes and chairs were arranged around a four poster bed. "Yes Geof what is it? You'll have to be quick I'm afraid. I'm still trying to get my PowerPoint presentation done for this evening."

"Sorry to disturb you sir but your wife wants to remind you that you have to be down at the railway station in twenty minutes for the 2 o'clock train to pick up Miss Lois' guests."

"Huh," Robert expressed in surprised. "Them! I didn't know it was getting on for that time. I need to finish this off. Are any of the chauffeurs available?"

Anderson blinked. "One or two sir. They're pretending to wax their cars while eyeing up the legs of our waitresses. Why? Would you like me try and acquire their services?"

"Yes Geof. Offer them fifty quid. Red Heath Station is only fifteen minutes down the road. They could be there and back before their employers know it. If they refuse double the amount. Money talks! One of them will do it."

"As you say sir. Erm there is one more thing. We have an insurance salesman downstairs, drinking the kitchen dry of tea. He claims you wanted to do some business with his company." The butler walked up to his employer and proffered a business card.

"I don't recall having made any appointment," Robert said with a frown, taking the card and reading the name and firm silently to himself.

"Nor does Mrs Crowe Sir. The man is a complete puzzle. Shall I ask him to leave?"

"Might as well. Get some leaflets off him then escort Mr Bisset to the front door personally."

Anderson smiled and gave a nod.

"Shame in one way because I like a mystery," Robert mused out loud, returning his gaze to the laptop, "I would have asked him to stay over for a night but with the guests coming in from all over for the party and to view the artifacts, there is just no room at this inn."

"There might be sir," the butler announced evenly, "there have been twelve cancellations so far. The Nicholsons and the Esterbys among them. And other arrivals state they won't be able to made it here any earlier than nine tonight. Roads, the weather and the lack of airborne transport has affected everyone's timetable."

"Well here or not at ten o'clock the press conference goes ahead. I won't delay it again for anyone." Robert declared.

"Very good sir. By the way if you're calling on Mr Homes later on, you'll find him in room four in the west wing."

"What the dickens is he doing up there Geof?" Robert asked with a deepening frown.

"He requested a larger room but I assume he just wanted more space to chase after his secretary."

"Hah!" Robert said. "She won't do much running. Any other problems I need to be made aware off or has Ashley swore you to silence old friend."

Anderson grinned. "She tried sir. I just don't listen to those kind of instructions."

"Great! I wouldn't find out half the gossip in my house if it wasn't for you so then. What's up?"

"Miss Lois doesn't seem to be working in the library or pulling her weight in helping out with the party decorations."

"Not surprised," his employer remarked. "Next!"

"The maids forgot to put soaps in half of the en suite bathrooms, Miss Isaaces wanted a television and video in her quarters, Mr Homes moaned about the journey he took in your brother-in-laws car, Miss Kapoor insisted on a brighter bulb for her bedside lamp so she could read her reviews, more guests have been complaining that we haven't vacuumed their rooms well enough and Mr Hannon said all his towels have been stolen while he was taking a stroll. And that's nothing to the trouble we're having with Mrs Snodgress..."

Robert grinned, wishing he'd never asked, "so apart from that. Everything's going swimmingly?"

"That's one way of describing it sir. Alas it's not mine. Now what about Mr Bisset. In or out?"

"Invite him to the party so I can speak to him at my own leisure. If we get full we can always throw a cot in the broom cupboard and he can sleep in there."

"Very good sir," the butler announced, "I know just the costume to lend him. I shall carry out your wishes immediately and inform your wife that you're abreast of the situation."

Robert nodded and began typing out more text as Anderson made his way out.

* * *

The butler closed the bedroom door quietly and strode down the corridor to where it ended at a junction. He passed suits of armor and tables decorated with vases of flowers. Anderson turned right at the intersection and was half way to the main staircase when he heard a haunting familiar voice shout at him from behind.

"Anderson! I want to talk to you now mister. I've got something to complain about."

The butler skidded to a halt, sighed then trying to compose himself, turned slowly, looked down and locked eyes with the woman before him.

"Aw Mrs Snodgress, haven't you got another hobby? Let me see how long has it been since I last spoke with you..." he said, tapping his wrinkled cheek thoughtfully with his index finger, "I know, it's been eight minutes. What can I do for you this time?"

The woman was about to speak when he pressed on, "Is your hair dryer not working again? Or is it that you still haven't got any hot water. I can assure you madam we do have electric power out here in the county."

Snodgress blinked and gritted her teeth at the insult. "Very funny for a lackey. I must admit I would have had better service if I'd been sleeping in a barn." The butler's left eye twitched from nerves. She smiled and continued, "I had a lovely day until I came here and saw that rat under your nose. It depressed me."

"All I can say madam is stop looking in the mirror."

Fuming, Snodgress pressed on, "you remind me of my second husband. He also wasn't the brightest button in the box. You know he fell for me like a short-sighted scaffolder."

"My condolences," the butler expressed without a hint of sympathy, "was he pushed or did he jump?"

Snodgress glared daggers at him. "I hear Mr Crowe keeps you around because you make him laugh. I haven't had the pleasure yet but if you were in my employ I would laugh as I sacked you."

"Thank goodness for small mercies. So," he went on, in a haughty way, not really willing to do something regarded as beneath his dignity but towing the line anyway, "I haven't got all day even if you have, so if you can tell me your problem in a little less time than it would take me to read War and Peace, I would be extremely grateful."

"My key card doesn't open the door very quickly. Miss Kapoor had to wait a whole minute outside her room before the sensor let her in. Had it taken any longer I would have had to climb through my window."

"Shame! I can direct you to a ladder Madam if you feel the need in the future."

"That won't be necessary you impotent sod," She replied. "You know I would demand my money back if this visit wasn't free of charge. I'm glad I'm going to the party tonight. The room won't look so bad once I've had a drink or nine in me."

"We're not a four star hotel," Anderson said, "you must take that into account. I really have to go or do you want to join me for a snack at tea-time? I'm sure we can find something for you to moan at."

Snodgress smiled and replied, "Oh dear! As tempting as that sounds I don't mix with the lower classes. I'm leaving my shoes outside in the corridor. I want them polished so I can see my face in them by tonight. Say they'll be ready by six-thirty." She arched an eyebrow waiting for his biting response.

Anderson nodded. "Fine Madam. I am absolutely sure none of us have anything more important to do than that. They'll be done even if I have to polish them myself." He nodded then spun and walked to the landing as Kalvinder Kapoor came out of her room and spoke.

"Alice! I been looking for you everywhere."

Snodgress turned as Kapoor drew to halt before her.

"What did the horrible butler say?" The film star asked, "is he going to do something about our complaints?"

"He is," her personal assistant announced calmly.

"I can't stand the man."

"Oh I don't know Kal. He's kind of growing on me." Snodgress said.

"Heaven forbid," Kapoor responded with a shake of her head.

"Anyone who isn't frightened of me and gives as good as he gets is all right in my book," Snodgress commented, "if I'd met someone like him years ago maybe I wouldn't have got through four husbands in a futile search for a person with that same attribute. Come on, let's go and check out our costumes. With our present luck, they're probably as crinkled as his face."

As they turned to backtrack to their rooms, the pair felt a strong gust of wind ruffle their hair and clothes and a faint hiss could just be heard faintly. Kapoor glanced behind her, but she failed to see the barest flicker of movement high above her zoom along the vaulted ceiling of the corridor and out of sight around the corner.

"What was that?" She asked her companion as they walked.

"Just a bit of wind." Snodgress answered calmly, striding on ahead. "A maid must have left a window open. What an idiot at this time of year. If my windows are open heaven help the butler is all I say."

Kapoor glanced about one more time then hurried after her assistant.

* * *

Lois grinned as she pressed the plunger down on the aerosol and hairspray shot out of the nozzle propelling her forward along the shadowy ceiling of the corridor above the two unsuspecting women below. She whipped past them then increased her body weight and depressing the aerosol enough to slow her momentum down, glided round the corner into the next passageway. A thick gray fog awaited her as she increased her weight and descended until she alighted on the carpet.

"Danielle," she whispered to the rolling haze, blinking as she found the depths impenetrable to her eyes, "I managed to control my density. I'm practically weightless when I fly. Are you there?"

"I'm here Lois," she replied as details emerged from the billowing mist, her faded body had the peaky image from a black and white photograph. Her friend was ghostlike and completed drained of colour. “I thought I’d have a go at creating a fogbank while everyone on this floor is in their rooms.”

Lois gasped as a shape grew vaguely, a distinctiveness of outline became visible around Danielle’s figure and a definition of colour rapidly developed in lighter tones before amplifying to sharply contrast with her surroundings. Danielle became more tangible gradually item by item, clothes, skin, hair until the young blonde was back in detailed resolution.

“Wicked power Danielle. Did the voices in your mind teach you to do that?”

“Yep! And so much more Lois. Bartok was right when he said the more we use our powers the better we’d become. I can control all sorts of water and sense where it is up to hundreds of miles away. There are gallons in the bog, droplets dripping from leaves, I know when it’s going to rain again and even sense the stuff in people’s bodies. Yours included. That’s how I knew where everyone was. It is creepy but I can anticipate the movement in the flow and direct it to by affecting the bladder of one man in room sixteen. He was just coming out to disturb us.”

“I’m hearing the same voices plus,” Lois revealed with a smile, “I’m becoming increasingly conscious of the flutter of a bird wings outside without being aware of why I know it.”

“Uh-oh I sense a maid coming this way,” Danielle announced smoothly. She clinked her fingers and the mist suddenly evaporated into thin air.

“I know,” Lois confirmed, seeing the fog hadn’t left a trace of itself behind, “it’s Anntte. She’s puffing and panting. That woman is so out of shape. Let’s get out of here.”

“I’m with you,” Danielle agreed, the pair walked off in the opposite direction.

“I’m getting like you Danielle. It’s subtle but I can tell by the air how you, Anntte and mom all breath in a little bit differently than anyone else. Before Bartok comes and takes what he wants I’m going to make sure Anderson dies first,” her eyes flashed murderously. “He’s so self-indulgent and completely up his own arse. He’s looked down his nose at me for the last time and I know just what I’m going to do to bring it about.”

CHAPTER NINETEEN

At 2.35 pm the very late 11 o'clock train slowed and eventually came to a halt alongside platform four of Red Heath Railway Station. Carriage doors were flung open and the crowd of passengers streamed out and headed for the exits. Josh Brennan and Russel Corbett grabbed their holdalls from the luggage shelves above their heads and led their party of nine along the emptying platform.

"Hey Josh," Yasmin Tweed said to draw the young man's attention. "I can't see Lois' uncle waiting around this long to pick us up. I bet he's gone and we're gonna have to fork out for a taxi."

He turned his startling preoxide-haired head back over one of his broad shoulders. "Yeah!" He said arching his eyebrow at her angelic blonde hair and baby-blue eyes. "Well he can pay us back. I ain't running a charity but I'll be making sure that I'm going to be on the receiving end of all of his goodwill."

"Don't forget what Lois said about the jewellry Josh," Corbett said with a wide grin and a wink.

"Jewellry? Is there something you forgot to mention Brennan?" Andrea Tucci asked. She walked behind them, her hair was much longer than Tweed's and was the rich colour of chocolate.

Brennan glared at his heavyset companion who was handsome in a harsh way as he brushed his long stringy hair away from his face. "It was going to be a surprise but Russel's let the cat out the bag now so I might as well tell you. Archaeologists have unearthed a few trinkets of jewellry in the grounds. Lois suggested if we go searching ourselves and find something of value then we can sell it and all get a cut."

"Sounds fair," Matt Levitt remarked, tramping along behind the crowd with two bags in his massive hands and others lodged under each arm. Tweed glanced up at the burly six footer and she was glad she wasn't dating him for his brain.

"That's the first place I'm heading anyway," Corbett revealed, stepping onto the treads of the escalator right after Brennan, "once I've shoved my bags in my room."

"I'm up for that," Dermot Thornton said, going up. "What about you babe?" He asked, his clean-shaven oval face grimaced as he dropped a rather heavy bag on to his foot.

"I am," Tucci agreed.

"Not so fast all of you," Brennan said in advance of explaining himself, progressing off the moving staircase. "Follow me and I'll tell you why."

Puzzled faces adhered to Brennan's heels as he crossed over to a pair of pay phones to wait for the others to ascend and gather around. Corbett drew up first. He had short, spiky hair that must have took him an a least an hour to get right. Although he looked down at Brennan, Corbett was barely three inches taller than his friend who was of average height and had a leaner build.

Tweed came next with her stunning looks and figure, then the stouter Tucci, the lean-hipped middle-heighted Thornton, the broader-shouldered, deeper chested Levitt and bringing up the rear were Prue Dwyer, Zoe Hawes and Sean Hardy.

"When Lois got in trouble," Brennan went on, his eyes roaming from face to face, "her mom Vertly began keeping a closer eye on her, mainly where she went and who she mixed with. That includes us. Now Vertly can't be around to spy on us all the while so we split into groups of three or four and take turns to do a bit of hunting. She'll never know Lois or us are up to no good."

"I want first crack then," Sean Hardy said. "Me, Yasmin, Matt and Zoe will be one team. It'll be dark in a couple of hours and we haven't got any torches so we should go out while it's still light."

Hawes and Tweed nodded together.

"Listen Sean," Brennan said with a chilling cold voice that radiated strength and authority, taking a step towards him and gesturing with his index finger, "you might think because Russel, Prue and I aren't in your precious college group, we don't have a say in running things. Well your wrong. Lois in my girlfriend and I call the shots. No one else. I hope you've got that because I'm not repeating it."

Sean Hardy blinked at the twenty-three year old and felt more and more agitated by Brennan's unnerving gaze. Hardy was above medium height with a superb muscular frame and a mop of brown hair highlighted with blonde streaks. He didn't back down from anyone but, as he regarded Brennan's chiseled cheekbones and intense brown eyes, his stomach muscles tightened. Something told him that Brennan was the kind of person who started a fight and kept on coming however hurt he might become until he finished it. Hardy glanced around for support and quickly saw that none was forthcoming.

"We'll do it your way then Josh." Hardy declared with a shrug.

"Good!" Brennan said. Corbett's grin began to turn into a smirk.

A Big Issue seller with a droopy right eyelid and wearing scruffy clothes but brand new shiny boots saw Brennan's crowd and believing he might make some quick cash, gripped his stack of magazines and strode from his pitch near the ticket machine and walked up to them. "Big Issue! Buy the Big Issue."

"Right gang! Let's go and see if..." Brennan stopped in mid-sentence and scowled, noticing that as he lifted up the magazines to show, the Big Issue seller had two gold rings on his finger. "Already brought one thanks."

"Oh thank you," Big Issue seller replied, his face dropping. He glanced around, saw some passengers coming off another train and rushed over to them.

"This way," Brennan said. Waving his group forward as he lead the way out of the train station. "Let's find out if there's been some transport provided."

Corbett walked alongside his friend and said. "Hey Josh. I didn't know you brought that magazine. The last time you spent a fiver, the queen's eyes blinked from being in your pocket for so long."

"I don't Russel," Brennan replied with a sigh and a thin smile at the joke. "I just said that to get rid of the loser. Did you see the ring he wore and the new shoes. That broke wasn't really hard up. He's probably got a sports car round the corner and a posh house."

The group stepped outside into dull sunlight as a bushy eyed, jowly chauffeur held up a board saying Wildwood Haven.

"That's us," Corbett announced loudly, taking in the parked Limousine before whispering to Brennan, "we're falling on our feet here Josh."

"Yeah," Brennan acknowledged. "For once Russel I agree with you."

They all clambered aboard and were soon off speeding their way towards their accommodation.

* * *

Hallie Sinclair ducked beneath the strand of police tape, clutching a sheet of paper in one hand and a bunch of wild pansies in the other, she lumbered across the road to where Owen Rydel stood talking to another Fire Office about a foot from the edge of the massive water-filled crater. Scattered debris still smoldered in the midst of scorched, browned grasses and charred tree trunks, some branches had been reduced by the burning to charcoal.

"...Water along with the gas pipes are still turned off," Findley declared from memory, "the bulldozer's been returned with our thanks, the supply tanker is half empty and two of the pumpers have gone back to the station."

"Okay! What about the thermal imagining equipment and sonar to help in trying to find the bodies?" Rydel asked, rubbing his tired, smoke filled eyes with his knuckles.

"Should be here in the next few minutes boss," the taller man revealed, "and Jackson's been flown by air ambulance to hospital."

"What's her status?" He asked, blinking to clear his vision.

"She's seriously ill with seventy-five per cent burns. Her husband and father have been informed. We got Gas Company Experts and our own team of Investigators wanting to come in to find the cause of the blast."

"I know the cause," the inspector said, drawing to a halt beside the pair, ready to divulge the information. "I'm Sinclair. The data I have is, at the moment, for your ears alone Chief Rydel."

"Leave us for a few minutes will you Mark," the Fire Chief announced calmly. "Congratulate the crews on a job well done."

Findley nodded and departed.

Rydel turned to address the inspector who, seeing silver in his short hair, didn't put his age to be above forty. "So what do you have for me detective? Apart from the fact that an extremely powerful bomb did this?"

"Nothing much," Sinclair uttered, taking a tentative step towards the crater, a little hesitant of where to put her feet. "The bomb was a very sophisticated booby trap and it was encased in a stolen Volkswagen Caravelle which had been used as a getaway vehicle yesterday morning by three armed robbers who made off with an estimated five million pounds. I am beginning to wonder however if Sentinel Enterprises have just pushed up the stolen amount so they can claim on their insurance."

"Hmmm," the Fire Chief muttered slowly. "These thiefs – could they have been with the Irish Republican Army or Al-Qa'ida? Because it would certainly explain what happened yesterday with the flyover."

"This doesn't bear the hallmarks of any of those terrorist groups. There was no Suicide bomber and there's nothing out here in the middle of nowhere to interest any IRA splinter group. I'm not a hundred percent sure, but I imagine my suspects wanted to create enough panic and disruption to allow them to escape. How did you hear about the flyover bomb?" She enquired, sliding her foot forward another step.

"My cousin is one of the investigators still sifting through every single piece of debris on the motorway."

She nodded in comprehension and stopped at the rim of the crater.

"Who had the misfortune of setting this bomb off?" Rydel asked, coming alongside the inspector who was peering down into the depths.

"One of my men who should have know better," she sighed. "It is all very hazy. One minute King was reporting to us that they'd found a vehicle matching the description, the next he mentioned another officer called Ryan disobey a direct order by going over to investigate the Caravelle, then the radio went dead. I knew Ryan." she looked at him before returning to gaze at the bowl-shaped cavity. "He was young, only a rookie, he was eager to please and out to make a name for himself," she sniffed disdainfully. "The bloody fool. He wanted great honor and admiration for doing something important. Well he's gone to glory now all right and taken the lives of three brave officers with him."

"I'll like a transcript of the communication if you've got a copy." Rydel ventured.

"Sure! I'll get my sergeant to fax you one over." She swallowed. "You had the chance to measure how deep this crater is yet?"

"No, just the width. it's about eighty yards across."

"Reminds me of the ones I've seen in books about the war," she told him. Suddenly shaking herself out of her reverie, "anyway if you find the bodies I want to be notified immediately." She kneeled and placed the flowers near the rim.

"I'll see to it personally," The fire Chief nodded grimly as she straightened. "So where are you off to now?"

"Back to the station to chase up some other leads if my people can't find a trail here."

* * *

"So where have you been for all this time Nathan?" Thaw asked seeing Bisset walk through the door and park himself on the nearest chair in the living room. Trumpet like tones and the brassy sound of music could be heard from next door. "Inside the manor. Talking to Ashley Crowe about her insurance," the older man replied, producing a cigarette from his jacket pocket and shoving it into his mouth, noticing that Thaw was now clean shaven.

"I bet that was a thrilling conversation," Klugman remarked, ripping off a portion of the adhesive tape from the roll with his teeth before tacking a long narrow piece of cloth to his torso.

"It was," Bisset admitted evenly, patting his pockets for a match. Arching an eyebrow at what Klugman was doing next with the roll of bandage. "She swallowed my cover story and I got a guided tour by the butler whose more of a snob than his employers."

"Did you see the jewellry," Thaw inquired, the only one of the four not busy doing something. He sat opposite the older man, leaning back with his hands behind his head. He wore black trousers, a leather jacket and brown boots. A pair of sunglasses were laying on his lap.

"The pictures don't do the items any justice whatsoever. Two more pieces have been included," Bisset said with a sigh, trying to hear himself think over the din coming through the walls, "a gold hair slide and a silver twisted ring. How long have we had neighbors?"

"Not long but it feels like for forever," Thaw said, "the house must be full if these bastards are down here."

"Nathan! How's security?" Cummings asked, stabbing a hole in a bed sheet.

"A couple of guards outside the trophy room and another inside plus several on foot patrol. And from what I saw I didn't spot any cameras inside the corridor but there are alarm boxes mounted on the outside walls of the house." Cummings nodded. "Has anyone got a match? My lighter's out of fuel."

Gillett nodded and came over with a box. Bisset smirked at the American's starting attire. Her hair was slicked back and tied in a French plait. She was wearing a dark T-shirt and hotpants with a white zigzag pattern in the front, and a thigh-strapped holster which held a .38 Smith and Wesson caliber revolver. She stuck the match and lit his cigarette.

"Thank you my dear," Bisset said, puffing away. "What's the get up for?"

"The party of course." She blew out the flame with a shake of her head, "you didn't think we were going to storm in there and take hostages did you Nathan?"

"Frankly my dear, I did." Bisset nodded. "How else will your goals be achieved? I endorse the robbery and stepping up the crime ladder to murder doesn't bother me in the least especially when I'm not asked to get in on the act too."

Thaw grinned. "It'd be careless of us to seize control of a house that large when we are so few in number and we don't know the whereabouts of all the guards. We don't need someone doing a diehard on us. The best way is to just go in costume and blend in with the masses then strike when the distraction goes off."

"I'm going as Lara Croft by the way," Gillett revealed. "This is Jerry's holster and boxer shorts – I've sewed up the flyhole." She patted the leather case as he tapped ashes into the nearby ashtray. "My gun and one of Kyle's T-shirts. As for the boots, I'll have to just make do with my high-heels."

"Highly imaginable," Bisset nodded, inhaling smoke into his lungs. "You should cut the mustard in that."

"What that mean?" Gillett said with a frown.

"You come up to expectations," Cummings remarked, his knife was cutting another wide hole in the white flat sheet. He was out of the overalls and now back in his regular clothes. Cummings saw the older man glance across. "I'm a ghost," he said, holding up the sheet with its two eye holes staring back to him. "It's rough Nathan yet highly effective."

"Indeed," Bisset commented with genuine interest. Blowing a ring of smoke into the air as he turned to Klugman who stood beside the staircase. He was sticking another strip of tape to the end of the bandage under his left armpit. Klugman wore strips of white cloth and other coloured material lightly over his clothes, wrapped around his arms and legs and chest, kept in place with sticky tape. He moved his limbs agilely and he'd left his hands and feet free to run or draw his handgun easily just hidden beneath a thick strip of gauze. "My, my Kyle! You do look like your mummy or did you cut yourself shaving."

"Hah," Klugman said, pressing the jagged end of the tape down more firmly with his thumb. "Get me a doctor, my sides are splitting.

If you're thinking of going to the crapper Bisset then go somewhere else because I've used all the toilet roll, gauze and ripped up the sheets I could get my hands on to make up this fucking costume."

"The Crowes have invited me as a guest, and have prepared an outfit for me." Bisset announced, eyeing Thaw again.

"Well about quarter past eight I want you outside in the parking lot," Thaw said, "acting as lookout for Adrian while he's acquiring us a car. The rest of us will be hitting the trophy room."

He sighed. "Fine! And do you mind telling me what you're going as Jerome?" He added as an afterthought.

"Well I'm not one for dressing up Nathan so I'm going as a certain leather-clad cyborg from the future. I got the shades, guns, and the bandoleer belt."

"Yeah," Klugman crackled loudly, "even if you haven't got the height, build or a thick Austrian accent."

* * *

"About time you got here Lois," Zoe Hawes said. Holding a can of beer as she opened the cottage door. The music was blaring before someone turned it down. "We've been settled in for an hour waiting for you."

"Couldn't be helped Zoe," she answered the elfin-faced young woman. Entering the living room where her mates were scattered about. "Had a bit of trouble dodging mom and dad. They keep wanting me to do work. Have you ever heard of such a thing?" There was laughter all round. "I left Danielle to run interference for me while I took one of the secret passages out of the house." She stepped further into the room and scanned the faces. "Everyone make it?" She added nervously, hoping against hope that they had.

"With everything free like this," Prue Dwyer said with a smile, standing with a Bavarian beer, "wild horses couldn't drag me away from this party girlfriend."

Josh Brennan jumped off the couch, went over and caught Lois' face between his hands before they kissed passionately. Lois could taste whisky on his breath as her fingers glided up to where his hair grew thickly at the nape of my neck while his hands lowered to groped her bum.

Watching their display of affection from where he sat Corbett smiled as he took off his earphones, music from Trilogy blared from the ear-pieces, "hey guys get a room."

"I intend to after this Russel," he replied, slapping his girlfriend's bum hard as the pair released each other. "By the time I'm finished with her she won't sit down for a week."

"Promises, promises." Lois said with a grin. Glancing around the interior of the cottage. The living room was alike in every way to the other two cottages in the block. "You all get your costumes okay? Because I'm sure my Aunt has arranged for some spares just in case."

"We're fine," Tweed remarked calmly, peeling the lid off a tub of yogurt. "When does the fun begin?" She added, shoving her spoon deep into the container.

"7 o'clock in the ballroom. Just come across and Anderson will let you in. I've prepared some party games just for us to celebrate this Halloween."

"As long as they'd not Ouija board or Tarot cards readings," Said Tucci, switching over the television channels with the remote. "X Files or the Others probably already did it."

Lois gritted her teeth at the couch potato. "It won't be anything remotely copying those programmes – I can guarantee that Andrea."

"Now you're here Lois. How about assigning slots so we can do a bit of treasure hunting?" Hardy said. Levitt nodded and came up to stand beside the shorter man. Brennan noticed the sudden support and he wondered who else might want to test his authority in the near future.

"You told them about the jewellry Josh?" Lois asked incredibly.

"Actually it was me," Corbett replied for his friend. "I let it slip out."

Lois blinked. "Okay! It's going to be dark soon so I'll show you in the morning. How's that guys?"

"Sorry Lois – it's not good enough." Hardy said firmly. "I talked to Matt earlier in the kitchen and convinced him that we could go while it's still light."

"You'll never make it. It's almost quarter to four." Lois said with a shake of her head.

"Lend us a torch then," Hardy pressed on, "and point us in the right direction. We'll be there and back before you know it."

"Fine Sean!" She replied. "If that's what you both want. I won't stand in your way. Josh give them a torch."

"What! Come on Lois," Brennan complained bitterly, "don't give in to these two idiots. We've got a plan. Let's stick to it."

"We all want to be rich Josh. I was going to go exploring earlier but I postponed it because of the train delay. In spite of thinking you're mad to attempt this, I'll draw you a map and both of you can follow it to the source. It starts behind the garages. Watch out for the archeologists, they don't work steady hours like the builders out there. I'd wait until the crews break up for the day in ten minutes time and then go."

"Be careful that you don't get spotted lover," Tweed said.

Levitt nodded and kissed her.

"No one as yet has explained to me," Thornton commented, "how we gonna shift the jewellry when we find it?"

Brennan smiled. "My uncle's a fence. He knows people who can melt the gold down and then we'll sell the stones separately. Anything I make out of this job will be all right with me."

After the map was created and Hardy and Levitt left, Lois and Brennan walked outside to talk.

"You took that well," Brennan said. "Mind you, you never mentioned the bog."

Lois smiled thinly. "Didn't I? Oh I can't remember everything. They'll soon be made aware of it. Let's walk! I've got something to show you. And no," she added, knowing he was getting aroused by her presence, "it's not that."

Brennan sighed with a slight curve of his mouth and followed her into the depths of the foliage.

* * *

Damodar lumbered through the wall of flame followed by two slithering reptile men whose long, cylindrical scaled bodies moved sinuously over the threshold, their muscular hands, clutching a block of marble about four feet in length and about half that in width. Bartok turned at the sound and watched Damodar gesture for the stone to be lowered. Their fiendish wedged-shaped heads twisted in painful grimaces and veins stood out in sharp relief along their arms as the marble block slowly descended to touch noisily down.

"You imbeciles," Damodar shouted, scars stood out on his hideously bald, ridged head, "if you've cracked the alter stone in any way then your measly hides will be dinner for the Chimera." The reptile men drew back then dropped to the floor in a low bow.

"And yours Damodar," the giant demon bellowed seeing the ghoulish humped-back figure turn and squat before him, "never forget that worm." His visage was stern.

Damodar gulped and replied. "I won't master. The legions are waiting for your command and here," he pointed at the block of marble, "is the stone as you requested. When will the time be right to use its power?"

Bartok didn't answer straight away. He waved a callused hand at the air in front of him. A section of the rock wall suddenly shimmered like heat waves, then the affected area faded from view to be replaced by a window of sorts depicting the shadowy landscape of another realm gradually becoming more dimmer in the subdued light. He grinned and deftly moved his talons in a lazy circle. The scene changed again to show the grounds of a large manor house, the outlines of which were fading in the encroaching darkness of early evening. Men wearing helmets and coveralls were leaving work in a steady stream. Another gesture and the picture altered to a closer view of the house where tents were erected and a number of women were rushing around, lighting candles on crowded tables.

Bartok glanced at Damodar still kneeling on the floor and said. "Twilight is approaching." Damodar nodded. "In just over four short hours we will break free and then I'll use the stone to amplify my abilities to finally build a new kingdom upon the ashes of the old."

* * *

Soon after dusk had settled, Ashley Crowe sat with her feet up in her small sewing room just off the main corridor on the ground floor. The chamber was larger than her husband's reception room where he greeted his clients, but not by much. A sewing machine dominated one corner while two chairs, a table were the other bits of furniture dotted about. Despite there being no window, a number of pictures of sea and landscapes adorned the walls to provide a view.

"I've never been rushed off my feet so much Vertly," she said. Sipping her drink as she reclined in her favourite arm chair, "I want to thank you for helping me with the chores. I couldn't have done it without you. Andrew and you will receive something from of this."

"Think nothing of it Ash," Vertly replied, slumped on the next chair. "I wish my darling daughter was more helpful but it's all excuses with her. I don't know what I'm going to do with her. I'm so tired. I could do with a quick kip." Vertly glanced at her watch and saw it wasn't there. "I must have put my watch down somewhere. Got the time?"

"Yeah," Ashley replied, reading the display. "It's five o'clock."

"Already. I think I'll have an hour's rest," she said, pushing herself to her feet. "Before I go up Ash, are you sure that everything's been taken care off?"

"Uh-huh," Ashley expressed with a smile. "The table and patio heaters are in place so are the gazebos and the decking. The ballrooms ready for the party and Rob, Andrew and Anderson should have the fireworks set in a little while. All in all we've done it."

"Great! If you see my worse half tell him where I am."

"Okay," Ashley replied. Sipping another mouthful of drink as her sister-in-law nodded and made her exit.

* * *

"Sean! We're lost man," Levitt declared, a hint of panic in his voice. The cone of light shined on the lines of the makeshift map before Hardy aimed the torch beam directly ahead of them. "This is a right cock-up. There's no trail through these bushes and Lois said nothing about a stinking bog. I should never have listened to you."

Clots of darkness drew back in the panning light revealing bog plants like Sundews and asphodels.

"Give it a rest will you Matt? You getting to sound like an old woman." Hardy said, pressing on forward.

"You'll have no teeth Hardy by the time I've finished with you," Levitt replied. Clenching his jaw and slowly following.

"Come on you big sissy. It's not far now." Hardy smirked as he concentrated in testing the firmness of the ground with every step he took. Mud sluiced beneath their trainers as tussocks of cotton grass drifted gradually behind them. Then all of a sudden Hardy heard distant voices. "Matt! You hear that?" Hardy whispered, sneaking a glance back over his shoulder.

"Hear what?" His companion raised his voice, looking slightly jaded.

"Oh never mind," he sighed, "just follow if you can do that," Hardy said, setting off again, the voices increasing in volume.

* * *

"Professor Keriry! Apart from the two guards flanking the path as we entered the dig, are there any other security measures we can tell our readers about?" Dawn Blye asked, holding up the mini tape-recorder to the older man's face.

Keriry blinked at the question. "None whatsoever Dawn. We are fortified by the nature of the land. The bog's deadly to everything except perhaps the wildlife."

Everett clinked his camera and another close-up of the Professor's features was captured on the roll of film. "Is there any other discovery you haven't shared with the Crowes?" He enquired, standing with the others in the broad hag surrounded by tents, boxy trucks, caravans, and an American (RV) recreational vehicle. Packing cases filled with artifacts were haphazardly scattered about the area. Nearby there were boxes containing tools, burlap and shellac.

"Why, as a matter of fact there is," he nodded with a grin, "please come this way."

The journalists were led to a table where a gold paten and an impressive silver chalice stood. They were embellished with gold, amber and enamels. Everett got closer and started taking pictures while Byle threw one more question at Keriry.

"Professor! Can you tell us about these pieces?"

"Of course. They were unearthed earlier by a student of mine called Mick Fulford. He's single you know," Byle frowned and Everett thought of a way to poke some harmless fun at his partner, "anyway I would say the pieces date back to the early part of the sixth century and similar pieces can be seen in Suffolk at the British Museum and the National Museum in Dublin."

"This Fulford guy will he be at the party tonight?" Everett grinned.

"He will," Keriry answered smoothly.

"Looks like you've pulled Dawn." Everett's grin broadened.

Byle groaned and shook her head. "Don't you start playing matchmaker as well. I get enough of that from my sister."

* * *

Damodar rushed into the armory, his sharp claws clinking on the marble beneath as he immediately dropped to the floor as Bartok tested the balance of a five foot broadsword.

"Great Lord," he said, shivering in fright. "One of your loyal hordes has reported overhearing a meeting in a glade between the invoker and a human male."

"Let me guess worm," the giant demon roared, swinging the war sword through the sulphur filled air. "He listened to the one called Lois say she wouldn't honour our bargain."

"Yes. How is this possible?" Damodar exclaimed in confusion.

"Yours is not the only source of information I have at my command," Bartok declared. Spinning on the balls of his feet, the sword arching until he embedded it in the wall in front of him. Glimmering golden sand poured from the crack and something not unlike a wail emitted while tears of dark green quartz spotted with red jasper trickled down the dying wall. "I have already ordered the undead to attack ahead of time." He withdrew the untarnished blade from the tear. "They have up to the witching hour to free us but they won't bear the responsibility alone."

* * *

Sean Hardy straightened, slowly emerging from behind a thicket, the torch beam was lowered at his feet. He converged with Levitt then the pair backtracked to a safer distance so they couldn't be seen or easily overheard from the encampment. Nearby the aromatic leaves of the densely branched, bog myrtle ruffled in a cool breeze.

"It's everything Josh said it was," Hardy announced excited, his eyes focusing on the site.

"Maybe," Levitt replied. Feeling a prickle of unease as he stared in the same direction. "It's too early to say. I wouldn't mind letting the rest of the gang see what we have then come to a decision afterwards."

"Fuck that Matt. I'm going to see if we can lift something now. You with me?"

"We can't Sean. You won't make it," he said. "Look we got to get back. It's nearly six o'clock. The return trip going to take fifty minutes in the dark, perhaps more..."

Hardy laughed. "Wait here then. I won't be long."

In a flash Hardy turned and disappeared into the foliage.

Instinct told him to return to the cottage but instead Levitt sighed at his friend's recklessness and shook his head before heading after him. Sticks cracked loudly as the pair moved through the slushy mud.

* * *

Tree branches were eerily backlit from the lights shining from the caravan windows. Hardy continued his impetuous dash, his torch trained to the fore in an attempt to circumvent the caravans and to eventually emerge on the opposite side of the encampment, where there were more tables littered with artifacts. Then in the darkness behind, his eyes not completely adjusted to the murk around him, Levitt accidentally tripped over an exposed rock and when he clambered to his knees, his hand bleeding from a narrow cut and his clothes and hair covered with mud and leaves, he heard Hardy cry out before silence reclaimed its territory over the bog. Thinking his friend might have had a similar fall, Levitt got to his feet, lit a match and peered with narrowing, straining eyes to see beyond the glow of the flickering flame as he groped his way forward between the bushes to where he felt the shriek had originated.

"Sean, Sean," Levitt whispered in concern. His nostrils flared with the stale, moldy smell of decomposing leaves and damp moss as he brushed his dark hair away from his high forehead. "Bastard's got himself knocked out. Well I ain't carrying him back," he muttered darkly to himself before silently admitting, "not if I can help it."

Levitt called out again, lit his third match and advanced, his feet treading upon sponge like soil while he felt more than a twinge of desperation as he parted countless fronds to emerge in a small clearing ringed in by stunted trees and bushes. Greyish peat mosses and heaths seemed to stretch across the ground before him. The flame extinguished, burning Levitt's finger and thumb.

"Shit," he uttered at the sudden pain. Blowing on his fingers as the shock made him briefly neglect the care he'd showed up to now when treading into the darkness, instead of finding firmer ground, his trainer came down on a floating mat of vegetation which immediately sank under his weight. Levitt crashed forward and splashed through the surface of the quaking bog.

As he descended into the basin, his eyes widened in absolute horror for out of the gloom Levitt gradually saw a blood mist emitting from Sean Hardy's flopping form. His arms were flapping loosely while his hair was waving in the current and his unseeing eyes were open, the pupils still dilated. His foot was pierced by a poniard that anchored him to the peat floor. The hilt of an antiquated sword stuck out of his chest. Air bubbles escaped Levitt's mouth and water rushed in as he cried out silently in fright. In that fleeing moment his instincts urged him to flee and on this occasion he complied. He whirled in the water and was about to kick to the surface when two shrivelled hands thrust up from the bog floor, splitting the peat asunder. Skeletal fingers grabbed hold of Levitt's ankles, the long yellowy talon like nails digging into socks and flesh, and drawing blood.

Levitt grimaced, thinking at first he'd been snagged by exposed tree roots but then he looked down to see where the problem lay, and saw a hollowed-eyed skull grinning back at him. More skeletal fingers shot out of the peat and seized his trainers and trousers. Bubbles continued to stream upwards as an ash-gray fog swirled madly inside Levitt's dazed mind. He extended his arms in front of his head in a bid to swim free, but his legs were held straight in a tight, vice-like grip and when he brought his hands down to his sides he found he couldn't budge them free. Levitt struggled, thrashing about, blood began seeping from his nose and mouth as water began filling up his lungs. The wizened arms pulled Levitt down to the bottom as he slowed and stopped moving as he slipped into black unconsciousness.

Even before he'd completely suffocated, another grinning skull with missing teeth and a hand clenching a large war axe, unearthed himself, and with a deft flick of a brittle wrist, the axehead sliced off Levitt's head. Despite fragments of vegetation ascending back up to float on the surface of the water, there wasn't enough to hide the mists of blood swirling below.

CHAPTER TWENTY

Throughout the bog, water bubbled and rippled before dappled withered flesh, the colour of mahogany, burst through and crawled or climbed out of the heath-topped basins. Scummy water dripped from crumbling clothes, swords and axes. Elsewhere mud cracked into chasms, and decaying heads followed by skeletal bodies forced themselves up from their graves to stride the earth once again, joining others who marched and rode towards the manor house. The stench of long buried death and decay adhered to the heels of this revolting army as they fared onward, their numbers growing as the ground belched up more cadavers. Bushes were trampled underfoot and ash, elm, oak and maple thinned around until the ground became firmer and the tree line came within sight.

* * *

"So Bryan, this Nathan Bisset was the agent who handled the both cases?" Sinclair said down her mobile as she was driven to the meeting. "Did he have any beef against Woodgate, Prestridge and Secombe or Sentinel Enterprises?"

Giddings didn't correct her about getting the names of the insurance firm mixed up, instead he pressed on to answer her question. "His boss and many of his colleagues have pointed out that Bisset bitterly complained about being passed over for promotion dozens of times. Younger and better sellers came into the firm and gradually took over most of his client list when he wasn't managing to get many results. This made him ill and he lose a lot of weight over it. His wife Blenda left him after twenty four years of marriage for another woman, and his two kids are racking up serious debts at university."

"Just when we were getting some really juicy bits off Dickenson and his staff, not knowing who to put in the spotlight first, we now come across someone else who is jealous, angry and who has access to routes, employee records, timetables and absolute knowledge of what the courier company carried for indemnity purposes. Hmmm! A new lead with a lot of opportunity and motive. Kept on with your other investigations Bryan especially finding out more about Jenkins and Rutten. But assign an officer to chase Bisset down. I want to talk to him as soon as you can arrange it."

"Sure guv," Giddings replied, "we have other good news. The sweat evidence from the driver's seat has finally been analysed. It was a bit of rush job like the post-mortem."

"And?" She said, seeing the car turn around onto another narrow road.

"We have a match from the DNA national database. A guy going by the name of Adrian Cummings. No additional aliases. He's got an arrest sheet as long as my arm. Robbery, GBH, arson and possession of illegal knives to name but a few. He has no known affiliation with any terrorist group and, this is the best part though guv, his file says that Cummings is six foot four in height and is known to have skills in woodcraft which he learned in this region when he was school here."

"That's all I need to know Bryan," Sinclair said. "Draw up a warrant then send an armed response team down to his last known address. I want him taken alive."

"I'll see to it personally guv. Talk to you soon."

The line went dead.

"Finally something is going right for me," she turned to address the young sergeant. "Anything on your side Keane?"

"Not much. Kitridge's turned up nothing on Cummings in the region and of the background checks she's carried out, so far all the regulars in the boarding houses have come back with a clean bill of health. There was however a newcomer sighted about three weeks before the robbery, a man walking a dachshund. No one paid him much attention and he hasn't been seen since."

"Prefect cover for a scout," she said with a smile. Peering past the head rests as a vague figure appeared out of the darkness, in front of a group of trees. "Tell her to keep up the good work."

The pale, face of constable Irving Cheney raised his arm to shield his eyes in the approaching glare of the highbeams as the Rover 75 roared up the trail and skidded to a halt before him. A cloud of dust rose from the tyres making Cheney cough. He held his helmet under his arm, revealing his ears which were as big as the handles on the Scottish football cup. The headlamps dimmed before Hallie Sinclair clambered out of her car, holding a battery operated lantern. She raced towards the lean officer with Keane and two other constables in tow.

"Got your message Cheney," said the inspector eagerly. Sneezing from the dust. "Report!"

"Guv! Perratt found tracks inside the wood that possibly belong to the perpetrators. This way! Stay in line behind me and kept to the signs," Sinclair frowned, "there are depressions and tree roots about that can easily twist an ankle or worse." He flicked on his torch and set off the towards the edge of the trees. Sinclair followed, thrusting her lantern to the fore while more torches were turned on from behind as their owners followed.

"The tracks are definitely human and there's more than one set because the footprints were blurry from the passage of others," Cheney said, pushing through more bushes, angling left as he followed a chalk arrow adorning a tree trunk.

"So the rain didn't wash everything away then?" Sinclair said with a nod, putting her thoughts into words as she placed her feet in Cheney's tracks. "Any that weren't smudged? We could take a plaster cast of?"

"Several!" Cheney revealed. Turning right at a batbox nailed to a trunk below which, another white chalk arrow was drawn across the bark, pointing ahead. "Some of the vegetation dropped down on the footprints. Due to the deepness of the impressions Perratt reckons the crooks are carrying at least one money pouch apiece."

"Maybe! But it would be my luck that we come upon a gang of hikers," Sinclair guessed, tramping on.

"Don't think it's hikers inspector," Cheney confirmed smoothly, ploughing through wind ruffled bushes as he tried to kept to the firmer ground. "You'll see for yourself when you get there."

* * *

Professor Keriry and Ginger Moore were just beginning to leave the dig site for the party, carrying the paten and the silver chalice when they heard the galloping of hooves. The professor's brow furrowed as he whirled to the trees to see who would be foolish enough to be approaching across bog land on horse back at this time of the evening. Overhead floodlights drenched the circle of vehicles and tables.

"What on earth," he uttered as fronds and thick high bushes fifty feet away in front of the pair separated and out of the gap riding at full speed was a skeleton horseman wearing a conical segmented helmet and breastplate of a Roman cavalry office. Moore flinched as she studied what he wore: a mud encrusted light mail skirt over a loose fitting, dirty long sleeved tunic with bands of colour about his arms and hem. The warrior held a javelin in one arm while a rounded shield and reins were clasped in the other. He sat astride a medium sized horse clad in thin circular plate armour.

Another Roman rider upon a similar mount appeared behind the first holding a bow and arrow. They both galloped at the frozen pair, swerving around crates and boxes. All this Keriry observed in a couple of seconds before seeing the sockets of the foremost rider infused with some kind of glittering blaze.

"Hell more like it professor," Moore said, dropping the paten as she came out of her initial shock.

"My God! It's alive, Dekarch," he sputtered.

"Yeah," Moore remarked, grabbing his arm and yanking him back as she began to run for her life, "he's also got a spear and is heading for us. Come on! Let's get out of here."

"It must be a prank Ginger," the professor announced agitatedly, still clutching the chalice. Being pulled along by his assistant, resisting slightly as he glanced over his shoulder at the rapidly approaching Roman. "Special effects like in the movies!"

"Well I ain't waiting around to find out," Moore said panting, noticing a gap inbetween the parked vehicles which she decided to head for. "Help!" She screamed, nearing her destination.

The Dekarch rode onward, his mount leaped across a hole. He saw his prey alter course from the path bisecting the tree line ahead and, in one fluid motion, drew his arm back and threw the javelin with more strength than he ever had in life. The hasta crossed the distance and with a moist blow, severed the professor's spine. Blood splattered onto the woman as Keriry collapsed, slowing Moore's momentum, his hand tightening his grip on hers, crimson spreading across his chest. There was the rasp of rusty steel as the horseman drew his long Spatha from its sheath, raising it on high for a forceful stroke at Ginger who tried in vain to release her hand from Keriry's dead vice like grip. She pulled and screamed again.

Outside the dig, the two security guards flanking the path, heard the shrieks, exchanged looks then ran back to investigate.

"Mrs Elmes said there would be trouble Sam," Shawn Paxton said, dashing on ahead.

"Sounds like it," Sam Fisher replied, chasing after his taller friend.

Abruptly the front leg of the skeleton horse dropped down a concealed rabbit hole. With the animal going forward, the brittle bone snapped just below the knee joint while the other folded beneath it. Balance and stability were lost, the head and neck acting as a counterbalance as the center of gravity shifted, plunged onward to crash into the ground, flinging its rider out of the saddle. Meanwhile the second Roman warrior, a little way behind, steered his mount out of harm's way and was about to gallop round to cut off Moore's escape when he saw two men appear on the path. Not entirely sure what to expect but not figuring on this, the warrior instantly loosed an arrow and the taller of the guards lurched as the shaft struck his chest. Fisher staggered and came out in a cold sweat, immobilized by terror by what had happened to his companion. Another arrow swished and soon an inarticulate death murmur sprung unbidden to his lips as he too fell writhing onto the ground.

At their rear there was a thunderous impact and the horse's neck shattered and twisted at an unnatural angle. Its large jaws cracked wide open and teeth flew into the air. The Roman collided into Keriry's back, and more blood gushed out. Moore exhaled as the warrior's empty eye sockets peered at her and a grin wreathed the lower half of his skull. His knee joints popped loudly as he got to his feet and advanced towards her, sword in hand. Moore's eyes bulged as the Roman took measured steps. She yanked and finally managed to pry her fingers loose as his blade sliced through the air towards her.

She ducked before springing into action, lashing out with a vicious kick. The Roman swerved his skull out of the way at the very last moment and, seeing an opening crept within reach while she was still off balance. He drove the Spatha into her stomach and ripped up. Blood gushed from the gruesome wound as Moore tottered back, glancing at her crimson painted palm and his sword dripping, before her legs gave out on her and she slumped to the ground. Out of the bushes strode a horde of the walking dead: warriors from all ages: knights in armour, vikings, anglo-saxon thegns and a great number of Roman infantrymen. They converged on the recently butchered and dying, their groping fingernails tore off strips of cooling flesh, ripped out steaming organs and anything else of use before they set off again towards the house.

* * *

"It's a bit early for all of us to go up to the manor," Bisset said. Brushing flakes of chocolate off his spangled, diamond-patterned tights of many colors before pulling up the baggy sleeve of his Harlequin jacket to glance at his watch. "It's only five to seven. I'm not complaining, I'll be glad to get away too especially with the racket from those kids next door. But what about the pouches and bags? You're going to need help carrying them nearer to the house."

"While you were picking up your fairy get up," Klugman said as Bisset frowned, holding his mask and wooden wand, "we decided we'd follow the neighbors when they go up because they're the only ones around here who could witness anything. I just came back from reconnoitering and the other cottages are empty. Once inside the ballroom we can wait until the party's in full swing then four of us can leave in ones and twos straight back here, grab the gear and stow it away in some bushes we've seen by the garages before returning the same way to pull off the heist."

"Four?" Bisset declared with a frown, "who's left out and why?"

"You are Nathan," Gillett replied. "You're now known by the Crowes and your disappearance – even for ten minutes – is likely to be noticed particularly in that Harlequin outfit you've borrowed. There won't be many people brave enough to wear something like that."

"Damned butler's fault," Bisset hissed, getting to his feet, "but not bad I suppose as plans go. I better get back myself. I told Ashley I was going to explore the grounds. Oh before I forget, are the charges still set to go off at eight-twenty five? Or have you all changed this part of the plan too?"

"The explosives will blow on time," Thaw said. "Just be where you ought to be Nathan. The rest we'll deal with."

Cummings came to the top of the landing and shouted down the stairs. "The neighbors are leaving and you want to see their costumes," he laughed out loud.

"Okay Adrian, join us," Thaw said, hearing him clambered down the staircase, clutching his sheet, before addressing the others. "Nathan lead the way, Sophie you next. Kyle, Adrian and I will bring up the rear. Go people."

"Right!" Bisset said.

The door was opened and out filed a clown and a video game character along with a mummy, a ghost and short, film robot from the future. Gradually they clustered together and holding onto their accessories, marched towards the light.

* * *

Dressed as a pirate and walking up to the French doors of the manor house thirty feet away, Brennan listened to the voices surrounding him as his thoughts revolved to the quiet glade where his girlfriend had shown him her startling powers.

"I hope Matt and Sean return soon," Tweed pouted. Wearing the apparel of Marie Antoinette, her high pompadour wig felt heavy on her head while her red hoopskirt was so wide that it pushed her companions further away from her. "I don't like my big lug out there. I wonder why he's not answering his phone?"

"Don't know Yasmin. At least you've left a note for them and laid out their costumes," Zoe Hawes said, walking alongside. Her short, buxom figure was covered with the linen garb of an Egyptian princess: A straight, narrow skirt hung to her feet, a gap in the dress showed off her flat tummy and a strip of cloth concealed her small, firm shapely breasts. It was suspended by a pair of leather straps, one over each shoulder, "you can't do anything else."

Zoe Hawes was nineteen years old with a rosy complexion and a oval face set with beautiful brown eyes above a pointed nose and full red lips. Her nails were red and manicured and her flat feet were encased within low-heeled sandals. She had decorated her eyes with kohl and covered up the pimple on her nose with pan stick. Silver jewellry encircled her long, dark wavy hair and her slender olive-skinned fingers. Fragrant oils had been rubbed into her lean arms and chubby legs.

"They must be okay," Dwyer assumed evenly, keeping pace up front with Brennan and Corbett who was wearing a viking outfit complete with sword, helmet and chainmail, "we would have heard something off Anderson if they'd been discovered."

Prue Dwyer was twenty three years old with an average build and a blue eyes and her face was topped by soft auburn hair falling about her shoulders. She had rounded hips, a small waist and shapely legs that were revealed in a little black dress that consisted of a short slit skirt and a tight sexy bodice with several of the laces untied in front showing the tops of her breasts. A witch's conical hat and a jet black robe hung down her back while she clutched a broomsticks in her right hand. Not far from her strode Dermot Thornton wearing a white polyester suit and button-down shirt made famous by John Travolta starring in a certain disco film.

"True enough Prue," Tucci said, her hair in braids and wearing a gray school uniform in the style of Britney Spears when she sang 'Baby one more time'. "Look the old fucker coming to let us in," she added, seeing the butler dressed as Napoleon Bonaparte, opening one of the French doors.

"Aw," Anderson declared with a smirk as the party approached. "You must be the friends of Miss Lois. I thought it was you lot coming up when the radio was switched off." He stepped back for them to enter. "Miss Lois is expecting you Mister Brennan and the rest of you in the library at 7.50. Until then you can mingle."

"Thanks corporal," Brennan said, entering the hallway beyond followed by Corbett and Tweed. A small smile touched the butler's lips as he appreciated the comment. "By the way my army needs their stomach filled. Any idea where?" The remainder of the party entered the house and crowded round.

"The ballroom me bucko," he added smoothly, "turn left and sail straight ahead. You can't miss it." He stared at Yasmin Tweed for a second in passing and said to her, "I suppose you won't be eating the angle cake madam?" and smiled.

"What," Tweed replied with frown, having no idea what the man meant.

"Never mind. Enjoy the party," he said before muttering "Peasants! I knew I should have chained up the cutlery."

As they left, Alice Snodgress descended the stairs as the Marquise de Pompadour and caught Anderson's attention. "Hey! You stuffed shirt. I've got a bone to pick with you."

Anderson exhaled deeply, turned, leaving the door ajar and gazed at her haughtily as Snodgress halted two steps from the bottom. "My word are you going for your hatrick madam?"

"Look Hans I told you before I don't like that form of address it reminds me of a brothel keeper," Snodgress said with a firm nod. She saw a Harlequin, a ghost and a mummy creep in while the butler was distracted.

"Well it's quite apt considering your wearing a dress of a royal mistress," he replied, seeing the woman blink then narrow her eyes as a woman in shorts and a guy in a leather jacket followed the rest inside and disappeared along the corridor, "but I'm digressing Mrs

Snodgress. What is it that jumps ahead of my assembled duties this time?"

"it's my shoes Sherwood!" She declared, pulling up the hem of her green hoopskirt to reveal them. "They're not very shiny and the polish smells like a cat has pissed on them."

The butler ignored her deliberate mistake with his first name and peered down at her high-heel shoes. He could see his face in the leather and could barely smell the beeswax. "I'm afraid you'll just have to grin and bare it. All the staff are busy with more important things with the party. If there's nothing else I have to go and watch the ice sculpture melt." He walked off to the kitchen, muttering, "I'll paint varnish on her shoes next time. The bitch will never know the bastard difference."

* * *

Puffing away on his cigarette, Lee Snowdon shivered in the chill of the evening air as he peered in the window of his employer's car to check if it was still locked up securely for the night. Satisfied he exhaled a plume of smoke then began to make his way back to the kitchens, weaving between the parked vehicles. Half way across the parking lot lit up by the glare of the 500 Watt floodlights mounted on the garage roof, the twenty-nine year old heard something squeak just beyond the range of the light. He paused to listen for it again and the sharp, high-pitched sound emitted louder as if whatever it was, had become increasing nearer. A third shrill sound came to his ears before, in the depth of the darkness, claw-like hands drew back thick cords by means of a winch and pulley as the perfect elevation was achieved, a lever was thrown and a massive crossbow bolt with a four-sided, iron head launched down a shallow trench and was sent forth with great force.

Out of curiosity, the lusty, young chauffeur walked towards the sound, frowning as he caught the hint of a swishing noise before glass began shattering. Snowdon blinked as additional car windows burst into pieces and the sound of tearing of metal rent the air. His throat constricted and paralyzed, he was filled with indecision – should he run or just stay put to see what was causing the damage? He waited, rubbernecking, narrowing his eyes and, at the moment his frantic gaze glimpsed the curving tip of a ballista and the skeleton warrior beside it emerging from the darkened woods, he took a frightened step back, and issued forth a whimpered gasp as raw panic gripped him. Then the long Garrot streaked through the rear windows of the station wagon directly ahead of him and the head punched past his guts and powerfully lifted Snowdon up off his feet. Blood spilled from the gaping wound as the point of the missile exited his back, clipping the bonnet of a Porsche and the boot of Mercedes-Benz before eventually smashing into the engine of a Rolls-Royce.

With his back propped up against the wing of the car, smelling the oil, hot water flowing from the gash in the bodywork, the chauffeur raised his head and his eyes swelled from the pain of his shredded abdomen. Crimson spurted like a fountain and flowed over his coiling entrails as his trembling hands tried to scoop them back into the wound. His breathing became shallow and raspy, and when he coughed more red foam frothed on his lips, his body growing colder from loss of blood. He faintly heard footsteps and his dulling gaze saw four skeleton warriors with drawn sword approach. The leader looked like a Roman. Long stringy hair framed his dirty skull and nails the length of knifes lanced out of bony fingers. He had one real, bloodshot eye turning in its bony socket and he grinned, displaying a tongue attached to the floor of the mouth. Lungs steamed and these organs inflated and deflated with a parody of life. Snowdon's final thoughts were that his sanity was leaving him then suddenly he was shaken with savage convulsions before he drooped forward to drape across the length of fletched wood, dead.

The undead walked up to the body, and the leader's borrowed tongue moved and clicked against his newly acquired gums before a guttural speech filled the air. "Fray the skin, remove his vitals, see everyone obtains some of the parts. I going to have that other eye..." he was tapped on the shoulder by a helmetless infantryman wearing sandals and rusty lamellar armour.

"Commander Patermunthis," he said in Latin, his tongue also having difficulty with the forming of words, "his hair! Can I have it? I've been bald for so long."

"Of course you can have the toupee Flavius," the commander replied with a nod, "don't let it be said that Julian Patermunthis doesn't give his men everything they want."

* * *

Constable Irving Cheney glanced up at another arrow drawn across the tree bark and followed it through a thicket of bushes and ferns to emerge on an animal trail. The inspector came next and blinked as she saw Kris Perratt within a swatch of light kneeling over a footprint and taking a photograph of it. Sinclair glanced to where the light was coming from and noticed that on the ground was his torch beam shining into his shaving mirror and reflecting the brightness over a greater distance.

"We've arrived Kris," Cheney announced.

"I heard you coming for ages. You sounded like a herd of elephants. What took you so long anyway?" Perratt replied, straightening and turning to greet his visitors.

"We had to drive round the blast site," Keane said, observing the smudged tracks in the mud before his eyes fell on a drying plaster cast, "and we got lost twice."

"Enough details sergeant," Sinclair rebuked him prior to addressing the tracker, "I am sure Mr Perratt doesn't want to hear about your terrible map reading. Now then Kris what have you found for me?"

"Footprints! A lovely size-twelve with a tack embedded in the heel plus a size seven and an eight. I took a cast of the larger one and took pictures of the other two. This trail is a repeated passage. At least three people have been through here in single file. From the weight of the foot prints I would say two of the them are right handed and the third is a lefty. I can also inform you of their height in relation to the width of the steps and possibly how heavy they are, once we've reduced the weight of the money pouches. I followed the tracks for two miles when Irving went back to fetch you. I believe the trail goes beyond that."

"Good! Cheney you and my two officers stay here and protect this section of the crime scene. Keane radio in our current position and ask for assistance then you, me and Kris are going to see where these footprints lead."

"Now the game is afoot," Perratt said, removing another tin from his pocket. He opened it up and inside was a preparation of powdered tobacco. He shoved some of it into his mouth before chewing.

* * *

Josh Brennan entered the library and instantly saw his girlfriend was dressed up as Wonder Woman. Danielle Huxley was standing beside her wearing a glittery bra and a few silks wrapped around her bum and hips. Silver chains hung about her ankles and midriff. A red gem was stuck in her belly button. Black candles stood on the two tables along with a thick book, crystals and a gong. Other things lay in the suitcase open wide on the floor.

"Nice to see so much of you Danielle," he remarked with a smirk, eyeing her all over as nearly all of the gang filed in. "If you want any help in getting out of that costume then you let me know. I'll be more than happy to assist in any way I can."

"Yeah me too," Thornton said, pushing past the others to get a better look.

"Men!" Tucci sighed with a shake of her head. "Oh for God sake. Get your tongues back in will you? It's embarrassing."

"Jealous Andrea? Because no one breathing, looks at you in the same way." Thornton inquired.

Tucci flushed and anger flashed into her eyes, "why don't you just go and play with yourself Thornton. That's the only way your dick is ever going to see any action in your life time."

"Quiet!" Lois shouted, suppressing a smile as she addressed them. "I wouldn't say that Andrea because anything, and I mean anything, is possible in the next few minutes if you listen to what I have to tell you." She glanced around, counting heads, hoping they already had several drinks inside them so they wouldn't be thinking all that straight when they heard her proposition.

"Yeah! Josh said you had an opportunity for us Lois," Tweed said, going over to the fish tanks and peering inside, "but he didn't state what..."

"It ain't dishonest it is?" Thornton asked evenly, "I know of your reputation. I'm not going to jail for no one."

"I'm not suggesting we break the law Dermot, in fact I'm able to promise you, your hearts desire. Power or riches or fame."

"How! What have we got to do to earn all this," Tucci asked, her brow furrowing.

"Wait a sec. Prue! Shut the door and where are Russel, Sean, Matt and Zoe? They are supposed to be here. Josh did you inform them of what was on offer."

The door closed with a clink.

"Russel and Zoe are coming I think," Brennan replied, shrugging his shoulders. "They stopped downstairs for an extra drink. Matt and Sean haven't come back from the bog. They'll be all right though, they've the map and a torch so the going shouldn't be tough."

"Hope so," Tweed muttered.

"Will that make any difference Lois? You'll still be able to carry out the ritual with just the six of us aren't you?" He saw her nod.

"Ritual!" Exclaimed Tucci with a shake of her head. "I hate wasting my breath because I said it before, count me out of using a Ouija board."

"How about proper magic from a spell book?" Danielle asked with an arched eyebrow. "You'll not be scared of that as well will you?" She pointed at *The Grimorie* on the nearest table.

"Poppycock!" Tucci said with a closed mind as she glanced over at the book, "no such thing. Where'd you get it from, a jumble sale?"

"Actually no," Lois said, detaching herself from the group and proceeding round the mat, "I brought it in a little book store when I went on holiday to America last year." She walked up to the tome and picked it up. "It tells you the usual stuff. How to get rid of warts, keep your skin flesh and conjure demons from a myriad of neitherworlds or realms to do your bidding."

"It's Halloween! Not April the first Lois," Tweed commented evenly with a easy smile. "What is it we're supposed to do? A bleeding kids game backed-up no doubt with nothing more than a poetry book?" Tucci said. "And I'm seriously missing out knocking back all the booze while I'm up here. Zoe and Russel have go the right idea by staying away."

Lois flipped open *The Grimorie* and scanned the yellowed pages as the door opened and Corbett and Hawes entered, clutching a bottle of beer apiece.

"You were saying Andrea?" Brennan said.

"We miss anything?" Corbett asked, taking a swig as Hawes closed the door behind her.

"We getting ready to summon a demon," Lois uttered, turning the pages until she found her bookmark.

"Include me in that," Corbett said, lowering the bottle as he advanced with Hawes in tow.

"Why not," she echoed, "it'll be a laugh."

"All right Lois," Tucci declared with a nod, "i'll tell you what, prove me wrong if you can. Let's act out this little fantasy role and see what a con artist you really are."

"That's fighting talk," Lois replied, a thin smile spread to her lips. "Danielle get the candles. Dermot raise the rug up gently. I don't want what's underneath to be disturbed."

He did so, and Tucci gasped at the large pentacle, wormwood and powered mushroom were sprinkled in the midst of the blue chalk lines. Danielle came forward and began placing the candles and holders on each of the five points in the circled symbol and then Brennan stuck a match and lit the wicks in turn.

"You actually believe this three ring circus of yours can work?" Tucci said with widening eyes.

"It will work Andrea," Lois remarked, observing Danielle next stroll to the circle and knelt to deposit a white crystal in front of the candle holders, just inside the pentacle. "It has before. Now joint hands and arranged yourselves about the figure." The group as one, complied. "With more of us lending our strength to the spell we should be able to keep Bartok here longer this time to grant all of your wishes."

* * *

"What do you think Adrian," Thaw said. Coming out of the trophy room to join up with Cummings before walking back along the corridor towards the ballroom. Two security guards flanked the front doorway behind them while another stood just inside the chamber among reporters and news crews setting up their microphones and camera equipment for the press conference. Each of them, Thaw saw, had been jockeying for the best position at the podium. More television cameras were being focused directly in front of and on high gantries down upon the priceless jewellry and artifacts lying in neat rows on the tabletop. From the walls, heads of elephants and lions looked down on the entire proceedings with blank disinterest.

"Keep to the plan. Wait until the distraction then do it," he ventured an opinion. "I doubt the guards will go anywhere but the news crews will want to see what the commotion is just out of pure instinct."

"Won't they just," Thaw agreed. "Did you and Sophie bring up the last of the baggage?"

"You bet," Cummings nodded then glanced at his watch. "All of it's behind the bushes. We also replaced the floorboards in the cottage so nothing looks out of the ordinary. Fifteen minutes to go! I think I'll grab something to eat before I get the car ready."

"Okay! Get a doggy bag for each of us," Thaw responded, striding alongside him. "I'm gonna round up the gang and get them all into position. See you out front!"

"Right!" Cummings remarked.

The monster mash was been played by the DJ as the corridor turned into the darkened ballroom. Thaw and Cummings parted and slipped through the crowd of guests as glitter balls revolved above their heads and lights in the ceiling bathed the dancers in vivid swirling patterns. Bats and rubber spiders decorated the wood-paneled walls along which stood tables covered with food and the occasionally small decorative jack-o'-lantern. At the far end of the massive chamber there were two doors that opened up to the city of tents outside, and through these passed guests, wearing costumes of every era as they helped themselves to the self-service food, danced or waylaid the waitresses and waiters carrying glasses of pink champagne, scotch, gin and ale.

Robert Crowe walked and mingled with his guests. He was wearing the robe and hood of an ancient Druid and clutching a wooden staff with a crystal ball on top. He nodded or simply said "Hello!" to a man wearing a magpie costume, someone dressed as a tree and Biljana Isaacs as Guinevere.

Connar Hannon sidled up to the super model and said. "I'm Admiral Horato Nelson! And you are?"

"Not interested," Isaacs said, walking after Robert.

Behind her, Mick Fulford in an ape costume wandered up to Hannon, "she sunk you there Admiral," he said with a smile. "I bet you a tenner that I can pull her?"

"Make it fifty pounds," Hannon replied, behind his mask, "and you got yourself a deal."

"Done," the ape nodded before the pair shook hands.

Across the room a pair dressed as Romeo and Juliet stared at Isaacs as she began catching up with Robert.

"What do you think Fletcher," Byle said thoughtfully, "do we accept what we received as gospel truth and confront Isaacs about her drug taking without any real evidence?"

"Definitely not," Everett mused, "we'll end up looking at slander charges if we came out with accusations like that, but it wouldn't hurt to show her the letter to see what her reaction would be."

"No harm at all," Byle muttered smoothly as directly opposite them Robert stopped in his tracks and turned when the music died and Isaacs called out to him. "Let's take a slow walk over there and grab hold of her when she's free."

Byle nodded and they both set off across the dance floor.

"Mr Crowe! When do you require me to do my spot?" Isaacs asked, noticing from the corner of her eye some flakes of dandruff on the bulging mass of material around her shoulders. She smiled, licked her palm and quickly brushed the flakes away. "Now that the press conference has been rescheduled?"

"Well about ten to ten Biljanana," he remarked easily, "you'll probably wear the same jewellry for the cameras as you did earlier for the photo shoot."

"Is that Kalvinder Kapoor joining me again?" She enquired, "because she threw a tantrum John McEnroe would have been proud off and that Mrs Snodgress..."

"I'm well aware of that windbag," he uttered, pulling a face, "I don't think I've heard the woman stop, not even when she comes up for air."

"Anyway Kapoor and I had a few words," she resumed, "on account of her picking the best of the rings, necklaces and bracelets."

Robert sighed and nodded. "Miss Kapoor was kindly asked to help with the modeling by my financial advisor or in fact her agent did on Homes' request..."

"Homes," she echoed. "As in Oliver Wendell the third? The oil billionaire and race horse owner."

"Correct! He believed it would be mutually beneficial for my company to crack the overseas markets if I had both of you involved in the publicity."

"I see," Isaacs declared thoughtfully, "well I'll be there on time." She sported a ghost of a smile before departing into the crowd. Byle and Everett followed.

Behind a robot, a mummy, a woman clothed in a space suit, knocking back wine like it was out of date, Kalvinder Kapoor dressed in the armor of Boadicea, and Alice Snodgress stood by the portals watching the dancers. Snodgress pointed at Romeo and Juliet and said: "You see those two! They're photo journalists and I imagine they're going to interview Isaacs."

"How can you tell?"

"Oh they got their hands on a letter I wrote saying Isaacs is taking drugs." The shorter woman replied calmly.

"Is she?"

"How would I know. I did it to make her pay for trying to upstage you Kal."

"Are you mad Alice," Kapoor said quietly, looking about to see if there was anyone listening, "you've got no proof that she does."

"No but the allegation is enough to get one on her."

"You've overstepped the mark this time. They'll have us for libel if they ever find out."

"They won't!" Snodgress reassured her, "I shoved the letter under the bloke's door when they went to interview the archaeologist. And to stir the shit further I wrote the letter in block capitals with my left hand. No one will be able to say we had anything to do with it. I love causing trouble. It's a knack I have. Another drink Kal?" She smiled sweetly.

The film star nodded before Snodgress spotted the butler and went off in pursuit.

CHAPTER TWENTY ONE

Smoke thickened from a spot of Lois' blood, spiraling upwards to the ceiling from inside the glowing lines of the pentagram as Lois released the hands on either of side of her and stepped back a few paces. "Danielle, Dermot, hurry and close ranks," she uttered, reaching over to deposit *The Grimorie* on top of the table then snatched up the gong and the padded hammer. "Interlock your fingers again while I put the finishing touches to the ritual."

The people sidestepped and did as they were told to Tucci's muttered grumbling as Lois mouthed a word of power and raised the metallic disk, striking a loud blow. A resonant tone echoed on the air then abruptly a blustery wind emitted from the bottom of the circle and began to disperse the smoke as it climbed to eventually reveal Bartok's disembodied head deceptively appearing, staring up at Brennan and Hawes projecting through the trapdoor, between the increasing brightening chalk lines.

"Keep the chain connected," Danielle shouted, tightening her grasp on Dwyer's hand, "the protection spell relies on it for a few seconds more."

"Wow! Far out," Corbett said with a broad grin, feeling the pressure Tweed was applying on his hand. "This has got to be real. I ain't drunk enough yet to hallucinate anything this cool."

The demon winked when Hawes inhaled suddenly with surprise and Tucci's eyes opened wide at the sight. Then his intangible torso and legs quickly floated through the floor, his gaze revolving as his head turned three hundred and sixty degrees to survey the faces arranged about him. Lois banged the gong once more and strode forward to the ring of hands. Bartok's ghost-like body slowly solidified as his overall density increased and he gained actual form and substance. His feet dropped a foot in height and stamped onto the trapdoor with a thump; the wood groaned under the weight.

"It's got to be a trick of the light or some dirt on my glasses," Tucci declared with a shake of her head, her face draining of colour, "this is scientifically impossible."

"It's not any of those things," Brennan replied before anyone else could. "It's magic. It's unpredictable."

"According to what I've read," Danielle said, "savage magic is difficult to control."

"Difficult!" Thornton echoed, "what have you got us into Lois?"

Lois sighed and ignored the comment. "Okay everyone step back," she shouted as the companions released their hands and nervously retreated. "Bartok is contained inside the pentagram and won't be going anywhere until I let him, isn't that correct my strapping servant."

The demon politely bowed to the waist then straightened. "As you say mistress I am in your thrall and you are mine, employed to perform services which are now due. I have already given you a sign of my good faith, the rest of your powers will be bestowed when I receive the price of our agreement. Free me so I may collect."

Lois' tongue clicked against her cheek. "Ah, that's a bit awkward at the moment. You see Bartok, all of my friends want the same gifts as me," the giant demon scowled as she continued, "and unlike me they aren't very trusting I'm afraid so what can you do? Either give in or just rot inside your old prison? I would hate to burn the pages relating to you. No one will ever let you out to play again."

The demon tilted his head back and laughed, a dreadful grating sound that echoed off the walls and made the hairs rise on the back of Thornton's neck. Dwyer's heart missed a beat and Tweed felt her body tremble from fright. Bartok suddenly grew serious and with a wave of his hand, all of the creatures in the aquariums started to grow and morph then disappear.

"I didn't think it was that funny," Danielle said with a frown.

"It wasn't. The fucker's up to something," Lois replied.

A pair of horns sprouted from his forehead. "I knew you would double cross me mistress Lois," the demon spat back with a ringing nasal quality his voice had lacked before. In the corridors outside, house plants ruffled and became animated without wind, and here and there tapestries and wallpaper on the ceiling adorned with roses and bushes, also stirred and writhed weakly. "That is why I took precautions to create a jail break, so to speak, using my friends in the marsh." Brennah exchanged glances with Lois who shrugged her shoulders. "Yet I see this prison has a way out I didn't previously consider until now."

He looked up at the light bulb and raised his fingers towards it. A low continuous, murmuring sound begun reverberating within the circle. In moments the bulb grew crimson and shattered, raining down glass upon the demon, drawing trickles of blood from shallow cuts. Zigzagging streams of electricity suddenly burst forth from the socket and shot down, ionizing the air in its path, arching away from Bartok to hit the invisible energy field about him.

"I would have upheld our bargain but not anymore," He said, feeling the tremendous heat from the discharges. "Soon I will walk the earth and wipe out all who are dull-witted enough to oppose me."

* * *

A tapestry decorated with flowers hung from the wall near the inner entrance of the ballroom, and when the light didn't flicker in its direction, prickly plant stems grew larger and thorns extended and became spikes; the blossoms slowly expanded, progressing towards maturity with sharply-toothed edges; and veins grew more pronounced on broadening leaves.

Outside a reddish, glowing ball about a foot in diameter, appeared out of thin air and floated for a second prior to zipping down and gliding along the ground, showing intelligence by ducking under table cloths and weaving in-between the city of tents towards the ballroom. When no one was observing it, the red sphere targeted a person warming himself by one of the heaters, disguised as the lead singer of Guns N' Roses. Tony Jordan was standing on his own and listening to the music, sipping beer from the bottle as the sphere zoomed closer and halted, nudging his left boot before disintegrating. A green nimbus surrounded the young man before he even realised it. He vanished without a trace, only to reappear a moment later on a slab of rock surrounded by a sea of fire.

"Where the hell am I..." Jordan sputtered in puzzlement, blinking at the crimson gloom and utterly flabbergasted, dropping the beer bottle to smash loudly at his feet.

Brimstone assailed his nostrils and took his breath away. Something flying in wider spirals spotted him, it swooped downward from the sky. With his mind at a complete loss as to where he was, Jordan shook his head as a shadow from a massive wingspan suddenly drifted across him. He turned and was forced to retreat a pace under the onslaught from a great rush of air. Looking up, he screamed when talons lunged and snatched him by the shoulders, claws ripped into his leather vest but only pricked the skin causing blood to trickle down to his neckline.

Then with the beat of wings and the thrash of its lion's tail, the mythical animal soared upward, lifting his burden effortlessly into the air. Jordan struggled, trying in vain to free himself from the iron grip but couldn't, feeling increasingly lightheaded as the island of rock dwindled far beneath him. A neck arched and a peal of laughter reverberated from the Griffin's throat.

"You're the first slave the master has sent back but not the last I fancy. Pray for the mines little one or you could be sacrificed on the altar stone. Some choice." The creature snorted at the mirth of his joke and flapped onward over the flickering sea.

* * *

"This dang boilermaker tastes like mouthwash," Homes complained, spitting the liquor back into his tumbler. "You there employee," his call brought a young skinny waitress over to them. "Get me another of these," he gestured with the glass, glancing at the woman's name badge, "and be sharp about it Annette if you don't want to see a pink slip in your wage packet tonight. Got it?"

Annette went pale, her long face grimaced and her dark ponytailed hair bobbed up and down. She took the proffered tumbler and quickly departed. Homes pulled out his pocket watch from the pouch of his Rhett Butler waist coat and glanced at the dial. Twenty past eight.

"Sissy where is Robert!" Homes remarked slightly louder than he meant, "I hate waiting around. Time is money don't you know."

Two red balls came into view inches above the ceiling. They glided towards the glitter balls and gyrated around them like moons orbiting a planet.

Dressed as Scarlett O'Hara in a green gown and a long red wig, Lynskey detected Robert Crowe between a man wearing a bright yellow Pokemon costume of a Raichiu, jigged with a buxom thirty year old woman dressed as a penguin. Cummings and Bisset carrying plates of food receded in the direction of the portals. Beyond, light from the garden torches made flickering patterns dance across the sides and the roofs of the tents.

"Aw shucks Oilver, have patience. He's coming now. All good things come to those who wait."

"Phooey!" Homes replied as the waitress returned with another boilermaker, he snatched it of the tray, took a sip and nodded his head in approval. "Better! You can go."

The woman hurried away and quickly became lost in the throng. Robert passed Annette and finally drew up in front of the pair. "Oliver, Sissy! Great party huh?"

"Not bad Robert. Did you make sure you provided the media with the revised edition of the press kit? We don't want them knowing some of the artifacts are coming back with us to the states."

"They won't!" Robert gave him a reassuring pat on his right shoulder, not noticing Thaw, Klugman and Gillett saunter one at a time out of the ballroom, towards the trophy room. "Professor Keriry has been keeping two sets of books in which he catalogues all his finds in. He's also been rotating his archeologists here and at the neighboring digs every few days so none of his people are around long enough to keep auxiliary records or check on what's been accumulated."

"You made a good call there," Homes reflected, swallowing the last of his drink, "once those baubles are in my private collection I'll keep my word and be your silent backer, getting you the best Public Relations experts my money can buy to promote our company back home. By the time I've finished Vulcan Projects will be a household name all across the country."

* * *

Another series of jagged spurts of lightning crashed into the barrier holding Bartok captive. The length of the wall crackled with energy but still it held against the onslaught.

"Fuck this," Hawes said, taking a step back before turning to run for the library door, "I didn't agree to something like this."

"Me neither," Tweed agreed, following at her heels.

Tucci and Corbett retreated back a pace apiece but stayed watching for very different reasons. Corbett was observing the patterns of the light storm; the jagged bolts of energy surging and swirling around the demon, the barrier ricocheting the effort and strength ten times over to collide into Bartok's face and torso. Tucci noticed spidery runes appear in the air above the outer edge of the pentacle, glittering for a second before vanishing, only to be replaced by another mysterious characters and not always in the same place twice. She wondered what the runes were and didn't have an inkling how she could explain their presence.

Brennan, Dwyer and Thornton slowly circumvented the captive and headed to where Lois and Danielle stood, watching the shield becoming visible with a bluish mother-of-pearl tint. Table lamps, fluorescent lights and incandescent lamps brightened the aquarium walls flickered then winked out as the light was redirected to another source.

"This isn't going according to plan," Lois said, opposite her companions, clutching *The Grimorie*. Her knuckles shone white with the pressure she was applying to the spine and the cover.

"Yeah and whose fault's that?" Danielle replied, her whole body trembling from fright. "What were you trying to achieve by betraying him? Now you've just pissed him off."

"So what Danielle! I'm greedy! Sue me. I wanted all the powers now, not later. Have you thought that if we let him go to collect his slaves he might not stop there? He could press on and keep on taking, finally leaving us a world we couldn't take advantage of ourselves?"

"Every waking minute since you proposed this venture," she replied with a nod.

Then the demon bellowed in rage as he saw colour seep upwards towards the ceiling. "No it can not be. All this power at my command and still I'm trapped here like a useless infant."

He banged his fists against the obstruction and again his clenched hands rebounded. Blood seeped from his nostrils and chest where smoke rose from smoldering, blackened fresh. Bartok roared as he called forth more electricity to do his bidding. Brennan edged further around, keeping to the shadows. Dwyer and Thornton brought up the rear. Blue-white forks of lightning produced a brilliant flash in the containment field against the encroaching darkness invading the library; the strands of energy strafed the glowing lines at his feet, and lashed into his body anew. The demon winced at the intensifying agony and little by little his illusion failed. His ears become pointed, his hair shrank, and his scales replaced skin.

"At least the spell of protection is holding," Lois said. The library shuddered.

"Maybe Lois!" Danielle replied evenly, "but the book doesn't say anything about that blue tint. For all we know the wards are weakening. I don't think the spell will last to twelve o'clock tonight and that's a guarantee."

Bartok kicked and punched the barrier again and again with sufficient force to reduce mountains into ash. He inhaled lungfuls of air and mentally urged his minions to cut a wide swath through the quickest route to him. He became aware of an answer while his forehead began to swell as blood roared in his ears.

"How long?" Thornton asked with a frown, coming to a halt beside the other two. Shifting his attention between the energy column and Danielle's face, "before the wards dissipate?"

The books lining the walls rocked before they started falling from the shelves in the after effects of another tremor. Blood flowed from the gashes in Bartok's hands but still he lashed out at the walls.

"I'm not sure," she shrugged in reply. "The way he's going at it, an hour perhaps?"

"Sixty minutes!" Dwyer muttered. "There must be a way in your book to send him," she paused as she saw the demon grow breasts, "erm it back to whatever hell it came from?"

"I didn't find one when I was consulting *The Grimorie* earlier. I could have easily missed a page or overlooked some text especially as I was tired after working late yesterday."

"Well get consulting girl!" Thornton declared. "We're up a creek here without a paddle."

"Your uncle got any guns Lois?" Corbett asked, snapping out of his reverie. "A few bullets will blow this sucker away."

"A shotgun possibly. I don't know where it is though,"she shook her head.

"I did the tour of the house while you lot couldn't be bothered to and I saw there were some swords and other things on the walls of a corridor not far from here," Tucci put in, "that would do for a bit."

"You ain't kidding!" Thornton declared with exuberance. "Show us Andrea and I'll made this bastard a eunuch before the night's out."

Tucci headed out at a trot into the corridor beyond. Thornton and Corbett followed.

"Rus! Save me something nice and sharp," Brennan shouted to his friend.

"Will do," came back the reply.

Leaning close to his girlfriend's ear, Brennan said, "any chance you can stop him with your air magic by drawing the oxygen out of his lungs like you did to the fox outside?"

"I'm not certain our friend over there is human. It's worth a try as a last resort," Lois said before addressing Danielle. "Let's get out of here and find a quieter place so I can hear myself think."

Danielle nodded and was the first to follow Lois as she dashed out the door, *The Grimorie* wedged firmly under her arm. Dwyer and Brennan swapped looks before pursuing. In the doorway Brennan lingered for a second and cast a swift glance back at the demon's elongating chin and maturing beard, cognisant of the fact that their very lives were now balanced on a knife edge.

* * *

Elsewhere as D.I.S.C.O was being played on the turntables, Annette picked up some empty glasses, deposited them onto her tray then set off towards the kitchen. A side-passage loomed up on the right and she nipped into it. The corridor was narrow and had a vaulted ceiling lost in the darkness above. Annette had not strode in far when she heard something akin to pieces of Velcro being pulled apart. Frowning, she glanced up and immediately screamed as a gigantic thing scuffled out of the shadow and down the wall towards her.

She saw that it was a cross between a reptile and an amphibian – a wedged-shaped head set with bulging eyes, a twelve foot long body squashed between both walls, and growing teeth; smooth undulating skin wrapped around thrashing tentacles and dark barred legs with webbed feet. In shock, Annette fainted, her tray clattered as she collapsed and lost consciousness. The monster continued to drag its developing feet, one of the slender tentacles quickly thickened and stretched to twice its original length and struck out; the end of the flexible appendage looping about Annette's torso and pulled her off the floor.

The young woman was quickly hauled up into its hinged mouth which opened wider to adjust to the proportions of her body. Teeth clamped shut, drowning out the snapping of bones and the ripping of flesh. Blood trickled down the edges of the creature's mouth. With a hasty swallow, the fleshy, wrinkled piece of skin hanging from its throat trembled violently. The walls of the corridor cracked, wallpaper ripped under extending claws and plaster flaked as the beast scrambled agilely to the ground and proceeded to the connecting passageway ahead.

* * *

Lois Elmes led the way along the corridor and as Corbett and Thornton followed Tucci ahead to the supply of weapons, the young brunette came to a halt next to a hanging depicting scenes of the second crusade. Yanking it quickly aside she revealed a small modest door inserted in an alcove.

"Where's this go?" Dwyer asked with a frown.

Turning the handle Lois pushed the door inward and began climbing up a narrow, widening staircase. "To the observatory. It'll be nice and quiet up there. Hobby of my uncle." More stone steps fell away beneath them. Their footfalls echoing off the closeness of the walls. "Been doing it for years. He's just not very good because the only comet he's ever found is the one in the high street," she puffed seeing the top come into view. "Here we are," she added, reaching the solitary room lit by a 100 watt bulb. Her companions piled up behind her.

"Hey we're in the highest tower," Brennan said as he took in the surroundings, "I can't bear heights."

"Well take a seat then and don't look down," Lois responded unconcerned, striding forward.

"I don't intend too," Brennan replied, seeing lights blink off and on from the machines, "where's the guy who runs all this shit?"

"The astronomer is at the party," Danielle said, stringing along behind Lois, "Hannon I think his name is. He's new to the job, took over from old man Dutt who retired last week."

The round chamber was dominated by the huge telescope the end of which stuck out of domed plexi-glass roof. The observatory was equipped with different types of instruments to catalogue the great variety of objects existing in space and the tremendous distances between them. A table was situated in the middle of the room about which stood three chairs. Danielle spread *The Grimorie* on the table top and Lois sat beside her and peered at the contents.

Dwyer walked up to the telescope and gazed into the eyepiece at the heavens and the clouds scudding across the view of the celestial bodies. The darkness pressed against the dome concealing the serious of events that were unfolding down below.

* * *

As the lightning continued to surge around him, Bartok dug his claws into his left thigh. Instead of blood, a yellow halo creep over the flesh and when his fingers withdrew, they tenderly held a wolf-head pommel. His hands retreated further and a hilt emerged from the top of the muscle along with a crosspiece and wide, grooved two-edged blade.

Soon a long broadsword was clasped within his right hand. He chortled then thrust the blade point at the barrier. Runes became outlined in red as the sword punched through and began to slice around the protection shield.

CHAPTER TWENTY TWO

Cummings and Bisset were just beginning to make tracks for the car park when they heard screams coming from the garden. Intrigued they proceeded to the portals and the tall man blinked when he saw skeleton warriors striding up the lawn, those in the forefront were lunging or hacking with swords; the single blows were dispatching the startled guests to their deaths. A man masquerading as Charlie Chaplin was stunned by a warrior's pommel before the Norman Knight plunged his blade down deeply into his back. Another guest – a strong, and agile jungle man – had his left arm sliced off and then his throat was severed from ear to ear. Two Roman corpses used their spears by hurling them at the wide-eyed and screaming party goers as they scrambled for the safety of the house.

Blood flew on the air and a young dark-haired woman dressed like the film star in Casablanca and an older woman in a Florence Nightingale outfit fell stone dead, toppling over a table and a garden torch. Sparks were thrown up and frames licked hungrily at tent canvas. Then something dived out of the darkness above, Bisset saw a glimpse of a monster insect with leathery wings and covered in bristles as thin as a needle and big as a man's arm which launched from the creature's side, raining down slaughter wherever it gazed. Guest's and warriors alike were pierced through with the sharp prickly spines but whereas the undead kept walking, pulling out the bristles and throwing them away, men and women received fatal deathblows and fell where they were stabbed in widening pools of blood. A man uttered a death rattle as his breath passed through mucus.

The screams outside grew louder and drew the attention of a number of the guests standing around the buffet tables. Couples frowned and exchanged glances while dancers suddenly stopped and turned towards the doors. Ashley Crowe, dressed as a nun, sighed and detached herself from the throng and marched up to where the insurance salesman and a ghost were standing. What if the outcry was because some fool had let the fireworks off early and some rogue rockets had landed in between the tents and injuring guests.

The law suit would cripple them financially. Crowe shuddered at the mere thought and braced herself against the worst. A Snowman, a tall Christmas cracker and others joined her out of curiosity.

Dinner plates dropped from shocked fingers. "What the fuck's happening and what is that thing flying overhead?" Bisset declared in panic as a blue-coated US cavalry man closed on the doors of the ballroom. More people followed the stocky man as Cummings grabbed Bisset's arm and pulled him back. A woman wearing a lavish costume fell, spurting blood as a sweeping slash of a blade sheared her head from her shoulders.

"I don't know. This ain't no re-enactment of a battle I ever heard off," Cummings said, reaching under his ghost sheet and producing a grenade with his free hand as he continued to yank Bisset back, pushing through the approaching mass of guests.

"This could complicate things a bit," Bisset said.

Cummings glanced at him. "You certainly have a gift of understatement. Nathan go and tell Jerome there's something weird happening here and we can't get to a car. I want us to meet on the main staircase in five minutes whether they've got the jewellry or not.We might have to fight our way out if we want to collect the bags."

"Gothca!" He replied then blinked and added, "what are you going to do Adrian?"

Cummings grinned wolfishly. "Buy you some time by acting as rearguard."

"Take care then," he replied before whirling about and hot-footing it as fast as he could shoving aside Kalvinder Kapoor and a middle-aged maid called Meryl along the way. Homes, Lynskey and Robert Crowe watched from the rear.

"I see you believe in delegating Robert," Homes stated.

"Oh yes! Ashley will sort it out whatever it is. That's what wives are for. Running round after us men folk."

Homes grinned and slapped Lynskey's bodice. "They have better uses, don't you my dear." Lynskey nodded and strained to produce a smile.

The cavalry man burst into the ballroom and bellowed, "run everyone." He dashed forward, pushing through the gathering crowd who couldn't see anything because the people outside were blocking their view as they charged into the ballroom. "Run for your lives. Death's coming!"

Judge Giles Pilkington wearing the costume of the killer in the Wes Craven horror thriller stared dumbfounded at the cavalry man. He knew the middle-aged barrister well because he had presented and pleaded cases in the Judge's court many times over the years and this outburst was so unlike him. He shouted, "Orbach! It's me Judge Pilkington, what's happening man?"

"You'll see your honor if you stop in here any longer," Orbach replied, hurrying away as fast as he could.

Cummings retreated some more paces. He had pulled his ghost sheet off and tossed it away. Now his Colt 45 was clutched in his right hand, beside his leg.

"Oh what utter rot," Ashley Crowe said, pushing through the gathering assembly in an attempt to get to the front. "Don't panic! He's probably had to much of our punch." The crowd was a shifting flow of bodies, milling and eddying, being roughly jostled as the guests shouted and screamed, going forward and back in a kind of compact scrum, fed by a desperate frenzy that drove some to kick and punch their way forward, treading on those who had been knocked down. "Let me through at once you hear."

"Maybe I should see what the problem is after all," Robert Crowe said with an anguished frown, proceeding to the center of the chamber. Cummings drew alongside him.

* * *

Zoe Hawes heard the approaching footsteps and opened up the bedroom door in inch or two to see who was passing by.

"Who is it Zoe?" Tweed asked in a whisper. Trembling in fear as she stood beside her. "That demon has broken free already has it?"

A shadow drifted across the floor of the corridor followed by another as Andrew and Vertly Elmes walked by dressed as Lord Bryan and his wife Anne Milbanke. Hawes closed the door to and shook her head as the pair passed. "It's Lois' parents," she mouthed silently. Tweed sighed and nodded.

"I've never had so much trouble putting on a pair of boots and a cravat in my entire life Vertly."

His wife smiled. "I saw Stan and Ollie once on TV, having a hard time with riding boots in a comedy short of theirs. I thought it was put on for the cameras now I know differently."

They progressed steadily down the passageway and turned left towards the staircase. Hawes threw the door ajar and peered left and right. The corridor was empty. "It's quiet. Let's hurry out of here while the going's good."

A red ball flew out from behind a pair of curtains and streaked after the women.

"You and me both girl," Tweed replied, following her out. "I am dropping off at the cottage first in case Matt's back. I want to grab a change of clothes and my belongings. If we try hitching a ride in this get-up, the drivers will keep on going, sure to think we've just escaped from the funny farm."

The globe latched onto Tweed and gave her elbow a gentle push. She faded a second later and the sound of her passage ceased.

"I see your point," Hawes declared. Striding along the corridor, not noticing the sudden absence of footfalls behind her, "we can use the back staircase and exit through the kitchen without anyone seeing us. What do you think Yasmin?"

When she didn't hear a response Hawes turned to see what was up with her friend. Her eyes went wide and she scratched her cheek in puzzlement as she stood alone in the corridor.

"Yasmin! Where have you run off to?"

Again no answer.

"Yasmin! I'll be at the cottage just time enough to phone the army. okay. After that I'm gone." She dashed off and didn't bother looking back.

* * *

"Two minutes to go Kyle," Thaw said, "here's where we head into the lion's den." He and Klugman arrived at the doorway of the trophy room and passed on through to the busy rush of voices. Gillett had entered first and was making her way behind the display table where a lanky security guard was standing at ease. His eyes drifted from the reporters and guests to latch onto the willowy, auburn-haired woman and observed her approach.

"Yeah!" Klugman replied evenly, "I'll move into position while you cover the door."

"Roger that," Thaw announced. Drawing to a halt on the pretext of examining the wall where a mounted head of a leopard hung next to one of an rhino. Klugman sauntered on between reporters and other news crews checking their tripods were the correct height, screwing on filters and adjusting front lights in an attempt to provide illumination. Klugman halted and glanced at his watch. Twenty seconds to go.

"Excuse me," Gillett asked the guard. "Can you tell me anything about these artifacts."

The rough-featured face blinked and shook his head, "not really love. I'm just here to guard the..."

The earth and the walls of the manor shook as the distraction detonated on the other side of the house. In the hallway outside Bisset wobbled on his feet as one of the security guards managed to seize an expensive pot before it fell off its pillar.

* * *

There was a massive boom and a tall tongue of fire blasted up and out, spewing material over a small army of Vikings and Saxons on the ground as they began surrounding their section of the house. The resulting shock wave blew the dead soldiers off their feet, their mottled, dry, withering flesh and moldering clothes were aflame in seconds. The blast had torn the side of the manor house off and the resulting rubble cascaded down on the burning warriors, burying them before they were incinerated. Windows in the towers blew out and smoke poured up into the air. The roar of the explosion engulfed the corridors and dust billowed into the massive oil-painting and tapestry chamber. Screaming and coughing began to be heard from one or two of the guests still residing within their rooms in the destroyed east wing while the bodies of three servants drenched in blood, were hurled down to the debris-littered ground below.

More Romans and Normans approached, flying glass was lodged in their sunken cheeks or sticking out of lank hair. A Viking had been impaled by a corner section of a metal window frame but he marched on with the other ancient corpses, not affected by it. Above them the monster insect flew through one of the bedrooms; the heat akin to a furnace, and sped on further into the house.

* * *

The lights immediately went out plunging the trophy room into semi-darkness. For three seconds an uncanny half-light from the bulbs of the TV cameras were the only thing penetrating the gloom until the power returned.

"That sounded like an earthquake. I think we're close to the epicenter," said a ginger-haired reporter from the Chicago Journal. He had a lived-in face that was perfect for radio and wore a wide-awake suit and black galoshes. "But I thought this area wasn't prone to seismic upheaval?"

"It isn't as far as I'm aware," an anchorwoman for one of the British newscrews said, "the tremors have stopped. It's funny but an earthquake is generally ushered in by foreshocks. There was no gradual increase in the power. It was like something blew up." She turned to address her team in a thundering voice, "come on! Let's find out where it originated."

Her crew nodded, grabbed portable equipment and followed her in frantic haste. The anchorwoman's words electrified the other members of the world media and her actions galvanized them to swear, spring up and scramble off after her. Thaw smiled thinly and watched as most of the crews departed, thinking he hadn't seen anything quite like it since he'd took his girlfriend to the January sales. The three security guards stayed in their places, a couple of camera men had also remained behind. Klugman glanced at Thaw and nodded then repeated the procedure to Gillett who drew her .38 Smith and Wesson caliber revolver from the holster and shot the rough-featured guard in the forehead.

As he was flung backwards, Klugman had already lifted up some bandages and pulled his 357 Magnum from his belt. Regulating his breathing, he levelled his weapon at the two stunned newsmen who turned at the crackle of gunfire. They screamed in incoherent panic as they saw the gun a moment before the Magnum exploded into life. Three bullets were fired in swift succession. Flesh, blood and hair moved through the air and then the pair toppled over in convulsive shudders. At the same time Thaw stepped into the hallway as the two security guards heard the hollow booms of the 357. He slapped the UZI across the back of one of the guard's head. Then a shot rang out as the third security guard was pulling out a nightstick. He jerked as a bullet cored into his brain from the rear. Bissett squeezed off the other round from his Derringer and the man's head pulped in a red spray, slamming him forward to the carpet. Dazed the second victim tottered before Thaw beat him about the head some more. He fell with his head caved in.

Behind him, Klugman had opened up a pillow case and mirroring Gillett, began to fill his with jewellry.

"Thought you didn't get your hands dirty Nathan?" Thaw said, seeing the older man's pallor was white from his exertions. "The music should drown out the sound of the shots."

"I wouldn't have Jerome but there was no alternate. We've got trouble. There are guys in the ballroom acting like Schizophrenics, ripping peoples insides out and preventing us from getting to the pouches or the car park," Bisset said. "Adrian said we should meet on the main staircase in three minutes time."

"Kyle get yourself out here. We've got ourselves some company. Who are these men?" Thaw asked with urgency in his voice as he addressed the older man, "what do they look like?"

Klugman came to the doorway with a handful of bracelets, rings and brooches.

"Something straight out of a horror film, butchering anyone who gets in their way." He opened up his Derringer, threw the used shells onto the floor then slipped his hand into his laddered tights and produced two more rounds. "They could be here for the same thing we are. The jewellry or works of art or even to kidnap somebody. There are lots of important people staying here. I've been introduced to a film star, models and the odd billionaire not counting the local Member of Parliament, counsels and a couple of aristocrats."

"Shit! I picked the wrong crime," Klugman said with a shake of his head.

"Look Adrian's going to hold them back," Bisset spoke on. Closing the breech of his gun paying no attention to Klugman's remarks, "but there's dozens of them. To many for him to handle on his own. It'll be only a matter of time before we run into some of them or they find our money."

"Okay we'll get going." Thaw said. "Sophie! We leaving with what we've got."

Suddenly there was the sound of breaking glass punctured by a woman's scream.

* * *

Ashley Crowe squeezed her way between the people and came upon an Abraham Lincoln lookalike in front of her as his muscles and tendons at the back of his legs were sliced apart. He cried out and dropped forward, grabbing Ashley around the waist so he wouldn't fall any further. Behind the hamstrung man, a huge figure loomed up and while Ashley swore and struggled to stay on her feet, Julian Patermunthis lunged with his short sword and Ashley's nose disintegrated prior to the blade punching out the back of her head.

"More skin for us Commander," the infantryman shouted as her corpse collapsed. Crimson droplets trickling from his new head of hair, down the side of his bony face where new flesh was stitched on. "I'll set about distributing the parts at once." He buried his sword to the hilt between a forty-five year old woman's shoulder blades. Blood gushed inside her space helmet and the Countess dropped to the floor after Flavius had ripped his weapon free.

"No Flavius," Patermunthis ordered, "we are commanded to free the master then you can take the spoils."

"Commander! Is our Lord far ahead?" Alongside the commander, Flavius and more legionnaires, one of which had the face of Matt Levitt stepped over the slain and advanced. Dozens of rotting cadavers came in pursuit, Vikings, Normans, Saxons and Celts.

"I sense he's somewhere on an upper level. Once we break through, we head there immediately." He feinted left then disembowel one of the merrier men who wasn't quick enough to flee.

During this drama 'Rock the Dinosaur' blared from the turntables but high on his platform the teddy-boy disc jockey saw his employer struck down. He lowered the volume and shouted into the mike: "Get out of here! People are dying! Call security or the police someone now."

"What!" Robert Crowe said to the announcement as guest's dropped their plates and hurried out the opposite exit. Homes and Lynskey came over to stand next to him, "can't be!"

"Better believe it mate," Cummings answered urgently, in a impassioned voice, about to venture an opinion to Crowe. "If you got guns, get them. You've got gatecrashers and your clientele are biting the dust all over the place. And it ain't special effects."

At the edge of hysteria the disc jockey left the record playing and joined the stampede to get out of the ballroom. Kapoor, Byle and Everett, Isaacs and Mick Fulford all attached themselves to the exodus headed to where they hoped there weren't any living dead. The fabric of the tapestry budged outwards as if a fist was behind it then purple blossoms burst through the ridges of the hand-woven silk and stretched towards the nearest of the departing guests. As soon as they were in range the flowers discharged fine, dust-like pollen at the masquerades, covering their faces in yellow grains. Hannon was one of three to crash into unconsciousness while a forth on the edge of the cloud felt woozy and staggered a step before she too tumbled. The crowd continued to run for fear of their lives and left those fallen behind. The red spheres sank, wrapped a beefy waiter and Kalvinder Kapoor inside iridescent light, and they immediately receded from view.

"Huh!" Robert uttered. Seeing the throng ahead thin as more guest's sprinted past them. Strange men dressed like ancient warriors approached. At their feet lay the blood-soaked figures of a number of men and woman. "But, but..." he stuttered, peering at Cummings for the first time and noticing he was armed to the teeth, "my wife has just gone up there."

"Then you're a widower. You can either run and hide or grab anything you can to defend yourselves," Cummings remarked gruffly, "they're gonna overrun the house before anyone has the chance to call the police. Fight or die, your choice. I'm doing the former."

Robert backed away slowly, and Homes and Lynskey went with him. Behind them, engraved hieroglyphs materialized and writhed in the hangings as thorny stems looped about an ankle or a wrist before dragging the drugged guests over to the heavy cloth where interlacing threads separated along the grain and lengthened into a mouth. Thorns dug deeply into flesh, ripping it apart desiccating the now lifeless bodies of Hannon, a maid and a penguin – the Chairwoman of the Government's Defense Committee. Blood soaked pieces of meat were slowly tossed into the mouth which moved as if it was chewing. Leaves grew broader and ruddier, the colour of the blossoms changed to a deeper tint of red wine and the tapestry itself blushed.

"Robert point me in the direction of your guns," Homes said, "I'll fetch them."

"They're in the garden shed under lock and key. The keys are upstairs in my library."

"Fat lot of use that does us. Sissy did you see those candles sticks when we first came in?" Homes spoke, seeing his assistant nod, "grab a couple and bring them back here on the double."

"Right!"

A plant stem from the tapestry lashed out lazily at Lynskey. Astonished at the sight, she twisted quickly aside and loped to evade it. Her fright was stronger than her fascination as she disappeared out of the doorway.

* * *

One floor above them, "this will sort out old frightful," Thornton said. He swished the broadsword through the air with his tensed two-handed grip.

"Put some armour on too Dermot," Corbett told him as he placed a basinet over the coif. He'd already donned a scaled hauberk he'd taken from one of the armoured dummies lining both side of the corridor. "I'm not taking any chances and afterwards I'm wearing his horns as a necklace." His lips twisted in a savage grin.

"Christ! That's horrible," Tucci said with distaste, her jaw extending truculently, "I'll settle on just having him sent back to wherever it is he came from."

Suddenly a very low hum could be heard coming from far off behind them. Thornton frowned and wheeled around as the sound slowly yet surely increased in volume.

"You two hear that?" He asked. Taking a hand off the hilt and reaching for a buckler worn on the arm of the dummy he'd taken the sword from.

"Yeah it sounds like a motor," Corbett stared in perplexity, down the passageway. The humming grew louder still.

"Or the same hum we heard when the demon was trying to escape," Tucci blinked and grabbed a short spear and a copper helmet.

"My thought as well," Thornton said, holding the round shield by its handle.

"Can't be!" Corbett bellowed with a shake of his head. He lowered his visor as a precaution. "How could he have passed us by without us seeing him? The library lies in the opposite direction?"

"Maybe he teleported out of the pentacle," Tucci managed to say as she edged behind her two companions, "there one second, gone the next."

"I don't pissing well like the sound of..." Corbett began but stopped, visibly shaken when something looking similar to an insect rushed around the corner of the T-shaped junction and headed directly for them. "Bastard hell! What's that?" His blood ran cold at the sight but it didn't stop him seizing the hilt of a scimitar, which exited the sheath with a rasp. He was relived to hear Tucci whistle in wonder, her beautiful green eyes dilated, and see Thornton's face go deadly white. Goosebumps running up his arms and legs.

The creature was four feet wide and was the height of a five year old child. It weighed more than fifty pounds and had one bristly oval body segment consisting of its head, thorax and abdomen with six skinny legs. On the tip of each was a large spotted green-black serrated pinchers. Two bat-like wings flapped to keep it aloft and five eyes blazed ferocious.

Bristles levelled and launched at the trio. Spikes clattered into the buckler, forcing Thornton to retreat a step. One stabbed Corbett in the thigh and he went down, gushing blood and swearing, "the only fucking place I ain't covered. Pull it out God damn it."

"Cut out your foul mouth for once Russ," Tucci knelt beside him, shoving a handkerchief into the wound, it became immediately saturated with blood. "You'll bleed more if I take the spike out. I'll put on a tourniquet," she went on, removing the tie from about her neck and wrapping it round his leg, in an attempt to stem the flow. He grunted as she tightened then fastened it securely with a knot.

As the creature briskly advanced towards them, the edges of its wings slapping the corridor walls, Thornton stepped in front of his friends and braced his legs apart, hoisting his sword and shield up to cover his chest. "This is not good, not good at all. Anybody have a thought on how I'm going to tackle it without putting myself on the menu."

"Hack its wings off," Corbett replied, his face paling and grimacing in pain as Tucci grabbed him by the arm and backpedaled down the corridor, semi-dragging him in the effort. Blood continued to seep from his wound, but not as much as before. Corbett spoke more bravely than he felt as he kept pressure on the wound. His instincts warring with each other: one was telling him to run while another urged him to inflict some revenge. "Its legs appear so narrow that I doubt they'll hold his full weight."

Tucci looked about her, saw the tapestries and had an idea.

Thornton swallowed, and watched the giant insect slow to a hover as it measured its foes. It estimated them in comparison to the others it had killed or injured then its body shuddered. "Well it's a plan. Achieving it is another matter."

"Leave that to me," Tucci announced quickly, puffing as she used all of her strength to heave Corbett to his feet. Corbett hung onto the tapestry and helped to pull himself up. "You just get him to keep his mind on you."

"No problem there," Corbett said, resting his weight on his good leg. "Dermot hasn't got a chance of being missed where he is standing now."

The creature flexed the serrated pinchers before propelling itself at Thornton. It closed to within spitting distance and behind his buckler, Thornton leaned forward and brought down a vicious overhead; the broadsword parted bristles and struck with a meaty chunk into the beast's head a moment before it was used to ram against the man with great force, flinging him backwards to collide into his companions and a few of the suits of armour. Two corridors away Zoe Hawes heard the awful clatter and howls of pain as she was about to descend the back staircase to the kitchen. Thinking Tweed had taken a wrong turn and hurt herself falling over something, she broke into a trot and followed the noise.

The trio fell over like bowling pins and the giant insect angrily turned in the air, its dense vital fluid splattering the walls. Then it completed the maneuver and lashed out with its pincers as Thornton rose, catching his head in a tight grip. Pressure was exerted until his skull exploded into a pulpy mess of blood and brain matter.

Tucci was the first to recover. She screamed "nooo!" Then kneeling, jabbed her short spear at the creature flapping above them. The weapon's head squeezed though empty spaces where the bristles had been fired, and buried deep into the soft flesh of the belly underneath. It squealed and flinched, slapping the air with its wings as it climbed. Hot blood spilled over her face and ran down the spear shaft as she continued to hold onto her weapon, and was lifted up from the pile of armoured arms and legs.

Claws popped out of the housing in its wings as the insect opened its bowels and dropped excrement over Corbett as he cut at its spindly leg. His blade vibrated as it cropped into bone, and the creature squealed again. Its height was affected by Tucci's additional weight until a pincer snapped the spear shaft in two and Tucci dropped to the carpet and rolled out of the way. Coughing up and spitting out the runny shit Corbett freed his blade and after clearing his vision as best he could with his sleeve, he lunged from behind to carve through one of the leathery wings and separate it into two. Blood spilled from broken veins and loose folds of the thin, fleshy membrane fluttered as the insect flew onward for a couple of feet before its mass became to heavy to bear and it lurched to one side, crashing to the floor with an almighty thump.

"Knew the bastard would be vulnerable when I clipped his wings," Corbett said, his heart pounding. "Help me up Andrea. I gonna finish this thing off once and for all."

"I'm not sure you should get near enough to try," Tucci admitted. Rushing to his aid, shifting her attention between Corbett and seeing the creature roll itself into a ball by the action of powerful muscles rising from the head and neck and loop around its rump. "Look at its position. The spines are projecting in all directions. Hedgehogs do that when they threatened." More bristles began growing in the spaces where others had been discharged. Gore clotted around the insect's pate.

"I ain't skirting danger," he replied. Crawling up the hanging and leaning on Tucci's shoulder and arm as he gradually hauled up to his feet once again. Blood seeping down his leg. "It's dead. It just don't know it yet." He took down a wooden tur shield from the wall mounting, reversed it and seized the two leather, grab straps behind. "Come on Andrea! Arm yourself."

"I'd rather let the police handle it."

He brooded for a second. "If we leave this object wounded, it could follow us and attack." Corbett said, limping forward. His sword glittered in the light as the beast, sensing trouble, inclined its pincers and good wing; and shoved, applying force on the carpet which began rolling up into undulating folds behind as the monster tried to push itself forward in a gentle swaying motion.

"Since you put it like that. I'll help chop it up," Tucci reflected with a reluctant sigh. Observing the insect from the corner of her eye tottering like it was drunk while it created more rocking movement by throwing its pincers to the front and quickly bringing them back again to continue the build-up of kinetic energy. "What's it doing? A workout?" She saw a mace with a spiked head on the opposite side of the corridor and went to reach for it.

Proceeding unevenly and laboriously Corbett advanced and his grip tightened on the hilt of the blade until his fingers ached. "It's struggling for movement. It's gonna be touch and go if I can make it in time." He dragged his leg onward two more steps, drawing his weapon back as he closed for a killing blow. His shield covering his chest.

Tucci ripped the mace off the wall, whirled and charged. "We'll see about that," She caught up with her companion in moments. Ahead the insect wobbled then with one further thrash of its pincers, it drove forward and ejected more spikes. They drummed into the shield and two grazed Corbett's forehead and arm while other missiles peppered Tucci's torso. She shuddered under the impact and collapsed, gurgling crimson blood. The monstrosity rolled on as Corbett stood his ground and let it come to him.

CHAPTER TWENTY THREE

Cummings strode ahead, raised his Colt 45 and fired until he emptied the magazine clip. Shells panned across the surging mass of warriors: two punched into the chest of a Viking, three more flattened against a Norman's body armour while more ripped into others who staggered as the force pushed them back first one step then another, but apart from that the bullets had no overall effect on the advancing mob.

"Damn they're still in the game. Must be wearing bullet proof armour," Cummings muttered to herself, holstering his Colt before unclasping two grenades from his belt.

A second later a handful of security guards rushed into the ballroom clutching nightsticks and M26 AirTasers. A bald-headed guard with a rotund figure and cool blue eyes drew up at Robert Crowe's side, surveying Cummings retreating figure and the approaching throng ahead of them. The rest of the guards stretched out to form a rough skirmish line.

"Am I glad to see you sergeant Diggines," Crowe said in relief. "We're beset by those armed men. They just burst in and started killing the guests." He was clearly distraught. "That one man there," he pointed at Cummings' back. "He appeared a few seconds ago at my side and fired into their ranks. I don't know if he's with them or against them. He could be discharging blanks for all I know."

"The police are on their way. We'll stop them. We've done this before. We'll work with the giant for the time being," Diggines said, "then once this is over I'll arrest him as a precaution. Come on lads! Let's try out our new stun guns."

* * *

Thaw and Klugman raced into the trophy room and saw a empty-handed Viking climbing through the broken window. In the foreground Sophie Gillett tottered forward a pace, a crimson froth trickling from her lips before her eyes rolled up and she toppled, crashing into camera equipment. The contents from her sack spilled out to glitter in the light. Thaw took a tentative step towards his dying girlfriend, seeing the broad throwing axe protruding from her back.

"Sophie!" He blinked and suddenly felt very weak in himself. "You bastard," he addressed the dead warrior who growled menacingly at them, "she was the best thing that ever happened to me." Livid with rage he directed his UZI and discharged the whole clip. Bullets stitched across the corpse, the impacts forcing him back out the window, leaving pockmocks in the woodwork.

Klugman heard a muttered grumble outside as he cautiously approached in a running crouch, his 357 Magnum to the fore. He knelt, let go of his pillow case and with his fingers put them over the radial artery inside her wrist. He couldn't feel any pulse. Thaw threw away the emptied cartridge clip, took another out of his pocket and slammed it home.

"Sophie's gone Jerome!" He said, squeezing off a shot at what looked like the same Viking clambering back through the window. The back of the man's head burst and he was thrown backwards into the gloom. Klugman unclipped a grenade and lobed it through the broken glass.

"Watch yourself!" He went on, covering his face to protect himself from any shrapnel as the explosion ripped apart the four warriors gathered around the window ledge and shook the teeth from a few others beyond. More camera tripods tumbled over and scattered limbs twitched and newly purchased eyelids blinked. Klugman peered up then got to his feet. "That's them all over." He holstered his gun, scooped up the spilled items and replaced them inside Gillett's pillow case.

"It appears we're now surrounded and separated from the money," Thaw said, raising to his full height from behind the pedestal. He was trying to occupy his mind yet he was boiling with anger over the lose of Gillett, "and we have to contend with another gang whose numbers exceed our own."

"That's as may be, but they aren't better armed," Bisset announced, from the doorway. Seeing that Thaw was suppressing sobs, the break in his voice and his short, gasping breaths revealed just how upset he really was, "I've seen that for myself."

Klugman straightened and clutched the pillow cases tightly, his military training resurfaced as he heard more glass being broken outside. "Don't matter! If one can murder Sophie with a throw like that then the rest are just as good. Let's motor!" He whirled about and strode over to where Bisset stood, "we need a new way off Wildwood Haven. Nathan, did you learn anything while you were been showing around."

"Not a lot from Anderson really," he replied, walking left and disappearing into the corridor beyond, "except he did let slip something about another fire escape route out of the house."

"Could be a secret passage," Klugman reached the doorway and followed. "If we can find the butler alive he can lead us outside."

Thaw was the last to leave. He sighed and for a fleeting instant let his face become twisted in pain. He swallowed, blew Gillett a final farewell kiss then composing his features, turned and ran after his companions. "If we can't find Anderson there's always the Crowes themselves," he uttered, catching up with them quickly.

"Now you're thinking," Klugman said, handing Thaw one of the pillow cases. He took it as they rounded a corner and proceeded down the next passageway, keeping in step with Bisset.

"I noticed you dawdled back there. Did you say your good-bye," he drew his gun.

Thaw sniffed, "yeah Nathan something like that."

"I sorry Jerome," Bisset said generally.

"Thanks! Let's hurry. Adrian's probably waiting for us." He picked up the pace and shot out in front. Ahead the crooks could hear frightened voices and the sound of footfalls quickening up creaking stairs.

* * *

"What do you mean you haven't got the caviar I want?" Alice Snodgress asked the butler as the pair walked with long steps through the electric eye and the kitchen door slid open, passing a maid carrying out more food for the buffet tables, "Sturgeon are the only appetiser I like."

"Well Mrs Snotgrass, we've got salmon and nothing else." Snodgress scowled and drew alongside him as he knelt and opened the fridge. "You're free to phone the nearest pizza place but I doubt they'll have any either. What tough luck you're haven't today," Anderson spoke on with a hint of mockery in his voice. Leading her further into the chamber between the worktops where three staff members were preparing more dishes for the party. Dirty dishes toppled and rattled in the sink. In the corner stood the risers of a narrow staircase ascending to the upper reaches of the house while another door between the microwave and the stove led to a walk-in pantry.

Snodgress' face darkened like thunder when he straightened and held a plate of tripe and onions. "I bet you're so unpopular even the Samaritans hang up on you."

Ian the head cook and the other kitchen helpers were enjoying this exchange.

"Actually madam," the butler responded. Placing the plate down before going over to a chopping board where a sharp knife and a long pigs pudding rested, "I wouldn't know you'd descended from apes unless I met your family."

"Why you good for nothing little..." Snodgress swore. Clenching her fists as the sounds of screams and footsteps approached the kitchen. Simultaneously as the deputy chef opened the door a crack it was shoved forcibly back into his face, breaking his broad nose by a Roman clasping the handle of a Fachion.

The deputy chef cried out in pain as blood streamed down his white coveralls. Registering their surprise Anderson and Snodgress glanced around. The other members of staff stopped what they had been doing, and peered into the chef's direction. One thought it was a drunk who had wandered round the side of the house.

"What's going on?" the butler shouted then exhaled sharply when his gaze focused upon the dirty, stringy-haired skull and emaciated frame of the warrior. Walking in his steps were a Norman knight and a Saxon whose bony face was covered with blue paint. Snodgress bit her lip. A second later the Roman closed upon the deputy chef and ran him through with a cleaver-like sword, ribs snapped, the edge of the long sword exited from his back.

He crumpled in a spray of blood as the front kitchen door slid open to reveal the DJ – his flashy neo-Edwardian style costume including his kipper tie and winkle-pickers were streaked with blood, none of which belonged to him. At his rear, pushed a woman in a Magpie costume and a man dressed as a tree, Byle and Everett came after. They were holding a vase and a bottle.

"Get out the way," Everett shouted and shoved the DJ, making headway into the room.

Byle jogged at his side with a face as pale as chalk. Breathing hard she said, "there are things following us and one of them just ate the waitress."

The door was beginning to slide shut when Raichu was caught by two slender tentacles and was quickly yanked back the way he'd come. A muffled scream echoed before the sound of crunching took over. The door closed.

"Fuck!" Everett sputtered when he saw the Roman advancing across the tiled floor slick with blood. The legs of the dead Chef still spasmed. Another pair of soldiers strung behind carrying javelins and short swords, "there's more of them in here."

Then the windows smashed as stones and clothyards blasted through into the kitchen. One shaft shivered in the neck of the head cook. When he plunged lifelessly to the ground, the DJ followed, falling as a stone pierced his forehead. Another arrow flew and caught Everett in the stomach as the kitchen door slid open again and an Alligator-like broad head and long blunt snout burst through the opening, the jaws had countless teeth as it snapped at a target a few feet away.

Anderson knitted his brows and shook his head in disbelief, muttering something distant. Snodgress shot an uneasy glance at a waiter who turned to flee but got cut down by the knight from behind, a crimson fountain issuing from the rip in his jacket. The two kitchen staff scampered inside the pantry and slammed the door against the attackers, ripping shelves off the walls and barring the door as best they could, the ends were thrust against the door while the others were wedged against boxes of fresh fruit and tinned fish.

Snodgress shoved her face into the butlers and saw bewilderment etched there, "Anderson! We need a way out of here now."

Anderson's lips moved yet only an unintelligible whisper issued forth.

Frantically her hand shot up and slapped his face hard. "Come on man snap out of it," She shrilled, her voice was taut with nerves. "Think man! God help me! You're my only hope."

The butler shook his head and slowly regained his senses. "What! Oh yeah. The staircase. It goes to the gym." He swiveled smoothly and moved along at a slow, steady trot over to the risers. Snodgress stooped to made a lessor target and kept close on his heels. "Doors off that led to all the first floor corridors."

The three warriors advanced in blood lust, fanning out and seeing the man and woman bolt up the stairs. To the warriors rear, four more soldiers emerged in the doorway. The feet of the man dressed as a tree slipped on blood and stumbled before a spear lunged and the man inside the costume shook in his death-throes. The magpie grabbed the handle of a saucepan and threw it with all her might at the Knight. It clattered off his diamond-shaped shield. She shrieked and banged into the butcher's block in her haste to escape.

Directly behind her, the monster galloped awkwardly forward towards its prey. The body of the incubus was growing, becoming thicker and scalier. Its legs extending as its momentum came to a jarring halt as it got stuck in the doorway, splintering the timber. It laboured, trying in vain to go on, but it couldn't move a muscle. A long bubbling tongue rolled across its teeth. Its tentacles were trapped by its sides. Meanwhile arrows were plucked from quivers as the undead aimed at the woman in the magpie costume as she ran for the stairs.

Unaware of Everett's wound, Byle was preoccupied with ducking a blade and watching where she placed her feet. She picked up the knife from the chopping board, avoided another slashing stoke by inches then stepped within the Saxon's reach and stabbed him in the ribs. No blood flowed from the injury and the warrior grinned at her as he approached, forcing Byle to retreat. Shafts were released and the Magpie gasped at the white hot pain. She stumbled to her knees and finally fell face down. Byle took another backward pace then her heel struck something solid. Dreading what it was she cast a quick look over her shoulder and her eyes widened in fright.

Byle just had time to scream before the monster lunged and its powerful teeth seized her. In moments the jaw closed, crushing her bones like twigs as the beast tipped its neck and devoured her. The warriors strode on and began ascending the stairs, dispatching Everett along the way.

* * *

Hawes rounded the corner agape at the sight of the bodies, the blood-soaked walls and of the unnatural thing driving onward. Keeping his anger suppressed and red filling his vision, Corbett only had time to thrust his steel and blind one of the insect's eyes before it screamed louder than ever and rammed into him, knocking him to the ground. Blood ran down his face from the cut in his forehead. The revolving mass of spikes and pincers reached Corbett's feet.

Hawes saw him just manage to shove his shield down to cover his legs when the creature rolled right over him, pressing the breath out of his lungs.

Bristles speared Corbett's feet but failed to penetrate anything else – the spikes only cut wide grooves in the shield and scraped harmlessly off the helm and armor. Horrified by the hideous being, Hawes was shaken out of her trance by Corbett's painful cry. Her gaze fell upon a loaded weapon leaning against the wall. Not sure how it worked or what range it had, Hawes snatched up the crossbow, aimed and fired the bolt. It lodged in the insect's flesh, rupturing another eye as it rolled away down the passageway, spilling red fluid in its wake. Hawes tossed the crossbow aside and ran down the corridor, stepping over the dead. She drew to a halt and knelt next to Corbett, surprised that he was still conscious despite the agony and blood loss. "It's me Russ," she said, quickly ripping off a strip of her petticoat and wrapping it about his feet. He grunted and winced, "I suppose that thing was a friend of the demon Lois conjured up?"

"Fair bet. We hurt the fucker pretty bad. Doubt it'll return this way." He coughed and bloodshot eyes gazed back up at her. "You're the last person I thought I'd see after you ran out of the library."

"Me too," she replied. Her words were punctuated with tearing sounds as she coiled the extra layers of her petticoat about the wound. She stared into his face and saw how pale it was from the pain, "I was going back to the cottage to change clothes and get out but I got separated from Yasmin and when I heard the din..."

"You thought it was her."

She acknowledged with a nod, "I'll go for help after I've patched you up."

"Please don't Zoe," he said, pushing himself up to his elbows, "I don't want to be left alone not here. Let's wait! That pissing butler is sure to be coming around at any moment complaining how my blood has ruined his precious carpet."

She nodded again. "Okay! And to be on the safe side I'll try and load the crossbow. But I think I've got more chance of explaining how my video works to my cat."

When the bleeding was under control, Hawes tore another length off her petticoat and tied all the dressings firmly in place before raising his legs higher than his heart by putting them on a chair she went and dragged from a connecting corridor.

* * *

The guards progressed forward as one, their movements showed training and practice as they trod on paper plates and squashed food under their weight. The AirTasers were pointed and when drawing apace with Cummings, the guards halted and waited until the mob came into range.

"You didn't manage to stop them then Mister..?" Diggines asked Cummings, shifting his attention, eyeing the grenades and advancing warriors who marched within eighteen feet of the skirmish line.

"Tiernan," Cummings lied with raised eyebrows, "they are probably wearing body armour that's why I didn't made a dent into them. Who are you?"

"Interior security. Those real grenades."

"Yep!" Cummings stated, "if your fancy gizmos don't stop those fuckers, these will."

The sergeant nodded and roared to his men. "Fire!"

Pairs of laser guided barbed hooks attached to copper wires shot across the distance and the hooks pierced two inches of clothing and attached to cold flesh. After that fifty thousand volts surged along the wires to paralyse the men. Instead of collapsing in pain, the unliving quickened their strides and closed the gap between them.

"The hell with this," Cummings blurted, turning to flee.

Diggines grunted in surprise at this development and didn't blame him for legging it. The sergeant hadn't anticipated the AirTasers not working. Making a snap decision he tossed his down and reached for his nightstick. "Draw batons and advance. We'll subdue them the old fashion way."

Officers blinked and exchanged glances before doing as they were ordered. Archers loosed shafts and a big-boned, swarthy guard and a lithe, blond-haired colleague dropped, jetting blood.

"Get out of here now," Cummings shouted to Homes and Robert as he hurried past, "I'll handle these killers. I'll see you outside."

Homes bobbed his head and they both scurried after him, stepping over sluggish vines coiling snake-like across the floor. Then the two sides clashed ever so briefly – yet nightsticks were no match for rusty blades and the deads renewed fury. Shields absorbed the blows and swords and spears returned with heavy strikes of their own, driving into flesh. Crimson poured and slowly one by one the guards stiffened lifelessly and fell limp to the floorboards. Diggines clubbed a Roman across Matt Levitt's face, white foam still clung about the mouth. The skin cracked and split as a Saxon got behind Diggines and stabbed him in the lungs. Just inside the ballroom Cummings stopped and pulled the pins from his grenades. As he saw the last guard fall messily, he knelt and rolled the grenades across the floor. Then he straightened, whirled and sprinted for the corridor.

Cummings had just scrambled out of the ballroom in the neck of time when the grenades detonated, blowing the ancient warriors apart. Arms, legs and torsos were scattered and the blast weakened a section of the floor. As more of the undead walked onto it, their shifting weight became to much for the floor to bear. It suddenly dropped to some hidden depth, taking fifteen of the soldiers with it. Reloading, Cummings poked his head around the edge of the doorway and saw through the billowing smoke that more men were entering from the garden.

"They've got to be on PCP or something," he concluded with a head shake, "can't think of another explanation that makes sense." He pulled the pin of another grenade with his teeth and lobbed it inside the ballroom before setting off to where his companions were. Rather than high explosives, a gas producing chemical burst forth from this grenade but this didn't stop the warriors for they simply walked with regular, steady steps to fill the corridor and began to invade the rooms beyond.

* * *

The strong spotlight from the hovering police helicopter shone through the bare trees and illuminated the carpet of leaves ahead of the small party of travelers. Kris Perratt moved with measured steps on the fringes of the drifting beam, displaying the grace of a prowling tiger, his eyes roaming about in search of anything out of the ordinary. Next came the inspector, holding her lantern to the fore and bringing up the rear was sergeant Keane.

Sinclair's mobile rang, "halt!" She shouted over the thump of the helicopter blades. Skidding to a stop, passing the lantern to

Keane before pulling the phone out of her pocket and glancing at the liquid crystal display to see who the call was from. She depressed a button, "what have you got for me Bryan?"

"Well guv, the ink wasn't dry on the warrant when we raided Cummings' address. Unfortunately he wasn't there."

"Surprise, surprise go on."

"His gran was though, and she reveals he hasn't lived at the flat for three months."

"How about," the inspector reflected, "a forwarding address for any mail?"

"He did. We've got the street and number. His destination was London and a Jerome Thaw lives there. According to penal records, Thaw was an old cell mate. He's been out for a year after serving time for burglary and carjacking."

"Uh-huh!"

"What's more there was another jail bird sharing the cell called Max Follett. His specialty was acquiring weapons, but Follett was in a car crash several weeks ago and he's been in a wheelchair ever since."

"Hmmm, Cummings was the guide and I feel that Thaw is definitely the wheelman," Sinclair said, "as for Follett I reckon he could well have been one of the original gang members then had to bow out and arrange a stand-in when he had his accident. I'll have the bastard charged on conspiracy."

"Sounds about right guv," Giddings remarked.

"Put out an APB on the trio and to play safe inform Interpol. They're to be quizzed about murder. I want a recent photo of the men released to the networks and set up a background check as well."

"I'll get right on it. We also turned up a logbook for a Mark Five, Ford Escort with the owner's name down inside as Kyle Klugman. He could be the stand-in."

"Good work Bryan," she said excitedly, absolutely meaning it. "Evidence is the key. I want the usual profile on this Klugman. Social security number, pets, all of it. Plus details about the car. Get back to me fast, understood?"

"Copy!"

"Anything on the whereabouts of Nathan Bisset?"

"Not at the moment! But I think we can possibly add his name to the list of accomplices to the hold up."

Sinclair blinked, "by what means?"

"The results from the spectrograph have been faxed over to me while you out of the office. Bisset's voice matches the one on his answering machine tape that his insurance firm supplied us with. The accent and the speech mannerisms of the speaker mirror the spikes from the audio cassettes of the hoax calls and the woman isn't far off being identified either. We've set the pitch key to her voice, the resonance and the volume all points to a yank, New Yorker and her extended oral tract informs us that she's tall. There's a few other things which are helping us put together constructive profiles of the felons."

"Okay Bryan keep at it. I'm going to see where this trail takes us. In all likelihood it's where Thaw and co stashed the Escort. Talk to you later," the inspector turned off her mobile and addressed the tracker, "Kris guide us on."

"About time," he muttered and took off at a quicker pace.

* * *

"What a crock," Brennan said with a shake of his head. Following his girlfriend and Dwyer down the stairs. "You're all so serious about this. But surely there's got to be a better plan?"

Beside him Danielle sighed and spoke, "none of us could think of one Josh. For our powers to work on Bartok, we have to lower the protection shield. He'll crack it apart eventually. I would rather take the offensive any day of the week."

"I can see what he means," Dwyer put in, reaching the bottom of the steps. "It depends a lot on Lois' control and if she can effect him long enough to move him in position and kept him there for the two minutes."

"Well it's all we've got," Lois reflected with a hardness to her tone. She pulled the door ajar and heard the echoing howls of screaming people and what sounded like explosions. "Damn! He's broken free."

Danielle flipped *The Grimorie* wide open and scanned the pages for certain text. "No!" She declared, seeing stars and runes alter colour and dance across the contents. "The big guy's still imprisoned, mind you according to the book he's behind all the trouble."

"How could he be?" Brennan asked with a frown. His voice slightly shrilled and cracking with hysterical excitement.

"God only knows," Lois replied, pulling aside the hanging and peering out into the corridor.

Dwyer halted alongside her and immediately took notice of something coming towards them. "Hey! Listen guys. You hear that sound?"

The companions quieted down and strained to perceived an irregular succession of soft sounds like papers being shuffled. Then the wounded insect came staggering into the passageway as if it was drunk.

"Now you don't see something like that every day," Dwyer said in a guarded utterance. Awed, she stared at the horror. Gore daubed its body and smeared up the dense growth of spikes as the monster bounced off the wall, its spikes digging into the thick pile of the carpet and out again.

"Lois," Brennan shouted, his skin clawing, "kill it."

Before she could reply the insect discharged more of its bristles. They flew straight at the companions but with a wave of her hand, the air solidified in front of them and the spikes crashed into the barrier like darts in a board. A second later Danielle focused her thoughts on the creature and it suddenly shrieked and reeled from dizziness as its veins and arteries became frozen and its lungs filled to bursting with water. There was a violent shudder, then the insect collapsed inward and deflated like a balloon. The many legs twitched aimlessly until finally it stiffened and lay still.

"Nice work," Brennan nodded with a grin, "Bartok hasn't got a chance with you two around."

"Let's hope so," Danielle said. Her blood was up and she had decided to bring a swift end to this dreadful adventure. She glanced expectantly at the faces about her. "It's time to finish this. Come along guys! Let's send that demon straight back to hell."

There were nods all round before she led the way down the corridor. Behind them the spikes tumbled from thin air onto the carpet, which cushioned their fall.

CHAPTER TWENTY FOUR

Homes directed Isaacs to "put that table there," and she knelt quickly and placed the table on the edge of the curved landing near to the chairs that were being stacked by Fulford. A Daveport was man-handled to the edge of the platform with a bureau. "Leave that space empty so the others gathering stuff downstairs have a way of coming through."

A man wobbled up carrying a dressing table and another was pushing an armchair towards the top of the stairs. "Where do you want this," he grunted with effort. "It's as heavy as a horse."

"Position it inside the gap when everyone is up safely." Homes looked around and heard more screaming. He stared at the barrier which was beginning to build up quite nicely and saw it was becoming slightly rickety. "You!" He pointed at a woman and man just straightening from bringing a forth a load of furniture. "Rip down bell ropes, tear sheets in strips if you have to. Just hurry we need to secure this barricade before it topples over. We've got to build it higher if we've a chance of holding off the killers until the police arrive."

They departed and broke into a run passing guests struggling with a highboy and a mattress, the latter of which was soon propped against a section of the decorative banister.

Thaw, Klugman and Bisset reached the bottom of the staircase and were greeted by a number of the guests hurrying up the steps, carrying tea-trays, footstools, bookcase, clocks and pictures. They were about to ascend behind the streaming flow when Cummings rounded the corner and shouted out to them. "Jerome wait up a second."

Thaw and the others turned and crowded around him as he slid to a stop. "Company's coming!" He panted. "I must have blown up at least twenty of the gang and it ain't slowed them down one bit. Don't know what they're on but they don't feel any pain and that's a certainly."

"What kind of numbers are we talking about Adrian?" Bisset inquired.

"A hundred maybe! When one fell, three took his place. Then the one I shot, got back up again. They didn't though after I started to blow them to pieces," he glanced around and didn't see Gillett.

"How far behind are they?" Thaw asked. The last of the guests ran up the stairs and passed through the gap within the barricade.

"A corridor or less!"

"What the fuck are we gabbing here for?" Klugman shouted.

"I am knackered," Cummings gasped, "where's Sophie?"

"She didn't make it." Thaw said abruptly.

"Let's move it up then to where there's some high ground we can defend. You can rest later," Klugman answered. Breaking into a run and scrambling up the stairs. They still held the two pillow cases. The others followed and presently all were on the opposite side of the furniture.

From the left corridor came Danielle and Lois leading the way for Brennan and Dryer.

"Any more stragglers behind you?" Homes said, walking up. He recognised Cummings from the ballroom and noticed the guns they all held.

"Didn't see any one else," Klugman replied, "we were acting as lookouts while you lot were erecting this rampart."

"I see!" The billionaire turned and motioned to bring up the furniture. "Right! Plug this hole up." The guests pushed the sofa and moved the wardrobe with failing strength, "and get whatever left to cover the banisters, like that mattress over there."

People rushed along the galleries and entered the bedrooms. Rounding the corner from the opposite side of the house, completely out of breath came Anderson and Snodgress. Danielle saw guns openly displayed by four men whom she didn't recognise.

"Lois! Do you know those guys over there by Homes?" She pointed, weaving though the mass of dashing guests.

"No!" Lois shook her head, making a beeline towards them, "but let's find out. They might be able to help us."

"Guns and sorcery," Brennan said, sticking to the woman's heels. "It's a nice mixture. One of them has got to get him."

"The problem's how is Lois going to persuade them to come to the library with us without sounding like we need a strait-jacket?" Dryer said.

Ahead of them. "Hey have you seen either of the Crowes or the butler about?" Thaw asked the American, not seeing Anderson and Snodgress emerge behind the rush of people. They were still both breathing rapidly from running fast.

"I don't know where Anderson is but I think Ashley Crowe is dead. Robert and a few others including my secretary, his brother-in-law and wife have gone to fetch some old weapons from his collection. Since you boys are armed, you're the only ones who can defend us all until then."

"My associates and I will do our best Mr Homes!" Bisset said firmly. Klugman grunted.

Guests leaned oil paintings, and mattresses against the balustrade which creaked under the weight of the latter.

"So these people are with you Bisset?"

"They're security consultants for my firm. I was wondering if Mr Crowe took you in his confidence about another fire escape route out of the house?"

He chuckled despite himself and stuck his thumbs in his pockets, "if Robert had, do you think I would be standing around here playing the last stand at the Alamo?" Homes said with a shake of his head.

"No I dare say you wouldn't Oliver," Lois declared coming to a halt beside them. The others crowding round. "I know where there's a door. It's in the library."

Below Vikings and Saxons started to file into the reception area from the rooms and corridors, and stare up at the staircase. Javelins were instantly thrown. Swords and axes glittered in the light. Arrows were swiftly plucked from quivers.

"Get to cover!" Fulford shouted, ducking down behind a overturned table. Anderson saw Lois and dropped to a running crouch. Snodgress did the same, perspiration breaking out on her forehead. Javelins that were tossed with inhuman strength punched through the mattresses; the foam rubber and coiled springs inside failing to stop the missiles velocity and three people groaned as the sharp points bore into torsos and heads.

In a sitting position, Bisset convulsed then stilled, falling forward, the Javelin point piercing deep behind his left eye socket, gaping and oozing blood. Thaw dodged behind the barricade and fired off a few rounds, dropping a Roman only to see him rise afterwards.

Klugman stood above the banister, blasted the crowd as it surged towards the staircase before kneeling back down. Shafts arched over the galleries and embedded in the walls and doors. A man dressed as a Christmas cracker crumpled and blood rippled out from his body. Anderson came to a standstill next to Lois and Homes. "We can't stay here. Those butchers have overrun the kitchen and are swarming up the back stairs. They'll be here before we know it."

Cummings pulled a pin and chucked the grenade at the rolling mass coming up the stairs. It detonated and flung six corpses into the air minus their legs at mid-thigh and the odd arm and head.

"Where do we go then," Isaacs asked, seeing another man fall in a crimson spray.

Using the confusion of the smoke and everyone ducking for cover, Lois peered through a space between the small posts of the balustrade, raised her hand and making ten warriors lighter than air, launched them up into the atmosphere. They shot skyward, smashing through the stained-glass window and continued to rocket until they reached orbit. In the corpses wake, pieces of the fire-breathing dragon rained down on the other cadavers who had clambered half way up the stairs.

"The library," Klugman announced, raising his voice. "Just point us in the direction girl." He hurled two grenades along with a couple more from Thaw and blasted nine warriors, mutilating them.

"We can't," Anderson blurted out in shock, "Mrs Snodgress and I just came that way. It was wall to wall death back there."

Fulford picked up a clock, straightened and hurled it at Commander Patermunthis stepping on the remains of the legionnaire called Flavius. It crunched into the Commander's recently acquired eye and he reeled under the impact.

"It's also the nearest door to the fire escape route Anderson," Lois argued forcibly.

An archer released his bow string and Fulford's lips gapped wide in short-lived agony when the steel point of an arrow burst suddenly from his chest. He staggered, gripping the shaft, blood gushing between his fingers before he pitched forward and tumbled over the banister to the floor below.

"I'm not going back," Snodgress sputtered.

"Who wants you to, you old vulture." Lois shouted. "I take anyone whose brave enough to come with me and that won't be many." Her words were meant to insult and cause an affront to their courage.

"Better do it quick while we've still got grenades to clear a path for us," Cummings said. "I've got four left."

"Seven!" Thaw echoed.

"I'm down to three," Klugman uttered, peering at the advancing mob. "It's now or never."

The clamor of battle grew louder. Danielle twiddled three of her fingers, and down on the right a pipe ruptured under the floor of the reception area, water gushed up, spreading wide in an instant and rising towards the roof before the towering wave broke and curved over to plunge down towards the flowing mass of undead. They looked up at the deep, rumbling sound as the mini tsunami ploughed into them; the warriors giving ground against the surging wave as it split ranks and slammed the individuals towards the opposite wall. Weak bones cracked and splintered from the impact.

"Nice time to go," Thaw said, "okay lady take us to this door of yours. Adrian you're rearguard."

"Right!" Lois acknowledged and sped off to where Anderson had come from. She turned the corner and arrows splintered around her on hardening air. Danielle followed closely shadowed by Klugman, Thaw and Brennan. In the middle Dwyer, a snowman and Isaacs struggled to keep up. Trevor Orbach plus Homes and Cummings kept constant pace behind. Snodgress and Anderson exchanged looks then hurried in the opposite direction secretly pursued by several crimson balls.

* * *

The police radio burst into life and the sergeant pushed a button and spoke. "Keane here!"

"Hi Justin it's Giddings," the voice crackled on the other end of the line, "put me over to Sinclair."

"Sure!" He stared at the inspector sitting on a log in the glow of her lantern, eating a small bar of chocolate. "Guv! it's Bryan for you."

She frowned and walked up to him, grabbing the proffered radio. "You've got good timing Bryan as always. We were just taking a break. How come you're contacting me this way?"

"Your phones out of action. Probably requires a recharge."

"More than likely. So give me what you got Bryan."

"We traced Kyle Klugman to the Isle of Wight. He wasn't there when our officers made the call. Neigbours say he's been gone over two weeks and they haven't seen the Ford Escort parked outside his house. But a police report tells us the car turned up late this afternoon six miles from Hereford. It was found by a local unit abandoned when it was caught in yesterday's flash flood. It hadn't been reported stolen. This has to be the vehicle they exchanged the people-carrier for."

Sinclair nodded. "Yes the pieces of this jigsaw are finally fitting together. So they got as far south as Hereford? I want to set up an Emergency Operations Center in the city and I'm taking one of our anti-terrorism units with us. Get Superintendent Lowther to sort that out. It should make her day to see me spending more department funds. Now then, did Klugman's neigbours have an inkling on when he might get back in town?"

"No guv but the milkman did. We phoned the dairy and Klugman cancelled his milk for five weeks, and his half-sister Tina Smullen is looking after his pet dog."

"Let me guess a dachshund?"

"Yeah! Smullen revealed her brother went to Hampstead for a job interview as a bodyguard."

"Bodyguard?" The inspector echoed loudly. "What training has he got for something like that."

"He was in the army for five years. Special forces until he hurt his ankle in a parachute jump and was drummed out of the service. We just made some general inquires and there are no bodyguard jobs in that part of London as far as we can tell."

"He's the weapons expert all right," Sinclair remarked. "Make some inquires at the army bases, see if any guns are missing from their armories. I want serial numbers if that's the case."

"Will do guv."

"Oh one more thing Bryan. I want you in my office at ten o'clock sharp tomorrow morning. I would like you to explain what you were doing on my personal computer yesterday when I was at the press conference."

"I haven't used your computer Hallie. I don't even know your password. Whatever this is all about, I can assure you that I've been set up."

"You disappoint me. I've caught you on video Bryan sending an E-mail to Dawn Blye of the *Daily Clarion* reporting you had information on a hot news item and were willing to sell it for a high price. And my password is simple. You've known it for years and I've never changed it. It's Elaine! My daughter's name."

There was a moment of silence then he spoke. "Shit! Looks like you got me over a barrel. When did you have the cameras installed?"

"Last year! It's a shame you've gone bad. Lowther wants your head on a plate to discourage anyone else thinking of going down the same path."

"I'm to be suspended I suppose and have charges of misconduct brought against me?"

"No suppose about it Bryan," the inspector told him, "you'll be suspended from duty immediately. The DPP is prosecuting this case. You're going to prison. They'll probably throw you in with the vulnerable inmates."

"Oh God!" He replied, knowing what that meant.

"You've made your bed now you have to lie in it. Carry on with the investigation then tomorrow bring in your passport and surrender your warrant card. I don't want you to be a flight risk. Be prepared for interviews. Keane will take over your workload. I'll speak for you in Court when the time comes Bryan but that's not for you, it's for your daughter Becky. I wouldn't want you missing out on to many years of seeing her grow up."

"Thanks Hallie."

"Discuss this with no one when you leave the office and don't take anything with you. Until tomorrow, bye." She switched off the phone. "Justin!" She addressed the sergeant, "you've just being promoted to my second in command."

Keane nodded and sat there, silently mulling over the extra responsible he'd been given until the helicopter came back from its refuelling to light their way ahead again.

* * *

The ground flew beneath Lois' shoes as she strode down the corridor. Dwyer stumbled when her left high heel snapped off. "Upsadaisy," Thaw said, helping her up and she in turn slipped off both shoes quickly and continued to run in bare feet.

"The library's just round this corner. The ninth door along." Danielle revealed to anyone listening.

At a junction the group deviated right and headed into the passageway. Unfortunately the companions had to skid to a halt when the door they wanted was behind a mass of walking corpses advancing towards them. Shafts flew on the air and Isaacs' and the rest of the group threw themselves to the carpet or ducked back behind the corner. The man in the snowman suit crumbled, blood spurting from his chest and throat and Klugman caught a fresh wound in his arm. The remaining arrows clattered harmlessly against the far wall.

"Great another scar," Klugman muttered, pulling a pin with his teeth and grinning. "Get back! This is gonna make us blooming popular." He flung the small bomb and doubled-back to hear the explosion shake the painting on the walls and shred the hangings with debris fragments. Warriors became disabled in the close confides of the blast including five of the archers.

Cummings raced up to Thaw. "Jerome! The ones on the stairs are breaking through the barricade. They'll be here soon. The other guests have ran off the other way."

"Okay," he replied, unclipping four of his grenades, "take these and delay them as long as you can then get your ass in the library."

"Two of these are smokers?" Cummings expressed his disgust as he gathered the bombs in both hands.

"Make do."

Cummings sighed before retracing his steps. Lois breathed in, peered around the corner and waved her hand, the corridor floor creaked as the new undead felt their rotting flesh gradually increased in heaviness. Their shoulders slumped, legs and arms grew to be like lead then they fell to their knees and finally dropped to the carpet as gravity became to much for them to bear. Behind, Klugman had already pulled out the arrowhead and discarded it, and was now binding the wound with what remained of his costume. Lois bent her arms back and pushed them forward. The gravity zone lengthened to take in the whole of the rear of the passageway. Romans tumbled, totally unable to stand up. Sweat beaded Lois' forehead and her palms suddenly became quite clammy.

"Now," she said, casting a glance back to Thaw and Klugman. "Throw your grenades while I can still hold them."

Klugman and Thaw approached the prone warriors, clawing at the carpet with effort. Thaw tossed a pair and Klugman lobed one before scrambling to withdraw. The explosions ripped through the flesh and blew holes in the walls. A door hung on one hinge while another fell inward to leave a gaping opening, revealing what was inside the library. Homes and the cavalry man wandered into the smoke in front of them and knelt to pick up swords. Brennan and the others joined in. Explosions echoed from around the corner and bellowing smoke preceded Cummings coughing as he clutched a double-handled axe and a Javelin.

Thaw drew his UZI and aimed it when he saw the hulking figure appear out of the dense clouds of fumes. It's only me Jerome," he shouted to the relief of Thaw who lowered his weapon. "Our friends are really pissed off with us now," he went on, "and they're still coming, only a bit slower than before."

"Good enough," Thaw uttered, whirling about only to hear Klugman swear when he saw what was inside the doorway. Thaw and Cummings broke into a sprint as Homes, Dwyer, Brennan and Orbach crowded around the others.

They saw Bartok's massive broadsword had cut through the blue barrier, and veins stood out like ropes in sharp relief along his muscular arms as he was presently bringing his blade down to slice apart more of the glittering shield.

"....What's that thing?" Klugman stated, shifting his attention between the demon's twisted face and Lois' countenance, his mind working over time.

Danielle replied, "it's Bartok. A high level demon from the Fire Plains."

"The Fire Plains?" Orbach echoed thoughtfully, "where's that?"

"In another realm!" Danielle continued, "we conjured him up earlier on and when Lois double-crossed him, it decided to employ magic to gather his own dead army from the swamp to free himself."

"Dead! Magic." Thaw uttered with a shake of his head. "No wonder we were having trouble stopping them. You can't kill what's already dead."

"You mean that you two and it are responsible for all the blood shed here tonight?" Isaacs remarked, horrified at the sight. "You should be ashamed of yourselves."

"You been lying to us bitch," Klugman announced angrily.

"You had this planned all along to bring us here and fight that monster," Thaw said.

Lois sighed, "I didn't mislead you even though I did omit a key fact – like him. The secret tunnel is on the opposite side of the room. All we have to do is get passed him and his black arts. And the next time you talk to me like that, I'll kill you by suffocation."

"Get in line girl," Klugman aimed his magnum at the glowing column and fired it six times in quick succession. The bullets sizzled in the energy before dropping through without any momentum to clatter softly at Bartok's feet. "You and I are gonna have words after this is over."

"Puny mortals," Bartok bellowed loudly at the noise before Lois could reply, his blade cutting deeper into the protective barrier. "I can count the minutes you have left to live and it's not much." He winked his left eye then something shimmered into being. An hourglass hovered in the air. From one glass bulb sand flowed upwards through a small opening to the other bulb. "Soon my sword will taste your blood."

"What have you and Danielle done with those fancy powers, Lois? Use them to destroy him now..." Homes declared firmly.

"He's only vulnerable when he's standing on consecrated ground for two minutes."

"Fat lot of good that does us with him in front and his army of undead behind us," Cummings said. Peering over his shoulder and seeing no sign for the time being of any more warriors coming along the corridor. "What I'd give to have a vicar around at this moment."

"No need. We have holy ground under the floor," Lois said. "This part of the house was built over an old church. We have a way..."

"Well then why didn't you say that in the first place?" Klugman answered, interrupting her before she'd been able to finish. He flipped the pin of his last grenade with his thumb and rolled it underarm across the floor. "Heads up! Coming through."

He barged his way between the crowd as they scattered on either side of the doorway. The bomb came to a halt when it collided against the energy shield.

"You moron," Lois shouted at Klugman, cowering behind the doorway, "we already had a plan do deal with him but now you've messed it up."

An explosion rocked the room and thick smoke rolled through the library opening. An instant later sprinklers rained down from the ceiling, dousing the flames flickering from furniture upholstery, clearing the smoke and improving visibility. Lois waved her hand in a lazy circle and the dark smoke and toxic gases produced from the synthetic materials were suddenly sucked up the fireplace and out the chimney.

"That's put paid to him," Cummings said with a nod as Klugman put his pillowcase beside Thaw's prior to snatching up a sword apiece.

"Your friend has only made him groggy," Lois said, "but we still might have a chance. Get in there and kill him before he awakens more of the dead and takes over the world."

"Err I'm not sure about this," Orbach commented loudly, gripping his sword tightly, "I don't believe in murdering somebody."

"Get a backbone man," Homes replied, "the lives of my family and my mistress are in peril and I ain't gonna let that happen. No siree!"

"Wait a moment You can't include me in this? I'm a model not a fighter," Isaacs pleaded.

"We all have to made sacrifices darning," Brennan replied, "get your head in the game. If Bartok wins, you won't have a career after this to go back too."

"Hah!" Klugman entered the room cautiously. "Amateurs. Just stay out of my way and I'll do it myself." The sprinklers ceased yet it was a gesture from Danielle more than a lack of water in the system.

The room was a tip. The books had been thrown from damaged shelves, chairs were blackened from fire, the glass aquariums and tanks were cracked and smashed, lights flickered in their depths and what remained of the carpet was waterlogged and smoldering. The rest of the floor was gone along with the pentacle and the energy shield, sunk into a hole in the middle of the room, the blast had caused.

Cummings and Thaw joined Klugman on the edge and looked down at the giant demon. He was in the act of slowly getting to his knees. Lois came up with the remainder of the crowd in tow with another idea in mind. "Quickly! You all must divert his attention before he realises what you're up too and uses his sorcery to escape."

Danielle glanced at her watch and said, "we've got one minute and forty three seconds to hold him for."

"I love a challenge," Klugman expressed his view. Eyeing the distance to the lower floor; at the same time he had emptied his weapon and was beginning to reload, "drop us down and we'll take care of this sucker."

Lois raised both her hands and all except her and Danielle were lifted off the ground.

"Why ain't you coming?" Dwyer shouted, holding her sword two-handily.

"I have to protect Danielle from the undead. She has to keep saying the spell up here without being distracted," Lois replied. With a deft twist of her four fingers, she propelled them forward, some faster than others to drift across the hole in a kind of widening circle. "You'll make less of a target split like this."

Thaw and Cummings discharged their firearms at Bartok as he finally got to his feet. He made no sound of anguish but the bullets ricocheted off his hide and up to slam into Orbach. He was peppered and he convulsed before going limp. Isaacs screamed.

"Uh-oh," Thaw grunted, "that's bad."

"Don't waste your ammo until the countdown has elapsed," Danielle raised her voice.

"Fine time to let us know we can't shot the bugger until later," Thaw reflected tensely.

Bartok looked up and grinned at the ring of people as they were lowered round him one by one until Orbach's body slumped to the floor. "I enjoy company dropping in," he spread his fingers out and his blade leaped from under some debris, the hilt smacked into his palm and his clawed fingers closed about it. His gaze wandered, turning to met the faces of his foes. Dust and lack of light prevented him from seeing that he was standing in an old church. "So you are the best champions this world has to offer? I feel sorry for it."

"Don't be," Klugman stated easily, "we're more than a match for you greenie. Any final words?"

"I ain't got any I suppose." Isaacs said.

Klugman sighed, "I was speaking to the freak."

"Er...of course."

Bartok chuckled long and loud.

"And I thought Cummings was thick." Klugman said, springing in, their blades clanging, producing sparks before he bounded out of reach.

Dwyer hefted a dagger, blade first and threw it. The demon saw a glint as it span end over end, and with a wave of his free hand redirected the knife back to where it came from. Dwyer fell to her knees, warm blood splashing over the embedded hilt. As she plunged sideways, Cummings lunged with the Javelin and the steel head blunted against his skin. Homes closed and swung a chair at the demon's back. It splintered but Bartok didn't react he just parried thrusts and feints off Thaw and Klugman then returned the attacks. Both men had speed and stamina. Alas, they still received several minor cuts between them.

Danielle continued to mutter words from *The Grimorie* while Lois concentrated and again increased gravity above the demon's head. He felt the change, turned with ease and out of a pointed arm speared up a column of ice which glanced off a hastily-erected air wall and froze the light fitting. Brennan cried out sharply and charged in with his blade high. Bartok smiled, deflected the sword then sent his own weapon in a low whipping arc and when the broadsword came out of the curving line, blood sprayed and entails spilled before Brennan joined them on the floor.

"Josh," Lois shouted angrily, "damn he never could do anything right." She turned to her friend. "Danielle! How long before the spell kicks in?"

"Anytime. Then Bartok's gone one way or another."

Three seconds later and feeling braver than she ever had in her entire life, Isaacs crept up behind the demon and kicked him in the shin. Bartok suddenly emitted a high yet diluted squeal of pain. He spun, gestured with his palm and sort of pushed Thaw without touching him. He flew backwards and crashed into the dusty objects littering the altar stone. The demon's gaze wandered then sighting a target, rotated his wrist and a whirling column of ice and snow flowed from his clawed fingers, lancing at Cummings and Homes. Cummings had long since discarded his Javelin and was now clutching the axe he'd pulled from his belt, ducked and rolled out of the way as Homes was caught in the blast. On the opposite side Klugman moved forward. He drew his gun and cocked the hammer. The blizzard had a temperature of minus three hundred degrees. Homes' skin suddenly lost all its pallor as he became very stiff. His eyes were stuck wide in surprise and his lips become frozen in a gaping rictus. Icy crystals surged to spread up his entire body and formed directly on the freezing surface as moist air contacted with it. Homes ceased moving as he finally frosted to the spot like a statue carved from ice.

Bartok glared at Isaacs as she scrambled away, his eyes blazed with anger and his mouth split wide, his teeth clenched. "So you steered me onto holy ground? Very clever! It still won't do a bit of good."

"That sounds like your two minutes are up, you damned cunt," Klugman said. His sword low and he squeezed of a round. The boom echoed loudly off the walls, "your balls are mine demon."

Bartok spun as the bullet ripped through his shoulder. Yellow blood and fly larva sprayed out the back. Cummings approached quickly from behind the demon who saw a red mist fluctuate in front of his flashing eyes.

"I'm going made this slow and painful fright-face," Klugman

warned, firing his gun twice more into the demon's stomach. The bullets bore deep, tearing into his vitals and Bartok howled in agony. Blood splashed down his legs. His face distorted and his soul shuddered with fury as a bloodthirsty desire for revenge drove a rush of adrenaline through his system, sweeping away the agony he suffered for the present moment.

Then the demon wrinkled his nose and a false grin spread across his palling features. "I think it'll be the other way round mortal." The hard-packed, earth floor beneath Klugman's boots cracked open and widened as a massive stone pincer shot up between his legs and clamped his genitals tightly before retracting and tearing them off. "Thanks for the idea."

With an expression of infuriated disbelief Klugman groaned. His legs bucked and he collapsed, crimson trickled from bitten lips as he managed to supported himself on one shaking arm. His blood pressure dropped and his breathing became shallower. Deep dark blood pooled around his groin and spreaded outwards. His muscles spasmed then Klugman fell flat on his face as the pain finally left him. A cruel, and unpleasant mocking laughter sounded before Bartok heard a scuff of a foot behind. He saw a lustrous blur when he spun about and was then driven to one knee as Cummings' axe buried deep in his ribs. Red fluid and flakes of bone flew from the wound but despite that the demon staggered to his feet, clutching his crushed ribs with one hand and his sword with the other.

"I warned him once not to play about. You saved me a job with Klugman," Cummings said warily, watching the demon swish his blade before him. "He needed killing and so do you. Whatever you are."

From the rear of the room Isaacs watched this battle with apprehension etched in her face. On her right she saw movement and Thaw stirred sluggishly as if he was in great pain. His face was white yet he edged off the altar stone with his UZI still in his trembling hand. She started to move towards him when she noticed a sharp point of a wrought-Iron crucifix imbedded deeply into his back.

He coughed and bloody foam specked his lips. He uttered "huh!" to express his surprise and disgust at the development then plunged lifelessly to the ground. Isaacs swallowed hard and moved to get the gun.

"Man of earth I am Bartok," he tottered forward a step and

another, his right heel suddenly began to slowly dissolve but he was so preoccupied with meeting the threat of Cummings that he failed to notice it, "and you are dead meat." Despite his injuries and gushing blood, he advanced and Cummings met him, swinging his axe in a figure of eight pattern like he'd seen in the movies. Next both of his horns became smoke and curled away.

Cummings feinted first and then swung his axe low at the demon's legs. He successfully parried and followed with a savage riposte at the human's head. Cummings dodged it, but the sword edge grazed his cheek. Red seeped down his skin. The demon's left heel started to match the other and smoke as it melted into thin air.

"Look Lois," Danielle pointed, "the bastard's unraveling, right on schedule."

"About time," Lois muttered. "If we'd lost anyone else, we would have had to fight the motherfucker ourselves."

Below her, their weapons clanged twice, and the shock of the impact surged up Cummings' arm. The top of Bartok's head evaporated as he wobbled on his feet. Then he thrust and the demon somehow twisted out of the way and with a backhand slash his blade descended, shattering Cummings' collarbone and went deeper still to peel his torso apart. Blood spurted and the axe fell from nerveless fingers. His eyes took on a glassy look prior to dropping at the demon's vanishing feet.

It was then that Bartok's gaze widened at the sight as his claws disappearing. "No this can not be. I have been vanquished," his voice came out slurred while his ankles dropped to the ground with a thump. Unusually he didn't lose his balance and fall over. He felt his head tingling and when glancing up, he saw part of his temple was gone too and the spell continued to flow down to the tips of his ears and beyond. He coughed up worms and more blood.

"We found a spell written in Hebrew. We changed it to English and now you're on a one way ticket out of here," said Lois matter of factly.

Half of his ears disappeared and the spell lowered to his eyebrows, "wait I'll give you the additional powers and wealth... Please don't sent me back to the Fire Plains!"

"Naw," Lois said firmly, "and who said we were sending you back to your old home?"

Bartok's eyes disappeared and his legs dwindled to his knees. He crashed to the ground again. "Nooo! you'll send me to..." His mouth, jaw and thighs went the way of the rest of him. Seeing all this, Isaacs pointed Thaw's UZI, squeezed the trigger and the shells punched into the demon's chest. His fading torso wobbled from the impact as it shrank.

"Yes we have," Lois said, hearing a pop of in rushing air as she observed a flash of light swallow up the last bit of the demon. She addressed Isaacs. "Nice shooting girl. Just stop there and I'll get you up," she gestured with a hand and Isaacs gasped as she was suddenly lifted up in an arc and was deposited by the doorway.

* * *

When Bartok faded from the realm of earth, his influence and control over the links he'd established dispelled like mist. The dead warriors faulted in their steps and fell, never to rise again. They slid down the staircases, cluttering up the corridors, littered the lawn outside along with skeleton horses. Red balls zoomed about then popped out of existence for all time. In the kitchen the monster lodged in the doorway commenced to rapidly shrink in size. Its colour changed and its overall shape transmuted, changing gradually, separating from one form to seven species: fish, frogs, and additional creatures from the aquariums, flopped, jumped or scurried away. The same happened to the remains of the flying insect up stairs.

Fire still raged from the side of the house, and the reporters, wearing blood-soaked clothes, wearily tottered from the smoke and settling dust cloud, stepping over moldering corpses and their stiffing colleagues as they drifted out.

"Well," the British anchorwoman said to her cameraman, her short auburn hair had been full of small tight curls but was now plastered flat on her head from sweat. "This is something you won't catch on CNN tonight. You did get all that didn't you Jim?"

"Yep," Jim replied, his face worked with emotion. Cluttering a video in a shaking hand as he walked unsteadily beside her. A bandage was wrapped around his head. "This will sent our ratings through the roof if we can get passed by the police."

"We will," she said, wincing from the bruises on her side where she'd been punched. "I'll stick the tape down my knickers when the times comes and let the ambulance take us and the evidence out of here."

Only four more people from various international news crews

followed them out of the room whose walls were coated with blood. One limped ahead while the rest labored as they helped each other to move.

"Who were they though? That's what I want to know," a sound engineer muttered, still in shock, "were they an army experiment gone wrong? Did it also affect the brain since they were only brandishing swords and spears?"

"I can't answer that Terry," the anchorwoman replied, proceeding on, "if the Chairwoman of the Defence Committee survived then that'll be one of the first questions I'll try and wring out of her."

The billowing sail caught the wind whipping through the rigging and strummed the ropes taut. The mast and hull creaked and groaned as the high, curving prow of the sleek, serpentine galley sliced through the stormy sea of fire. Polished oval shields atop reflected the rows of oars withdrawing from the flicking flames but the intense heat didn't burn or even blacken the sloping timbers from stem to stern. Upon the heaving deck, the captain stood at the helm and in the semi-darkness, revolved the wheel to keep the canvas in the gale. Below the poop, scaled sailors climbed up the rigging to the crows nest, scrubbed dirt from the planks and rowers grunted and strenuously hauled the oars up to the tholepins.

The galley crested another swell and as it descended into the next trough, buckets of bubbling water toppled over to splash across the deck and sizzled as it dribbled down through the metal grille into the dark depths of the submerged hold. Seated on hard benches, Geof Anderson pulled on the rusty links, testing the strength of the chain fastening him and the other prisoners to the great iron rings set in the hull behind them.

He sighed heavily and released the series of rings, "it's no good Alice," he panted in the heat, "the only way we could break it was if we had a sledgehammer."

Snodgress nodded and her nostrils flared, the shackle encircling her left wrist rattled slightly as she wiped the sweat from her brow, "at least you tried Geof which is a hell of a lot more than others here are bothered to do."

"Hey that ain't fair grandma," Tony Jordan shouted, weighed down with chains, opposite her, "I've done my share. You just weren't around to see it. I plan on escaping," he assured her, with determination in his voice, "but I'm playing a waiting game until we reach the mine I heard one of them mention."

"Then what?" The cowboy asked, peering at him, "am I missing something because I wish you would tell me." His hands tensely gripped the edges of his bench, "all I know is we're currently surrounded by an inferno I wouldn't recommend skinny dipping in and heading towards a foreign country where we could be stranded for months or years to come. I've read about the slave trade. I didn't think I'd be a part of it. The Crowes certainly know how to throw a party."

The trembling captives exchanged glances and a few more of the group began to whimper in overwhelming hysteria as confusion and horror played across their faces.

"Look! There's no point in quarreling among ourselves," Kalvinder Kapoor blurted out, attempting to make peace by reconciling the opposing sides as she sat beside the rock star, "we have to learn what we can about this situation we find ourselves in. My career has allowed me to travel extensively and I've never seen so many volcanos in one place not even in the Pacific basin where they're most common."

Interest flickered in the eyes of the party guests.

"Kal's right," Snodgress agreed, jutting her chin in the air, "I doubt the whereabouts of the fire plains is in any of the tourist pamphlets in the high street. I admit I was a little disoriented when we first arrived in respect to the time and the place but not to Geoff's identity. From what I glimpse I didn't recognise any of the landscape and those goons that put us down here were dressed better than Dr Who rejects. I've never seen anything quite like them either."

"Well the thing that flew me to this ship felt real enough," the young waiter said, scratching his jaw. "There's no way that was an actor in a foam rubber costume."

"It wasn't," Yasmin Tweed said, learning forward out of the shadows. Her heart thumping against her ribcage. "What you saw was a monster and on deck are demons and Snodgress is quite correct. We aren't even on earth anymore but on another planet if you can call this realm that. It's Bartok's home and we're trapped here now just as much as he is or was."

"Catchy name," Snodgress declared, eyeing Tweed with uncharacteristic nervousness. The young woman stared down at her hands.

"It's ridiculous lass!" An elderly gardener gasped in the humid air. "It's so contrary to nature and reason that it's simply laughable. An alien land indeed."

"I ain't lying," Tweed stated passionately, her head snapping up, "I witnessed him with my own eyes be conjured inside a pentagram."

Anderson frowned thoughtfully as he gave her a suspicious glance, "You're one of Lois' friends aren't you?" Tweed nodded and he groaned, having an inkling where this would lead. "Cor talk about a model citizen. This Bartok, was he behind the army that broke into the house?"

"An army!" She uttered, raising her eyebrows in surprise. "Er...he might have been but I can't be sure. I got zapped while he was still escaping Lois' spell. Anything is possible. Where did the men come from?"

"Who could say," Snodgress answered, with a shrug. "How was the demon summoned?"

"Yeah," Anderson agreed, his temple throbbing, "I wouldn't mind knowing that myself."

"By black magic. It's a long story and very freaky."

"We're not going anywhere girl," the cowboy remarked, lifting the chain that bound him.

"Okay! It all started with *The Grimorie...*"

* * *

With a litter made up of spears and fastened together with trouser belts and tied-back curtain cords, the conscious Russel Corbett was carried by Robert Crowe, Lynskey and a couple of the others who had gone to fetch the weapons. Able bodied guests brandished swords and pikes kept an eye out for anything still surviving while Hawes loped alongside the litter and held Corbett's hand. Behind them were Isaacs, and Andrew and Vertly Elmes. They were helping along the additional walking wounded, supporting the odd guest who couldn't stand unaided, their faces tight with pain.

"I just can't get over it," Vertly said, dragging her tired feet, "we were trapped in the bedroom but those killers didn't come in to attack us? I don't know what to make of it."

"It could have been a moon eclipse or the mistletoe over the doorways for all I care," Andrew replied, "I'm just glad we survived the night. I'll tell you this much Vertly. It's opened up my eyes and I've decided I'm coming off my diet. If you don't like it then tough. You're not holding me prisoner to my needs ever again."

Vertly frowned, "yeah right."

"You'll see. This time I mean business."

Directly ahead the back staircase creaked under the weight of Danielle and Lois. Corpses were draped across the steps.

"So how are we gonna explain all the bodies and the damage the house has suffered to the police," Danielle said. Picking her way down gingerly between the arms and legs.

Lois pulled a face as she came next, whirling blue and white lights pierced through the stair window. She glanced down, through the glass at the patrol cars as they screeched to a stop outside the kitchen garden, crushing herbs and vegetables under the tyres. "I don't know Danielle," she shook her head, "I really don't know."

The pair continued to descend the steps and at the bottom, their attention focused on the uniformed officers as they burst into the kitchen with automatic pistols. The rest of the guests filed down, seeing flaming streaks flash across the night sky and disappear. They weren't meteors as many believed but the animated corpses Lois sent into orbit now burning up in reentry. Corbett, through great pain and blurred eyes turn, happened to glance up to the staircase ceiling where he saw dust motes swirl into a pair of eye sockets, and spread to form a grinning mouth. He blinked, babbled something indistinct and pointed at the sight. Hawes' gaze followed where he aimed but the apparition vanished before she saw it.

Hawes shivered and swallowed hard, hoping what he saw was just a trick of the light and shadows or was simply caused by his delirium and exhaustion, and not something else which could be far more sinister...

Printed in the United Kingdom
by Lightning Source UK Ltd.
108226UKS00002B/1-15

9 781905 237463